The

GIRL
from the
ORPHANAGE

The Orphanage Of Secrets © 2022 Robert Barclay.
All Rights Reserved.

No part of this book may be reproduced in any form or by any electronic or mechanical means including information storage and retrieval systems, without permission in writing from the author. The only exception is by a reviewer, who may quote short excerpts in a review.

This book is a work of fiction. Names, characters, places, and incidents either are products of the author's imagination or are used fictitiously. Any resemblance to actual persons, living or dead, events, or locales is entirely coincidental.

Printed in Australia

First Printing: June 2022

Shawline Publishing Group Pty Ltd
www.shawlinepublishing.com.au

Author Page: www.robertbarclay.com.au

Paperback ISBN- 9781922751232

Ebook ISBN- 9781922751294

 A catalogue record for this book is available from the National Library of Australia

The GIRL IN THE ORPHANAGE

ROBERT BARCLAY

A GRIPPING AND DISTURBING STORY ABOUT EXTRAORDINARY WOMEN

The news shatters Katy Yehonala's world. Her husband, Simon, has been murdered in a remote Cambodian border township. What was he doing there?
Unable to sleep, melancholy draws Katy into his study, seeking solace. A remembered smell, a half-read book, something. What she finds is an unfinished manuscript called *Chavy's Story* hinting at Simon's secretive work and tells the harrowing story of a young village girl trafficked for sex.
Katy and Clara travel to Cambodia in search of answers. The riddles buried in the pages of *Chavy's Story* unmask a forgotten horror from Katy's childhood and for Clara, a beautiful Italian charity worker threatens to upset a lifetime of modesty.

Chavy's Story will change Katy and Clara's lives forever.

"Masterful and gripping, as if the author anticipates everything we as readers will demand. And he delivers... Exceptional follow on to The Diary of Katy Yehonala..."
Kelly, Indiebook Reviewer

Acknowledgements

The Girl in the Orphanage is a novel about heroes, courageous women and men who risk their lives on the frontlines fighting the evil of child sex trafficking and the children who live to tell their stories. The inspiration for the novel is one heroic child.

Many organisations do this unsung work. They were there before light shone into the dark corners of abandoned humanity, living a precarious existence unimaginable to most of us. One of whom, incidentally, introduced me to eating tarantulas, a delicacy Katy and Clara, wisely in my view, choose to decline in the book.

A sincere thank you to UNICEF and your Director of Child Protection in Phnom Penh at the time, Silvia Pasti. Silvia spoke with me about the immense challenges around the country's privately-run orphanages and my novel would not have been possible without your help. UNICEF's work changes lives.

I have dedicated *The Girl in the Orphanage* to these champions of humanity and the survivors.

The novel is set in Cambodia, a Buddhist country. To my friend, the Venerable Bhikkhunī Nirodha, I am indebted to you once again for your insights into Theravada Buddhism and its sometimes-contrary rituals in different countries. I hasten to add I hold you blameless when my homage to storytelling lured me from the Middle Way.

Thank you once again to my friends at Shawline Publishing. Particularly to Samantha Elley, whose hubris-hunting red pen and hawk's eye prevented me going on long walks with my best friend, the English language, and distracted readers from the story.

To Sonja Walmsley, who again put aside her book reading addiction to help me tell my second novel in a more reader-friendly way, and to Danielle Sanelli, who kept me on track during stressful times, thank you both. Danielle, for your sins, your alter-ego, Elena Accardi, appears in the novel. I confess to taking outrageous and entirely unfounded liberties with your lifestyle choices with Elena.

Introduction

Katy Yehonala has found her contentment in Melbourne, in the Red Peony Garden, where she and Simon plan to spend their days. Their daughter, Clara, has achieved world acclaim as a concert pianist and lives in Paris.

After Simon is murdered in a nondescript border township in Cambodia, Katy discovers an unfinished manuscript. The name pencilled at the top calls the document *Chavy's Story* and the pages reveal a web of events leading Katy and Clara to a private orphanage in Phnom Penh.

Their tenacious search for the truth about Simon's death alarms the Australian and Chinese embassies but intrigues a distinctly off-colour New Zealand-born investigative reporter, Jim Preston. Together, they set out to discover what is true as they unravel the deadly riddles of *Chavy's Story*. On the way, they find nothing as it appears and a brutal political and criminal web imperils their lives.

For Katy, the pages of *Chavy's Story* lay bare a long-buried demon from her childhood, and Clara discovers the truth about herself which challenges her inhibitions and taboos as she struggles to fight and finally embrace her deepest longings.

The Girl in the Orphanage is gripping and disturbing storytelling, a story about extraordinary women and a reminder of what is still happening to children out of our sight, robbing them of what all parents take for granted.

The Girl in the Orphanage is the second novel in The Butterfly Dynasty series.

1

THE DAY BEFORE YESTERDAY

There is but a single day in each woman's life when she is permitted to look upon the ecstasy and agony of her life and see the capricious hand of God. Today turned out to be the one conferred upon Katy Yehonala.

The lights dim, an unspoken signal to the audience. Seated again after the interval, a palpable sense of expectancy permeates the vast concert hall. Even the musicians of the famed Beijing Symphony Orchestra look between themselves, waiting. Tonight, a new concerto by the celebrated Chinese composer, Jiang Kui, is to have its première; the final performance on the program after an evening celebrating the composer's genius. Seats for the concert sold out weeks before.

   Standing alone in the wings, a beautiful young Eurasian woman experiences a surge of adrenaline pulse through her body. She shrugs off her desire to flee, a fear she still feels seconds before walking onto a stage. Instead, she takes a deep breath, draws her shoulders back and steps into the waiting spotlight. Those fortunate to have tickets, or, like the Chinese Premier and his wife enjoying the privileges of power, applaud generously. They have all come to hear China's national treasure, Clara Yehonala, play Jiang's latest work.

She wears a long, emerald-green silk dress and walks with an imperious, feline grace, her sleek hair and magnolia skin numinous in the spotlight. Not for this virtuoso the immodest distractions of cleavage or exposed thighs; her sublime music speaks directly to every soul in her audience. Miss Yehonala's only whimsy is a delicately embroidered silk shawl the newspapers say once belonged to the Dowager Empress Cixi, from where she traces her illustrious parentage.

Bowing to the audience, she acknowledges they will be friends for the next forty minutes, sharing a spiritual connection through her music. In a tender moment, she lightly kisses the shawl and lays it reverently on the Steinway grand concert piano and greets the conductor, Maestro Michel Gaultier, and the concertmaster.

Motionless at the piano, Clara Yehonala holds the hushed audience in her hand. After the applause, the silence is unnatural. Ten seconds pass. Twenty. A single note echoes. Then the sublime opening of Jiang Kui's third piano concerto fills the expanse of the mighty concert hall.

In a different world, four thousand kilometres away, two white SUVs slide quietly through the unlit backstreets of a nondescript township called Krong Chey, a stone's throw from the border with Vietnam. Their lights are off. Inside are two Cambodian police officers and three charity workers. One of them is an Australian. His name is Simon Bailey.

They pull over at the entrance to a narrow alleyway and switch off their engines. Now they wait. There is a different kind of silence here, the menacing one. Each nerve ending taut, they focus their attention on the alley's darkened entrance as if it might whisper a secret. With the air conditioning off, beads of sweat prickle on their foreheads and cling shirts to their skin in the oppressive pre-monsoon humidity. Simon Bailey's watch shows an hour before midnight.

'It's time.'

These men have driven from Phnom Penh without informing the local police. In their line of work, they know how dangerous it can be to trust anyone. Halfway down this alley is a locked cellar and inside are seven children, trafficking victims, on their way to Ho Chi Minh City. Children who wealthy paedophiles will rape of their innocence before their captors sell them into seedy brothels for the gratification of a poorer class of predator.

Their operation begins.

The rescue is going as planned. They usually do.

Two policemen enter the building and force the watchman to hand over the key to the cellar. The Australian man hurries down the stairs to release the terrified children who escape into the alley.

This time it is different.

Two men step from the shadows.

'Hurry, hurry,' calls one of the workers, urgency in his voice. 'Into the cars, quickly. Run!'

Shots ring out. In the gloom of the stairway, a primal terror twists the stomach of the Australian man. He knows he is trapped. He is a man from a different age, brave enough, still believing in a code of chivalry. He steps into the alley, hands raised in surrender. Forced onto his knees, he stares into the indifferent eyes of a man devoid of honour or compassion. The gunman walks behind him and, for a second, the Australian man feels a cold pressure against the skin on the back of his head. The gunman fires. Simon Bailey crumples forward, face down into the dirt and litter. He dies instantly.

One of the young girls screams as she reaches the safety of the first SUV.

'*My shame, my shame*, no!'

She tears herself away from the two charity workers and races back along the alley, throwing herself on Simon Bailey's lifeless body, convulsing in tears. The same gunman takes deliberate aim and fires twice more. He smiles, but not with his eyes.

Unhurried, he walks to a waiting vehicle, which screeches away towards the border. The staccato clatter of a motorcycle follows a few moments later.

Simon Bailey is Clara Yehonala's father.

2

YESTERDAY

How could I ever forget yesterday?

My day started well enough as Sundays usually did, sitting on my patio at home on the outskirts of Melbourne with a cup of floral tea, enjoying the sights and smells of our garden. Those early mornings were a Katy ritual.

Autumn's colours were flowing through the leaves like crimson, purple and gold-coloured inks mixing in a glass of water. I remember hoping Melbourne's blustery winds would stay away until my husband came home, anchoring the remaining leaves for another few days. I sipped my tea, watching the sails without boats falling and smelt the first of the damp autumn chill. Simon and I loved rugging up and kicking through the leaves, though it always seemed the fallen summoned their lingering companions to earth before our time of enjoying them was ever enough.

I met Simon as a student in England more than twenty-five years earlier. Our love of nature and each other began with the English countryside. Unfortunately, I lost him a year later. Not from carelessness or the demise of a fleeting romance, as you might easily believe. I had flown home to China when my dear Granny Chen died. Then my mother fell ill. Filial piety and family obligations never allowed me the opportunity to go back, keeping me confined in dutiful captivity. With regret, but without complaint, I might add. Inevitably, we lost touch. Yet, despite the passage of time, I kept him in my heart even as veils descended, year by year, blurring my memories.

Now I'm in my early forties and no longer "drop-dead beautiful" as Simon once flattered me during my student days in England during the eighties. And what Chinese girl wouldn't melt under the spell of forest green eyes and an Australian accent?

My face has always been more sculptured than soft, like Mama and my Manchu forbears, though not too bad-looking, considering. I can't masquerade as anything extraordinary these days, but can still turn an occasional head. Just enough to keep my shoulders back, a habit ingrained from childhood. After all, I am a Yehonala.

Simon and I met again five years ago when fate intervened in the mysterious way it does. He also met his daughter, Clara, for the first time. Xiaoli - her birth name - had been as much a surprise to me too, popping into my consciousness after getting over jet lag from my rush back home, later as the cause of my expanding waistline. How all our lives might have been different had I not kept my secret so well.

They adored each other and Simon's and my love affair continued where it left off all those years before as if nothing had changed, except the accumulated evidence of time. Our shared pleasures have since been nurtured by careful and regular care, creating joy as the three of us grew together.

Simon was away in Cambodia again and I had been looking forward to him being home on Wednesday. He ran a charity there, the Sunlight Foundation, and he'd campaigned for years to raise the plight of children sold into the sex-trafficking trade, often getting himself involved in matters better suited to a younger man.

He was nudging sixty now. Far too old, in my opinion, to be charging around in the dead of night like the archangel Michael, rescuing children from the teashops and smoky karaoke bars in the backstreets of Phnom Penh. However, we both shared a passion for what we believed in, with matching stubbornness.

Much to my relief, I finally persuaded him to leave his *Boy's Own* adventures to others. In the future, he promised to devote himself to fundraising and my dearest hope, spending more time with me around the Red Peony Garden, our little business on the banks of the Yarra River, forty or so kilometres east of Melbourne.

We bought the place when it was a run-down plant nursery and hobby-farm spread over about a hectare. We spent three years recreating a blend of Suzhou's ancient imperial gardens, places we enjoyed lost hours when we'd lived in Shanghai after our much-delayed marriage.

I named the garden to honour Mama's memory. The one hundred double-bloom peonies drew thousands of visitors each November, when their magenta and scarlet flowers, as big as dinner plates, overflowed the walkways, filling the air with intoxicating fragrances.

The Red Peony Garden came to be popular with visitors on their day trips to the nearby Yarra Valley wineries or on their way to the musty antique shops and cottage restaurants in the Dandenong Ranges. Especially Chinese tourists and those émigrées who had fled New China with old money. I supposed, like me, they imagined the peaceful garden as a forever-lost world; a Shangri-La hidden behind whitewashed walls and its red-painted moon gate entrance, guarded by two fierce-looking, grinning stone lions.

My favourite time of the day has always been the early morning before we opened the gates. I would sit in my waterside pagoda, sipping tea and watching the koi glide beneath the lotus and water lilies in the lingering mist. The morning sunlight caught their multi-coloured scales and they glinted like jewel boxes. Over the years, the koi had grown tame and rose to take food from my hand, rolling over like playful puppies so I could scratch their rubbery tummies.

Afterwards, if Simon were here, we'd enjoy a meandering, arm in arm walk under the willows, weeping their morning dew into the water like a lover's tears. Or we'd take a last stroll around the garden's bamboo-fringed arbours and restful courtyards before opening the gates and happily sharing our pleasure with visitors.

I left the day-to-day management to the ageless Mr Wang, a gentle Buddhist and expert on all aspects of the garden's design. He's been there from the start. Mr Wang believed his life's mission began and ended with the visitors' enjoyment and together with his assistants, they never overlooked the tiniest detail to ensure the garden's *feng shui* perfection.

I'm a lot younger than Simon and had inherited money, even though an ill-fated romance in Lagos had seen the balance savaged a few years back. A previous life, best forgotten. Together with Simon's trading business in Hong Kong, we had the financial freedom to do as we wished though we were both kept busy, him with the charity's work, me indulging my love of the garden.

Gardens had been Mama's great love too. I knew she watched over me with a contented smile on her face. I spent much of my time in the greenhouse, where I grew rare Asian plants as a hobby and chatted to visitors about traditional Chinese gardens, exotic plants and fruits unknown to most westerners.

Most satisfying of all, after so many twists and turns, my life's journey had settled on a destination. I summed up my life as contentment.

News of Simon's death came on the same Sunday. In the afternoon. Two Federal Police officers arrived at my door telling me a gang of traffickers had killed him during the rescue of seven children in a rural Cambodian township. They said the criminals were smuggling the children into Vietnam and someone had alerted them about the rescue attempt. The gang shot one of the girls as well and she died before reaching the local hospital. I screamed like a harpy at them for letting Simon get involved in such dangerous activities, venting my rage and disbelief over my fractured world. They forgave my outburst and I apologised for my behaviour. I didn't envy their job.

The Australian Embassy in Phnom Penh wanted to fly Simon home. I knew it wouldn't be what he wanted. Too much of his heart lived in that tormented country. I told them I would fly to

Cambodia the next day to bury Simon in the land he loved and asked if they would let the embassy know. After they left, there remained one painful matter to deal with. Our daughter, Clara. I needed to call her.

I must say here we Yehonala women don't have an unblemished track record with fathers. For one, the Red Guards murdered my grandfather during the Cultural Revolution and forced my mother to watch. I can't begin to imagine something so terrifying for an eighteen-year-old girl to endure. My own father died soon after we returned from our grim exile to a village gulag near the Siberian border after I turned twelve. And now this.

Clara grew up without knowing her father at all for her first twenty years. She'd met him for the first time when Simon and I also found each other again, purely by happenstance, those five years ago. Afterwards, she breezily announced she would be the first Yehonala girl to grow up with a dad. For his part, he promised her he didn't plan to die and she had set about making up for all the lost years. He lied to both of us.

By now, Clara's fame as a pianist kept her travelling continually. Some said she was the most gifted virtuoso in living memory; all agreed there were none comparable today. In curious Jungian synchronicity, Simon had once even seen her play the Last Night of the Proms at the Royal Albert Hall. At the time he had no idea his cheers were for his daughter, however, he did his part raising the roof after her booming *Heroic Polonaise,* an encore she still remembers as her most triumphant, getting caught up in the euphoric fervour of flag-waving British pomp and patriotism.

People knew Clara universally as the Jade Princess, partly due to our family's lineage to the last Chinese empress Cixi, another Yehonala woman inattentive with fathers, losing hers when she became the emperor's favoured concubine in the Forbidden City at sixteen. The other reasons were her stunning Eurasian features and the air of demure mystery surrounding her, stage-managed by her agent, Max Santini, a woman of indeterminate age and manic energy, whom Clara adored. Max protected her as well as any bear mother did her cubs.

The Girl in the Orphanage

In a tragedy of parallels, the night Simon died, Clara had been performing in Beijing. I'd been watching her on CCTV, the Chinese TV channel, full of pride and feeling blessed by my life, blissfully unaware Simon waited to die in a grubby alley in a Cambodian border town with a name I couldn't pronounce. We cried together for a long time. Tears for remembered last conversations, tears for things we talked about, for things we should have talked about, for complaints I made about him spending so much time away I wished I never said to him. Tears for the why-why-why. She promised to meet me in Phnom Penh the next day. We were going to need each other.

My emotions eventually subsided to more of an ocean swell than waves crashing onto the shore, but unable to sleep, I had wandered into Simon's study. I suppose I must have been looking for a personal memento I could touch, or a remembered smell, or seeing what his last activities had been. A half-read book, some doodling on a piece of paper, a coffee cup. Something familiar.

What I found turned out to be the unfinished manuscript of a book he'd been writing. The last pages were still crisp, as if he had been adding to the narrative. Curiosity became the handmaiden of my sadness; I curled up on a sofa and started to read *Chavy's Story*, the title he had pencilled into the top corner.

The story began in the 1970s, around the time I knew Simon was in Vietnam and Cambodia during the war, before we'd even met, and finished at what appeared to be the present day. As I read the first few pages, I wondered who this "Chavy" could be and why this family seemed important to him. Could it even be a true story?

At crossroads in my life, or at those times I thought I wasn't strong enough to pick myself up after stumbling, there's always a small voice whispering in my ear telling me I was facing in the right direction and urging me to keep walking. This time, the child's voice called urgently. I sensed an invisible hand tugging my sleeve with such insistence I finally understood. Chavy's story, Simon's legacy and Katy Yehonala's destiny were the same.

I must follow this road wherever it led. I would finish Chavy's story and discover the truth about Simon's death.

I gazed around our rooms, so familiar to me, wondering if it would be for the last time. Would they ever feel the same? I went into our bedroom, pulled a suitcase down from the shelf above our clothes and started packing.

I carefully placed the manuscript in my carry-on bag.

My favourite seat on an aeroplane is next to the window. I could say my choice has to do with the view; looking down from heaven and watching the sun rise or set is surely one of life's joys, urging you to believe in God. A more prosaic truth existed: I'm a lily-livered aeronaut who needs to watch the plane land through the window. Waiting blindly for the sudden *bump* of impact from the centre aisle invariably leaves me a nervous wreck.

The thought has me blinking and shaking my head. How amazing it is that one's mind can distract to the banal and suppress the overwhelming.

My Qantas jet flies high above Australia's heart, about midway between sunset and sunrise, heading north. I confess to being anxious, not about flying, more about being unprepared for what I'd committed myself to and if I had the strength of character to ride the emotional roller-coaster I'd climbed aboard. I was thankful Clara would be there with me, at least for a few days. Her bright personality and offbeat humour would keep us both calm and collected. Always sensible and practical, I could depend on her to manage the arrangements for Simon's funeral, an ordeal I felt sure I couldn't do by myself.

I needed courage. Even the temporary Dutch kind would do to stiffen my resolve for what lay ahead. Considering a large brandy, I decided instead to rummage inside my carry-on bag. Pulling out the manuscript, I stared at the first page, changing my mind about the brandy. Napoleon's company was exactly what I needed.

Thus, fortified by my crystalline-gold backbone, I picked up where I'd left off the night before and continued reading…

3

CHAVY'S UNFINISHED STORY

'We called you Chavy, a name which means "little angel". After the murderous times of the past, perhaps a little divine inspiration for the future was in our minds. And to complete an even handful of girls, your little sister Rangsei arrived two years later. We all called her Peou.'

Back then, Cambodia was a frightening, malefic dreamscape, fit only for Dante seeking inspiration for his *Divine Comedy*. I was born onto those stepping-stones of Satan and into my tortured country.

My own nightmares waited patiently for me.

3. HOME

Me and Peou were not survivors of the Killing Fields like my Khmer parents and three older sisters. Both of us were born after the family returned to Kampot. For me, the horror of Mum's stories became my family's memory of history. I wished I had been born into those days because when times were hard, which were often enough, my older sisters retreated to a sacred space only they knew and they guarded the gates with spiteful boasting, leaving Peou and me feeling shunned and lonely.

My family returned to a traditional Khmer farm in a village along the Prek Chha River, near where it emptied into the Gulf of Thailand. To be honest, the farm's just a small field attached to the house divided into a rice paddy, vegetable patch and an enclosure for ducks. Farms similar to ours stood nearby. We and our neighbours shared an old, bony-shouldered white ox to furrow our fields after the dry season before planting rice and vegetables. Naturally, my parents would have preferred Peou and me to have been born boys for the demanding farm work, but we girls were all the labour on offer. We rolled up our sleeves like everyone else.

A Khmer farmhouse like ours stands on stilts. The ground floor doesn't have walls, just a tiny kitchen and storeroom in the centre, next to the rice mill. We had hammocks slung between the stilts for resting during the heat of the day and the space provided a place for parking our two rusting bicycles and my dad's mud-spattered motorbike. We had no ground floor living room because the river overflowed its banks during the rainy season and coffee-coloured water lapped around our farmhouse for several days.

After the water receded, we shovelled buckets of thick mud from under the house and tipped it into the paddy field and onto the vegetable patch. River mud smells rich and mythical, of decayed leaves and fresh earth. I loved the smell and the dark, oozy material squishing between my toes, although the mud constantly sucked off my flip-flops. Mum said the river mud made the rice and vegetables strong.

We all lived together on the first floor, up a sturdy wooden stairway, safe and mostly dry when the monsoon rains came. The plank walls needed repairs, so Mum hung batik sheets over them, making the rooms bright and colourful. Mum and Dad slept in one room and we five girls nested behind a wall made from a hanging sheet. My older sisters constantly bickered about who would sleep with Mum when Dad went away. Peou and me slept cuddled together on a padded rug like two bananas.

Dad went away a lot since he worked on a fishing boat. Often they followed the fish into Vietnamese waters, earning money to support our family. If the police caught them, they paid a fine and lost their fish. When that happened, he often stayed away for two weeks; the horrible local kids called me the kid with no daddy.

'I have a daddy, but he's across the sea in Vietnam earning money for the family,' I always replied to them with teary anger.

'If your daddy wanted you, he would stay with you. But instead, he left you and ran away.' They knew how much their sword-grass words cut me.

I felt so upset when the neighbours' kids mocked me but extra excited when he came home, so I convinced myself I didn't mind because he always brought clothes for us. Although they weren't nice clothes, we were joyful about our family reunion. Especially me, the reason being I could show the nasty children I had a real daddy after all. I believed he loved me the most since I didn't talk much and respected everyone. I'm a smart kid too, which I hoped made him a little bit proud, even if he never said so.

Each morning before school, my older sisters worked in the field picking vegetables and weeding the rice while Peou and me fed the ducks and collected the eggs, wearing our too-big rubber boots in the mucky duck pen. Collecting the eggs always turned into a fun game of hide-and-seek thanks to the ducks who liked tucking them away in secret corners. Well, fun unless one or two chased Peou when they were in a bad temper, forcing her to hide behind me until I shooed them away.

Before the sun had hardly woken up, Mum and one of my sisters rode the bicycles to the market carrying eggs and vegetables. Looking back, I expect people might think ours was a hard life. But, to me, it was simply life. The others thought paradise best described our home compared to the war and the refugee camps, snapping at me if I ever complained, so I never did.

After my older sisters went to school or helped Mum sell eggs and vegetables at the market, me and Peou stayed home by ourselves. We knew the rumours about bad people who kidnapped children when there weren't adults with them, so whenever I heard about a stranger in the village, I took Peou's hand and we hid in the storage shed to protect her from a danger I didn't understand. When the stranger left, we came out again.

We often went to the neighbour's farmhouse to play because their kitchen smelled of delicious cooking and I wanted extra food to feed my sister. Occasionally, they gave us a bowl of congee or fried rice, though usually, they ate together, ignoring us. To take our minds off the mouth-watering smells and our growling tummies, we'd play games in the surrounding jungle until Mum or my older sisters came home.

We weren't big enough to climb the trees for fruit, looking up wishfully at the coconut palms and the out-of-reach delights growing on the wild mango, papaya and breadfruit trees. If we were lucky, I could knock one down by throwing a stick, or one had become overripe and fallen. The lowest-hanging ones were always gone. Unfortunately, my puny arm wasn't strong enough for my sticks to reach the higher branches.

Me and Peou loved the sounds and fresh smells of rain when the monsoons came; the heavy drops drummed like a thousand *samphors* playing on our rusting iron roof. I'm sad to say our roof leaked and the gutters quickly overflowed, sending torrents of water cascading over the edges. For fun, we'd pretend we were hiding in a secret treasure cave behind a waterfall, undressing and dancing naked under the overflowing gutters to get cool from the steamy weather, shrieking with laughter as the water splashed off our faces and shoulders. Wonder and innocence filled my childhood life in those days.

When I turned six, my oldest sister took me to register at the Trapeang Number Two primary school. Going in with a cheery face turned out easier said than done. After staring at the other kids on my first day, I was nervous and shy because they were all big and too noisy. Still, when you make a great leap ahead, you must promise yourself to try, right? So I tried hard and did well, even though being the smallest kid in the class brought me the wrong kind of attention.

My sister cut my hair short like all the farming kids and I'm afraid to say, I looked more like a skinny little boy. My family felt sorry for my small size because Mum didn't breastfeed me as a baby as she didn't have enough milk. After she'd gone to sell vegetables in the market, my sisters took me to the neighbour's house and asked them to breastfeed me as they hated to see the tears on my face and listen to me crying so hard with hunger. They told me this was the reason I'm so small and not too healthy. Even being so small, when the teacher asked me to read, I read as loudly as I could. My big voice made the others laugh, coming from such a miniature person.

During break times, I sat by myself watching the other kids play. I didn't join in, as they liked fighting each other and playing rough games. Sometimes when I brought snacks, they hit me and stole them. I wanted to fight back, but they were all bigger than me, so I would cry. Once though, a boy bullied me and this time, instead of crying, I got angry and threw a chair at him. The chair hit his head, making his nose bleed. He screamed in pain, so I grabbed my book and pencil and ran home as fast as I could, proud of myself, but too scared to go back to school for two days until Mum asked the teacher to protect me. To my surprise, the bullies left me alone afterwards. Three young girls even decided to become my friends. We became a girl gang and together we were strong.

At the start, I walked the two kilometres to school with the neighbourhood farming kids and being so small, I had to walk and run at the same time to keep up. I didn't dare go to school alone; getting lost in the jungle shortcuts where the thick green vegetation blocked out the daylight frightened me if I walked by myself. Soon, I found a girl in my class who lived near my house and we walked to school together. Kanya became my best friend. Her mum ran a local shop and her family had more money than us, but she didn't do well in class, so I often helped her by doing her homework. Whenever the teacher found out, she punished us with a few hits of her stick or made us stand in front of the blackboard on one leg. Now and then we talked so much we got lost in the dense jungle on the way home from school. Luckily, the villagers got to know us and brought us home when they heard us calling for help.

At mealtimes, my sisters criticised me for picking at my food. The problem being we lived in a fishing village and I didn't like fish. It smelt terrible and made me feel sick. When my mum cooked other kinds of food for me or added spicy herbs and vegetables to hide the fishy smell, my sisters made fun of me.

'We are poor. How can you be so picky about food?'

'We're not rich, so don't be a fussy princess.'

'These foods are specially cooked for Madam.'

'Isn't she a special queen bee?'

Whenever Mum had to cook food for the whole family, then cook different food for me, I felt sorry for her. She had to endure so much.

After dinner, me and Peou helped my older sisters wash the dishes and clean the house. No matter what my sisters said to me, I always helped them. When Mum split wood with the axe, I collected the firewood, or when she cleaned the vegetables, I brought her the water and dug the scraps into the vegetable garden. When I helped my mum, I was proud of myself, like a grown-up doing adult work. I loved to see Mum smile.

I dreamt of becoming a teacher. In my imagination, I stood next to the blackboard with the chalk, adding up numbers and showing my class how to solve their homework problems. Although my parents didn't support me a lot, I still tried my best and studied hard, so when I became a teacher I could earn enough money to hire people to grow vegetables and rice for us. Mum would be able to rest.

When the teacher asked questions or asked a student to do our homework on the blackboard, I always raised a hand first. I also put my hand up when I didn't know the answer, even though the teacher got angry with me.

'Chavy, why do you raise your hand when you don't know how to do it?' yelled she.

'Because I want to stand in front of the blackboard. When you teach and I stand next to you and look at the other students, I feel like I'm a teacher.'

My words would make her laugh. She told me if I studied hard and did my homework, it might be possible to be a teacher when I grew up.

Our family life got worse when I turned nine. My dad and his fishing boat boss broke up. With no job, he stayed home and started his own business growing more ducks. He started drinking alcohol.

When he drank too much sombai, he hit us. I didn't hate him; I pitied my mum because she worked even harder, yet he still beat her. A few times, my sisters protected Mum from my dad; they hated him when he got drunk. He scared us, yet my mum begged us to forgive him. He loved us, she explained, and he worried about us being so poor. Afterwards, he felt upset about hitting us, but he still did when he drank the next time.

My poor mum was tired, not just her body, but her mind, too. I cried silently when they fought each other, using my reading book to cover my face. I couldn't study when they fought each other, so I waited until midnight after they had gone to sleep. Living in this situation made me miserable and I needed a person to talk to who could understand my sorrows.

One day, I saw a number on a *Finding Friends* advertisement taped to the window of the local village shop and I called on the public phone. At first, a surprise appeared on my face because the number had a woman's name attached and a man answered. Still, he seemed to understand my problems. I called him on weekends, though my family didn't know about it. I never thought he might be a bad person, instead trusting his words came out of his heart; I believed he thought of me as a sister, as I thought of him like my brother. When we talked with each other, he tried to get me to visit him. I wanted to but always refused since I knew my family would never allow me to go there alone.

4. THE PINK HOUSE

At the end of the year, the teacher announced me as the highest-ranking pupil in my class: The Number One Student. I glowed with pride and couldn't wait to tell my parents. The school even organised an award ceremony to give prizes to the top three students and invited everyone's family to come. Before the ceremony started, my teacher asked to meet my family.

'I'm sorry, they are busy. They cannot come today,' I replied with a trembling voice, trying to hide my glum face.

All the other parents came to encourage their children. My dad refused, drinking with his friends being more important and I felt so upset with him. I understood my mum's situation, even though I was disappointed with her, too. She had to sell vegetables to earn money for the whole family. The times were extra hard now my dad had no fishing job.

After the ceremony, I held my prize tightly and ran home as quickly as I could. I didn't want the other children to see me crying because I didn't have parents who came with gifts and flowers as theirs did.

Home, alone and heartbroken, I decided to call my best friend. He understood my sadness and asked me earnestly to meet him. He said he wanted to see my face and told me he didn't live far away. I thought I could meet him and be back before my mum got home. He took me into the coffee shop and listened to my woes like a good friend. Later, I got worried about the time, so he kindly offered to drive me home. As we were about to leave, he gave me a cup of milk. I drank it and soon I became sleepy.

I woke up with a heavy, sticky weight pounding all over my body, crushing the life from me. I could hardly breathe. I had no clothes on. I saw the heavy weight on me was a man. He breathed like in a running race and I screamed in fright and pain because my insides were being ripped apart. I tried to sit up but couldn't lift my arms or legs as his sweaty body pressed down on me, pinning me to a hard mattress on the bed.

Terrified, I screamed more. There were two other men. They were naked, too. I could smell alcohol and saw their eagerness for me between their legs. One of them covered my mouth with his hand to make me quiet. I tried to bite him. He slapped me hard until my mouth and nose were swollen and bleeding. I could taste blood in my mouth. I tried to wriggle away from him. I couldn't and fell silent.

The other two men laughed while they held me down. A second one raped me. I wanted to go home. I tried to talk to them because I didn't want to die there. My cries were useless. The third man dragged me to the bathroom. He raped me again on the cold, mildewy floor and threw me back onto the bed when he finished with me.

A lot of money lay strewn on the table from the first man who had paid for my virginity. I sat naked on the dirty sheet watching him put his police uniform back on and leave, my blood and their stains on the sheets next to me. I could smell the sickly-sweet stink of their attack. I wept from the pain and humiliation of my rapes and the shame I had brought upon my family.

In the morning, my two captors took me to another place. I heard them say they were going to sell me. I didn't know where I'd been taken; I knew my farm and family were far away and my mind and body were too tired to fight any longer and throbbed with pain, inside and out. They tried to feed me rice soup and didn't rape me like before, so I waited in silent fear for what would happen next. Finally, one of them left to make their trade for me. The one I knew stayed on guard.

'I want to go to the toilet.'

He shouted at me to be quiet.

'I'm hungry.'

'Wait until my friend comes back.'

I tried to talk to him.

'If your mother, daughter, or sister were in the same situation as me, how would you feel?'

He shouted at me more.

'Don't talk so much. If you're hungry, wait here. I'll buy food for you. Don't try to run away. If you do, I will catch you, and I will kill you.'

He left, locking me in the room.

My chance to escape had arrived. I couldn't go out the front door since he had locked me in, but I managed to force open the bathroom window enough to squeeze my little body through and dropped down from the first floor into an alleyway.

My flip-flops fell off when I landed. In too much of a hurry to care and too scared he would come back before I got far enough away to put them back on, I kept running. The rocks and broken glass cut my feet quite severely. My feet hurt and the cuts bled as I stumbled towards the street. My heart pounded in my chest, but I knew I would be safe and free once on the main street. Before I got there, my vision blurred and I crumpled to the dirt like a puppet cut loose from its strings.

The bright light hurt my eyes and rough hands dragged from the boot of a car. My hands were tied together and I had a scarf around my mouth to stop me from calling for help. He took me inside a Pink House, shoving me into a windowless basement where other young girls and two little boys cowered around each other in the stark light of a single neon tube. Their faces were expressionless, indifferent to my arrival. I saw I wasn't free at all. My terrors had hardly begun.

Buddha's grace abandoned me for months. My new captors treated us brutally, beating us, giving us drugs to make us obedient and the days, weeks, whatever the time, passed in a grotesque haze. Customers would arrive to stay in the rooms upstairs for a night and occasionally they stayed for a few days. Men raped me more times than I can remember. As each new guest arrived, they forced us to put on colourful dresses, gave us earrings and bracelets to wear and a woman put lipstick and rouge on our faces and ribbons in our hair. We looked like pretty dolls. They sent us into a large room where we sat on benches, waiting for the men to come in and pick which one of us they wanted. Life became living like an animal in a zoo.

There were westerners, Chinese, Japanese, Thai and Vietnamese men who regularly came. We had to be nice to them and the local people as well. They ordered us to be extra nice to high-ranking Cambodian police officers. I remember one very fat man. An important Australian government official, they told us, and he came quite often. Our keepers said we must call him Papa Georgie. He always took two or three of us for his pleasures. Papa Georgie never treated us gently.

If a girl got sick, a man came to take her away. Sometimes girls became ill from the drugs and sometimes from a disease. Sometimes they tried to kill themselves. I never saw them again. New kids would arrive as replacements; the new girls were always terrified like me when I first came.

Every single morning when I woke up, I promised myself I would fight to stay alive to see my family again. I also tried my best to protect the new girls by telling them to sit behind me in the viewing room. If it looked like the man would pick them, I got up quickly, pretending he had selected me. Later, two of the older girls helped me by doing the same thing to protect new girls from the men. Our trick often worked, especially if we smiled, but we couldn't shield them forever, or the little boys at all. Eventually, everyone suffered the same fate.

One day, a miracle happened. Different people came into the Pink House. They were policemen accompanied by nurses, and they were making a lot of noise. At first, we were frightened and we huddled together in the corner of the basement, hugging each other. Then came a different feeling, I suppose I could say relief. We were not going to be put on display because the policemen were putting handcuffs on our captors and taking them away. The feeling should have been joy, but we had all buried our childhoods long before. After the nurses checked us, they wrapped us in blankets and the men carried each of us to a waiting bus, which took us all to a local hospital. It was night time and the flashing red and blue lights hurt my eyes. Our cellar had no windows, so time held no meaning for me.

I remember an older western man picking me up in his arms and carrying me to the bus. He had a kind face. In broken Khmer, he told me his name was Mr Simon and he smiled. I was safe now, he said, and he would take me home to my family. I curled into his arms like a baby. I didn't know how to cry anymore.

5. THE ORPHANAGE

Two days later, I returned home to Kampot with Mr Simon and an interpreter. I bowed at my parents' feet, asking them to forgive me for making them worried and saying sorry because I couldn't keep myself a virgin like other Cambodian girls. My mum hugged me.

'You did nothing wrong, Chavy. We are to blame because we didn't take loving care of you. We're sorry. We didn't know what happened to you and wanted you to come home. We thought you were dead.'

My mother touched my face to make sure I wasn't a dream, saying I looked as thin as our vegetable hoe. I had been gone for four months. I didn't know how much time had passed. It seemed like a long time to me.

Even though my family welcomed me back, I knew life would never be the same for me in my village with the shame I'd brought on my family. There would never be a husband for me here when I grew up. Mr Simon knew too. With the interpreter, they told my parents he would pay for me to take English classes, so later I might find a job as a tour guide, or in a hotel, where speaking a little English would help me earn good money for my family. His charity would also give extra money to my mother each month to make sure my family would look after me.

I studied English very hard for two years and taught Peou my lessons when I got home so she could learn too. Living by hiding from people made me tired. I hated seeing men, even my father and stayed by myself or with Peou, even though living in my private darkness made me scared and lonely. I began to hate myself. I couldn't remember the happy child I used to be, the one who loved to splash in the rain. I saw darkness around the lights instead of the other way around. Soon there were no colours in my world at all. Depression sometimes overwhelmed me and my health got worse. My mum kept encouraging me, although I didn't always listen to her. Once or twice, the pain in my heart became so strong I thought about throwing myself in the river to be at peace again. Mum still took care of me.

'Did anyone say bad things to you?' she would ask.

I always shook my head and she'd wipe my tears away.

'Don't worry about what other people say about you, Chavy. Even what your sisters say. They talk without thinking. You're their sister, please forgive them. Don't think too much and study hard.'

I would often hear my sisters blaming my mother.

'Why do you take care of her this much?'

'She also has hands. Why can't she eat by herself?'

'She's not a baby anymore.'

'She's so fake. She always wants attention.'

'We don't want to hear her crying like a crazy person all the time.'

My tears rained down when I couldn't hold them back after hearing what they said.

Finally, the noise from my older sisters and the looks from the people in the village forced my parents to send me away. They said they had found Peou and me a job as maids for a rich family in the big city of Phnom Penh.

As soon as we arrived at the house, I knew it wasn't a respectable place. From the stories the girls at the Pink House told me and how the servants looked at us, I knew our jobs were not to be maids. Now I needed to protect my little sister. So on the second night, after the house became silent, I woke Peou, whispering to her to be as quiet as a mouse and we ran away. Hours later, too tired to walk any longer, we found refuge inside the walls surrounding a large building where we fell asleep, curled up together in the doorway like two spoons. In the morning, the people who worked there found us and took us inside. The sign over the gates called it the Vitara Orphanage.

The manuscript ended there. Katy lay back in her seat, sadness draining through every part of her. She blinked away the tears.

In the isolation of the cabin, honey-coated appeals churned in her mind, testing her resolve.

'Why are you answering a call for a journey you are the world's least qualified person to undertake?'

'Why are you putting Clara, the only family you have left, in danger?'

'Why don't you attend Simon's funeral and return home to the safety of the Red Peony Garden?'

'Is this Khmer girl any of your business?'

Katy didn't know the answers. Could she be blaming herself for what happened? Should she have taken more interest in Simon's work? Would he have been more careful if she had?

She remembered another occasion when she made a reckless decision - a time when she asked Simon to take her to see the English countryside all those years ago. She hardly knew him then. They were leaning on the parapet of the Albert Bridge in Chelsea, watching the River Thames swirl and eddy around the pylons in the moonlight. He quoted something about "travelling the world to find the beautiful, but the first place we should look is into our hearts" by a philosopher she'd never heard of, while he tried to convince her the English fought their wars to defend the hedgerows.

At the time, Katy didn't know her impetuous request would change her life. As it turned out, her destiny and those of the people she would come to love became etched in stone after their unscripted moment. The Chinese people know this as *yuánfèn*, the hand of fate.

Despite the fears tempting her to abandon her quest, she drew herself deeper into the dearest memories of her life. Katy *would* answer the call. She hadn't picked this battle but knew in her heart so long as she was in it, she would see it through to the end.

Katy Yehonala would walk her road to Damascus.

4

THE JADE PRINCESS

Beijing Capital Airport is a welcome destination. I gazed down through the window of my Air France jet as we banked low above the smoggy *hutongs* and already clogged boulevards, preparing to land after my overnight flight from Paris where I'd recently made my home. I checked my watch, 7 am, and breathed a sigh of relief. No delays. I had plenty of time to relax and practise before my performance at the concert hall in the evening. We touched down gently and taxied towards the terminal.

Premier Liu Xiang and his powerful wife, Qin Liangyu, would be there with their daughter, Liu Yu. I was friends with Yu, or Vivien Liu, as she became when she attended Wellesley College. Vivi was a year younger than me and a vivacious, delightful woman, quite unspoiled, unlike so many of the "princesslings" in China and we were both involved in similar charitable organisations. We weren't best friends as our paths seldom crossed, but we shared similar interests and a bowl of soup when we were both in Beijing or when we met at charity functions. I was one of only a handful of people who knew she was a very discreet gay woman and I also liked her partner, the actress Carolyn Wu, star of the immensely popular *Legend of the Dragon Princess* historical drama series.

Vivi's father was a new style of Chinese leader, the youngest ever to hold the position. I'd met him at concerts before and other times on fund-raising events after the devastating Wenchuan earthquake back in 2008, before he became Premier.

Don't get the wrong idea. He and I weren't close friends by any stretch of the imagination. Even so, a large bunch of roses from him always waited for me after my Beijing performances. Nor did I nurse any silly fantasies of Premier Liu shopping for red roses and writing me messages personally, but he loved classical music and his patronage was important. He also knew of my immense pride in my Chinese heritage, especially my Manchu bloodline, even if watered down by a helping of Aussie corpuscles. As a result, my performances always lifted in the magnificent Beijing Concert Hall, as if the prodigal daughter had come home.

Except for Dad, I don't know much about the western side of my family, but the Chinese one grew up in the northern city of Shenyang, the ancient Qing capital, until we moved to Beijing when I became Uncle Sasha's student at the conservatory. Up until two years ago, we'd held onto our Shenyang home as well, where my dear old Nanny Wu lived out her remaining years.

Shortly after 9 am, the taxi dropped me at home. "Home" is an apartment my mother bought a decade or more ago. I stay here whenever I'm in China; it's a short walk across Tiananmen Square to the concert hall and to the Conservatory of Music where I studied as a ten-year-old.

One of these days, I'll get around to selling this apartment too I suppose, and move everything to my parents' home in Australia. I'm only ever in Beijing for a few weeks a year and miss spending time in Melbourne.

Our treasured nineteenth-century Pleyel piano moved to Beijing from Shenyang with us. *Laolao,* my grandmother, taught me to play music on this beautiful museum piece before she died, so it has sentimental value well above its monetary one. I loved coming home to Beijing for the Pleyel as much as anything else; its velvety sound reproduced pure Chopin. When I played, the music instantly transported me back to my happy childhood days in Shenyang with Nanny Wu, my mother, and *laolao.* Then, my raucous keyboard banging and little Maomaochong's howling were followed by the banging of sleep-disturbed neighbours during my not so virtuosic beginnings. Growing up, our tiny white poodle, Maomaochong, my darling "caterpillar", had been my best friend.

Although reserved by nature, like all Chinese girls of the time, I didn't suffer false modesty about my talent as a classical pianist. After all, the ageing Russian musical genius Aleksander Berkovich himself, my grumpy, dearest Uncle Sasha, recognised my talent when I was nine. A long story my mother related in the diary she published, much to my embarrassment. I don't recommend you read it unless you happen to like stories about precocious children.

He told her I would be the greatest Romantic pianist of the century; I'm grateful Ma decided not to pass *that* snippet of hair-raising karma on to me at the time! I knew Uncle Sasha and his wife, Anna Kholodenko, the legendary Ukrainian cellist - my aristocratic *babushka* - were enormously proud of what I became and he mentored me until he died a decade later. Their fond memory, including Uncle Sasha's bear-growls whenever I bungled an impenetrable melody, followed by babushka's scowls at him for his ill-temper and making me cry, hold a permanent place in my heart.

The musical media know me today as the Jade Princess, a reference to my descent from the Manchu empress, Cixi, the other Yehonala woman of some fame, or infamy, depending on which history book you read. Max Santini, my agent, has made much of this and taught me early in my career performing has as much to do with theatre as it does with musical ability. I'm sure Max's carefully crafted portrayal of me accounted for a large part of my celebrity. She called it my brand, like Clara Yehonala is a musical version of Louis Vuitton. Here I readily confess my occasional homage to Louis Vee; I'm easy prey to my designer vice whenever Max and I stroll down to Place de Vendôme near her apartment in the first arrondissement, or if we wander along the elegant Rue du Faubourg Saint-Honoré, home to the *haute couture* brands of Valentin and Chanel.

The piano has been my life and joy since childhood. My mother tells stories about *laolao's* playing, giving her the one respite from my violent squirming and kicking during my early escape attempts from inside her, so I suppose being a musician from birth is no exaggeration, even an understatement.

Walking onto a stage now as a fêted pianist is like nothing else in the world. I feel the sense of occasion in every nerve, the awesome responsibility when the spotlight falls solely on me. Nothing can be unperformed the moment I sit down and I know the conductor, audience and critics dissect each note. None of them as sternly as me.

At first, the possibility of failing so publicly terrified me. What eleven-year-old wouldn't be quaking in her boots performing in front of their mother? Not to mention a thousand other people. As my celebrity grew, another feeling dominated. I understood I had forfeited my right to be less than perfect, whether or not jetlag had me wondering if I knew night from day, which happened more often than you might think. Like a trapeze artist without a safety net, I learnt to cope with those pressures while barely in my teens.

Well… sorry, I'm lying to you. And as anyone will tell you, I never tell lies. As a matter of fact, those demons narrowly missed taking my life. A gruesome story, but thankfully one with a happy ending. I may tell you all a bit later. We'll see. These days I'm far more assertive than my mother would ever believe and I surprise myself all the time. I've overcome the five thousand years of conditioning Chinese girls have endured. Well, almost.

Now, back to Max, my agent and friend. Dearest Max had somehow managed to keep all my marbles in the bag through my worst times, which incidentally, also brings me to my new home in Paris. It's Max's home and we live there together. A recent turning point in my life shall we say, though we've been close for all of my twelve years or more *on the road*.

Except for Uncle Sasha, there have never been influential men in my life, only women, so it didn't seem odd to me to find myself attracted to Max even though she was much older. At first, doubtless from all our demureness-conditioning, I felt more confused about my feelings than affection. We'd tiptoed around for a couple of years until three months ago when I agreed to move in and we'd see what happened. Let me say I'm hardly the *femme fatale* or Mills & Boon type, more a deer in headlights, especially in my underwear, but so far, so good. We don't see much of each other as my life is usually taken up living in airports, on aeroplanes, or out of suitcases in, nowadays, chic hotel rooms. Music has always been my escape as well as my greatest love, anyway.

I often hear from people who imagine classical pianists living in gilded cages, far removed from normal lives. If those people met me in real life, they'd find me disappointingly ordinary. I'm not floating in fairyland lost in a transcendent melody, adorning the gossip pages of trashy magazines with a Formula 1 driver in tow, or high on drugs and alcohol. Instead of champagne breakfasts, cocktail parties and using all those free tickets, I love nothing better than wearing my old jeans, jersey and woolly socks to lounge around and mull over sudoku, or I'm on a quest for a quiet dumpling restaurant in the local Chinatown. I'm a lament for those who picture their virtuosi sitting atop Mount Meru at the centre of the universe.

In the last year or two, I've discovered Harry Potter. I love losing myself in JK Rowling's imaginary worlds created by language, not unlike my own in many ways, Harry P's in words on paper, mine written in notes on the grand staff.

I've got no time for social butterflying, even if I yearned for such a lifestyle. Apart from Harry P, one of my few concessions to non-musical pleasures is an occasional visit with Max to her hometown of Montalcino, a picturesque, medieval hilltop town in Tuscany. Her parents have a vineyard there and in their warm-hearted, exuberant Italian way, they fuss over me like their favourite pasta. They own horses too and I love to ride in the rolling hills among the cypress trees and olive groves. The other place I love is Melbourne. If we're ever all there at the same time, hanging out with Dad and Ma and sharing a bottle of shiraz is even better.

I realise it sounds like my feet never touch the ground. Let me admit I adore my transient life working with gifted musicians, though not for the reasons you might think. The truth is, it's mostly a lonely existence and any *diva* pretensions disappear whenever I sit facing my piano in a hallowed place like Vienna's *Musikverein* or my sentimental favourite, the *Salle Pleyel* Concert Hall in Paris. To be looking into the mind of Liszt or Rachmaninoff is to feel humbled before the greatness of the composition and my private struggle to win the composer's consent. The subtleties in these divine creations inspire me; I feel blessed by my musical gift and the sacrifices are easy.

Now, back to Max again. No, I haven't told my mother about her, mainly because I have no idea what to say. Incidentally, before you start jumping up and down, this is *not* a lie, the odd omission doesn't count. I don't think she's too worried about having a grandson, at least not compared to most Chinese mothers. Still, relationships such as between Max and me aren't part of her normal life. Or mine. Besides, I owe her far too much for her sacrifices for me to disappoint her. I can't decide whether I'm admitting to cowardice or holding more altruistic motives.

Adore her as I do, I'm also aware as much as she is, her relationships have ranged from misadventures to disasters over the years. Like me, she never had a father to guide her romantic exploits and I suspect she's spent her life searching for an idealised version of one. Whether by fate, choice or accident, except for Max, I've avoided being seduced by her example or finding myself a participant in similar follies.

Dad's the exception. He's the best thing ever to have happened to her and me. She met him, Simon, while a student in England. Even then, she almost blew the opportunity when *laolao* became sick after Granny Chen died. She left England and him, to go home to China. When she arrived back in Shenyang, she discovered me crawling around her uterus and didn't tell him – so now you know the story about how I lost my dad for the next twenty years. Whatever the psychology behind it for both of us, Dad's a man we both love without reservation.

On Saturday night, my performance at the Beijing Concert Hall again seemed like a homecoming. The guest conductor, Maestro

Michel Garnier, and I knew each other. We'd also played Jiang Kui's works before and understood our tempos well. The afternoon rehearsals had been intense since Jiang's concerto was fearfully challenging in parts, but I'd been learning the piece for months and we were looking forward to the night. I thought Jiang's latest work his best, ranging from a soft, sensual piano opening with beautiful cadenzas for me, to a majestic finale Beethoven might have roused himself from the earth's gentle embrace to applaud.

To my great amusement, as well as being enormously flattered, the irascible Jiang Kui asked Max if I would perform his work. Jiang's genius, self-proclaimed as well as accepted, was no secret to anyone; my amusement was due to his legendary antipathy towards female pianists. His *tits and thighs* scorn of a few notable ones became such a running joke they avoided his music altogether. We'd spoken many times about interpretations of the piece. As a result, I'd decided to play the cadenzas with more sensuality to help temper his poor image and Michel had agreed to do the same.

My red roses were there following the performance. I gave them to the gifted young concertmaster who had led the violins and orchestra faultlessly. Premier Liu and Madam Qin honoured us when they came by to compliment Jiang Kui and me and Vivi and I had a friendly catchup over a glass of champagne. She invited me to a karaoke night with Carolyn and her other girlfriends the following evening.

Jiang himself beamed with joy at the concerto's reception. He even told me he liked my green dress. I told *him* his bow tie was the wrong colour. He roared with laughter and we toasted each other while we had our pictures taken.

My watch showed past 11 pm when I finally left after mingling with those VIPs and media at the *après*. Contrary to what my friends believed about my life, no swanky limousine waited at the stage door to spirit me home after I'd bathed in "flashlights and adoration".

Comfortable instead in my old jeans, well-travelled hi-top Vans and hooded sweater, I dawdled home alone across Tiananmen

Square with my shoulder bag, passing people who didn't know me or paid me any attention. Like the dumpling restaurants, walking alone at night must be one of the few times I got to know life as a normal person. I smiled to myself, closed my eyes and took a long breath. Clara Yehonala, another pedestrian out late, enjoying a stroll on a balmy evening like anyone else.

I let myself into the apartment and ran the shower, feeling the hot water massage my shoulders and the day's tension trickling away. Afterwards, I switched on the TV, half-hearing a story in breaking news about a western man who had got himself killed, idly wondering why anyone in China would be remotely interested. Slipping into comfy old pyjamas, I dried my hair and went to bed.

Whatever Clara's other eccentricities might be, being an early riser isn't among them. She sleeps until late, then drags herself sleepily to the kitchen to make coffee. She's looking forward to seeing her musical friends at the conservatory later in the afternoon, followed by her fun night of karaoke at the KTV before flying back to Paris in the morning. While waiting for the coffee machine, she idly clicks on the TV and checks her mobile phone.

'How odd, nine missed calls from Max and even two from Vivi Liu and it looks like dozens more from everyone I know and from many I don't. I must...'

She glances at the television screen.

In the split second of comprehension, her face falls from mild concern to nightmarish, overwhelming horror.

She watches herself break right before her eyes.

She's clawing her face, her hair.

A scream wrenches free from her soul. Another. Another.

They ricochet around her apartment. They are primal, of raw intensity, of desperate need, of searing pain and they escape into the street outside and drown out the world.

Clara's face and a picture of her dad stare back at her from the TV screen.

She hears her telephone ringing…

5

A CURIOUS WELCOME FOR KATY

Arriving at Pochentong Airport wasn't a new experience. Clara and I had been to Cambodia three years earlier after agreeing, me dubiously, to see what my new husband had been up to there with his charity.

My sweet-talking husband somehow managed to convince his new wife and daughter into visiting a place where I fully expected to meet my worst nightmares: heinous desperadoes selling us into a life of sex slavery, getting ourselves blown up by landmines, or exotic bacterium devouring us from the inside. After listening to stories of his adventures, how come I turned out to be the one having palpitations? His still-besotted daughter would have stormed the Gates of Hell without a first thought if he asked, let alone a second one.

Our Khmer guide, Rithy, stood waiting for us when we arrived. He said his name meant "powerful strength", a physical comfort, if not an entirely reassuring one, by the fact we needed him in the first place. Now, here I am again with, I must say, well-founded misgivings.

Today, my destination proclaimed itself as Phnom Penh International Airport. A more grandiose sounding name than before, announcing times had moved on. Well, I reminded myself, they had for me too.

As soon as I walked onto the aerobridge, a solid wall of humid, suffocating air hit me. I sucked hard, gasping for oxygen. The rains hadn't yet come, although the ominous, blue-grey clouds billowing on the horizon, shifting their shapes even as I watched, advertised the first monsoon storm on the way. Or perhaps the Gates of Hell did plan to prove a point.

The air conditioning inside the terminal was fighting a valiant battle against May's stifling weather and though outnumbered, had somehow captured a handful of degrees advantage. After locating my bags and paying for my visa, I looked around for the hotel shuttle and sanctuary from the devil's sauna.

'Mrs Yehonala?'

I turned to find a man standing behind me, immune from the steamy air and crisply dressed in an open-neck shirt and pleated pants. He looked to be about thirty years old, tanned and fit-looking, with the poise of a man in control of his personal space. I instantly regretted not visiting the restrooms to freshen up, a striking example of my vanity, one of the deadly sins I prefer to think of as a virtue.

'Yes. Are you from the hotel?'

My surprise to find an Australian, for his familiar accent betrayed him, would be the driver of a hotel shuttle must have shown on my face. He looked faintly amused.

'Good morning, Mrs Yehonala. No, I'm afraid not. My name's Martin Lewis. I'm from the Australian Embassy. Ambassador Nelson asked me to see you safely to your hotel. It's the Palace View, isn't it?'

'Well, yes, Mr…Lewis? I've booked the shuttle to take me. There's no need to trouble you.'

'It's no trouble, I assure you. And please call me Martin. Don't worry about the shuttle, there's an embassy car outside. Its air-conditioning might be just what the doctor ordered.'

Nearing meltdown, I could hardly disagree with the diagnosis and let him whisk me through a side door to a waiting car. The driver took my bags while I settled into the mercifully cool interior.

'May's the worst month of the year,' he needlessly informed me, 'though they tell me the first rains may well arrive this afternoon. The wet season doesn't usually start for another fortnight, but the skies don't lie. After the storms, the city will be bearable again.'

He exhaled as if in relief for this miracle, although from what I could see, he'd not leaked a drop of perspiration. A second one ran between my shoulder blades and trickled down my spine.

'Mrs Yehonala, please pardon the surprise. First of all, might I extend my sincerest sympathies and those of the Australian Government to you and your daughter for your loss? This tragedy must be a terrible time for you both.'

'Thank you. To be honest, beyond the first shock, I haven't had time to think much about what happened. I'm still half-expecting Simon to call me and apologise for the mix-up, though I assume bringing me good news isn't why you're here.'

'Ah, I wish it were the case. But no, the story is quite true.'

'Why *are* you here?'

'Well, let me put you in the picture. When Agent Gauci telephoned yesterday, saying you wanted to hold your husband's funeral in Cambodia and with your daughter's arrival as well, I'm afraid it rather set the cat among the pigeons, so to speak. Embassies don't deal well with last-minute emergencies, you see. Do you remember Agent Gauci? She came to see you Sunday.'

Who could have forgotten Melinda and her colleague, Glenn Davies? They were the Federal Police officers who brought me the news of Simon's death. Was it yesterday? Maybe the day before, I couldn't remember. I grew curious to know why Simon's funeral would be a last-minute emergency for the Australian Embassy. Even I knew unless someone were well-connected or their favour needed cultivation, embassies don't provide officials and shiny cars with chauffeurs for them. As far as I knew, Simon and I were neither.

'Martin, you haven't yet explained about cats and pigeons. I'm tired and distressed about what lies ahead, as well as confused. I don't want to add crankiness to my list of problems. Or yours. So, as you offered, could you please "put me in the picture"?'

'No problem. Well, let me start by allaying at least one of your concerns. Ambassador Nelson has instructed me to put the resources of the embassy at your disposal. With your permission, we'll manage all the funeral arrangements for you. Now, as regards the rest, I'll drive you and your daughter to meet the ambassador tomorrow morning and he'll answer all your questions. I beg you not to press me further. There's little else I can say.'

'Where's Clara?' I asked him, becoming alarmed. 'Is she alright?'

'Oh, yes. I assure you, your daughter's absolutely safe.'

He glanced at his watch. A Rolex. Somehow, I doubted he'd bought it in a street market.

'She's about to board an Air China flight from Beijing to Phnom Penh as we speak and will be arriving here early this evening. I took the liberty of booking her into an adjoining room to yours with a connecting door. I thought you'd like the convenience of having her close by.'

Calmer now, I thanked him. 'Yes, you're very thoughtful. Will you be picking her up as well?'

'Alas, no. Miss Yehonala's a Chinese citizen; the Australian Embassy would be going beyond our jurisdiction to get involved with a foreign national in another country. However, we have spoken to the Chinese Ambassador. They had already booked your daughter's travel and arranged for their embassy staff to meet her flight and bring her to the hotel. I'm told Premier Liu knows your daughter personally; seems he regards her as a national treasure in China. He spoke directly to the ambassador so you can rest assured her journey will be trouble-free.'

'I don't understand. Are we in danger?'

'No, no, not at all. No worries,' he hastily assured me, offering one too many guarantees of a danger-free visit for my comfort. He read the scepticism on my face.

'It's more to do with protecting you from the media,' he reassured me. 'You may not be aware, the story of your husband's death, coupled with your daughter's celebrity and your family history, made headlines in the world's media. The newspapers here are sniffing a story too and we don't want them to make a fuss. Allow you both the privacy you need at this stressful time. You know the sort of thing.

'In fact, one of the reporters from the *Phnom Penh Times*, Jim Preston, was waiting at the airport to ambush you. I had a quick word in his ear, but he'll be back when your daughter arrives, along with others, I expect. You can rest assured the Chinese Embassy staff will be diligent in keeping her away from reporters. The quaint expression we use is "taking an abundance of caution" to protect the privacy of our citizens.'

I knew less than nothing about the wheels of diplomacy, indeed, tactfulness being my least endowed charm, according to Clara. Even so, I doubted two ambassadors and China's premier lost a moment's sleep over one Australian man dying far from home and my curiosity became aroused a second time. Also, I knew Clara was the last person who needed protecting from the media even without Max Santini hovering around. Despite a natural inclination to speak my mind, I decided to bite my tongue. At least for now.

'Martin, is all this a diplomatic way of you saying the embassy would rather have flown Simon home to Australia?'

'Mrs Yehonala, it's a diplomatic way of saying you're a citizen of Australia, entitled to all the resources at our disposal when you need them. We're simply here to support you. Well, here we are at your hotel. Let me help you get checked in and settled.

'A final word, if I may,' said he, leaving the room. 'This is a wonderful hotel with some of the best food in Phnom Penh, as you may remember from your last visit. Once your daughter arrives, you might prefer to dine here rather than explore the temptations of the city, at least until you meet Ambassador Nelson tomorrow. It would be best under the circumstances. I'll pick you up at 10 am. Goodbye, Mrs Yehonala.'

This unflappable young man intrigued me. How did he know I'd stayed here before, three years ago? I agreed to heed his suggestion. For a while.

Exhausted, I lay down on the bed, trying to make sense of the unexpected events since stepping off the aeroplane. Grief still bubbled inside, kept in check by the lack of sleep, confusion and alien surroundings. I dozed fitfully. Hours later, the sound of the connecting door opening snapped me awake. Clara stood there looking like she'd not slept in a month. She ran to me and we hugged, both finally free to howl our eyes out in private.

'Ma, what are we going to do?'

'It's okay, *baobei*; we'll be fine. We always manage.'

'Why? Why are we so cursed? He promised me he wouldn't die. He promised he'd never leave me. He promised he'd always be here for me. I hate him for doing this to me. Why couldn't he keep his promise to me? There's a hex on being a father in the Yehonala family. In our family, it means if I ever marry, I'll lose my husband, and my children will lose their dad and...'

'*Hush, baobei*, we'll be okay. Let's rest together for a while.'

'I decided on the plane I'm never going to get married, Ma. I'm not even going to find a boyfriend. Ever. It's too sad. I loved Dad so much. I waited twenty years to meet him and now he's been taken away. Like all the other fathers. It's not fair...'

She collapsed in my arms, still sobbing. We lay together on the bed for a long time, holding each other close, not even trying to stop the tears, losing ourselves in the companionship of the room's satin evening gloom.

'You know, when I stepped off the plane, at least five Chinese men were waiting for me,' whispered Clara to me later. 'They already had my bags, rushed me through the visa office and away from the airport. They wouldn't tell me why. What's going on, Ma?'

'I don't know. This man from the Australian Embassy, Martin Lewis, met me. He said reporters are eager to write a story about you and Simon and they need to protect us from them. I expect the Chinese people were doing the same thing. He's taking us to the Australian Embassy tomorrow morning and the ambassador will explain what's going on.'

'I'm hungry. Can we go out and find something? We could stretch our legs and try the street food.'

'I have a better idea. Let's get food sent up and a nice bottle of wine. Sound good to you? It's so clammy outside.'

Even as I spoke, thunder rumbled overhead and a fractured ribbon of lightning illuminated our darkened room. Almost immediately, the heavens broke releasing a torrent of vertical rain in the still air as the first monsoon blotted out the view, making the choice for us and avoiding awkward excuses.

We settled on the balcony sharing bowls of barbequed fish and lemongrass beef, drinking a favourite Australian shiraz. The pounding rain continued to shroud the city in its noisy, blurry mask and at least for now, our earlier pent-up grief spent. We relaxed companionably next to each other, saying nothing for some time, listening to the monsoon's musical rhythm.

'Perhaps I should have agreed to bring Simon back to Australia; I've got a feeling the next few days are going to be hard for us. I'm sorry, I wish it could be easier. It won't be and we're going to need each other.'

My daughter, my best friend, looked at me.

'I'm sorry for what I said before. You know, about hating Dad. I didn't mean it. I needed to lash out at someone. Don't worry, I'll never let you down. We both know what you did is what Dad would have wanted and… can I sleep in your bed with you tonight?'

A mother and her daughter eyed each other, committing to an oath of solidarity, clinking glasses to seal a pact.

'Yes, the company would be nice; I think there'll be plenty of times over the next week neither of us will want to be alone in the night.'

They took breakfast in the small French-colonial bistro next to the pool and returned to their room, relaxing on the balcony and waiting for Martin Lewis. After a good cry and a night's sleep, they both felt and undeniably looked better. The luscious, tropical smells from the gardens below drifted on the morning air, breathable once more after the cleansing downpour the night before.

The Palace View overlooked the ornate, yellow and white King's Palace with its intricate Khmer spires and multi-layered golden roofs in an elegant part of Phnom Penh. Beyond the palace, the mighty Mekong River bustled with its motley armada of wooden barges ferrying families, vegetables and whatever else kept the city's heart beating. A calming view to quiet the most stressed of souls.

'I saw two Chinese men in the foyer, the same ones who met me yesterday,' said Clara, savouring a delicate flower tea. 'They need to go back to spy school if they're from the *Guoanbu* because they stood out like westerners with chopsticks. I'll be happier once we know what's going on.'

Katy smiled. Clara had recovered the quirky sense of humour she loved about her. Together, they would deal with whatever lay ahead.

'The man I met at the airport, Martin Lewis, told me Premier Liu had taken a personal interest in your well-being. China seems to consider you a living legend, so you can bet no Chinese bureaucrat is going to risk you even breaking a fingernail. You might have to get used to them.'

'In that case, they're already lining up for a stretch in a *Laogai* holiday camp, fingernails are a sacrifice all pianists make for our art. Anyway, I'm quite used to people following me around. It's a pity Max isn't here. She'd quickly see them off.'

'I suspect the formidable Max Santini might have met her match with those two. We'll need to look after ourselves.'

'Ma, I just want to lay Dad to rest and say our goodbyes. It isn't a lot to ask, is it? Why can't people leave us alone?'

'I don't know. Hopefully, we'll…'

The telephone buzzed.

'Martin Lewis is downstairs waiting to take us to the embassy. Perhaps we'll find the answers.'

6

CLARA BARES HER CLAWS

'Good morning, ladies, I hope you rested well. I believe the day is going to be less humid after last night's storm. Not as wearing on everyone, I expect.'

'Good morning to you, Martin. Before we go any further, if you're our bodyguard, jailer, taxi driver, or whatever your job is, I insist you call us by our first names. My name's Katy. This is my daughter, Clara.'

'Great, first names are so much easier; I'm happy being called Martin. I'm delighted to meet you, Clara. Sorry it's under such unfortunate circumstances.'

He shook her hand, holding on to it and his eye contact taking too long for a casual introduction. Was he showing a chink in his diplomatic armour?

'Whenever you're ready Martin…'

Clara freed her hand, offering a lop-sided, tolerant smile. I'd never paid much attention to her wearing her public persona before, causing a quick refresh of a mother's idealised image of her unpolished little girl.

Two Chinese men pursued us out of the hotel, their car close behind as we drove away. Ten minutes later, our car turned into the modern steel-grey and glass structure of the new Australian Embassy building and disappeared into the cool shade of the basement. An express lift opened to a reception area where an immaculately dressed Australian woman led us to an office designed to impress powerful friends or, I supposed, to intimidate lesser mortals. Several people were already waiting. One, a tall, self-assured man with a professional smile and going-through-the-motions eyes, came over.

'Ah, good morning Mrs Yehonala, Miss Yehonala. My name's Robert Nelson, the Australian Ambassador to Cambodia. Welcome to Phnom Penh. Allow me to introduce you to Ambassador Zhao from the Chinese Embassy and Elena Accardi. Elena is the head of UNICEF's child protection agency in Cambodia. You already know Captain Lewis.'

'*Captain* Lewis?'

We shook hands and the ambassador invited us to sit down, offering tea and coffee. The performance seemed to be a show for us, though why I couldn't imagine. I glanced at Clara and saw her thoughts dittoed mine.

'On behalf of us all, indeed of our governments, our sincerest condolences on your loss. It is tragic beyond words. But rest assured, we will provide every assistance to you and leave no stone unturned to bring the criminals to justice.'

I sighed, hoping we'd been called here for more than an assault on clichés and platitudes.

'Clara and I are grateful, thank you; Captain Lewis and the Chinese Embassy staff have been *diligent* in making sure we were able to settle into our hotel. Ambassador Nelson, why has my husband's death created such diplomatic attention? We would only have asked you for consular help to arrange the funeral.'

'Well, normally, such would be the case. However, I'm afraid the matter is a little more complicated, mainly because of your family background, the international celebrity of Miss Yehonala and as might be expected, the nature of your husband's death.'

Ambassador Zhao continued.

'Mrs Yehonala, your daughter is a household name in China, even around the world. Things she does often become news.

Premier Liu, even the Chairman, take a great interest in seeing China's shining stars celebrated at home and especially abroad. Premier Liu's aware of Clara's musical gifts and knows her behaviour is always exemplary and I might add, her image is a powerful symbol of China's growing presence on the world stage.'

The urbane Zhao, a generation and an education later than the revolutionary Chinese government officials of twenty years ago, looked perfectly at home in this environment. I took an instant dislike to him. He turned to Clara.

'Miss Yehonala, your arrival here for your father's funeral has already made headlines in the world's media. We need to be comfortable...'

Clara raised the palm of her hand in a gesture worthy of an apprentice traffic policeman on Melbourne's Collins Street.

'Ambassador Zhao, before you continue, please listen carefully to me. I am proud to be a daughter of China and my involvement in good works there. I also take immense pride in my Manchu heritage and will never do anything to discredit either. I am deeply offended if you are suggesting I might do otherwise. My *celebrity*, as you call it, has nothing to do with me saying goodbye to my father. Before anything else, I am my father's daughter, not China's. I will tell you, sir, right now, I care nothing about newspaper stories. I care only to share a moment with my father for the last time, which I am going to do with my mother. I do not care in the least whether we make you, China, the Australian Government, or anyone else, *comfortable* or not. Now, please tell my mother and me why we are here.'

I looked at my daughter as she stared down these two powerful men, defiance etched into every fibre of her body. I saw Martin and Elena Accardi wince. Clara evidently picked up similar misgivings about Ambassador Zhao.

'Clara - may I call you Clara?' soothed Ambassador Nelson. 'We're not wishing to prevent you from honouring your father. On the contrary, I promise you. If you allow me, I'll ask Martin to explain the dilemma we have. Martin, would you mind, please?'

'Certainly, sir.

'Clara, Katy, let me first reiterate the ambassador's comment. We all want you to have the privacy you deserve.'

Clara fixed him with an icy stare.

'I feel there's another *however* coming, Captain Lewis?'

'Yes, well, you see, your father's, Mr Bailey's, death has brought into sharp focus a side of Cambodia's life we're all working hard to wipe out - the evil of the child sex-trafficking trade. Clara, your musical genius, the story of meeting your father after twenty years and your family's genealogy back to the Qing dynasty rulers, have created the kind of story the media love. Here in Cambodia, it's the same, which is why we've gone to so much trouble to keep the media away from you.'

'Why does it matter? Who cares if the newspapers use my story to write about the trafficking trade? I certainly don't. Anyway, surely publicity would be a good thing.'

Clara refused to be side-tracked by flattery from Martin, continuing to glare at him.

'Excuse me, Martin. Perhaps I might continue.'

Elena Accardi turned towards us. Clearly, a change of strategy was called for. Martin Lewis looked relieved.

'Normally, Clara, yes it would. For more than three years, UNICEF, with the support of charities and governments, Australia and China among them, have been pushing to have laws passed to protect children and improve child welfare. You might think people would see this as a good thing. But in Cambodia, there's strong resistance in some quarters.'

I wanted Clara to know her fellow mutineer remained primed for battle. 'I still don't see why us being here is any problem. So far, you have done nothing except add more stress to an already stressful time for us. If there's nothing else which is none of our business, or unless there is anything which is, please take us back to our hotel.'

'Mrs Yehonala,' said Ambassador Nelson, barely containing his irritation.

He paused.

'This information I give you is in confidence. There's a lot of power and money invested in leaving the situation the way it is. Next month, there will be a vote on the proposed new laws in the National Assembly. If they pass, the Cambodian Government will be able to prosecute some powerful people and expose a lot of entrenched corruption behind the trafficking and drug trade.'

'Ambassador, I'm not quite so naïve as you may think to believe governments are incorruptible; there isn't much *confidential* to me about politicians and bureaucrats having greasy palms. Why don't you tell us why it's any of our business?'

'As your daughter said a moment ago, your husband's funeral ought to be an opportunity to reinforce the need for the new laws. However, it is a two-edged sword. Our Chinese friends, led by Ambassador Zhao, have been leading the way in pushing the Cambodian authorities to make the changes. On the other hand, a careless word, a criticism of what the government is proposing, may swing enough votes to undo the work of the last three years. Particularly coming from Clara, who has a powerful voice which will carry around the world, and even more so in China, who the Cambodian government rely on for support.'

Nelson looked at us, then at Zhao, annoyed he told us more than he planned. Zhao sat as inscrutable as an ancient Zen master. His stare gave away his displeasure, though of whom I had no idea.

'This is the reason we kept you from the media before we had the chance to talk,' continued Nelson. 'There will be those trying to take advantage of anything either of you says or try to put words in your mouth, to discredit the government's record and hence build suspicion about the motives behind the new laws.'

'You both seem to have forgotten my father is dead because the government *does* sit on its hands about the child sex business. What are you asking us to do, say what a fantastic job you're all doing? If you're asking me to meekly wring my hands and be silent, I can tell you to think again. Nothing is further from my mind. I doubt my mother feels differently.'

'Most certainly not, Clara,' an annoyed Nelson responded. 'We want to release a statement to the newspapers, from you both, to reinforce what we are trying to achieve.'

He handed us both a single sheet of paper.

'We want you to say nothing except what is in the press release to anyone. Frankly, my concern is this will be difficult. Naturally, the temptation will be to criticise the Cambodian Government for what happened to Mr Bailey. I would doubtless feel inclined to do so myself in your position, so I understand why you might want to express critical feelings.'

'If you were ever in our position! I hope you never are *in our position,* sir. Are we also to keep our shadows?'

'Clara, the ambassadors want to leave me and the Chinese Embassy staff with you,' said Martin. 'At least until the funeral is over and you leave the country. We think by then opponents will lose the opportunity to undermine support for the new laws.'

'On the detail,' continued Nelson, 'I've arranged the funeral service for tomorrow afternoon. I've asked Ms Accardi to invite the various heads of the charities and government organisations to attend, as well as journalists. It would be impossible to keep them away. The Cambodian Minister of the Interior, Mr Suong, will also pay his respects to Mr Bailey. Ambassador Zhao and I will also attend. It will not be private, I'm sorry. I hope you understand.'

'Mrs Yehonala, Miss Yehonala,' said Zhao, 'we're asking for your help. Naturally, we have no power to order you to say or do anything you don't wish to, but an enormous amount of good, or bad, may come from this sad event.'

I looked at Clara. She still looked as though she might disembowel someone. Her expression softened slightly. She nodded. Everyone seemed relieved. Nelson continued.

'What I can do and have done is to arrange for you both to visit the funeral home so you may have the private time you need. Martin will drive you there this afternoon or at any convenient time for you.'

'Clara and I both pray something good might come from this tragedy, so we'll do as you ask. In China, we have our traditions when a loved one dies. One of these is *shoulin*. Ambassador Zhao will explain this custom to you if you wish.'

I noticed Zhao's respectful nod.

'I would be grateful if you will contact the funeral directors; I'm sure they'll understand our traditions.'

Nelson smiled, relieved with our agreement. Deciding now presented an ideal opportunity to conclude, he got up and we said our goodbyes.

We left the office and waited in the reception area, leaving Martin in earnest discussion with the two diplomats. As we chatted to fill in the time, Elena told us she had grown up in northern Italy, in Trieste, and had worked for UNICEF around the world for nearly ten years.

Elena Accardi was a classically beautiful woman, around thirty, with olive skin, high cheekbones and light brown hair which tumbled over her shoulders. She dressed in the way only Italian women know how to do, wearing almost no makeup except subtly around her eyes. Nor did she need any; I imagined her spending much of her life enjoying or fending off attention. She was also clearly passionate about her work, made more so by her extravagant hand gestures when she spoke. I felt an instant affection for her.

I saw Clara did too. She bit her lip, gazing at Elena, whose eyes looked deeply into Clara's for a few moments. Her breathing became softer, the pensive look melting into a smile between them as soft as I've ever seen from her. Her body squirmed just a little as her muscles relaxed. There was something about that gaze, as if in those few moments their souls had made a bridge. Then it was gone.

'My agent, Max Santini, is also Italian,' said Clara, seeming eager to speak. You're similar to her, high energy...'

'You're too polite, Clara,' replied she, interrupting, wearing a slightly bewildered smile. 'Santini? Sounds like a Florentine name. Tuscany is so beautiful - landscapes, history, music, lots of high culture.'

'She's from Montalcino, a medieval town in Siena. It's quite breathtaking. Sorry, how stupid of me, of course, you know where it is. I've been there a few times.'

'Ah, little wonder she makes her living in classical music. Andrea Bocelli, Puccini… Even Dorotea Bocchi grew up there.'

'Yes, I met Dorotea there once. She and Max are friends. Max's family has a vineyard growing *Sangiovese* grapes, at least I think I got the name right. My dad loved wine, so I usually brought him a bottle of Brunello whenever I went home to Australia.'

'Would you meet me sometime, Clara? We could chat about the joys of Italy.'

Elena's offer came as a surprise, I could tell, even to herself. I noticed an elemental look passing between them. They stared at each other as if they'd seen a ghost.

'Oh… yes…I'd like to… When things are more settled. Okay?'

Clara's nervousness surprised me after her confrontation with the ambassadors. I also wondered why she'd never mentioned anything about Italy to me. Before I could ask, from further along the corridor, a door opened. A seriously overweight, middle-aged man lumbered his way towards us.

'Hello Elena, I haven't seen you for a while. How are you, *poppet*?'

'Fine thank you, George.'

I couldn't help noticing her feigned smile.

'George, let me introduce you to Katy and Clara Yehonala. They're here for Simon Bailey's funeral tomorrow. His wife and daughter.'

'A terrible business, I'm so sorry.' He held out his hand in a hasty greeting and kept walking. 'My apologies, I'm running a little late.'

I thought being oversize in this climate must be exhausting and wondered why he would even want a posting here.

'George Sorensen's a cultural attaché,' explained Elena. 'But we all know him as Georgie around here. He's on his second posting to Phnom Penh and came back earlier in the year after two years in Thailand. Georgie loves working in Asia, probably not so much this time of year, I imagine.'

I felt the hairs on the back of my neck prickling.

'Will you be flying back to Australia straight away, Katy?'

'Pardon? Sorry, my mind's somewhere else. No, not immediately. I want to find out more about Simon's work here, meet the people he worked with and see what we can do to continue his work. I want to see Simon's legacy and his charity work continue.'

'For heaven's sake, don't tell Bob Nelson you're staying. He'll go into meltdown if he thinks he has to be responsible for either of you a second longer than necessary, particularly after Clara put both ambassadors back in their boxes. I'm sure they thought a little pep talk in the Australian version of the Oval Office, as we all call it, would have you sufficiently cowed into doing what they wanted. Instead, we all got a surprise. Ambassadors don't like thorny problems pricking someone, especially themselves.'

Clara looked amused. 'Don't worry, we aren't planning to ruffle anyone's feathers. Except when people are playing games with us like those two are.'

Suppressing my grin, I turned to Elena. 'Simon did a lot of work in Svay Thom, Elena. I remember last time we were here, we met an American lady, Rebecca - sorry, I don't remember her other name. Will she be coming to the funeral?'

'I know the Svay Thom mission well and Rebecca Maddison. I've already invited her and her husband, Ross. I didn't know you knew her. She only arrived in Cambodia two months ago.'

'Simon, Clara and I met her three years ago, a few months after they got the Pink House closed down; I suppose she's back for another tour of duty. Would you ask her if she would like to talk about their work together? Also, last time we had a guide, more like a bodyguard, a large Khmer man called Rithy. If he's still around, could you ask him to come?'

'Rebecca already asked me if she could say a few words tomorrow. Closing the loathsome Pink House down was the first major success we had. Before my time here and the event which kick-started the drive for better laws to protect children. I read the reports and know your husband was one of the first through the door when the police finally raided the place. I'll call Rebecca this afternoon.'

'You ladies ready to go?'

Martin rejoined us, a barely concealed rebuke written on his face. Presumably, the ambassadors told him they don't appreciate being put in their boxes by people he was supposed to be looking after.

'If you don't mind, Martin, could I get a lift back to my office? It's on the way.'

'No trouble, Elena, happy to be of service.'

Elena and Clara continued chatting as we left, Clara slipping her arm through Elena's in our age-old gesture of friendship. Once in the car, they exchanged telephone numbers. After dropping her at the UNICEF building, I asked Martin to stop briefly at the hotel, then we drove to the funeral home. As soon as we arrived, a sepulchral western man greeted us, introducing himself as the Director, Alan Doole.

'Madam, we've been expecting you; our commiserations for your loss. My colleague here, Wang Hsin, is familiar with your traditions and will help you in every way he can. Please come in.'

I carried my bag inside and we sat ourselves down in a private reception room. I had already spoken to Clara about what I needed to do. Even though she insisted she would stay to help me, I prevailed on her to leave. She could join me later and we would sit *shoulin* together with Simon until the morning.

'Martin, in China we observe traditions for our loved ones, not so much in these modern times, perhaps. In my family, they are still important. There are things I need to do. Please take my daughter back to the hotel; you can bring her back this evening.'

He looked at me, then at Clara, thinking he couldn't protect two people at once if they weren't in the same place. No doubt the ambassador's words were still ringing in his ears.

'Let's leave, Martin. Now, please.'

If nothing else, Martin Lewis proved a quick study, my suggestion appealing to him as diplomacy's higher calling and no doubt preferable to inviting a pleasantry or two from Clara.

'Mr Doole, when those people killed my husband, another also died.'

'Yes, a young Khmer girl.'

'What happened to her?'

'The ambulance brought her here with your husband. I'm sorry, we know nothing at all about her.'

'Where is she now?'

'We cremated her this morning. As no one is likely to claim her remains or have left instructions, we'll scatter her ashes in our memorial garden tomorrow.'

'Mr Doole, I wish my husband's remains placed in the care of temple monks in Phnom Penh. Can you arrange this for me? I'll make a significant donation every year to ensure they respect his memory.'

'I see. It's rare to inter a layperson in a Buddhist temple, though not unheard of, particularly if the family does good deeds and makes a proper donation. I'm aware of a temple abbot in Phnom Penh who might grant your request, particularly if I mention your family's ancestry to the Buddhist Qing rulers and explain the good works of your husband for the children of Cambodia. I'll speak to the abbot at the monastery this afternoon.'

'Also, I want the remains of the young Cambodian girl to accompany him and receive equal care and respect. Can you arrange this for me too?'

I handed him an envelope. He weighed the contents and smiled.

'I will do my best, Madam. It will be helpful the young girl is a Buddhist.'

'Mr Wang, please take me to my husband.'

We entered a clinically clean, cold storage room with its stainless-steel tables, tiled floor and sterile benches. I experienced a different chill when I saw the funeral director had already brought Simon's empty coffin into the room, the sudden weakness in my legs forcing me to grip his arm. I assured Mr Wang I was okay and he left my side to open a shiny door and wheeled out a trolley carrying Simon's covered body. He pulled back the sheet.

Swallowing hard, I looked down at my husband's grey form carrying the bruised marks of his death. Doing my best to sound convincing, I told myself I was ready and determined to ensure my husband would be properly prepared for his journey.

'Hello, Simon. It's just me. I'm going to take care of you.'

I blinked away the tears beginning to blur my vision.

'We can't have people thinking badly of you, can we, my darling? Or believing you have bad habits.'

I opened my bag and pulled out a towel, three washcloths, and a bottle of rose water. Mr Wang brought me a bowl of water.

Afterwards, I dressed Simon in his favourite clothes. First, a summer shirt we'd bought in Wenzhou years before; he loved the delicate bamboo print pattern and silk texture. Next, a pair of Country Road cotton chinos, well worn, which I remembered from so many times sitting on the patio having a glass of wine or working around the garden together. Then a pair of brown shoes he'd bought at a Salvos store. I knew he loved pottering around second-hand shops; our home had more than its fair share of what he generously called *bric-a-brac*. I used a shorter word to describe his treasures.

Finally, I pulled out a heavy-knit, olive green jumper. Despite the weather, I wanted him to wear this on his journey; the green always brought out the colour of his eyes. I struggled to dress him by myself, managing eventually with Mr Wang's help and we lifted him into the coffin.

'Mr Wang , please take my husband to the reception room.'

I breathed a sigh of relief to be out of the antiseptic air and to have Simon resting in respectful surroundings. Here, Clara and I would spend the night. I lit four candles and sat with my memories of our companionship. Eventually, it may have been hours, I sensed Clara's presence in the room. She stood over the coffin, looking at Simon.

'I didn't hear you come in, *baobei*.'

'Dad looks at peace, Ma. I remember him just this way.'

She had changed into a plain white, cotton dress and removed her makeup. Even so, she looked radiant in the candlelight.

'I made Martin drive me to a Chinese emporium; I thought you might not have remembered to bring spirit money. I also had him take me to a restaurant and I bought food and a little wine. Wang Hsin's preparing it now.'

Our custom included sharing a last meal as a family. Clara placed an extra bowl of rice with chopsticks in the coffin so Simon wouldn't be hungry on his journey, and I put three coins in his left hand to pay the ferrymen as he crossed the three magic rivers. Silly things, I suppose for people in our modern age, but preserving the proper order still runs deep in traditional families like the Yehonalas. Finally, Clara gave him a large amount of spirit money; he would be respected as a wealthy man when he arrived. We were almost ready.

I told her I'd found Simon's manuscript and his medals in the back of a drawer the night before I left. I showed them to her. She read the citations quietly to herself and placed them in the coffin, and we pinned the newly polished medals on his chest. At the end of his journey, his ancestors and ours would receive him with honour.

'What about the manuscript you were telling me about?'

'Simon was writing a book he called *Chavy's Story* about a young Cambodian girl. I think she may have been a person he knew; I'm not sure. Maybe he came to Cambodia this time to finish the story. I thought you might want to read it.'

'Give it to me, Ma. Now, leave me here, please. Martin's waiting outside. Go home, rest, and get ready for tomorrow. I'll be fine here by myself; I'll see you in the morning.'

This time Clara insisted.

7
ENDINGS

I looked up into the faces of about thirty people seated in the chapel, their eyes fixed on me. I noticed the furrowed brows of the two ambassadors and the surprise on Clara's face. I had said nothing to them.

I took a deep breath, gripping the slanted top of the lectern for support and hoped the words would come. Clara instantly got to her feet. She came over to stand next to me, linking her arm through mine. She smiled, speaking softly in my ear.

'Take courage, Ma. Whatever you're going to say, we'll say it together.'

I began.

'This lovely man we are saying goodbye to today was many things. Mostly ones nobody knew about because modesty was his way. To me, I know Simon as my husband. To my daughter, Clara, he is simply Dad. One of those *things* I know gave him the greatest joy.

'Many years ago…'

I stopped, feeling warm tears trickling down my cheeks. I bit my lip, composing myself. Clara squeezed my hand gently. I looked up, feeling Mama's eyes on me.

'…Many years ago, Simon and I first met in England. I was a young student. And Simon? Well, at the time, I didn't know for sure. He had a broken leg and lived in a bed and breakfast hotel in Chelsea. A friend of his told me he once fought in a war. A war not far from here, across the Mekong River in Vietnam. Being curious, I asked Simon about it.

'Those who know Simon will know getting him to grandstand about what he's doing is impossible, as Rebecca reminded us a few minutes ago. So you won't be surprised to hear he was the same in those days. Instead, he told me a funny story about the war, a story about drinking too much beer one night and swimming around in the darkness, painting red kangaroos on American warships in the harbour. I called him an idiot.

'Three nights ago, when going through some drawers at home getting ready to come here, I found an old box. Inside were several medals he'd received before painting his silly kangaroos. It has taken me more than twenty-five years to accidentally discover my husband has always been a hero. He's wearing those medals today, including the two the Americans gave him. One he received for helping save the lives of ten children and their teacher from a burning school less than a hundred kilometres from this very spot. The other for taking bombs to pieces, his job at the time. He's wearing these medals now because we Chinese believe our loved ones deserve to enter the afterlife accompanied by the honour they earned in this one. Pinning those medals on him last night is the only time I have done something I know he will disapprove of me doing. He'll complain about showing off. For my small sin, dear husband, I'm sorry.

'Why do I tell you this particular story? Well, it's because the good in the world is usually made up of unrecorded acts of sacrifice. Simon is, has always been, a quiet warrior for what he believes in and tragically, it is why he died.'

This time, I couldn't stop the tears. I didn't try.

'...He loved Cambodia and spent his life helping to repair the lives of its children. There's a saying about the darkest hours being before dawn. So let me say to Minister Suong and all those here remembering his life, I know Simon is looking down in joy as the charities, UNICEF and the government continue their work to ensure children get the childhood they deserve. I intend his work will go on, so what happened to my husband and the little girl who died with him, will one day never happen to anyone else's family.'

The day had been a long one for both of us. As they promised, the Australian Embassy had organised the service, including a marquee set up on a private lawn outside the chapel with refreshments.

The funeral director led the ceremony, then Robert Nelson made a short eulogy, followed by Rebecca. After I finished, they took the casket away and we moved outside to meet everyone. Robert Nelson and Cambodian Minister Suong left after making their farewells, wishing us both a safe journey home. Zhao remained to speak with Clara for about fifteen minutes, though their conversation looked to be more like socialising than sympathy. After he left, Clara came over, her two escorts nearby.

'Can you believe it? He invited me to lunch and wants me to visit the Chinese Embassy for a photo session.'

'He knows you're a favourite of Premier Liu and also knows having a photo with you will help his career. I imagine Cambodia isn't the posting ambitious Chinese diplomats queue up for.'

'Well, if his idea of diplomacy is chatting up the daughters of bereaved families, he's likely to find himself stamping tourist visas in Tasmania next. Anyway, it was a deeply touching service, Ma. I didn't know you were going to speak; your story about him was perfect, exactly like Dad was and it's how I'll always remember him. I'm sure he won't mind about the medals.'

'Thanks, *baobei*. I don't think I could have got through it without you next to me.'

She smiled.

'We're family, Ma. You know, those three diplomats all looked worried you would say something not in the script. I don't trust them, especially Zhao. They're not telling us the truth, though I can't work out why they're lying to us.'

'I agree with you. And why I'm staying in Cambodia.'

'*Wode ma ya!* You're what?'

'I'm going to find out what happened to Simon, and I'm not leaving until I do.'

'*Madame* Yehonala?' A man, a stranger, held out his hand.

'My sincerest condolences to you on your loss, *madame*. I knew your husband slightly and I am an admirer of his work.'

'Thank you, Mr…'

'Pardon, *madame*, my name is Rémy Aubert. I'm the pastor of a small mission in the Svay Rieng countryside, south-east of here.'

To call Father Aubert an old man would give the wrong idea entirely, though old he certainly was. Angular rather than thin, his sun-weathered skin stretched across his face like oily parchment. A small, silver cross hung on a chain around his neck under a crinkled, cream-coloured linen suit and a light cotton open-necked shirt, despite the humidity. A short white beard and neatly parted hair framed a gaunt face. However, his clear blue eyes, shining with an inner joy, washed decades off his age.

'Thank you, Father Aubert. I'm pleased to meet you. May I introduce my daughter, Clara?'

'*Mademoiselle* Yehonala, it is my pleasure. Pardon, I hope you aren't offended by the term? I see my government is trying to ban calling young ladies *mademoiselle*. However, I refuse.'

'Father Aubert, I'm a young woman living in Paris. I shall be outraged if you do *not* call me *mademoiselle*. Where would Paris be without romance?'

'Ah, we are sure to be friends,' smiled he. 'I hope the legacy of your father's work will bring you solace in the future. He was a good man. I've noticed the newspapers are already publishing stories about him, as well as you. I pray you are both left in peace, though I see the journalist from the *Phnom Penh Times* is here, no doubt looking for a story. I suppose there are other reporters around. At least you have Martin Lewis here to keep the wolves away.'

'Oh, you know Martin Lewis?' asked Clara.

'We're not friends, though we have met on a few occasions, *mademoiselle*. I shall be in Phnom Penh for a few days before

I return to the mission. If you would like to meet me again, I would be delighted to know you both a little better. I may be able to let you know more of the work Mr Bailey did here.'

He handed me a card with his telephone number.

'You can call me any time, *madame*. Put your faith in the glory of God, bless you both.'

Elena Accardi joined us. 'It was a beautiful service, Katy. You both have my deepest condolences,' said she, kissing Clara and me on the cheek. 'Watching you together and listening to your words was such an emotional experience for me and I imagine everyone else. I don't believe I would have had the courage to speak as you did.'

'Thank you. I must say I'm relieved to have got through it in one piece. My daughter's mainly to blame for keeping me upright.'

'You're quite a team. I see you two have met Father Aubert.'

'Yes, who is he?'

'You can guess he's French, though he was born in Cambodia. I'm told his family left after independence in the fifties and moved back to France. He studied medicine, became a pastor, then returned here to set up missions to help street kids in the slums of Phnom Penh after Pol Pot got kicked out. People say he knows more about this country than almost any westerner.'

'Sounds like an amazing man.'

'They thought him saintly in those days. Nowadays, I'm afraid I'm not a huge fan.'

'Why? What happened to him?'

'For the last ten years, he's been working alone in the countryside, a missionary of the bible-bashing, fire and brimstone school. I'm not certain, but I heard he's involved with agricultural projects as well. I don't know much about them, I've never been to his mission.'

'How come he went to the countryside?' asked Clara.

'Gossip abounded, but who knows the truth? I'm a Catholic myself and carry enough guilt simply for being born to be concerned about rumours of Father Aubert's lifestyle choices.'

'He mentioned he knew a little of Simon's work.'

She smiled and nodded. 'Who knows? Wouldn't surprise me, though. He seems to know most of what goes on in Cambodia. He built his wooden chapel in the middle of nowhere down near the border with Vietnam, so best to see him before he goes back or you might never have the chance. People tell me he rides his motorbike around the villages behaving like a holy Hell's Angel, especially if you're a Buddhist. Acts more like a radical Mother Teresa without the gender, budget and media coverage and spends his days ministering to sick children, doing his best to bring God into the locals' lives. I'd say the good pastor is a mixed blessing to the world.'

Elena's dry humour served as a perfect antidote for the messages of condolence passing for conversation today.

'By the way, Martin mentioned to me he's staying at your hotel for a few days. He seems to be taking his job of looking after you quite seriously. Did you know?'

'No, I didn't. Clara noticed a couple of Chinese men hanging around, looking awkward. Martin must have kept out of sight. I quite like him; can't say the same for his boss.'

'Mmm, he's quite handsome too, wish I were wired differently. Maybe he's got his eye on your daughter. What do you think, Clara?'

'I think if a man comes near me between now and doomsday, I'll be joining the Missionaries of Charity myself.'

'A worthy calling, but such a waste, *bella*.'

She winked. Clara noticed something on her shoes.

'Don't worry, you'll be fine. Martin's job is keeping out of the way. I have a sneaking suspicion he's what's known in the trade as a *spook*, sort of like an apprentice 007, you might say. I wonder if he has to kill me now I've told you?' said she, a blithe grin illuminating her face.

'I'm beginning to feel like the villain in a James Bond movie myself.'

She smiled. 'Listen Katy, give me a call later and we can have lunch together. I know an unusual place you'll love. Simon did speak to me once or twice about his work the last time I met him, let me see, possibly a month ago. I remember the meeting because I'd given a talk on Cambodian orphanages to my UNICEF colleagues and he asked me about one in particular. I don't remember which one. I'm sure it will come back to me.'

'Thanks, I'd like to.'

'*Benissimo!* Now, I must be off, I'm afraid. My prayers are with both of you. I'll look forward to seeing you again soon.'

As Elena left, the journalist from the *Phnom Penh Times* came over. Martin materialised next to me without even a puff of smoke.

'Hello Martin, still on guard duty? Mrs Yehonala, Miss Yehonala, my name's Jim Preston. I expect Martin has already mentioned me? My sympathies to you; this must be a terrible time for you both.'

'Nice to meet you, Mr Preston.'

'Call me Jim. I read the press release the embassy sent around. I'm not much into insipid motherhood statements, might I talk to you?'

'Jim, I hardly think this is the time, or the place, for this conversation,' interrupted Martin.

'There have been rumours about police involvement in the shootings. Do you have a comment about ?'

'Enough, Jim!'

'Will you be staying in Cambodia long, Mrs Yehonala?'

'Martin's right, this is hardly the time, Mr Preston. But in answer to your question, yes, I intend to continue with the charity's work in Cambodia. Please give me your card, perhaps we might meet later.'

After he left, I turned angrily to confront Martin Lewis.

'Police?' I snarled the word at him. 'A little detail perhaps slipped your mind, Mr Lewis. Or should I call you Captain Lewis? Is there anything else we're not supposed to know?'

Fighting to control my boiling anger, I stormed away to find Rebecca and Rithy, leaving Clara and him together in an animated conversation. I doubted he gained a sympathetic ear. Calmer, Rebecca and I arranged to meet later in the week at the Svay Thom mission. As we were preparing to leave, Alan Doole, the funeral director, came over.

'Mr Doole, thank you for hosting such a respectful service for my husband.'

'An honour, Madam. Much good has been spoken of Mr Bailey today.'

'And the temple?'

'I spoke with the abbot. He agrees and thanks you for your generosity. He asked I ensure you are familiar with the correct traditions of their temple - dress, behaviour, rituals and so on - which are essential for you to understand. Wat Bagan, the temple, is an awe-inspiring building, one of the oldest in Phnom Penh, built around 1500 and holds the remains of Suriyopear and his son, Chettha, two Khmer kings of the period. I'm sure you'll find Wat Bagan a proper rest. The monks themselves are from an ancient Buddhist order, which originated in Myanmar.

'The abbot says they will build a stupa for him in a respectful place in the temple's garden. We'd call it a crypt and will take about a week to complete. In the meantime, the abbott said he'll take personal charge of the remains of both your husband and the young girl in the monastery as you have no home here in Cambodia. I'll deliver the ashes tomorrow into his care. If you give me your contact details, I'll call you when the final consecration is to take place and I'll be happy to attend with you to guide you on the day.'

Clara finished her conversation with Martin Lewis and came over.

'I've been thinking about what you said earlier.'

'Oh?'

'Ma, you're not Miss Marple and I'm no Detective Mei Wang, but you're going to need help. I'm convinced there's a lot going on we don't know about.'

Tension rippled between us on the drive back to the hotel. Martin Lewis's attempts to dismiss Jim Preston's comment about police involvement in Simon's death, putting it down to a reporter looking for a new angle on a story, irritated us. The thought of being patronised by him *infuriated* us.

8

BEGINNINGS

I had a restless night, we both did. Ma and I talked until she finally fell asleep in the early hours while I tossed and turned fitfully until sunrise.

The stress of Dad's funeral and, obviously enough, his loss was to blame. I knew there was enough hurt and anger inside me and it was all I could do to keep it bottled up. And yes, I know perfectly well hiding grief away isn't healthy, nevertheless, we Yehonalas have turned our kind of coping dysfunction into an art form. I also knew there was more troubling me.

Elena Accardi. I couldn't get her out of my head. The feeling that passed between us at the embassy was euphoric, or something else I don't have an English word for. It had brought heart, lungs and vocal chords to a screeching halt. I felt it again when her leg pressed against mine in the back seat of the car afterwards. I can still remember her perfume too, sandalwood, from when she kissed my cheek at the funeral yesterday. I'd never experienced anything so primal, even in my most intense immersion in music or in those still remembered traumas and hallucinations of my early teens when Max had kept me safe from myself. Had Elena felt it too? I was almost certain she did. Surely she did.

It was around 11 am when my telephone vibrated softly on the bedside table. When I saw who it was, the heat rose in my neck and face. I walked quickly to the balcony so as not to wake my mother.

'Clara, it's Elena.'

'Elena? Oh...'

'I know this is a terrible time for you with all you're dealing with, I'm sorry for bothering you...'

'You're not bothering me, I was just thinking about you. *Oh God, why did I have to admit that?*'

'You were? I...*um*... I was wondering if you would like to meet for a coffee. We may not have any other chances before you leave. There's a café I know near your hotel, the Temple Coffee shop, you won't have to travel far. If you're not too busy.'

'Your timing couldn't be better. You have no idea how perfect coffee sounds right now after last night. On one condition, you come to the hotel. I'm not very presentable, best I don't scare any more of the good citizens of Phnom Penh than I need to. There's a little French bistro here in the garden, which is pretty enough to distract your attention from the Clara zombie, but you'd best be prepared.'

We arranged to meet in an hour. I wondered what was on her mind and I can't even begin to describe the fidgety anticipation I was feeling. Trying not to disturb my mother, I closed the door to the bathroom as quietly as I could, had a long shower and tried unsuccessfully to camouflage the ghoulish black circles around my eyes and cadaverous complexion with some expensive potions. Eventually, I shrugged my shoulders and decided the best solution would be tomorrow and a decent night's sleep; a loose pair of paisley print forest green pants I'd bought at the market with a plain off-white blouse would have to do for chic. And large sunglasses, if all else failed and Elena stared too aghast at me. I scribbled a note for Ma and hurried to the lift.

I was fifteen minutes early; Elena was already waiting for me at a table by the pool.

'Before you say a word, I know I look like someone who broomsticked in. I did warn you. *You*, however, could at least have chosen not to look like you stepped out of Vogue.'

She stood up and kissed my cheek.

'Didn't I tell you I've a soft spot for bewitchers? I had a meeting this morning with some Cambodian government officials and charity heads about the new child protection laws. It always pays to look your best for them, especially the Cambodian men. I came straight here, otherwise, I'd have worn my sackcloth.'

'I think you'd make sackcloth into a fashion statement. Thank you for confirming my sorry state,' I said, 'and here I am thinking we're friends. Coffee? They also make a delicious green mango salad here. I'd be happy to share one with you. It's enough for two, unless you'd prefer something else?'

'Sounds perfect, I can brush up on my chopstick skills.'

I looked at her and she met my gaze. Did I detect a similar look in her eyes now as back in the embassy? It quickly disappeared, but too late for me to be mistaken. There was an awkward silence hanging in the space between us.

'So Elena, what does UNICEF's head of child protection do, aside from what seems obvious?' I asked her, the first banal thing I could think to say.

'A lot of my work's trying to keep support growing for the new laws, like this morning's meeting, which was also how I came to be at the embassy meeting,' answered she, seeming relieved. 'Bob Nelson wanted me there.'

'How come you were part of their scheme to keep us quiet?'

'It did seem that way, didn't it? I thought he was making a bigger issue of the problems than I thought necessary, but I don't pretend to know the diplomatic world he and Ambassador Zhao live in.'

'Why are these new laws so important to everyone and causing such a fuss, if we're to believe what the ambassador was telling us?'

'They're essential. Once the laws are approved, it will be a huge first step in protecting Cambodian children. The other stuff he was talking about, I can't answer you; the laws are far-reaching so he may be right about them dealing with corruption.'

'My mother and I think none of you was being honest with us.'

'Clara, *I* can promise you I wasn't lying to you. There aren't any child protection laws in Cambodia and seeing them put in place is the most important thing in my life. Half the children in this country have experienced severe beatings, a quarter have suffered emotional abuse and one in twenty have been sexually assaulted or trafficked. My job is trying to get everyone to endorse a national vision for the changes, so the new laws have some teeth. If, as Bob Nelson told me, getting you not to stir up bad publicity would help my cause, I'm not going to apologise for helping them.'

'I'm sorry, I wasn't being fair throwing you in the same pot as the others. I can't begin to imagine how stressful your job must be and the sort of things you get to see.'

'You know, you and I are similar in many ways.'

'What do you mean?'

'Clara,' she lay her hand on mine, 'for one, I'm not as blind to your conflicts as you may think.'

'Is it so obvious?'

'Maybe only to me, especially after the way you spoke about Max Santini back at the embassy. And if your mother doesn't know who Dorotea Bocchi is, I do. She's one of the gay icons of style in Italy and a loud voice for women not to be afraid to decide for themselves about how to live their lives.'

I nodded.

'My mother doesn't know about Max's and my relationship. I'm not even sure it's right for me, especially with Max. I'm terrified of a relationship with a man after what's happened in our family.'

'I can tell you one thing,' she went on, 'I do know a little of your family history. Simon told me once about the time he first met Katy when I asked him why he involved himself in charity work. He said, alongside his war experiences, your mother inspired his work. I know she's an incredible woman, a trait running in your family, apparently. I can't tell you what to do, except when the time comes, you might find her more understanding and supportive than you think.'

'Some consolation, I suppose. You don't happen to have any courage pills to take with your advice, do you?'

She laughed. She had a delightful laugh, reminding me of a schoolgirl in the playground.

'I'm the last person to ask about courage, Clara. I know the work your father did with kids, but I didn't know about you until recently. When I invited Rebecca to the funeral, she told me what your family does for her mission. I'll admit I did some checking up on you afterwards and found out about the voluntary work you do in China with needy children and youth groups.'

I picked nervously around the contents of the salad, avoiding her eyes.

'Many of us do charitable work in China, I'm not really so special. Elena, why did you come here today?' I asked, unprepared to look directly at her.

'I wanted to see you again before you left.'

'Why?'

'Because I think you're an amazing woman. Also, something happened between us and... Well, the best way to say it is I couldn't help myself.'

Now I did look up and saw her looking at me, an expression I couldn't put a name to, something between affection and sadness.

'I...well, now you've seen me in my unpainted form, I expect you're sorry you bothered.'

'No,' said she, 'and I'm serious. I saw the same reaction on your face as well. I came to see you because I'd never forgive myself if after you leave, you thought you were the only one who experienced what you did. I think you deserve to know how incredible you are. If there's any sorrow, it's because it won't matter in the end, because you'll be leaving in a day or two, and I'll never see you again.'

'Elena, now I'll give you my public confession. I spent the last two nights telling myself nothing happened between us, and it's impossible, and I might be wrong, and it's wishful thinking. I should also tell you I'm not leaving Cambodia, not yet at least.

I'm staying here to help my mother find out more about what happened to my father and to make sure his work carries on.'

I knew I was in a vulnerable state, not only to Elena but to any powerful emotions while my defences were down. Lessons well learnt ten years ago. Still, defences aren't armed guards, are they?

'No Clara! You must leave. No, I didn't mean to say that. *Oh mio Dio*, I would never have told you if I knew you were staying and we'd be seeing more of each other.'

At that moment my body warmed, like I was sitting in front of a blazing fire. Elena was a woman I desperately wanted to know and I willingly lowered the rest of my guard and opened myself to fate's caprice.

'I did feel what you did, Elena. And to hear your words is what I wanted to hear. Let's start by deciding on this lunch you suggested with my mother and worry about everything else as we go.'

'*Oddio. Oddio! - Clara, non capisci...* Now I am truly sorry I came to see you. No matter how I feel about you Clara, it can't be.'

9

A DEAL WITH THE DEVIL

Clara and I were sitting in the hotel garden under the tropical greenery late the same day, watching the clouds building up for the afternoon deluge. I could see having a short respite earlier today with Elena had revived her spirits from the previous night's torments. We were discussing our strategy over a chilled glass of wine. Or, more accurately, the fact we didn't have one.

'Where do we start?' I asked.

Only after the obvious question did it occur to us we knew next to nothing about what happened. And even if we did, we had no idea what to do or how to do it.

'I thought about this earlier, Ma. In a way, it's similar to solving sudoku puzzles.'

'If arithmetic's the answer, we're doomed. You know I'm one of the four out of three people who struggle with numbers.'

'Don't worry,' said she, grinning. 'Sudoku isn't about numbers, it's about possibilities. One thing you *are* good at figuring out. Remember how you and *laolao* planned your wedding when you found out you were having me?'

I looked blankly at her.

'Don't you see? Back then, you had to work out possibilities from the choices open to you, decide on the best one and organise how to do it. Oh, speaking of which, I'm glad you made the choices you did,' added she with a cheeky grin. 'Sudoku's the same. It's all about identifying the possible choices for one of the boxes, eliminating them one by one until the correct number's left.'

'You almost sound like you know what you're doing.'

'We'll learn as we go along,' said she, lifting her drink.

We clinked glasses.

'*Gambei*!'

'I wish I'd watched more television. Simon loved Inspector Morse. He always knew what to do.'

'Dad loved classical music too, didn't he? You know, I must have been four or five the first time I saw sheet music. What a jumble of nonsense. *Laolao* taught me music tells stories about how composers lived in their inner world, what they were trying to whisper to me in their music and how they wrote it full of surprises, jokes, twists and turns, all in emotional codes about their passions. Once I understood, I discovered a secret language full of clues about how to read their words and sentences and how to tell their stories - when to hurry through, when to reflect on a clue and what riddles they left to uncover by yourself. I'll bet Morse solved his mysteries the same way. With Morse and sudoku, how hard can it be?'

Clara winked at me like we were Lancelot and Gawain, setting out to unearth the mysterious Sangreal. Our foolhardy naïveté at the time still amazes me.

'What about your concert schedules?'

'I called Max last night. I told her I needed time before I'd be ready to go back. She understands and is going to cancel my bookings for a month. I want to find out what happened too.'

'The other thing is we should be remembering Simon, being in mourning for him and…'

'Ma, the best way to respect Dad's memory is to find out the truth. If we wait, we're going to find it harder.'

After my earlier mental bravado about following destiny, reality dawned. We were standing at the doorway of a journey, ready to take the first step into the unknown without a compass.

Hopefully not as lambs to the slaughter, which *would* have been our opinion had we bothered to think more about it or had the benefit of second sight. So, bursting with all the innocent daring of the clueless, 'alright, what's first?'

'Well, sudoku has nine possibilities. At the moment, we have hundreds. We need to get them down to something a bit more manageable.'

'Let's go and see the reporter, Jim Preston. We have no idea who else we can trust around here. He might give us a few clues.'

'You're a star. Give me his number.'

Clara phoned and an eager Jim Preston agreed to meet us. I called the waiter over to write down the address he gave us to show to the tuk-tuk driver. We arranged to meet the following morning.

'What about Martin? If he knows we're meeting a reporter, he'll go bananas,' Clara reminded me.

'Easy, we won't tell him. Besides, it's none of his business. Anyway, he's probably left the hotel now the funeral's over.'

'I'll check.'

She wandered over to the reception clerk. After a minute's conversation, she came back, grinning.

'We're safe, Martin checked out this morning. I haven't seen any sign of those Chinese bloodhounds today, either. Still, we'd better keep our eyes peeled. I doubt they're going to ignore us until we leave town.'

'You're right. I'm not convinced their protect-us-from-the-media story is why they're hanging around in the first place.'

Sisowath Quay wasn't far from the hotel. When we arrived, the reporter was waiting for us at a table outside the coffee shop, across the road from where the wide Tonlé Sap River joined the mightier Mekong. He stood up, smiling broadly, including his eyes.

'G'day, glad you decided to meet me. Call me Jim.'

'Nice place, Jim. I'm Katy and this is Clara.'

The streetscape bustled with colour and vibrancy; the river side of the road a promenade lined with palms, our side a thriving waterside hub of colonial-era shops, bars and restaurants, their tables overflowing onto the footpath. The noisy, social atmosphere reminded me of Dijon BC - before Clara - back when a wide-eyed hotel management student travelled on a wine tour of Burgundy with her shameless friend Amy Chan. Ah, dear Amy, who opened my eyes to a lot more than vineyards…

'Thought you might like the Fresco Café, has the best croissants in Asia. As you live in Melbourne, you probably know Pellegrino's so you'll find the coffee here's like cat's piss. It's the best we can do in a third-world country. Have a pew.'

We ordered the croissants. True enough, they were melt in the mouth delicious. We opted for fruit over feline juice.

Jim Preston looked fortyish, trim, with the layback style and tongue-in-cheek, cynical humour found in Australians and misunderstood by everybody else. He reminded me of Simon when we first met. Despite his colourful turn of phrase, I felt comfortable straight away.

'Given ASIO the slip today, ladies?'

'For now. They must think we're not dangerous subversives anymore.'

'You might want to think again, Clara.' He tilted his head to the side.

Two obviously not Chinese tourists sat down in an adjoining café.

'Don't stress about it.'

We tried to ignore them. No doubt Martin Lewis would be paying us a visit later, bringing his displeasure along for company.

'You're from Melbourne too?' I asked.

'Nah, worked there for ten years on a couple of the local rags. I'm originally from Mount Maunganui, a small place in New Zealand no one's ever heard of unless you mistype an address on Google.'

'How did you end up in Cambodia?'

'You make it sound like the ends of the earth, Katy. I love it here, been working at *The Times* for the last five years. Got married to a beautiful Cambodian girl two years back who treats me like a god. What's not to love about Cambodia? I live like a maggot in bacon.'

Interesting image. He did look like a man content with the world.

'There's plenty for a reporter to do here with all the crap going on in South-East Asia. I also cover stories in Vietnam and Thailand for the paper, speaking passable Khmer and a spattering of the Vietnamese lingo helps. So ladies, down to business. Why'd you agree to talk to me?'

'First of all, I think we're supposed to say all this is off the record, aren't we?'

'You've been watching too many movies, Clara. All I have is my reputation which, believe it or not, means a lot to me despite what Martin may have told you.'

He grinned a lop-sided smile, disarming us both completely.

'If it makes you happier, I'll write nothing unless you say it's okay. Deal?'

I looked at Clara, who for once didn't have her antenna twitching. Instead, she looked him straight in the eyes.

'Jim, we know anything we say about my father's death will get you headlines until these new laws go through and will get us in trouble with lots of people. Including, for me, the Chinese Government. The thing is, we believe there's more to the story of my father's murder than we're being told. Zhao already asked us to say nothing except what's in the press release. Chinese officials mean *ordered* when they say *asked*. So we need to know we can trust you.'

'Clara, I give you my word. In blood, if you like…'

We looked at each other and the ghost of a smile appeared on Clara's face. She nodded. We needed to trust someone. An investigative reporter wouldn't be the worst choice.

'Okay, we have a deal. And no need for the omertà. In return for your word, Clara and I won't talk to anyone else in the media about this story. Supposing there is a story. You'll need to trust us for the moment.'

'Fair enough. Now, first up, why don't you tell me what our diplomatic friends told you about these new laws?'

'Well, we met the ambassadors, Nelson and Zhao, the morning after we arrived. They were paranoid about what Clara and I might say to the media about Simon's death, which is why the press release came out. Martin Lewis and the UNICEF lady, Elena Accardi, were there too. They tried to convince us that new laws due to be debated in a month were good for the country but have a lot of opposition. They told us if we came out criticising the government, there's a chance the new laws would get rejected. So we agreed to say nothing.'

'I've met UNICEF's answer to Monica Bellucci a few times. Can't imagine her on the side of any bullshit, especially if kids are involved. Elena's one of the good guys. Well, she would be if she hadn't broken the hearts of every single guy in Cambodia, plus a few married ones, with her lifestyle choice. What did they tell you these laws were about?'

'They told us if the laws get passed, the government will be able to prosecute some powerful people and expose a lot of corruption behind the trafficking and drug trade,' said Clara, suppressing an urge to interrogate Jim Preston about Elena.

'Hmm. Well, at least the corruption part's true. I'll be brutally honest with you, except for the PR, Australia and China don't give a shit about the local Cambodian trafficking and drug trade problem unless it ends up on their doorsteps. Many in the Cambodian Government do, UNICEF does, but the Chinese and Australians only care about what hurts their strategic interests in Cambodia.

'Right now, for example, developing the port of Sihanoukville is taking everyone's attention,' he told us. 'The Chinese are building a major shipping container port for their new global trading routes, as well as adding a base for their navy ships so they can patrol the South China Sea shipping lanes to piss off the Americans. China trains the army, the police, teachers and politicians; it's like a coup, though no one dares say as much. Australia's caught in the middle, trying not to upset their biggest trading partner while keeping their eyes open to earn brownie points, sucking up to their American masters as they've always done. Might even be part of Martin Lewis' job description.'

'What's all this all got to do with us?'

'Good question, Katy. I've got a few ideas and you have my interest. China's the biggest provider of foreign aid and Beijing's giant state corporations have invested billions of dollars here in dams, oilfields, highways, railways and so on and private Chinese firms run the Cambodian commercial landscape. Have a drive around Phnom Penh to see the Mandarin posters advertising luxury condos, new hotels and cancer hospitals. Chinese money controls Cambodia's economy, not its political maturity. My guess is that's why you're a problem.'

'The Chinese billboards are pretty hard to miss. What does political maturity mean?' asked Clara.

'It's a nice way to say the Cambodians don't always do as they're told. These new laws are a local issue and corruption exists in the woodwork of the place. I don't think you and Katy need to worry about Beijing getting upset with you, as I said before, bad as it sounds, their agenda's too big to care about a few kids or the odd corrupt general. Your problem's someone local. Zhao maybe, especially if he's doing deals with crooked officials. Not to say I wouldn't be concerned, depending on why they want to keep you quiet and who they are, you should be crapping yourselves if you started stirring the pot. Most of the smaller projects are with private Chinese companies and still worth millions, so there's a lot at stake. The contracts get awarded by what we Kiwis call the brown paper bag method.'

'Are you saying Zhao's taking bribes?'

'Do bears crap in the woods? I'd be more surprised if he wasn't. Why you're such a headache to them has got me beat, unless the success or failure of the new laws will upset a few private arrangements.'

'You think us blaming the government for Simon's death could influence the laws?'

'Nah, Buckley's chance unless an embarrassing press story came to light, but I can't see it happening. At worst, it's more likely there's a police chief or two who might find themselves exposed by bad publicity and they're Zhao's or someone else's mates. You need to understand the generals control life here and they're usually trying to outdo each other for power. If the new laws passing or failing, say, helped or hindered the wrong one to take control of one area, all the side deals would have to be renegotiated or might see the light of day. A neat way to get rid of a rival. Many of the generals and politicians running the joint were in Pol Pot's army during the Khmer Rouge days. They have novel ways to negotiate with people who buck the system.'

'So being responsible for a psychotic general losing his influence is not a promising career choice?'

'Too right. See the river over there, Clara? It's full of people wearing concrete boots who should have made better career choices. Still, could be Zhao just wants you to be kept safe. Having Premier Liu's favourite Jade Princess found floating in a stormwater drain on his watch wouldn't be great for his Politburo ambitions. From what I've heard, he's a rising star with powerful friends. Now, tell me again why you came to see me.'

'We think my father may not have been killed because the rescue of children went wrong and we want to find out what did happen. And just so you know, we're not interested in concrete Jimmy Choos or meeting other ends, watery or otherwise.'

'Pleased to hear it. Pity though, *that* would make a great story,' said he with a droll grin. 'And I get why you don't want to go to the cops. Incidentally, do you have any evidence? Us reporters always like factual sort of things,' he added with the same lazy smile, this time edged with a challenge.

'Not yet. And yes, we know it sounds like one of those conspiracy theories from a bereaved family. Except we know Simon was writing a book about child sex trafficking involving a young Khmer girl he called Chavy. At first, me and Clara weren't sure if it was a novel, but since we've been here, we think she may be a real person because at least two of the people and places in the book are real. We think he came to Cambodia this time to finish the book.'

'And now he's dead.'

'Yes.'

'Ladies, this may be a bloody stupid thing to say, given what's already happened to Simon. You do understand what you're getting involved in could be a health hazard?'

'Do you know George Sorensen?'

'Nope, can't say I do. As far as I know, he works as an attaché at the Australian Embassy, not too athletic to put it kindly. He's never come up on my radar. Why?'

'He's a person Clara and I met at the Australian Embassy a few days ago.'

'Will you help us?' asked Clara.

'Let me sleep on it.'

10
KRONG CHEY AND CROCODILE SHOES

'Ma, an ordinary genius might have overplayed her hand.'

'Have you been reading those *Women's Weekly* magazines again about how to be a good daughter?'

She winked at me.

'Don't need to. I had the Yehonala playbook.'

'Kept me on my toes, too. Mama could have given Emily Post a few pointers.'

'I meant throwing the line to Jim Preston about George Sorensen.'

'Jim Preston's a reporter who told us he'd got a good bullpoo detector. We won't get him to help us with a fairy story about what might have happened to Simon. Besides, this kind of thing happens all the time according to him. Hopefully, right now, he's checking out George Sorensen for us.'

'If he does help, you'll need to get a touch more adventurous with your swearing.'

'I saw you blush. He's a lot like Simon; salty language seems to come naturally to Australians. Kiwis, too, apparently.'

Clara and I were back at the Palace View, sitting on our balcony sharing a bowl of seasoned nuts and sipping a glass of mango juice in what had become a ritual, governed by the weather as much as anything else. Even now, the thunder rumbled overhead and the storm clouds had opened, obscuring the Royal Palace and shrouding the river behind a veil of noisy rain. A few cool drops splashed off the balcony railing onto the warm skin of our arms.

'Let's forget Georgie for the moment. We need to rethink Zhao.'

'Why, *baobei*? It's not a major surprise he's a bit shady.'

'Not that. Remember me telling you he wanted to get a picture taken with me?'

'I remember you weren't impressed. We decided he wanted to ingratiate himself with Premier Liu. Getting you into bed probably wasn't too far from his mind, either.'

'Don't worry, they're all the same; I'm quite used to getting propositioned. I've changed my mind about him being a failed diplomat in the backwoods of Cambodia. After meeting with Jim, we've misunderstood how important Cambodia is to China. He's here because he's on the rise, not because he's a loser. He wants the photographs as an insurance policy to make sure no one harms me, which is why he has these Chinese men following us around. I'll bet he thinks the photos will warn anyone with ideas to hurt us that we have powerful friends.'

'Which means someone believes we need protecting.'

'It also means someone else thinks we're troublemakers,' added Clara.

'But who? Could we get Jim to organise pictures and a story for his newspaper?'

'Ma, you *are* brilliant! Speaking of Chinese friends, how do you think those two Chinese men knew we were meeting Jim Preston at the Fresco Cafe? They weren't hanging around when we left the hotel.'

'I've been thinking about the same thing myself. Do you remember when you were on the phone with Jim? We got one of the waiters to write down the address for us. My bet is they passed it on to them, or Martin; we need to be doubly careful in future.'

'We're both getting paranoid. How about we get a taxi and head down to the night market for a little shopping? I'm getting to love these cotton batiks; they're perfect clothes for the climate.'

'Okay, *baobei*, there's a million little restaurants around there too. We can try a *fish amok* or find some blue crab chilli while we plan our next moves now ASIO's lifted the dining bans.'

'What?'

'Something Martin brought up when I arrived. I'll tell you about it later.'

After breakfast, Katy and Clara, dressed in their new batik skirts, light tops and wide-brimmed straw hats bought from the market the night before, flagged down a tuk-tuk. Clambering in the back and holding on tenaciously, they bounced and chugged their way to Svay Thom, revived by the cooler morning. Last night's storm had cleansed the air and the vegetation shone as if the earth had breathed in the rain, giving life back again.

Three years had passed since they were last in Svay Thom. Rebecca didn't seem a day older to Katy, although the Pink House now bustled with activity, the ground floor transformed into a small factory where young girls were sewing clothes and the first floor converted into four spacious classrooms teaching hairdressing, dressmaking and shopkeeping to young women. The mission had also bought the land next door and work was well underway to build a school for local children.

'Not all we're doing is successful yet,' said Rebecca, 'but we've come a long way since you two were last here. The girls sell the clothes they make, and we're teaching them the skills to run their own little businesses. We don't make a lot of money, still, we're slowly getting there.'

'Is it safer now?' asked Katy.

'Much, thank the Lord. We've been able to get more of the local community leaders involved and found money to help people when they get into financial trouble; we're sort of interest-free moneylenders. Many in the Tonlé Sap fishing community now come to us instead of going to the local loan sharks, which stopped some child trafficking. It's still going on, although not like before.'

'What did my father and the Sunlight Foundation do here?'

'Simon donated directly to us, as you know. He also wrote and taught English classes for us whenever he came to visit. The charity's different and involves rescuing kids from brothels. Rithy helped him.'

'So, Rithy works for Simon. I see. If I continue to pay Rithy's salary, can you find a job for him in the mission? At least until we get things sorted out.'

'We'd love to. He's like a piece of the furniture; wouldn't be the same without him around. He asked about his future yesterday, I'll give him the good news. Come with me, you two. I want to show you something.'

Rebecca took them to the area of the new school construction; already the frames of the classrooms were taking shape.

'Eventually, we'll have four classrooms here to teach children and adults life skills, English, and basic trades. We're also building a community centre where the local leaders can plan how to make the community safer for kids. We've established a fund to help make the programs work.'

'We'll be proud to help any way we can,' said Katy. 'We'll be supporting your work as Simon did. Financially, anyway.'

'I hoped you would. With your permission Katy, we want to name the community meeting hall The Simon Bailey Centre.'

Katy's emotion rose to the surface, threatening to overflow. Sensing Katy's battle, Clara answered.

'I couldn't think of a higher honour for my dad, Rebecca.'

'Neither could we. So now, let's head back to the Pink House. Rithy's there and I know you both want to talk to him.'

They met Rithy on the top floor, unrecognisable from the barren space of three years ago. It felt different with no burly guard on hand to protect them from incursions. A happy buzz of activity flowed through the place.

Rithy greeted them with a smile and the traditional *sampeah*. He still had his strong physical presence, coupled with the warm friendliness of the Khmer people.

'*Lok* Rithy, it's good to see you again,' said Katy.

'Mrs Katy, Miss Clara, it is my honour. Please, just Rithy.'

Since they were last here, Rithy had married and had two children, a boy and a girl. He proudly produced their photographs. They rented an apartment near Boeng Kak Lake, two kilometres from the mission and his wife, Jorani, taught in the local primary school. Jorani's mother lived with them.

'You're a lucky man, Rithy; your family is beautiful. We're also here because of family. Will you help us understand what happened to Simon?'

'I will tell you what I know, Mrs Katy. I went to Krong Chey that night with Mr Simon.'

'You were there?'

'Yes, I always went with Mr Simon on these raids. We'd never been so far from Phnom Penh before. Usually, we're in this local area and he surprised me when he said we were going to a border township.'

'Do you know why he wanted to go to Krong Chey?'

'Only that he knew about these young girls who were being smuggled into Vietnam, Miss Clara. We have a good relationship with the local police chief here and he provided two officers to come with us.'

'How did Simon hear about the girls?'

'I cannot say. He only told me they would be staying in the Krong Chey building overnight while the Vietnamese gangsters made their trade.'

'Why didn't you ask the local police to rescue the children?'

'We were always careful to work with the police we trusted, Mrs Katy. When we asked local police to help us, the children would often disappear before we arrived, so we stopped telling them when we were coming. Unfortunately, many of the police departments are corrupt or are part of the criminal gangs.'

'Can you tell me and Clara what happened that night?'

'We got there quite late. We had two SUVs and planned to send the policemen into the building to get the key to the cellar. We would open the door, release the girls and drive away. Very simple. If we found no one there, we had a crowbar to force the door. We parked at the end of the alley so we wouldn't be noticed and the policemen went into the building and arrested a man who gave us the key. Mr Simon went into the cellar to release the girls while I waited in the alleyway. When the girls came up the stairs, I hurried them towards the SUVs.

'Two men were hiding in the shadows and started firing their guns at us. I made it to the safety of the cars with the girls, but Mr Simon got trapped in the cellar. When he came up the stairs, a man shot him. Before I could stop her, one of the girls ran back up the alley to help Mr Simon and the same man also shot her. Then the men walked away. Not even running. I heard them drive off towards the Vietnamese border. Soon afterwards, I heard a noisy motorcycle ride away.'

'Didn't the police with you do anything?'

'They arrested the man with the key and stayed inside the building, Miss Clara. In a few moments, it was all over. The local police arrived and we handed the man we arrested to them. I told them the story and they ordered me to leave.'

'What happened to Simon and the young girl?'

'I didn't see. The local police called an ambulance which arrived as we were driving away. We needed to take the other girls back to Phnom Penh to a shelter.'

'Rithy, I want you to take us to Krong Chey.'

'Mrs Katy, I don't think you are wise. It's a border town and not safe because Cambodian and Vietnamese criminals live in these places. We never told their police we were coming because they cannot be trusted.'

'We still want to see where it happened and go to the hospital,' Clara insisted. 'I understand if you don't want to take us, I'm sure we can find another driver.'

After Rithy's warning, Katy didn't feel quite so sure about going.

'No, I'll take you there,' said he, though his reluctance to make the trip clear enough. 'I'll see if I can get a police officer to come with us in case there's a problem.'

They agreed to meet at the hotel in the morning, and Katy and Clara returned to the Palace View as the first heavy raindrops fell, announcing the afternoon monsoon.

Rithy arrived in the mission's white SUV after breakfast. Rebecca had plainly given him the news about his job as his smile beamed broader than usual. They checked the street until sure no one looked as if they were waiting to follow them and set off, keeping their eyes on the road behind. Unfortunately, Rithy's friendly police chief told him he had no officers available for what he called babysitting duties.

Krong Chey lay nearly three hours away on the border between Cambodia and Vietnam, a kilometre or two off the main highway running between Phnom Penh and Ho Chi Minh City. Under different circumstances, the drive would have been delightful. The afternoon storms had made the jungle vegetation and rice fields the most vivid of greens and the heavy air had anchored the dust on the road. The highway lay like a blood-red ribbon ahead of them.

As their SUV got further south into Svay Rieng province, the landscape changed to marshland. One of the poorest provinces in Cambodia, the residents made their living as subsistence farmers or by fishing between the regular floods of the Mekong River. Even now, water had flooded the fields from the rains and swelling streams.

Katy and Clara hadn't spoken much on the way, concerned with the emotional stress of walking in Simon's footsteps in the place where traffickers murdered him. Rithy's silence must have been because he thought he should have tried harder to talk them out of the trip in the first place.

Krong Chey turned out to be a small town, consisting of the main street with narrow, unsealed side streets and power lines haphazardly strung off poles, many at odd angles. Some had various posters pasted on them, either torn or dirty or both. The place had seen better days. The town centre consisted of old houses, bars, rickety shopfronts, garages, and open-air markets under canvas roofs and dusty from the trucks which made regular passage through the town. It smelled of barbeque skewers, ripe fruit and exhaust fumes. The usual scooters skittered about and the street market bustled with people. Turning off the main street, they drove into the grim-looking backstreets until Rithy pulled up under a spindly tree. Here, no children played. Not even a stray dog wandered the deserted alleys. Whatever they were expecting, this creepy corner of the township gave them pause to consider their earlier eagerness.

'There's the place,' said Rithy, pointing to a narrow alley fifty metres ahead on their left. Katy glanced at Clara, who now also looked apprehensive about venturing outside.

'Will you come with us Rithy, or do you want to stay here?'

'I'll come, Mrs Katy. I beg you not to stay too long.'

The three of them got out of the SUV. A few beer bottles, soft drink cans and cigarette butts lay strewn on the red dirt surface among the stones and dusty weeds; since the storms, watery potholes had opened up. They stepped carefully around the rubbish and puddles and after about a fifty metre walk along the alley, they stopped between the high walls of old, run-down buildings. The space about Katy felt oppressive, suffocating her. Her head lolled from one side to the other and dizziness swamped her. She brought her hands to her eyes to guard them, covering them to keep her balance.

'I'm right here, Ma.'

Clara linked her arm through Katy's in a gesture of support, her own as well as Katy's.

Rithy indicated an opening in the wall of a brick building. They saw stairs descending into a gloomy space below. Although the name bore no resemblance to its nature, a faded sign proclaimed it the Paradise Storage Company. A drab place, anyone could easily have mistaken it for an abandoned warehouse; the entire alley lay in the shadows of other high buildings with barred, grimy windows. They stood there for several minutes, unsure what to do.

'Ma, this place is ghastly. I don't want to be here.'

'We can leave now, *baobei*. Rithy, we can…'

'What are you people doing here?'

Startled, they turned to see three policemen had walked up quietly behind them, barring their way back to the SUV. One officer spoke in Khmer to Rithy.

'Mrs Katy, he said it is too hot outside. You must go inside for a cool drink. I am to wait here with two of them and they say you must leave your phones with me. Mrs Katy, Miss Clara, you must go with the officer.'

Katy gripped Clara's arm, anxiety beginning to gnaw her insides. She swallowed, feeling her throat dry.

'Ma, let's go with him; I can't believe they're going to harm us. We've done nothing wrong.'

Clara didn't look or feel as confident as she sounded. They followed the policeman into the building and were told to sit down behind a cheap table in a windowless, humid room. Katy leaned against the back of the chair, next to Clara, the perspiration sticking her forearms to the plastic tabletop. A girl brought in glasses and a jug of water. She closed the door as she left. They were alone.

Five minutes later, a lifetime to them, they heard a noise outside. More than enough time for both of them to have let their imaginations run wild. They jumped involuntarily when the door burst open. Two men came in, one a sweaty policeman, and judging by the stripes on his shoulder and swagger, a senior officer. With him stood another man, a Vietnamese, dressed in an open-neck floral shirt and linen pants. He had a snake tattoo around his neck and slicked-back hair. Katy noticed his shoes. They were crocodile skin and polished to a mirror shine, which looked malevolent in this grimy building. A shiver ran through her body, even in the steamy room. The Vietnamese man spoke.

'I have seen your pictures in the newspaper, so I know who you are. I know who you both are and why you came here. What I am going to say, I am going to say once.'

His voice carried the quiet menace of a man who did not need to raise the volume to intimidate. He fixed his gaze on Clara.

'Such pretty hands. I know you play the piano and are quite the star. You should understand you are playing with fire now, not your piano. Those who play with fire are burned. Always badly. I'm sure you have heard this saying.'

'It sounds like it might be a song title.'

'Ah, you are a comedian, too. You will discover I enjoy a little humour myself.'

He glanced at the police officer and nodded. Without warning, the policeman brought his night-stick crashing down on the table, millimetres from Clara's fingers. The reverberations sent the glasses and jug crashing onto the floor, splintering the plastic table and splashing water and glass fragments on their legs and feet. The noise resounded like a gunshot. They both jerked backwards instinctively, Clara pulling her hands back, holding her clenched fists protectively under her chin. She felt warm wetness trickling between her legs.

'I see you are not laughing at my joke. Accidents happen here to comedians. All the time. You would be wise to remember, Miss Yehonala. As for you, Katy Yehonala…'

He reached into a pocket. The metallic *slit* of a knife blade springing free froze her in terror, strangling the air around her, making it impossible to breathe.

'Perhaps you also have a joke for me?'

Katy stared in horror at the knife in his hand, a metre from her face. Panic paralysed her. She noticed his long fingernails; they were spotlessly clean. She wondered why his clean nails mattered to her.

'What happened to your husband and the *troublesome* Khmer girl is not unusual for those who go to places they should not go.'

He leaned forward, his face now centimetres from Katy's; she smelt cologne and stale cigarettes. He laid the cool steel against her cheek. She flinched, feeling the sting as the tip of the blade pierced the skin under her eye. She breathed the scent of the wound first, a primaeval sweet smell, then felt the warm blood seeping down her face.

'You are an attractive woman, Katy Yehonala. I will allow you to remain so for the moment because I'm a kind man and I appreciate beauty. Do not, however, mistake my kindness for weakness. If you two poke your noses where they do not belong again, weakness is not what you will remember me by, I promise you. You and your pretty daughter will be satisfying the sexual urges of my men and you will spend your lives, short ones, doing useful work in a Bangkok brothel.'

He stood back and started to leave, pausing in the doorway. He turned to face them, his smile lacking any trace of human emotion. Katy realised the root of horror was pitiless indifference; she stared into the face of pure evil.

'Krong Chey is my town. Neither you nor your foolish companion outside, who came here before, are welcome. Do I make myself perfectly clear? If not, or if you have more jokes, I'm sure my colleague will be happy to give your daughter a sample of the romantic attention you can both expect next time.'

The policeman leered at Clara's body and stepped towards her. She recoiled in panic as he leaned over and grabbed her arm and pulled her roughly to her feet. They nodded vigorously.

'I see we understand each other. Now, you can leave. My suggestion is at once. Not only Krong Chey, Cambodia as well. I never warn people twice.'

Clara fell backwards limply into her chair. He left them sitting at the table, both white with fear, and left. His companion followed him out the door into the alley. They were alone.

Katy looked at Clara while attempting to wipe away the blood from her cheek with her fingers, managing only to smear more across her face.

'I suppose he's not stopping for tea, then?' stammered Clara, dredging up some gallows humour to hold herself together.

Katy saw Clara shivering, not from anger, but fright. Katy understood. She felt the same.

'Okay. Enough. Enough!' cried Katy, not even trying to disguise the near hysteria in her voice. 'Clara, we must stop. You're the only person I have left in the world. Simon's memory isn't as important as losing you. The Vietnamese man... is a psychopath!'

'I'm glad you kept that part to yourself, Ma. I doubt psychopaths like being called psychopaths. He might have got upset and frightened us,' babbled Clara shakily, still trying to make a joke of their encounter. 'At least we learnt something important today.'

theirs, three indistinct figures inside. They both saw Rithy leaning against the SUV nursing his ribs, grimacing in pain. The nightstick had issued a final warning.

'We must go to the police.'

'Ma, it may have slipped your notice, we've already met the police.'

first day as too-intrepid sleuths, in relief more than celebration.

The humidity had been building all day. Now, the sultry late afternoon air was claustrophobic. The whole city waited eagerly for the afternoon storms to clear the air and by the look of the clouds writhing in the sky overhead like puppies under a blanket, it wouldn't have long to wait.

'Let's have a shower Ma and go out for dinner.'

'It's going to be like the Huangguoshu Waterfall outside in a few minutes.'

'Okay, we'll skip the shower,' said Clara, grinning. 'I noticed a hotpot restaurant not far along the street outside the hotel. I haven't had one of those since we got here. Besides, don't you know the old song, "Singing in the rain"?'

'I suppose it's better than singing "Candle in the wind" which was my pick a few hours ago.'

'You're a million laughs. We could do a music-hall double act.'

They both knew it wasn't side-splitting repartee but with emotions stretched to breaking point, comedy was as good as anything else to paper over memories of their lucky escape. The first clap of thunder rumbled across the sky as they stepped outside. The air cooled down as the first drops of rain fell, forcing up the umbrella.

The Palace View was on a picturesque boulevard copied straight from a Renoir painting, like much of the Phnom Penh streetscape in this once elegant French Quarter. They hurried past several colonial-era mansions nestling behind high walls and their overhanging jungle trees, leftovers from a different age and showing signs of decrepitude. Lightning jagged over their heads and the heavens opened, obscuring all except the pavement directly in front of their scurrying feet. They huddled together and ran. Before reaching the restaurant, their sodden shoes were squelching through ankle-deep water and they could barely hear each other's voices above the booming rumble of thunder and hammering rain.

The Ting Yuan hotpot restaurant proved worthy of soggy feet. The Chinese owner soon had a cauldron of spicy, cherry-red broth bubbling away ominously, resembling the pool of eternal torment prepared for King Yama's sinners. Today at least, the underworld deity and his ten courts of judgement would have to wait a mite longer for the Lady Yehonalas.

They ordered trays of sliced meats, seafood, leafy greens, lotus roots and mushrooms and helped themselves to a liberal choice of dipping sauces. To a tattoo of beating rain and surrounded by curtains of water cascading over the edges of the courtyard canopy, they tossed food into their brew and settled into a feast.

'I can feel my faith in men restored,' admitted Clara as she spooned wagyu beef and enoki mushrooms from the spicy broth and passed a bowl to Katy.

'What do you mean?'

'Well, take Rithy, for example. First, he's beaten up, earning himself cracked ribs for his trouble, then he's apologising to us for putting *our* lives in danger.'

'He probably thinks it's not good for job security to get your new boss murdered on your first day,' said Katy, still trying to laugh off the memory. 'The good news is we don't need to doubt his trustworthiness.'

'True. Now the problem will be convincing him to help us again. With his young family needing him, who could blame him for avoiding us like a head lice epidemic.'

'What I meant before - what did you mean about losing your faith in men?'

'Oh, that, I...*um*...'

'Has someone hurt you, *baobei*?'

Katy poured each of them a glass of wine, expecting a tale no parent wants to hear about a child they love. Instead, Clara thought for a while, quite unlike her, before deciding on the answer.

'No. No, at least not before today, it's nothing like you're thinking. I'm, you know, worried about getting married one day and my kids losing their dad. We Yehonalas haven't been super successful with dads over the last hundred years.'

'Not a flawless record, I'll admit. We haven't done badly as women, have we?'

'No, I think I'm happier in the company of women. You, Elena, Max especially. She and...'

'I just want you happy, *baobei*.'

'I am, Ma. I promise you.'

'Keep your hands in your pockets in future.'

Clara looked relieved about the change of subject. The confession playing on her mind would keep for another day.

'The Vietnamese man we met today terrified me. I was two years old the last time I peed my pants and I'm still shaking after today's nightmare. But you know, after I thought about it, I'm sure he never tried to hurt me. Only scare us.'

'That part of his plan worked a treat.'

'It might have been different if I wasn't so well known. I think he knew if they hurt me, it would have brought a lot of trouble down on their heads. Do you remember what Jim Preston told us? Chinese money keeps Cambodia going. We train their soldiers, the police and run the legal and illegal industries. So no, they won't hurt us unless we force them to.'

'I like your optimism. We're going to need it.'

'I'm thinking your idea about getting pictures in the *Phnom Penh Times* is looking more like divine inspiration every minute.'

'Not to mention a priority. Unlike you, I don't think we'll survive acting like a pair of nitwits again. I'm sure if he knew a way he could have committed the perfect murder, we'd not be eating wagyu beef and listening to the rain right now.'

'Let's not talk about Krong Chey anymore. I read Dad's book about this girl, Chavy, from start to finish in the funeral parlour.'

'Even after what happened in Krong Chey, finishing the story and finding out what happened to him is important to me. I owe it to Simon because I never got involved in his work here. I realise now I should have. Perhaps he thought he could never tell me everything he did, like I wouldn't be interested. If I had, this might not have happened.'

'No, Ma. You're wrong. Dad was who he was, you said so yourself at the funeral. Finding out what happened is important to me because I loved him, same as you, not because we let him down.'

Katy wanted to believe Clara. She knew Simon could be a single-minded old romantic when it came to things he believed in.

'A bit like Don Quixote, wasn't he?'

'Except for the white horse, Ma. He wrote two things in the book which are important in the story we don't know about yet.'

'Georgie?'

'Yes. Dad wrote about the Pink House, which we know is Rebecca and Ross's mission house, so we know part of the story is true. The next question is whether Georgie from the embassy and Papa Georgie from the Pink House are the same person, or if he's a made-up character.'

'We know Chavy described Papa Georgie as a fat Australian government official, and Sorensen seems to have been here at the right times.'

'It's hard to imagine him as a murderous gangster.'

'How many murderous gangsters have you met, Clara?'

'Good point. Only one so far. And he's not the George Sorensen type, though being a paedophile is even more disgusting to me.'

'To be fair, Simon might have modelled his Papa Georgie on George Sorensen and before the book got published, planned to change the name of the character.'

'Maybe. Hopefully, our scheme to get Jim Preston involved might come up with answers, one way or the other.'

'So let's keep the foot-roasting of George Sorensen for later, *baobei*. At least until we know if he's guilty.'

'Seems fair. If Sorensen is Papa Georgie, I vote for castration by rabid rats. Foot-roasting is for wimps.'

'I'm glad you're on my side.'

'The other part we know nothing about is the last thing Dad wrote.'

'The Vitara Orphanage?'

'Uh-huh. Where does the orphanage fit into the story? We don't know if the place exists yet; a half-decent detective would have checked it out first. We forgot all about it. Not to forget the million-dollar question…'

'Chavy.'

They both voiced her name at the same time.

'Do you think she's real, Ma? If she is, I've a feeling her story is going to break our hearts.'

'It already has.'

The night turned late, the wine glasses exorcised of the last grape and a worthy battle fought and won against the hotpot. Clara had also purged Katy's lingering guilt about Simon's death. The rain still pounded down. She looked mischievously at Katy.

'Singing in the rain?'

'Why not?'

With the umbrella safely furled from the dangers of getting wet, they removed their shoes and linked arms, slushing home in the torrential downpour and jumping in the flooded gutters like street urchins while making a valiant attempt at Gene Kelly's signature tune. They were a bedraggled sight when they arrived at the hotel, shivering in their near-transparent clothes and trailing a tributary of the Bassac River in their wake through the lobby, laughing, if not hysterically, at least cathartically.

Back in the room, they showered, dried themselves off, and crawled into bed together, cleansed inside and out by an offbeat choice of crisis therapy.

'Are you okay, *baobei*?'

'We're both still in one piece, Ma, but I think you should brush up on your parenting skills.'

'And you could brush up on your potty training. I suppose today could have ended up differently?'

'But it didn't. What's our plan now? Aside from me not wearing expensive *La Perla* underwear next time we do dumb things.'

'Remember, tomorrow we're having lunch in a place I'm told we're going to love.'

Neither of them noticed the red light on the house phone.

12

TARANTULAS, RED ANTS AND ORPHANAGES

'The message at the reception desk was from Jim Preston asking us if we could drop Dad's manuscript off at the newspaper tomorrow,' I called out to my mother as she stepped from the shower.

'Well, something's got his attention,' replied she, re-appearing in a dressing-gown and drying her hair with a towel. 'Getting a call must be a good sign.'

'Don't get too excited, Ma. If we're right about the hotel staff passing on messages about us to the Chinese or Martin Lewis, they got this message too and will assume Dad's book is important, which might not be good news for us.'

'Well, we don't know for sure if they're passing on messages. Besides, what's done is done. We'll take the book with us today and leave it with him on the way to lunch with Elena. We can let him know about yesterday's little adventure.'

'It might be safer if he had the manuscript. Just in case.'

'In case of what?'

I wondered myself.

We clambered into a tuk-tuk, bracing our feet against the twists and turns as we puttered and bumped through the narrow streets, manoeuvring surgically through tight gaps in the traffic.

Like our tuk-tuk, events were moving at a pace not totally under our control and getting less so by the day on several fronts.

When we arrived at the *Phnom Penh Times* office, we found no sign of Jim Preston. One of his colleagues told us he'd gone to Bangkok and wouldn't be back in Phnom Penh until tomorrow. We decided to leave the manuscript; I still thought it would be better in his hands than ours.

Elena had recommended we meet her at a restaurant called Romdeng with a promise of something a bit different. She was filling my thoughts and I was eager to see her again. We weren't disappointed. An elegant, two-storey colonial building greeted us, set in a lush jungle garden with a koi pond close to where she'd booked a table. However, the charming location wasn't the promise of "something a bit different" we imagined. If we wanted to step outside our culinary comfort zone, we'd come to the right place.

'*Ciao* Clara. Wonderful to see you both again,' said she, not quite as convincingly as I expected, or hoped. 'Katy, what happened to your eye?'

'A careless accident in the bathroom yesterday. Nothing to worry about. What a delightful place this is.'

'After what you've both been through, I thought you two might like to see one of the success stories of volunteer work in Cambodia. A group called *mith samlanh* started Romdeng, it's a local organisation working with street children. Their name means *friends* in English.'

I was only half-listening as, like my mother, we stared aghast at lunch on the adjoining table. Unless my imagination was running riot and I prayed it to be true, those people were munching on giant black spiders. Elena saw our faces and chuckled.

'Tarantulas. Delicious, I'm told, especially barbequed with a lime sauce topping. People tell me they're crunchy with chewy insides if a little oily. I've never been game to try them myself; I break into a cold sweat any time I find a money spider in my bedroom.'

One of the diners looked like a catfish.

'They're great favourites with locals and a delicacy the tourists pretend they ate for bragging rights when they go home. There's also crispy crickets, red ants, frogs, even buffalo on the menu if arachnids aren't your thing,' added Elena helpfully as possible options.

'Not quite what I had in mind when you said something a little different.'

'You'll be pleased to hear there's more on the menu than creepy crawlies, Katy. The remarkable thing about this place is ex-street kids run the operation, learn hospitality skills and how to run a business. The older kids even make the tables and furnishings and all the profits go back into helping more kids get off the street. Romdeng's a great story about what can be done when people set their mind to it.'

My mother quickly recovered from the visual advertisements of the menu, though even during her time in exile as a child, I doubted she'd been served up such novel protein options.

'I've eaten sparrows, bullfrogs, even snails in my life,' said she, thinking along the same lines, 'plus a few things I never plucked up the courage to ask about. I thought I couldn't be surprised anymore.'

Elena looked at me with the same soulful smile at the hotel and turned to my mother.

'How are you settling in, Katy? Are you still staying on for a while?'

'We both are, despite the dietary delights on offer. There are activities at the Svay Thom mission we'd like to get involved with and we both want to find out what happened to Simon.'

'Yes, Clara told me your plans. Any progress? I've heard nothing from the embassy.'

'We're still waiting to hear news.'

I could see my mother's reluctance to mention anything we'd been up to until we knew who we could trust. Including Elena, who we knew moved in embassy circles. It would have been a struggle for her; discretion didn't top the list of my mother's dominant genes, ranking alongside diplomacy. Airing her unvarnished opinions ran deep in her Yehonala DNA, a trait surfacing in mine.

I studied Elena's profile as she spoke to my mother and felt a touch to a lonely place deep inside me. Why is she looking as if she'd rather be somewhere else?

'What do you recommend on the menu?' I asked her.

'It's all good. On the insect front, the beef with red ants is delicious. When I came here with my partner, the ants were the only beasties with more than four legs I could manage. You don't notice them in the spicy basil stir fry.'

'Elena has a partner?' A wave of nausea washed over me. I quickly looked away, knowing the shock must be written all over my face. How could I have been so wrong before? Elena reached under the table and her hand squeezed my leg.

'Why don't you order for us, Clara?'

I tried hard to distract myself, to appear normal, despite the sting of those words stabbing into me.

'…Yes…how about we do it the Chinese way? We'll order dishes to share. That way, we can try the ants, just to say we have.'

The food I ordered had once walked, swam or flown in the Chinese banquet style, plus a vegetarian dish, steamed rice and duck rolls for an entrée. A jug of chilled lime juice took up the remaining square centimetres of the table.

'Are you sure you two don't have Italian blood running through your veins?'

'Eating has always been how Chinese families get together,' said my mother. 'Do you know, when we meet anyone, our greeting is "have you eaten?" We don't bother asking how you are. We think food fixes most complaints.'

'We Italians are the same. I remember as kids in Trieste, family gatherings meant mountains of food. *Nonna* Accardi got rabid if we kids started arguing around the table, not uncommon, as our family gatherings were more like celebrating the Assumption of Mary. She would stand up in horror, waving her arms and yelling, *Gesù é al tavolo*, which means, Jesus is at the table, her way of saying how dare we desecrate a sacred family meal and our Italian roots. It said as much about the importance of food to the family as it did about her religious beliefs.'

'Ancestors and food are also the closest Chinese families come to religious rapture these days. Does your husband work with UNICEF too?'

'I don't have a husband, Katy. My partner works for a Swiss aid agency called Mercy International, but I haven't seen her for more than a year. I'm afraid we're both fallen Catholics destined for eternity in the nine circles of torment.'

I am caught in a camera flash, stuck in time. My limbs can't move as if someone else is controlling them remotely, nor can I shut out their voices.

'She's Swiss herself, from a town called Neuchâtel. At the moment, she's in Somalia's refugee camps with the child victims of the famine and civil war. It's her life. She's a remarkable woman and makes me proud and scared every day to know her. Mogadishu's about the most dangerous place on Earth to be right now.'

'Oh, I...'

'Don't worry, Katy. I decided it's cowardly to be afraid to care for someone worth a thousand of the people who criticise me for my choices. A big call for an Italian Catholic,' added she.

'Please stop this conversation or I'm going to scream.'

'Now I understand what Jim Preston meant. He hinted about you breaking the hearts of all red-blooded men in Cambodia,' said my mother, ploughing on cluelessly into a river already churning from winter storms.

'Dear Jim's never lost for a newspaper headline...'

I saw Elena drowning in the same torrents. I must head off my mother's diplomacy-devoid curiosity before she stripped this excruciating conversation utterly naked.

'Let's talk about my father. Did you remember the name of the orphanage he asked you about?' I asked Elena, my voice carrying a barely concealed hostile edge I couldn't contain. My mother's sideways look gave away that her sensors were on full alert.

'I knew it would come back to me,' answered she ruefully. 'It's called the Vitara Orphanage, a privately run place in the Phnom Song district on the city's outskirts.'

'Sorry, I need to go...excuse me for a moment. *What's happening to me?*'

I almost ran to the toilet, making its privacy before being violently sick. I needed to get myself under control. I'd never felt such explosive emotion boiling inside before. After a few minutes of deep breathing and splashing water on my face, I thought I might be ready to return. When I sat down, Elena glanced at me with intense sadness in her eyes, as if she could see into my soul and read each naked emotion written there. They were talking about the orphanages.

'...no, Simon never told me what interested him about the Vitara Orphanage. I thought it odd, as he only got involved with the children in karaoke bars, teashops, or backstreet brothels, as far as I knew. Many charities are worried about the orphanages, so I didn't give it much thought at the time.'

'Why are charities worried about orphanages?' asked my mother.

'Well, orphanages are a big problem for child protection organisations; their lack of regulation puts children at risk. There's exploitation, malnourishment, lack of education and sexual abuse going on all the time. Believe it or not, paedophiles have set up orphanages here in the past. The government ones are usually managed well, the private ones cause the problems. They cover the range from badly run to criminal enterprises.'

'Aren't there regulations controlling orphanages?'

'They're not enforced, Katy. Anyone can set up an orphanage here. The worst places have been closed down over the past year, but it's slow going. Do you know nearly three-quarters of children in Cambodian orphanages aren't orphans at all?'

'What?' I interrupted. ' So why are they in orphanages?'

'It's been an unfortunate side-effect of Cambodia becoming popular with tourists. People want to volunteer; they even pay money to work in them. It's no coincidence the number of orphans in Cambodia has also risen. In fact, it's doubled in the last five years. In a poor country, using children as tourist attractions is an easy way to make money.'

'Kids belong at home with their families, not in orphanages,' I snapped at her. A helpless comment, as I well knew. I began to realise neither my mother nor I knew half of what my father had been doing in Cambodia, or the heartbreaking work people like Elena did every day.

'Try telling a single mother living in a village, struggling to support eight kids on less than a dollar a day,' replied Elena, far more kindly than I deserved. 'These orphanages exploit victims of poverty by convincing parents to hand over their kids with the promise of education and a better life. Many are run like a business using kids as the product. They get sent out to dance for donations in popular tourist areas or perform shows in the orphanage.'

'Why are criminals interested in orphanages?' I asked, calmer now. 'Seems like a lot of work for not much profit.'

'You couldn't be more wrong. Donors give millions and money laundering's common. The kids also make souvenirs for the busloads of tourists who visit and collect donations at the gates. Orphanage tourism is booming and a lot of money changes hands. They've also been a godsend for paedophiles who can pay a fee to take a child, unsupervised, out on a "play date" for the day. Where there's an opportunity, the criminals move in. We know there's child trafficking, but as far as I know, no orphanage has ever been prosecuted.'

'Will you take Clara and me to visit the Vitara Orphanage?'

'Why on earth would you want to go there?'

'Well, Simon had an interest in the place and we want to continue his work. Maybe he planned to donate money to the orphanage.'

Elena looked at both of us a little suspiciously, weighing up whether we had other motives.

'I suppose I could. These places always like UNICEF visiting for a photo opportunity. Great PR for their donors. And with you

Clara, I expect they'd jump at the chance to have your famous face on their next fund-raising flyers. I'll need to check if there are warnings about the place. It wouldn't be a good look having any of us promoting a shady orphanage.'

'It would be better for you and Elena to go together, *baobei*. Would you excuse me for five minutes? I need to make a visit too.'

I knew my mother too well. She may not have guessed all that was going on between Elena and me, but she had guessed enough to know we needed some time to talk to each other. Elena looked away wretchedly from me, her lips in a grim line.

'Your mother's a very perceptive woman.'

'Elena, how could you?' I mumbled, my voice barely a whisper.

With my head in my hands, I struggled to stop the surging tears from giving away any pretence of self-defence. 'How *could* you? How could you throw what I said I felt for you back in my face?'

Smarting from my sense of betrayal, anger spilt over. 'When I went to the toilet, I threw up. Do you have *any* idea how much you hurt me? How can someone as kind and sensitive as you be so cruel, especially knowing how much everything else has taken out of me? I just don't understand. Is this your way of telling me to keep away from you? If so, all you had to do was say so, or not call me in the first place.'

'No, please don't go away. I've done a terrible thing, but I'm not lying to you about my feelings. Now, well, right now, I wish I could take you in my arms and hold you and tell you not to worry...'

'Oh really! You have an ingenious way of showing how much you care about my emotional state,' I spat at her.

'I said I wish I could. Except I'm not brave enough. Please let me try to explain, not to make an excuse because there isn't one, aside from admitting to you I'm a jellyfish. It took all my pitiful ration of courage to meet you at the hotel and only then because I honestly believed I'd never see you again. When you said you were staying, I didn't know what to do, so I took the coward's way out and just kept quiet about Adriana.'

'But why?'

'I thought it wouldn't matter for a few extra days until you left and we could stay friends and have space and time. Everything happened so fast. I even believed it was for your benefit instead of my selfishness. Even though Adriana and I have barely spoken for a year, I tell myself she and I are still together and I don't know how to stop loving her. I know it's not healthy and may not even be true anymore.'

'Why not simply tell me? I can deal with worse than being told you're not interested in me.'

'But that wouldn't be true. The trouble is, I'm not a convincing liar except to myself. Having a partner just slipped out and when Katy asked about "my husband"… well, I just spilt everything. Clara, I beg you to forgive me. I'm unspeakably sorry our conversation about Adriana hurt you coming without any warning. I saw how it affected you. It nearly broke my heart to see your face.'

'I'm not sure I can forgive you. The only reason I'm not leaving right now is because I'm not much better than you. We've not been completely honest with you, either. I suppose we had our well-meaning reasons too.'

'You mean going to the Vitara Orphanage is more than a social call?'

'The truth is, we think it's connected to my father's murder. We don't know how. He mentioned the Vitara Orphanage in a book he was writing.'

'I had no idea he was writing a book.'

'Neither did I until a few days ago.'

My mother returned and all the fiery potatoes got dropped. She looked at me. God only knows what she saw, but she sat down as if nothing had happened.

'Clara's been telling me about your interest in the Vitara Orphanage, Katy. I'll promise to keep your suspicions to myself. I'll also help you visit the place or in any other way I can. Please be careful, though. The places we child protection agencies work are never quite what they seem.'

We got back to the hotel under the darkening skies of the afternoon monsoon, arriving with five minutes to spare. My phone buzzed as we stepped out of the lift. Glancing down at the message, I stared.

'*Cuore mio Clara, be patient with me. Please. Love Elena.*'

'Is everything okay, *baobei*?'

'Yes, Ma. I think so.'

We opened the door to our room. I froze. Everything wasn't okay at all.

'We've had a visitor.'

13

BURNING EARS AND NEW MATES

Clara had always been obsessive about things like closing drawers, doors and zipping up zippers, so when she insisted the pocket on her suitcase should not be partly open, I had no doubt our visitor had forgotten to close it. The maid possibly, though unlikely. Their job's way too important to risk rifling through a guest's bags and failing to hide the crime. A random intruder? Also unlikely. One possibility remained.

'This means the hotel staff *are* passing on messages. Why would anyone be interested in Simon's manuscript?'

'Whoever it is, they must be worried there's more in Dad's book than there actually is. But what? And who's alarmed enough to break into our room to find out?'

'It must have been Zhao's Chinese Embassy staff or Martin Lewis. My guess is they may not be on the same side.'

'More to the point, who's on our side?'

'I have a cunning plan to find out.'

I picked up the phone and asked the duty manager to come to our room. Five minutes later, there was a knock on the door. Clara let him in.

'My name is Samay, Madam Yehonala. How can I be of service?'

'Please have a seat, *Lok* Samay, I'm hoping you can help us. We seem to have been careless. Before my husband died, he wrote a book about Cambodia and one of the newspapers here wants to publish extracts. Unfortunately, we've mislaid the book and CD somewhere. We may have left them by the pool, perhaps in the restaurant, or in the garden. Hopefully, not in a tuk-tuk.'

I gave him a vacuous smile with all the innocence of an empty-headed woman I could conjure up.

'Would you be good enough to check if anyone has found them?'

'I'll ask the desk staff to enquire for you. What is the name of the book?'

'It's called *Cambodia's Secret Child Sex Trade*.'

'Oh!'

He looked shocked. Was it by the title?

'We'll do our best to find your book, Madam. May I also say how sorry we were to learn of your husband's death? It's been in all the newspapers.'

'We're both grateful, *Lok* Samay. And thank you for your help; the book is the only copy we have.'

After he left, we returned to our evening routine of sitting on the balcony with a drink and spicy nuts, feeling safe in the noisy embrace of the rain. Even a little back in control. Or at least, a story we told ourselves.

'Is my nose growing?'

'Like a weed. The CD added a nice touch.'

'Let's hope it keeps whoever came in our room worrying someone else found the manuscript and CD first. You'd better send a message to Jim Preston's phone. Tell him to contact us on my mobile phone or yours in future. I'm sure we can trust him with our numbers. After all, we don't want him phoning the hotel switchboard again, thanking us for the manuscript.'

'I think there's more of Inspector Morse in you than you're letting on, Ma.'

We both wondered what tomorrow held in store.

The next day turned out to be an educational one, vastly improving Clara's and my Anglo-Saxon vocabulary. Jim Preston called us in the morning, suggesting we get together for coffee in the afternoon at the Fresco Café. We found a secluded table and shared our suspicions about hotel staff passing on messages and our idea to say we'd lost the book.

At first, he seemed quite pleased with our creativity. However, our smugness rapidly dissolved when we added the details of our visit to Krong Chey. On a scale of one to ten, with *furious* at the entry-level, well, you may already get the picture. We thought he would burst an artery.

'We all have the right to monumental stupidity, ladies,' he roared, 'but you two fucking idiots are abusing the bloody privilege! Did one of you leave the dipshit bag open in your room that day?'

Clara and I both squirmed under his glare while he warmed to the task.

'Even a fucking half-wit would have known they'd be watching the fucking alley if crims used the place for trafficking kids across the border. Didn't you think? Thinking isn't illegal, you know!'

'We realised afterwards,' I mumbled.

'A fat lot of fucking good it is having rear vision mirrors! How about you, Clara? What if you had finished up with a pair of crushed hands? Or you Katy, with acid splashed on your face? You're damned lucky your friend Rithy only got a couple of cracked ribs. Your fucking celebrity isn't going to protect you if you start turning over the wrong rocks in this country,' he now bellowed at us. 'And before you go blundering around next time and do get to meet your fucking ancestors, let me tell you the basic things you need to know about investigating anything.

'Rule number one is don't go doing bloody stupid-ass things likely to get you killed. Rule number two is to go back and read rule number bloody one again.'

'We want to visit the Vitara Orphanage next,' said Clara.

'God, give me strength! Didn't you two amateurs hear a word I said?'

'The time just flies by chatting to you, doesn't it?' said Clara with a cheeky smile.

He rolled his eyes, followed by a kind of grunting laugh.

'Sorry. I guess I've seen too much happen to people over the last five years.'

It looked like his temper or his list of swear words may be getting exhausted.

'Calm down, Jim. No need to throw all your toys out of the pram. Clara and I know we were lucky in Krong Chey and I promise you we've learnt our lesson. Why do you think we're telling you?'

'Look you two, investigating a story is a slow process. When it could get you on the wrong side of seriously ruthless bastards who murdered two million of their fellow citizens a few years back - and in case you've forgotten - Simon Bailey last week, it needs to be a *careful*, slow process. It takes time, hard work and you can't do it by charging around like the Chinese version of Charlie's bloody Angels. We'll need to talk to people, find documents if they're available and spend as much time as it takes to piece the story together. I know you want answers...'

'Do you mean you're going to help us?' ventured Clara, testing the water.

'I'm not going to help you get yourselves killed if that's what you're asking. If you're willing to listen to a reporter with a little experience in these things and agree not to go feral again with more bloody kamikaze missions, we can talk about it. I'm not joking about you floating in a stormwater drain making a good story. It's not an article I'd enjoy writing.'

'Sounds like we're best friends again,' said Clara, a not-contrite expression on her face. 'We'll be good.'

'Kill me now! Will you stop acting like a cloud sailing on the summer bloody breezes and cut your crap, Clara. I know I'm wasting my time trying to stop you from doing whatever dumb-ass thing you're going to do, but I'm serious about not wanting to write your obituary. Okay?'

'We *both* understand.'

Clara nodded, this time without the smile after I cast an evil eye in her direction.

'I'm sorry, Jim,' said she. 'I didn't mean to be smart-alecky. We admit we were stupid and had no idea what we were doing. The truth is the Krong Chey man scared us to death. We're still having nightmares.'

'From what you told me, whoever you met would have scared Rambo. Right, first of all, I'm beginning to agree with you. Something smells about Simon's death. Second, I think there might be a story here. I went to Bangkok on another story yesterday and decided to talk to my contacts about young George. I found out his last posting was Bangkok and checked to see if he'd left skeletons lying around Thailand. Yes, Katy. You're about as subtle as a meat axe.

'Anyway, I heard a whisper around the backstreet sex shops about a fat guy with a penchant for renting a few young girls at a time. Seems he's not too gentle with them, either. Right nationality, right age, more or less the right description, right size. There's nothing to hang George Sorensen for yet and certainly not enough evidence to raise flags at the embassy in Thailand or he'd be cooling his heels with the Aussie Federal Police. If it is him, he's good at covering his tracks, but it gave me enough to dig a bit deeper. The man they were talking about hasn't been seen around Bangkok for the best part of a year.'

'About the time he left Thailand to come back here.'

'Could be, Katy. Could as easily be a coincidence. When I got back from Bangkok last night, I started reading the manuscript you left at my office. This Papa Georgie of yours also likes to have two or three kids and is rough with them. The coincidence seemed too much for me. I'm thinking *Chavy's Story* isn't a novel.'

'What else did you find out?' asked Clara.

'I went through old newspaper articles about the raid on the Pink House a couple of years or so ago, the one Simon Bailey got involved in. After some more digging, I found out who the owners of the joint were and where they are now.'

'Aren't they in prison?'

'Nope. Only those who worked in the place were locked up, probably so it would look like the wheels of justice were turning.

The two owners, a Cambodian man and his Vietnamese wife, never made it to the big house at all.'

'Why not?'

'Usual reasons. Powerful friends would be my guess. Simon's book said there were a couple of generals and police chiefs who were customers; I told you how this place works. You can bitch all you like about the world's injustices, what's done is done. What's more interesting is where those fine pillars of Asian society set up shop for their brand-new career.'

'Let me guess, they run the Vitara Orphanage. Now we know why Simon became interested in the place.'

'Slow down, tiger. We don't know why he wanted to check it out, besides, I can't imagine how he could have found out about the owners. There are fifty reasons he could have been there, which means we don't bolt down rabbit holes without thinking first. We need to be *careful*, remember?

'Anyway, top of the class for you, Katy. As it happens, our friends have their grubby fingerprints on half a dozen orphanages around the country. No great surprise they don't work in them, but my contacts tell me they're the money behind the operation.'

'We have a plan,' said Clara.

'God, give me strength! If it's anything like your last work of bloody genius, I can hardly wait.'

'No, you'll like this one. You'll even get an exclusive story in your newspaper.'

We explained how Zhao had asked for photographs with Clara after the funeral and told Jim our first impression about wanting them taken to win favour in China with the Premier. However, after learning more about China's relationship with Cambodia, we now thought the photos were more likely insurance for Zhao to make sure we were left alone to protect his ambitions.

'Nice to know you listened to at least one thing I told you,' said he, grunting with mock approval. 'And the photo-op's a great idea. My editor will buy it too. Zhao can tell us all the wonderful things he and China are doing for Cambodia and you can say all the right things to support him, plus a few things about your life, family heritage and so on. Good PR for both China and you, especially as I'll be writing the story. And it will make anyone think twice before they give either of you a hard time again.'

'You see Jim, we can be obliging as well as giving you high blood pressure,' said Clara. 'Now you can stop worrying about us. I'll call the Chinese Embassy to set up a meeting for us all.'

'Right. I'll organise the photographer. Don't get too confident, ladies; we don't know who's behind Simon's murder yet. To be honest with you, the good guys only catch the bad guys every time in Hollywood. Also, whoever it is might not give a fu… care a lot about Zhao's lovefest with Clara.'

'What about George Sorensen? Do you think he might be visiting the Vitara Orphanage now for his "fun"?'

'Well Katy, if it *was* him at the Pink House, it's likely he's mates with the owners. He'd need them to ensure his privacy given his job at the embassy. So it may be where he goes, either there or to one of their other places. The Vitara Orphanage is far enough outside the city to be discreet and Sorensen is extremely careful about covering his tracks if he's a paedophile. If he is Papa Georgie, it would be a safer place to go, or to a quiet hotel nearby, so the owners can bring kids over from the orphanage.'

'We have another plan,' I said. 'We're going to ask Rithy to follow him. We think he'll only go there after he's finished work in the evenings when it's less likely anyone will notice. It shouldn't be too hard to watch his home and follow him on a scooter.'

'He rents a small villa in the Boeung Keng Kang district, not far from Sisowath Quay. If you can, try to get a photograph or a video, but for God's sake, do it from a safe distance. And please, no heroics, ladies, remember my blood pressure.'

He wrote the address on a card and handed it over as well as a photo he'd got from somewhere.

'Don't worry, Jim, there won't be any fucking heroics.'

'*Aiya! Did I…*' I saw Clara's mortified expression. Jim looked impressed.

We decided to walk the short distance back to the hotel, stopping on the way for an ice cream. As expected, I didn't have long to wait.

'Ma, when I said you needed to get more adventurous with your swear words, I didn't mean starting with the five-star ones in a café. You're my mother and I expect better parenting from you.'

'Sorry, I didn't mean to embarrass you. I got a bit over-excited as we seem to be making progress. It slipped out and surprised me as much as you, I promise I'm not planning to make a habit of it. *Um*…though I must say, swearing's quite liberating.'

'*Liberating* isn't exactly the word I'd pick, Ma. I accept your apology, though it's not the way we Yehonalas were brought up. You should know the rules better than me.'

I walked meekly beside her, licking my ice cream, my inner child feeling eleven years old again after facing Mama's wrath. I had once disobeyed her in public, a capital crime in the Yehonala manual of good order and discipline.

'Sometimes I feel like your mother,' scolded she, turning towards me.

'You sound like her, too.'

She grinned like a Cheshire cat and linked her arm through mine. Whatever our misfortunes have been across the generations, I knew the family name rested in safe hands.

In the morning, Katy and Clara headed out to Svay Thom to check on Rithy's injuries, hoping to win his support for their "stalking George Sorensen" hustle. Despite a casual mention to Jim about asking Rithy to help, they were far from confident he'd want to enlist himself in another meet-your-ancestors expedition with his new bosses, even if this one should turn out to be a touch less perilous.

'How are you feeling, Rithy?' asked Katy, returning his sampeah. 'Have you been to the hospital?'

He grinned, evidently not feeling too much the worse for wear.

'It is bother about nothing, Mrs Katy. Jorani and Mrs Rebecca are fussing over me like I am a child. I am Rithy, strong like the elephant.'

'We're pleased to hear it. We have another job for you if the elephant is willing.'

'If it is not in Krong Chey, I am pleased to help you, Mrs Katy.'

'It's not in Krong Chey. Let us explain first and afterwards it will be up to you. We won't be upset if you don't wish to do this job. Okay?'

Katy explained they needed him to watch George Sorensen's villa for a few hours each evening and why they wanted him followed. If Sorensen left, he was to keep a safe distance and report where he went. Sounded straightforward enough, even to Katy.

'This is no different from work with Mr Simon. We watched places for hours, planning how to rescue the girls and catch the ringleaders. No trouble for me, Mrs Katy.'

'Do you have a scooter?' asked Clara.

'I can borrow one easily enough or take Jorani's.'

'Borrowing one won't do. Jorani may need hers and we must keep this job secret. No one must know what you're doing, not even Rebecca and Ross. As it will take your evenings, you can tell Jorani you're working for Clara and me like you did with Simon, but you cannot tell her who the person is you're following. Is this going to be okay with Jorani?'

'No problem, Mrs Katy.'

'We'll pay you for the extra time,' said Katy. 'Now, take us to the motorbike shop.'

By the middle of the afternoon, the scheme was hatched. They agreed to start the following night and arranged to meet back at the Palace View the next afternoon.

'Convincing Rithy turned out easier than I thought it would,' said Clara on the way back to the hotel.

'He wants to be working again. I'll bet he never went for a checkup either; I don't think he likes anyone treating him like an invalid. Now, how do you feel about riding on a scooter in the rain at night?'

'Me?'

'Well, we should take Rithy some food and help keep watch. If George Sorensen decides to go out while one of us is there, we can ride on the back as another pair of eyes.'

Clara beamed like the birthday girl.

'You mean like Audrey Hepburn in *Roman Holiday?*'

'Sort of, though more like a madwoman's voyage through the Yangtze Floods, I expect. In the morning, best we buy two of those blue poncho things people wear here in the rain.'

14

NIGHTS OUT

'Clara?'

'Yes?' I mumbled drowsily, gathering my scattered faculties and irritated to be roused from a lazy sleep-in.

'Good morning, it's Martin Lewis. From the embassy.'

'I only know one Martin Lewis; I don't need to work out which one you are. And it's one too many if they make a habit of waking me up in the middle of the night. What do you want, Martin? I hope you have a good reason to disturb me so early.'

'Oh. Sorry. Well Clara, as our official business is over, I hope, *er* wonder, if you might like to, sort of, have dinner with me. And by the way, it's nine o'clock in the morning.'

Am I his bureaucratic project with all the boxes now properly ticked off?

'Are you *sort of* asking me on a date, Martin?'

'I…*um*…suppose I am.'

'You woke me up for that?'

The line went quiet.

'Was he lost for words or thinking twice?'

'We haven't always seen eye to eye over the past week. I thought, well, I…'

'Just a moment, let me find somewhere a bit quieter.'

Whatever else Martin Lewis might be, I decided an ace love

rat didn't appear to be among his accomplishments. I muted the phone and rolled over.

'Ma, it's Martin Lewis,' I hissed. 'He's asking me out on a date. What am I going to do?'

'Lucky you. Well, you should go. He's almost sure to have another motive, like finding out about the book, or he knows we're talking to Jim Preston, or he's heard about our visit to Krong Chey.'

'So you don't think it's my irresistible charm?'

'It's certainly not because of your phone manners. There's an old saying, *baobei*, keep friends close and your enemies closer. Have a nice time. You might also learn something.'

'I don't think I'd rate highly as a Mata Hari. Besides, I...oh never mind.'

'Sorry to keep you, Martin, and for my grumpy voice. I suppose we could. I mean, yes, I'd like to. Pick me up at seven-thirty if you like.'

'Great. See you later. Bye.'

I stared blankly at the inert phone in my hand. *'Why on earth...as if I don't have enough romantic problems.'*

'While you're talking to your admirers, you may as well get up and give the Chinese Embassy a call and arrange for the photographs. We should also see Rémy Aubert if we can; he might know more than we think. At the funeral, he told us he'd met Martin a few times.'

My mother and I had been enjoying our sleep-in, a plan now to be abandoned. I dragged myself out of bed, found Rémy Aubert's card and got comfortable on the balcony in my pyjamas. No-one answered. The call to the embassy turned out better and the receptionist put me through straightaway to Ambassador Zhao. He said he planned to meet Minister Suong on a business matter later in the week, which would be an ideal opportunity to take the pictures. We arranged a time to meet in two days. I phoned Jim to confirm the arrangements.

'As we're not going to be allowed to spend the day lounging in bed like a pair of lazybone pigs Ma, I'm going to have a shower and get dressed. Let's go down to the Peking Canteen for a bowl of dumplings. We can find a shop for the raincoats around there as well.'

I disappeared into a steamy torrent of water with my fabulously decadent Mademoiselle body wash for the next fifteen minutes, afterwards lounging on the sofa with lime juice and mangosteens, waiting for my mother. Life's little prizes for getting up with the sparrows.

'While you were in the shower,' called she from the bathroom, 'Alan Doole, the man from the funeral home, phoned. The monks at Wat Bagan have finished the memorial for Simon and they want to hold the service at ten o'clock tomorrow morning. I said we'd be there.'

'All that seems to have happened so long ago, doesn't it?'

In the late afternoon, Rithy reported in for stakeout duty.

'How's the new scooter, Rithy? Have you mastered the controls?'

'Indeed, Miss Clara. I am quite an expert in the traffic. I'm now ready for the working.'

The three of us sat on the balcony drinking tea while we agreed on our plan. We would watch the house until 11 pm, then Rithy could go home. If George Sorensen made an appearance, Rithy would contact us if one of us wasn't with him and follow, ensuring he kept out of sight and get the address of where George went. In the traffic at night and in the rain, a simple enough plan without too much risk, barring pneumonia. We exchanged phone numbers and gave Rithy the address and Sorensen's photograph. We were all set.

'I'll come tonight, Rithy,' offered my mother. 'We can check the streets together so we'll know where you'll be. Are you comfortable with me riding on the scooter with you?'

'Oh yes, Mrs Katy. You will be safe with me.'

'Don't forget your new poncho, Ma. Looks like you might need it.'

After they left for their evening vigil, I stayed on the balcony, wondering about my evening with Martin Lewis. I agreed with my mother about him having an ulterior motive in mind for asking me out. Still, I felt a flutter of anticipation about the night. No, do not wear a look of astonishment, I don't mean *that* kind of flutter. More the confused kind, given I'm trying to come to terms with my current choice of gender and dealing with the random Elena images floating around in my head.

In any case, it's not like I've never been out with a man. I'd had plenty of opportunities for dating before Max and I got together but avoided anything, shall we just say, "invasive", after a practice session or two when I quickly caught on to the idea we were supposed to end up in a bedroom. Don't get me wrong, I hadn't signed up for the purity pledge, more because indifference ruled what I laughingly call my sex life. Even poor Max thinks my sexual handiwork leans more towards frigid than frisky, though in all honesty, I must say I try my best with the limited erotic tools at my disposal. Besides, with my schedule, I assumed the men who asked me out were only interested in bragging rights to fit in with what little time I had anywhere, an affair sure to have me featured in a gossip magazine or plastered over the internet, even if they could evade Max's protective claws.

To tell you the truth, my biggest sexual battles were in China fighting off middle-aged, or older, political or business heavyweights. Ending up as a trophy girlfriend for adornment rights around the banquet table is a common enough fate for all of us in the public spotlight if we happened to be young, pretty, and willing to make the devil's bargain for help up the success ladder. As a result of my disinterest for a leg up, or more to the point, one over, I'm doubtless one of the oldest virgins in China, although a crusade to rectify my sexual shortcomings loomed low on my to-do list.

Well, I *had* committed to this Martin date, so I'd best make an effort and hoped this one wouldn't incite me to murder. At any rate, it couldn't be worse than one amusing a sweaty Krong Chey policeman with a body odour issue. I took another shower and sorted through my clothes for what I thought might be dating ones in the tropics, picking out a burgundy-coloured silk dress with spaghetti straps and a pretty scarf I'd found on a shopping expedition to the Russian Market. After applying a little makeup and digging out some strappy low-ish heels, I waited, mentally preparing myself to deal with either a lecture or an attempt to coax me out of my clothes. The room phone buzzed.

'Clara, you look stunning.' I hazarded a guess about the disrobing option.

Martin looked different away from his usual role, whatever his job turned out to be. The open neck cotton shirt and cream chinos suited him; I hadn't paid attention before. He looked passably handsome. I judged him to be around thirty and he appeared more relaxed than he sounded on the phone earlier, thank God, with carefully uncombed hair, looking fit and untroubled by the humidity. He also looked confused about whether to kiss my cheek or shake hands, so I chose for him. Public displays of affection outside the fickle glamour of the onstage, arty crowd, were not in my amorous repertoire. Best he found out early.

'Thank you, at least until the rain undoes my camouflage. It's nice of you to ask me for dinner. Where are we going?'

'To a French restaurant called Anise, a little place with a western, Asian and Cambodian menu. I didn't know what you preferred to eat, so thought I'd cover all the bases.'

'Well, I've never been out with a spy before. I suppose we both have lots to learn about each other tonight.'

'How would you know? I wouldn't be much of a spy if I gave myself away on a first date.'

I gave him a smile and a couple of marks for having a sense of humour and a quick mind.

'A *first* date, Martin? I thought I signed up for one. Did I miss the fine print?'

'Shall we go? I've got a car waiting outside,' said he, sensibly ignoring my limp attempt at humour. I realised, to my disquiet, I was a little nervous.

We made it safely to the restaurant moments before the first spots of the nightly deluge. I had a moment of sheepish concern for my mother, hoping Sorensen decided to stay home tonight, saving her from a waterlogged scooter ride while I went out, with a particle of luck, enjoying myself.

Anise turned out to be delightful. We had a small, outside table with bentwood rattan chairs under a softly lit veranda, surrounded by tropical undergrowth. The pounding rain lent a charming, comfortable ambience to the night. Lovers might have called it intimate.

'Clara, let me first say I'm off duty. I've got a feeling you doubt my motives for asking you out.'

'Hmm, an unusual thing to say on our first date, Martin. If I'm to believe it isn't to keep tabs on me – do I have the right expression? – I'm curious as to why.'

'I'm a masochist,' offered he, then saw I wasn't particularly amused. 'Could also have something to do with you being a beautiful woman. Is that a good enough reason for you?'

'Silly me, and here I am hoping you're interested in my mind. Anyway, I think you should stick to being a masochist, so when you discover I'm not interested in having sex, I can always get out the horsewhip.'

I smiled at him, meaning it to be a sassy quip. With a hint to tread carefully.

'I didn't anticipate we'd be talking about erotica so early in the evening. I'll need to revise my small talk.'

He winked at me and smiled.

'Hmm, I quite like him. Martin, I'm willing to suspend my doubts in the interest of having a nice evening. Let's get a drink and order. I'm starving.'

I scanned the menu.

'I'm happy with the French menu and a glass of shiraz. Australian would be nice. Or the Brunello if your budget runs to atmospheric. I assume you're paying even if I don't sleep with you?'

He looked at me quite oddly, apparently not sure of the right answer. I assumed he meant yes.

'I have a friend who owns a vineyard in Montalcino where they make it and I do my bit to keep them in Ferraris. Oh, there's nothing on the menu I wouldn't enjoy, except *escargots*. I'm happy to leave the ordering in your hands.'

'Do you have a rule about keeping people off-balance?'

'No, sometimes I can be plain-spoken, I caught it off my mother. Come on Martin, smile. Aren't we supposed to be having an agreeable evening?'

He laughed. 'Actually, I'm having a wonderful time. You've read the menu already?'

'You need to learn at least one thing about concert pianists tonight. We can all sight-read a whole concerto in minutes. A menu is child's play.'

'I've never been out with a world-famous pianist before, or even an unknown one, as you just discovered. The good part is you won't get asked lots of boring questions about classical music. I can't even play Chopsticks. I'm more a fan of living musicians and a bit of jazz.'

'Strange as it might seem, I don't find classical music boring. And it may surprise you to know I play and sing in a rock band for charity each year. It's a lot of fun. I only need to play a few chords and no one notices if I miss one occasionally. Except me. Is Anise the place you come to sweep all your dates off their feet?'

'I'm afraid the dates are few and far between. You're the first volunteer in a long time.'

'Oh? Just so you remember, I volunteered for dinner, not dessert. Still, you're not *that* bad looking. Do you have poor personal hygiene habits I'd find out about back in your apartment one day? *Aiya, you know being a smart-aleck is your favourite trick to keep people on the back foot.* Be nice! Sorry, Martin.'

'I must admit, it's harder than I thought to find a woman who enjoys the earthy charm of the football change room. Is French food a favourite?'

'I live in Paris when I'm not travelling. Phnom Penh feels a lot like the old quarter to me since I've been here, so I'd like to enjoy a little nostalgia. I have an apartment in Beijing as well and I'm sure you know my parents, my mother now, lives in Melbourne. I like to visit there too when I can.'

'I'll remember to order a nostalgic meat pie 'n chips if we ever meet in Melbourne. Your life sounds exciting, at least to someone who doesn't live your lifestyle.'

'It always *sounds* exciting, even to me, and I'd be lying to you if I said it wasn't. It's not always as glamorous as you might imagine and I'm not fond of the glitz. I usually eat at backstreet dumpling shops where no one bothers me; my life is quite solitary which suits me most of the time. My real home is 10,000 metres on my way to some hotel or other between concerts.'

'You don't have a boyfriend?'

'Ha! Who would ever want a girlfriend they saw once in a blue moon? *Well, it's not exactly a lie, is it? He did ask about boyfriends. Why am I not telling him the truth?*'

'More surprising things have happened, Clara. You don't miss being in a close relationship?'

'Oh, now and again I wonder about what's missing in my life, like maybe a puppy or a new pair of Jimmy Choos. It passes. How about you? Robert Nelson called you *Captain* Lewis. Why aren't you sailing around on a boat wooing pretty girls in exotic ports?'

'Ship.'

'I beg your pardon?'

'The navy likes them to be called ships, not boats.'

'Thank goodness. I thought you were swearing at me.'

'I'm not *that* heroic. Besides, I'm an army captain, not a navy one.'

'What's the difference?'

'About $200,000 a year with not a girl to woo in sight. We army captains are quite junior officers. I grew up on military bases around Australia and Asia. My father's a brigadier, quite senior, his father too. Joining the army seemed a pre-ordained career choice for me.'

'You'd be better off as a navy captain if you want to impress a Chinese girl. Besides, if you're in the army, shouldn't you be running around the jungle chasing shadows and being eaten by mosquitos instead of trying to seduce me?'

'Where did you learn to be an expert on military strategy?' said he with a boyish grin. 'Most of us take years to learn the job.'

'Oh, Martin, you may have to run to keep up. You just learnt my little way of letting you know I'm interested in your life.'

'Ah. Well, my job at the embassy is to help the military attaché. Unlike me, he *is* quite a senior officer. I volunteered for this diplomatic job and I speak a couple of languages, which helped. The job's about keeping my eyes open; nothing like in the movies, I'm afraid. Sorry to disappoint you. We just read papers, attend diplomatic functions, those sorts of things. All very open, no microphones in bedposts or meeting strangers in dark places saying things like "the eagle flies at midnight". I don't even own a poison-tipped umbrella.'

'How disappointing. Our second date is looking unlikely, not even any naughty pillow talk to make me blush. Tell me, how does looking after people like my mother and me fit into your not-so-secret world?'

'I got volunteered. Pretty much everything we do in Cambodia has to do with the army; I found myself in the right place at the right time, or wrong time and seriously regretted the job after our first encounter at the embassy. Lucky Elena Accardi bailed me out. Yesterday, I decided you can't possibly be a viper-tongued spitfire all the time, so I risked my ego again. After you answered the telephone, I decided the jury was still out.'

He made me laugh for the second time. I apologised for my quick temper.

'I can go from mad to not quite so bad when I put my mind to it. Just not when I get woken up too early.'

'I'll remember next time. Part of my job with you included doing my homework and I learnt about your father's war record. Not surprising his fighting spirit found its way into your DNA.'

'If you did your homework properly, you'd know my shy, retiring nature comes from the Yehonala women's blood sloshing around my veins. I come from a formidable line of them.'

We chatted for another hour, the time passing without me noticing. And believe it or not, I was still enjoying his company. Finally, we ordered a last coffee.

'You'll be heading back to Melbourne soon?'

'No, not yet. More likely to Europe when I do leave. My agent's pressing me to go back before she has to reschedule more concerts. We're waiting till we hear news about my father.'

'I hope I can see you again if you're staying in Phnom Penh for a while. I'll try to do something exciting in the meantime to impress you. Listen, Clara, I know you've been talking to Jim Preston. It isn't my business any longer, however, I know this country and how it works. It would be best if you didn't give him anything to publish which might upset anyone.'

'Like my father's book?'

He looked momentarily taken by surprise, but recovered quickly.

'I don't know anything about a book, so I can't answer your question.'

'Do you know who broke into our room looking for it?' I persisted, seeing he looked uncomfortable.

'No, I don't. How do you know a burglar broke into your room?'

'They left a zipper undone on my suitcase. You're not shocked to hear it happened? You're not even mildly indignant a person broke into our room and rummaged through your date's underwear?'

'You might be mistaken; probably the maid tidying up. There's usually a simple explanation for these things. Nothing's ever quite what it appears.'

'Including you, it seems.'

'Depends on how I seem to you, I suppose.'

'Well, for one thing, I was hoping for a more gallant response, especially from someone who just said they want to impress me. You know, like the ambassador said, "leave no stone unturned". Martin, please let's not finish a lovely evening squabbling. I've had an enjoyable time tonight and we've met lots of good people in Phnom Penh who said kind things about my father. Unfortunately, we missed one person we wanted to see: Father Aubert. Do you know him?'

'Father Aubert? No, can't help you there. I saw him at the funeral, but I've never met him.'

'Never mind, I don't suppose it matters. Martin, it's past ten o'clock. My mother and I have an early start tomorrow morning. The monks at Wat Bagan are holding a memorial service for my father.'

We arrived back at the hotel and Martin walked me inside.

'Should I ask him to come up for coffee? No Clara, what are you thinking? That's a bad idea on so many levels.'

'Perhaps we can meet another time, Clara - if I don't call you too early? I had a great night.'

'Who knows? I did too, thank you.'

'Will I still be needing my suit of armour next time?'

I dropped my reserve and raised my defences, theatre-kissing him on the cheek and hurriedly stepped into the lift before the awkward nightcap conversation did come up.

'It always pays to be prepared. Goodnight, Martin. *Yikes...*'

My mother had already wrapped herself in an oversized dressing gown and armed herself with a glass of wine. She poured another for me. I could see the poncho glistening in a puddle on the floor and her shoes hanging from the shower in the bathroom, trickling water. I also noticed her wringing-wet jeans draped over a chair on the balcony.

'How was your night, Ma?'

'Oh, wonderful. Take a look around and you can see how much fun I've been having. George Sorensen went out for dinner with another western man and I got half-drowned. I don't feel a bit like Audrey Hepburn.'

My phone buzzed. A long message about her day. Ordinary. Nice. Reassuring. I'd answer when I relaxed. We were doing this a lot.

14

WAT BAGAN AND BALD CHICKENS

The temple soared above a vividly emerald jungle garden like a phoenix rising. Golden spires, gables and curling finials reached high into the blue sky, its tiered, red-tiled roof and white walls numinous in the bright sunlight. Katy and Clara gasped in wonder at the fairytale picture.

They arrived early wearing plain white dresses and no makeup, as Alan Doole had recommended the day before. He waited for them outside.

'Good morning Mrs Yehonala, Clara. You're in plenty of time.'

'Wat Bagan is simply magical, Mr Doole,' said Katy, neither she nor Clara able to remove their gaze away from their awe-inspiring surroundings.

'Yes, for me, Wat Bagan's the most beautiful of all the temples in Phnom Penh. Now, we must go into the garden to wait for the monks; I'll offer a few words of advice as we walk. There's little for you to do as I've made all the arrangements. If you're unsure, simply copy what I do, or ask me quietly.'

They walked together on the grass between tropical plants, lush after the rains, noticing several memorials in quiet alcoves, all immaculately looked after, surer now they'd made the right decision. Eventually, they arrived at a three-metre, two-storey monument in a secluded corner of the gardens, adorned in flowers. A crowned Buddha statue gazed down benignly at them, carved into a recess at the base of the stupa's gold-painted spire.

'The ashes of Mr Bailey and the young Buddhist girl are already inside the top storey of the monument. I placed them there before you arrived and arranged the flowers and fruit bowls. When the monks arrive, sampeah with your fingers together, raised to your eyes, and bow your head. Don't speak and don't, whatever you do, try to shake hands, touch them, or even walk across their path. It's forbidden for women.'

'What happens during the service?' asked Clara.

'First, the monks will arrive in a procession. You'll hear them chanting one of the sutras in the Pali language, which they think of as the Three Jewels - finding comfort in the Buddha, the teachings and the community of the faith. After the monks assemble, the Abbot will give a *Dhamma* talk about the idea of impermanence and the duty we have to live the Middle Way according to the Buddha's teachings, which will go on for about fifteen minutes. At the same time, the monks will be chanting a verse about misfortunes rising and drifting away and living in harmony with this truth brings the highest happiness. The Abbot's message will be death is not the end, only an end to the body and the spirit remains to carry on in another realm. It's a beautiful, moving ceremony. I hope my explanation will help your understanding if you don't know the Khmer or Pali languages.'

'I'm so glad you explained it to us. Is there anything we need to do?' asked Katy.

'At the end, there's an important ritual where you both take part; it's why the empty bowl and a jug of water are next to the stupa. I'll give you a sign when it's time. Clara, you will pick up the bowl and your mother pours water into it. Let it overflow the top of the bowl until the jug is empty. The monks will be chanting about overflowing rivers being like cascades of good merit flooding into Mr Bailey and the young girl to end the ceremony. Remember to sampeah and bow again as they leave and don't say anything. Follow what I do if you're not sure.'

They heard the chanting of the approaching monks. Katy felt a lump in her throat; Clara reached out nervously for her mother's hand.

Afterwards, they walked back across the grass. Katy asked Alan Doole to pass on their heartfelt appreciation to the Abbot and advise how she could best arrange an annual donation to the temple. The money settled, he offered them a lift to the hotel and they settled in for the brief ride. Back at the hotel, Katy and Clara relaxed in the bistro with a cold drink.

'Ma, the service was so uplifting. I felt sad and elated too. I'm glad we were able to put Dad to rest in such a peaceful way. The temple will be a beautiful place to visit each year on Qingming.'

'After all the worry and stress, I think he'll be happy there. There's space for all of us, too.'

'How about we have our funeral conversation in fifty years?' Clara smiled as her phone rang. She had a brief conversation and put the phone down.

'Speaking of worry and stress, the call was from Martin Lewis. He said he's got news for us and will be here in a few minutes.'

'I never asked you before. How did your date with him go?'

'I'll tell you all about it after he's gone. First, you tell me about *your* night.'

'Well, the good news is Rithy's a skilful rider. I'll also admit I had fun riding on the back of a motorbike, like a child again, at least until the biblical torrents arrived. The other good news is George Sorensen's street has coffee stands and food shops with a clear view of his villa. It's easy to see him coming or going.

'A car with another man picked him up about eight-thirty and they went to a restaurant for dinner in the riverfront area. We stayed across the street until they left and followed them back to the villa. By then, it was past ten o'clock and we thought it unlikely he'd leave again, plus we were like drowned rats, so Rithy brought me back. You can try it yourself tonight. Rithy's coming here on the way.'

'It's the least I could do after having a dry night myself. *Shhh*, here's Martin.'

'Hello, what brings you here today? Last night you told me you're no longer on the case.'

The waiter brought over a glass. Katy poured lime juice for him.

'Some hemlock?'

'I dared to hope we're on better terms now, Katy. Your daughter's nice to me.'

'Is this true, Clara? We must talk later about the follies of youth. I'm quite prepared to be nicer as soon as I'm sure you're honest with us, Martin. A fair offer?'

'Since Clara let me know you were going to the temple today, I came to see you both because I thought you might like news about the investigation into Simon's death.'

'Yes, we would,' said Clara, squinting her eyes reproachfully in Katy's direction.

'I've been informed the police in Krong Chey charged a man with the murder. Seems another man arrested at the time, the one guarding the girls, told the police who did the shootings as part of a deal to face a less serious crime. According to the report, the murderer turns out to be a small-time trafficker and drug dealer.'

'What will happen to him? asked Clara.

'If he's convicted, he'll go to gaol for a long time. Cambodia doesn't have the death penalty, more's the pity sometimes. The Australian Government will push for a maximum life sentence. I hope this will bring some comfort to you both.'

Katy could feel her blood beginning to boil and got ready to confront Martin. Clara saw the danger and saved him and themselves.

'Thank you so much for letting us know, Martin. Yes, it's good to hear the police are doing their job. I can see my mother is quite emotional hearing this news, especially so soon after this morning's service. If you'll excuse us, I'll take her back to the room.'

'No problem. Can I call you later?'
'It's fine.'

'Ma, I know what you're thinking. The good news is he obviously doesn't know we went to Krong Chey. The bad news is we don't know if he's deliberately lying to us or if he's been given the wrong information.'

Katy and Clara were back in their room. Katy had calmed down. She still hadn't forgiven Martin for not telling them about the rumours the police were involved in Simon's death and his latest information, or deliberate lie, infuriated her. She thanked Clara for keeping the peace.

'Are you saying I hold off on his foot-roasting for a while?'

'I'm honestly not sure, Ma. I know he's lying to us about two things. First, last night, he told me the one time he'd ever met Rémy Aubert was at the funeral. You remember, Rémy Aubert said they'd met several times before. The second when he let slip he knew about Dad's book, or so it seemed to me; he got defensive when I mentioned it. Surely, he must have been the one in our room.'

'Could there be someone else we don't know about who's interested in the book and getting the messages, not him?'

Katy surprised herself trying to find excuses for Martin.

'How would Martin know about the book at all if someone else altogether was looking for it? No, your idea doesn't make sense. And why would he lie to me about not knowing Rémy Aubert? We need to meet the pastor; he also said he knew about Dad's work. We may as well meet everyone who came to the funeral. I'll try his phone again.'

Clara dialled the number, getting through this time. Rémy told her he'd already left Phnom Penh and returned to his mission in Prey Kam, a village in Svay Rieng province. He'd be happy to meet them if they drove down, telling them to call ahead if they'd like to visit.

'I'd rather stick needles in my eyes than go to Svay Rieng again.'

'At least it will save crocodile shoes the trouble, *baobei*. This time we won't tell anyone, not even Rithy. Instead, we'll hire a car for sightseeing and tell the driver afterwards to take us to Prey Kam. We'll call Rémy Aubert on the way. Tomorrow, you've got your photo thing at the Chinese Embassy; we'll book the car for Thursday morning.'

'I think it might be a sensible idea to let Jim Preston know,' said Clara. 'I don't think my ears could stand him shaking his beads at us again. Good insurance too.'

They agreed it made good sense. Katy phoned, telling Jim their plan. He wasn't over-excited by the idea, but thought they should be safe enough if they kept quiet about the trip. Katy pictured his droll smile when he told her he hadn't written about homicidal clerics in years and read somewhere they were an extinct species.

'Think of it this way, if you get yourself knocked off, at least you'll have a priest nearby for the last rites and I can assume the good pastor is one of the bad guys,' were his parting words. His unique brand of Antipodean humour tested her patience.

'Well, all done, *baobei*,' Katy announced as she hung up the phone. 'And not a single swear word in the entire conversation. Parlour English must be what passes for reassurance in Jim Preston Land. Now, tell me about this date of yours.'

'I've got a better idea. Let's call down to get a couple of masseurs up here first. I'll tell you all about my date with Captain Lewis while someone's untangling my shoulders. Don't worry, Ma, I'm not about to elope. You know what they say, you can't pluck feathers off a bald chicken.'

Two hours later, Katy's phone chirped, letting her know Rithy had arrived. Clara picked up her poncho and headed out the door. At 11 pm she returned, hung her Vans in the shower, and her jeans over the chair outside.

'He likes eating out, but so far, he doesn't have children on the menu. Any wine left?'

15

I'LL DO MY CRYING IN THE RAIN

'Clara, I want to go to Kampot. I decided after the service at the temple I need to see where Chavy grew up and find out about her life. We've read about her, but we know nothing about what's happened to her.'

'When are you going?'

'I thought I'd leave on Friday morning after we've been to Svay Rieng to see the pastor. I'll come back either Saturday night or Sunday morning.'

Clara and I were sitting in the café downstairs having a late, leisurely breakfast before getting ready for the afternoon photoshoot at the Chinese Embassy.

'I know Chavy's the key to the story, sort of a golden thread wrapping things together. I can't put it into words. I feel there's a hand tugging at my sleeve, urging me to find out.'

'Do you want me to come with you?'

'If you want to, though I think this is my journey. I feel it's too personal. You don't mind me going by myself, do you?'

'No, Ma. On the contrary. Don't worry about me, I'll be sitting around the pool, shopping, and sleeping like a dead person without your snoring. Sounds heavenly, a change of pace for a couple of days will do us both the world of good.'

I knew Kampot lay on the Gulf of Thailand and Chavy's farm somewhere along the Prek Chha River, but little else. After breakfast, I went to the reception desk to ask for a map. Back in the room, I spread it over the table.

Would it be possible for me to find Chavy and her family? Where do I start? I recalled Simon had written about the primary school Chavy's older sister had taken her to enrol when she was six, so I telephoned Jim, asking him to go through the manuscript to see if he could find any more information. Did Simon write the name down? I couldn't remember.

He called me back a half-hour later, the Trapeang Number Two primary school, he told me. At least I had a start. I hoped Chavy turned out to be her real name, not one Simon had invented, or there would be no chance of finding her. Being honest with myself, coming up empty-handed seemed more likely. I tried to lower my expectations.

'Why are you interested in the school?'

I told Jim the same as I'd told Clara. I wanted to go to Kampot because I needed to learn more about Chavy's life.

'Other than curiosity, Jim, I can't explain. The school may be the only link to her, though I don't know how many years ago she went there. We don't even know her family name. I feel we owe her more than half a name in half a book.'

'I've wondered about Chavy myself. Bloody girl gets under your skin, doesn't she?'

'Yes, Jim, getting under your skin is exactly what she does.'

'I'll give you a little advice you might find helpful. Kampot province, like Svay Rieng, is among the poorest in Cambodia, mostly small produce farms and fishermen living in village communities. They're suspicious of strangers, especially in the countryside, as you might remember Chavy telling us in the book. Find a local, one born in the countryside, a man preferably, not one of the scripted tourist guides and think of a good reason for your prowling about asking questions. If not, you'll find the place will clam up tighter than two thumbs up a pig's…'

'Stop right there, Jim. I get the picture. It isn't pretty.'

'Good luck, Katy.'

I could feel the smile in his voice.

'Oh, before I forget, is Clara going with you?'

'No, why?'

'Well, I've got two tickets for a classical concert at the Chaktomuk Conference Hall on Saturday night. The National Orchestra's performing with a foreign conductor, Antonin Cernzy, so I guess it will be more than amateur hour. Not my thing, I prefer my songs with words. Clara's welcome to them if she's at a loose end. I'm sure she misses the roar of the greasepaint and the smell of the crowd.'

'Thanks, I'll have her call you.'

'Call who about what?' called Clara from the bathroom.

'Jim has two tickets to a classical concert on Saturday night and said you could have them. The conductor's Antonin Cernzy. You'll need to call Jim if you're interested.'

'Anton? In Phnom Penh? How wonderful! I'll call Max straight away and have her tell him to call me.'

She began at once pacing around the room like a cat, talking excitedly to Max. Clara must be missing the concert hall more than she'd been letting on. I got back to my map. Not the correct scale to show a school, yet I couldn't help feeling a glimmer of hope.

A half-hour later, I heard Clara's phone.

'Hello…What?… Yes, of course it's me… I'm fine… yes.

'No, I should be back soon…no, everything's okay…she did?

'What time?…where are you now?…oh…it happened to me there once.

'You're so mean… no…the Palace View…with my mother, naturally.

'I'd love to… dinner yes…no, just dinner, don't waste your breath asking.

'Yes, telephone me when you arrive…yes…yes… see you soon.

'Can't wait…safe trip…*Ciao.*'

She put the phone down and looked at me, a badly concealed grin across her face.

'Anton.'

'Oh, really?'

'*Shhh!*' said she. 'Anton's a talented young Russian conductor and needs to take any booking he can. Which is why he's conducting here. Also, he's very handsome, looks like a young Antonio Banderas and has a huge following of female admirers.'

'How do you know an unknown conductor? Are you one of the lovestruck women falling at his feet?'

'If anything, it's the other way round. I first met him at the Gnessin School in Moscow when we were both students. People thought him destined for great things when he got older. I offered to fill in at one of his concerts in Toulouse three years ago when the soloist became ill because none of the other big-name pianists wanted to risk their reputations.'

'What's wrong with him?'

'It's a funny story. Anton was better known in those days for his offstage performances with pretty musicians. Max objected to me playing, convinced it would be a bad career move, by which she meant she worried about a photo appearing of me half undressed in the back seat of a taxi. She was furious when I insisted on playing and came to Toulouse to guard my virtue. As it turned out, the cellist was extremely pretty, which saved me from a fate worse than virginity, according to her. He got wonderful reviews and has been grateful ever since. Thank goodness the musical press was in a good mood or I'd have been looking for a new agent.'

'What's all the excitement about?'

'Don't stress, Ma, Anton's different these days. He asked me if I'd be interested in warming the orchestra and helping with rehearsals. He thinks I must be bored. He's also worried about the soloist, a local, who he says is talented but inexperienced. According to Anton, he plays adagios like he's in a marching band. Anton thinks I might help him practise his solo piece.'

'So you won't miss me?'

'Nope. *Um*...I mean, of course, I will,' lied she. 'Except I *have* missed the concert hall.'

'Well, he's certainly put a sparkle in your eyes. The camera's going to love you.'

And it did. We met Jim and his photographer at the gate to the Chinese Embassy compound and were escorted to Ambassador Zhao's office; Minister Suong was there with another photographer to take photographs for their personal collections. I stood in the background like the ugly girl at a high school dance while Clara basked in the attention, entirely at home, posing like she'd been coached in media events. And exceptionally well, by the look of it.

After drinks and small talk, Zhao gave us a prepared statement the newspaper could use. Jim read it, nodded and asked a few more questions. He assured Zhao he would publish the story in the weekend edition of the paper where it would get the widest attention and be carried around the world in the online papers and news agencies.

All the diplomatic missions were in the BKK district, so there were dozens of cafés catering to taxpayer-funded residents with expense accounts. After leaving the embassy, we found one out of the humidity and settled down for coffee.

'Zhao gave me a press release about a new agreement with the Cambodian Government he wants in the article, which is fine. I'll write it so Clara doesn't come across as a puppet of Chinese government policy. More a human-interest angle about how you're enjoying the country's beauty, the warmth and friendship you've received from the Cambodian people, how well the government has helped with the investigation of your father's death, blah, blah. The story, plus a little more about your interest in continuing to help the children of Cambodia, should have you smelling like a vote to an Aussie politician. Being friends with Minister Suong is like a passport to Buddhist nirvana in Cambodia, so for anyone thinking about popping you off to the choir invisible, the article will have most of them think twice. Remember, ladies, *most*, not *all* of them, think twice.'

'Thinking about people I'd like to pop off, Clara went on a date with Martin Lewis the other day.'

'No kidding, Clara? Isn't fraternising with the enemy a hanging offence in China?'

'Seems like whatever we do, someone wants us out of the way; aren't even prisoners on death row entitled to a decent last meal? What's important is he let slip he knew about Dad's book. Also, he lied to me about not knowing Rémy Aubert.'

'When you meet the pastor, don't be surprised if they've got their stories straightened out. It's interesting though, about the book. Dunno what to make of it. I'll see what dirt I can dig up on the good Father Aubert. More to the point, what's your George Sorensen project produced so far?'

'Waterlogged feet,' said Clara. 'We twice followed him to restaurants. Eating out is all he's been up to so far.'

'If he's who we think he is, he won't disappoint. Hang in there.'

'Oh, Jim, thanks for the concert tickets. I'm so looking forward to going. I know Anton Cernzy quite well. Do you want to come with me?'

'Don't tempt me. Here, take them. If Sophea found out I'd spent the evening with a beautiful young woman, they'd be fishing me out of the bloody Mekong River. No, take your new best friend, don't you Chinese say the snake you see doesn't bite you? A spot of culture wouldn't do an Australian much harm.'

'One last thing, Jim. Martin also came to see us yesterday, telling us the police arrested a man for Simon's murder. Is it true? We don't know if he's lying to us deliberately or not.'

'Yep, it's true. I got the same report on my desk this morning and it's the story the paper will run with, for obvious reasons. It's timely because the whitewash story coupled with the Zhao article will work nicely for you, even if not for the poor bugger who got stitched up. Though I expect no one will shed tears for him.

'As far as everything else is concerned, ladies, don't make any waves, especially about casting doubts on the official story. If anyone asks, your message is how relieved you are the police are doing their job, how thankful you are the criminal's been caught, or something as sugary. Can you both manage a simple message without creating a firestorm?'

'I can, I'm not sure about my mother. When things are best left unsaid, not even the Prince of Darkness knows what might jump out.'

'I shall be the Queen of Tact.'

'Do your best, Katy. It will be easier to keep digging around for the truth if nobody suspects you know things aren't as they seem.'

'Funny, Martin Lewis said the same to me the other night at dinner.'

Back at the hotel, I booked a car for the following morning, telling the concierge we wanted to spend the day visiting the tourist sites around Phnom Penh. Clara and I went to the room to prepare for our third night of George-watching. I glanced at the sky. *Sigh...*

The punctual, piano-key smile Rithy turned up and we set off, me clinging onto his waist as we weaved through the traffic pretending we were in a video game, arriving at our coffee shop as funereal clouds spawned an early night. The air smelt heavy with moisture. Sheet lightning intermittently illuminated the sky, flashing silently through the clouds, thunder rumbling around us a few seconds later.

Tonight, we didn't wait long for the rain or George Sorensen. We'd not even finished our coffee before the same car as before pulled up outside the villa. We quickly slipped into our ponchos and crossed the street to the scooter as the first heavy raindrops fell, watching George Sorensen squeeze his bulky mass into the car. The rain got heavier. Before long, our front wheel was cutting a bow wave through the flooded streets, sailing among the busy monsoon armada. After about fifteen minutes, while stopped at a red light, Rithy turned around.

'Mrs Katy, tonight is different. Their car is heading away from the city centre in the direction of Phnom Song. This is the way towards the orphanage house.'

My heart began to race with the new reality. No longer a slightly surreal, abstract quest we were pursuing, we were following a dangerous paedophile who must be on his way to rape children. Were those grey shapes in the car the men involved in Simon's murder? If so, they would have no hesitation doing the same to us. The enormity of the situation hit me. I blinked rain away from my eyes, shivering, peering through the storm at the hulking, misty form of George Sorensen. Their car, stationary two metres ahead of us, waited benignly at the lights like others in their haloes of splashing raindrops and silhouetted by fitful lightning.

My stomach churned knowing what horrors would happen to children tonight; ones we were powerless to prevent. Who could we trust to tell? We could only be there tonight to record from the shadows, to bear witness and prevent it from happening to other children.

'Don't lose them, Rithy.'

'Never fear, Mrs Katy. I won't.'

I took out my phone. As carefully as I could, I started taking videos of the journey. Photographs would be vital. I stopped noticing the rain clattering noisily on our ponchos and trickling off my nose.

Another twenty minutes passed. The car turned into a side street, stopping at the back entrance of a large house. Rithy pulled over behind a parked car and switched off our lights. I held my phone's camera towards George Sorensen's car, hoping the images of them entering the building would be visible through the rain. They disappeared inside.

'What is this place, Rithy?'

'It is not the orphanage, Mrs Katy. I don't know.'

'Let's walk around to the front and have a look. First, we must get the address.'

'We backtracked along the side street and around the block to where the building's front entrance faced onto the main road. A large, colonial-era house stood behind a high wall, probably once home to a wealthy French merchant. The high iron gates were closed, a chain and heavy padlock ensuring privacy to anyone inside. There were lights on upstairs. Through a lowered blind, I saw the indistinct shape of a large man. At least two smaller silhouettes were moving around. I tried to take a video with my shaking hands. Rithy took the phone, doing it for me. Someone drew the heavier curtains closed, shrouding the house in darkness, hidden behind sheets of rain. I photographed the front of the building and the street sign.

Uncalled, the face of a village girl from the past flashed into my consciousness. I began trembling. I cried out to Rithy, 'We must try to get closer; we mustn't be late today.'

He looked at me curiously. I linked my arm through Rithy's so we might look like a couple on our way home. We crossed the street, pausing at the iron gates. Through the wrought-iron bars, I could see a child's tricycle laying on its side in the courtyard next to a faded, coloured ball. I took a picture. Without warning, an emotional hurricane surged inside me, fighting to break free. I turned urgently to Rithy, pleading with him.

'We must stop what is happening inside! We must break in. We must find the children. Don't you understand? Don't you see? I can save her this time…'

I seized the bars, shaking the padlocked gates with all the strength I could find. A light came on, the front door opened and light flooded onto the porch. A long shadow fell across the front garden. Rithy forcibly dragged me away, out of sight from inside eyes. He grabbed my shoulders in a vice-like grip, staring into my eyes.

'Mrs Katy!' whispered he intensely. 'Tonight, it is too late for these children. What is done cannot be undone, no matter what we do. Here are dangerous men. We will not help anyone if we cannot tell the children's story. We must get away. Now.'

I trembled uncontrollably, crippled by my remorse. I finally understood many things tonight. He hurried me away, half dragging, half carrying me. Once back at the scooter, I called Clara. She instantly recognised my panic.

'What's wrong, Ma!' screamed she down the phone.

'Get Jim to the hotel,' I stammered. 'Now. Wait for me. It's okay…I'm okay.'

I hung up. Exhausted. Impotent. Again.

'Rithy, take me back to the hotel as quickly as you can.'

Rithy hurried Katy towards the lift, past the quizzical looks of the concierge staff. She ran into the room, collapsing into Clara's arms, burying her face in her shoulder, unable to stop the flow of tears at the helplessness and shock from the night. She hardly noticed Jim in the room. When she did, she blindly held her phone out to him. He took it, scrolling through the pictures, not saying anything.

Clara sat Katy down on the sofa and put her arm around her as she fought to control her rasping breaths. She knew she needed to calm herself. She wasn't helping anyone.

In her mind, she could see a picture of Mei, the little girl in the Jilin village, her childhood friend. Tonight had brought Mei's memory back in the most horrifying way.

She heard her Mama's voice.

'You know what I expect of you, May-ling. It won't do for you to fall apart in front of these people.'

She turned to the door, fully expecting to see her standing there, a stern expression on her face, shoulders back, fiercely proud of their family name. But it was Clara's voice drawing her back. Ordinary. In control.

'Jim, please look in the fridge, find whatever you can inside. Anything will do and pour the drinks. The stronger, the better. A double one for my mother. Ma, let's get you out of this poncho and dried off. Jim, find a towel for Rithy.'

'Don't worry, Miss Clara. The rain is nothing. Please take care of Mrs Katy.'

Katy vaguely noticed Jim pour the contents of the miniatures into glasses. She took hers in shaking hands, slopping some on her chin as she drank. Jim took beers for himself and Rithy.

'Rithy, sit down. Now, tell us all about what happened tonight.'

After Rithy finished, Jim spoke gently to Katy.

'Katy, nothing I can possibly say will make this experience go away for you. Besides, I don't think you'd believe me anyway if I started spouting Mother bloody Teresa homilies. But I promise you, George Sorensen will never put his hands on any more little girls.'

16

SHADOWS FROM THE PAST

'Jim, the experience is behind me. The question now is, what are we going to do?'

'Christ, your drink must have had decent jungle juice in it. Welcome back. Are you sure you're okay?'

'I have been better. My problems are of no matter for the moment.'

They all looked at me like Mother Teresa *had* indeed dropped in, not Mama.

'What matters is George Sorensen, not me.'

'Katy, I've been looking at the videos and photos you took. I don't know how you managed it in the storm. You did an outstanding job. Unfortunately, the rain has obscured the number plates of the car and any half-decent defence lawyer would have no trouble arguing it isn't George Sorensen in the photos. I'd have trouble picking him out of a line-up myself.'

'After all this, we have nothing?' Clara looked dejected.

'I gave you the bad news, now for the good part. We have the address of the house and we have pictures of someone going in, who could be Sorensen. We have kids and someone, possibly Sorensen, upstairs with them. Powerful images, politically embarrassing images. Perceptions matter here.'

Clara sat up, renewed enthusiasm in her body language. I did too.

'So what? You already explained it's not enough to arrest him,' said she.

'It isn't. Still, we don't want to leave even the slightest chance he'll get off by accusing him now, do we? We'll have one chance in a courtroom. We want him to rot in hell.'

'Clara's for castration by rabid rats. How do we make sure we get him?'

'Nice touch, you might be onto something. Here's the plan. Bright and early tomorrow morning, I'll be visiting our friend the ambassador for a discreet meeting. As they say in the best Mafia movies, I'll make him an offer he can't refuse. I'll tell him the newspaper's been tracking Sorensen for a while and we have evidence of his paedophile activity in Phnom Penh and Bangkok. I'll show him the photos to prove it; the more convincing ones Katy took.'

'Won't he simply send Sorensen back to Australia?' asked Clara.

'He won't dare. I'll threaten to publish the story saying there's been a cover-up by the embassy. I know my editor would back me up. No, Bob Nelson won't want his illustrious career to end with a posting as the janitor in the Botswana Consul's office. He's much too ambitious. He'll promise me to get someone to watch Sorensen's villa, maybe Martin Lewis, to report when he leaves next time as well as get the local police and AFP to stake out the house and raid it when Sorensen shows up next. I'll promise to write the story and he'll claim all the brownie points for the arrest and bask in the glory.'

'Are you sure?'

'When you've been around these people as long as I have Clara, you'll learn self-preservation trumps everything else. Once Sorensen's arrested, we may have a chance to get more information from him about Simon's murder.'

'How about us? Won't our involvement get Rithy, my mother and me back on the concrete shoe roster? We're not exactly top of the embassy's Christmas card list at the moment, either.'

'The best part about having a reporter as your best mate is no one need ever know where I got the information. Even better than learning new words. Unless you're keen to see your photos in the newspaper again?'

'We'll pass.'

'Thought so. Now Rithy, take a day off tomorrow. You've earned it, Sorensen's unlikely to go out two nights in a row. The day after, I want you to watch his villa again. When he leaves, I want you to telephone me, okay?'

'Why do we need to keep following Sorensen?'

'Katy, in my business, you leave nothing to chance. There might be another place he goes or someone else he's mixed up with we don't know about.'

'Okay, Mr Jim. Do you want me to follow him to the house?'

'Only until you're sure you know where he's heading. Call me a second time and go home. There's no point in putting you in danger or letting the police see you and start asking awkward questions; we can leave the heavy lifting to the AFP. Katy, I'll need to copy all your pictures and videos onto my phone to show Nelson. Once Sorensen's picked up, delete them all, or delete them tonight if you like. We don't want to leave evidence around you three knew anything about this shit. Okay?'

'You'll get no argument from us.'

'Another thing. Be careful around Martin Lewis. He's starry-eyed about Clara, but he's no dope. If he gets the job to watch the villa, you might accidentally let something slip, even in your body language. Speaking of Martin Lewis, if he's been in your room, you can bet he won't have any ethical issues about scrolling through your phones given half a chance; an even better reason to remove the photos.'

'We will and thanks, Jim. Sorry about my dramatics earlier.'

'Dramatics? Dunno what you're talking about. Well, I think we might be done here. Rithy my friend, as it's stopped raining, how about you give me a lift back home on your red rocket?'

'My pleasure, Mr Jim.'

Clara and I were alone at last.

'Do you think it's nearly over, Ma?'

'I hope so. Except one thing's bothering me. How does Jim know Rithy has a red scooter?'

'I think we have more on our minds to worry about right now than the colour of Rithy's motorbike.'

We settled down on the balcony, both quieter than usual. I didn't need to be a genius to guess the reason for Clara's silence, nor did it take long before she asked.

'I've never seen you so distressed before, Ma. You frightened me tonight. I'm sure what you and Rithy went through must have been traumatic, but you knew what we were doing by following George Sorensen. You also knew what the result would be. Do you want to talk to me about it?'

'It's silly, really.'

'Not to me. You're my mother and I love you. Now we both know you drive me crazy with the dumb things you do once in a while and you drink way too much red wine.'

She smiled.

'But you've never been out of control. Not ever. Not once in my life. Tonight scared me, Ma. I need you to be what I know. You're all I have in the entire world and I depend on you. With Dad gone, it's you and me again. Please don't take that away from me.'

I reached over and took her hand, kissing her fingers gently.

'I promise you, my darling, I'm not going anywhere. Pour a glass of wine for me. I'm ready to talk to you about tonight.'

I stood up and leaned my elbows on the balcony, looking across at the misty Royal Palace and the bustling river traffic. Clara came and stood beside me, propping her elbows next to mine. I remembered Simon and me on Battersea Bridge a long time ago.

'I've never told anyone this story before, not even Simon. I was eleven years old at the time and we were in the Jilin village. Do you remember me telling you before about Auntie, the old Buddhist lady who told us stories?'

She nodded.

'I had a friend there, a village girl called Mei. We were the same age and we were inseparable. One day, Auntie sent me to fetch Mei because she hadn't turned up for work. When I got there, her house seemed eerily quiet, like one of those places nobody lives in anymore. I went inside and found her uncle asleep on a chair, passed out from too much *baijiu*. An empty bottle sat on the table. I remember how spooky the ceramic bottle looked with the sun shining through the window, gleaming like a display in a museum. I tiptoed past him into the back room and found Mei curled up in the corner in a little ball. She was naked. I'll never forget her eyes.'

The emotions were threatening to spill over again. I paused, taking deep breaths to force them down again. I went on.

'...Her eyes. They were white, like saucers, staring through me as if I didn't exist. Not so much a cold stare as a vacant one, like she'd died, yet her body hadn't realised. Her uncle had raped her.'

I stopped speaking again. I closed my eyes, remembering the sight of her in the corner.

'...She said, "why didn't you come for me this morning, May-may?" I just looked at her. I didn't know what to do. She told me she would be coming to work soon, so I nodded and left. She arrived later with a smile on her face, but never again looked the same way I knew her before. You see, I always went to her house on the way to the fields. We would walk to work together every day, holding hands. This one morning I was too lazy to get up early enough and scared of being late to work, so I didn't go to her house. Her uncle raped her because of my laziness. I've lived with the blame all my life.

'Tonight, at the house... Inside, young girls were being raped too, just like Mei got raped because of me. I couldn't forget her stare or the feeling of me *not being there* out of my head. All my guilt came flooding back to me. I realised I've never forgiven myself for not understanding Mei's terrors when I should have, for abandoning her, for being late, for being lazy, for being selfish, for not saving her. I didn't stop her horrors then and I was powerless again tonight to stop the same horrors happening to other little girls a few metres away. Like before, I did nothing to save those little girls tonight, either. That's why I lost myself.'

I stopped talking, wiping my eyes.

'Oh, Ma...'

In the silence, I turned toward Clara. I saw the silent tears streaming down her face and her trembling shoulders. Looking back towards the misty river with its procession of life, we were quiet for a long time. She spoke softly to me.

'You were eleven years old, Ma. You weren't responsible for what happened to Mei any more than you were to blame for Dad's death. And you didn't abandon those young girls. You saved dozens of other girls tonight who will be safe because George Sorensen will never touch them again, ever. Ma, you can only...'

She stopped speaking.

'I don't feel like anyone's guardian angel, *baobei*.'

'Now, I'll tell *you* a story.

'A couple of years ago, Dad and I were sharing a bottle of wine. Actually, we were starting a second one. I almost had him telling me stories about the war, so you can guess he'd drunk a glass too much shiraz. Instead, he let on why he *didn't* talk about the war. He said in war, ordinary people were forced to make choices and anyone who hasn't experienced war could never understand.

'I asked him what he meant. He told me about those codebreakers who solved the Enigma puzzle during the world war. How one time they decoded a message about a submarine attack on a convoy taking place an hour later. Seems there were hospital ships too. They realised dozens of men and women were going to die unless they were warned and changed course. But if they abruptly changed course, the Germans would immediately guess their code had been broken and would use a new one, extending the war and thousands more would die. I can't even begin to imagine what torments were going through the minds of those poor people.'

We took a sip of our wine and watched the boats on the river and the people strolling along the riverbank.

'But you can, can't you, Ma? Even so, you're not responsible for other people, or their situations. Monstrous things happen every day to people, occasionally for the best and often for the worst of reasons and sometimes just because they do. That's the work of fate, Ma. You, me, all of us can only ever do our best. Try to be kind to yourself, okay?'

'Thanks, *baobei*. Being able to talk about it has been like opening a window and letting a fresh breeze blow through. We Yehonalas have a long tradition of locking the wrong things out of sight.'

'You know, we don't need to see Rémy Aubert tomorrow; we can go another time. Seeing him won't make much of a difference right now. I know what will.'

'What do you mean?'

'You're going to Kampot tomorrow. Go there, Ma. Find Chavy and give her a name. Take as long as you need and don't come back until you're ready. I learnt something myself tonight. I now know why Chavy is so important to you, even if you don't know yet.'

18

IN THE FOOTSTEPS OF GHOSTS

Once clear of the city, the traffic thinned and the potholes multiplied. Thankfully, no dust clouds swirled in the wakes of today's traffic, blocking visibility and seeping fine grit into the car. The rains had settled the red dust damp and heavy on the ground.

I relaxed, content with Clara's insistence to make this trip. Not so much because I'd find Chavy or her family in a Dr Livingstone kind of way, more a feeling of walking in her footsteps, bringing a sense of who she is, or was, to life. Clara's intuition about Chavy's life also being my quest for peace loomed large in my mind. I allowed myself a pleasant feeling of anticipation and let the tension drain from my shoulders.

After an hour of heading south, we were deep in the countryside's flood plains. Isolated, rustic farmhouses on stilts blended with jungle and vivid fields, vibrant after the rain. Occasionally, we drove through interchangeable townships strung out along the highway, all painted claret by trucks during the dry season. People shopped in their galvanised-iron covered markets, run-down haberdasheries and food stores, while women sat under blue plastic awnings offering their produce to the passing trade. Scooters buzzed in random bee patterns, avoiding each other in an unwritten right-of-way code. We stopped at a roadside stall where I bought a Coke for the driver and me.

The distant Elephant Mountains came into view, a corrugated horizon rising over the flood plains. An hour later, we entered Kampot city. I hoped it wouldn't turn out to be a larger version of the worn-out towns we'd been driving through all morning. My spirits lifted the moment we reached the town centre, a roundabout curiously dominated by a huge durian statue.

Kampot turned out to be a delightful French provincial town with wide, tree-lined streets dotted with cafés, tropical gardens and homes in an eclectic mix of colonial and Asian architecture. The driver pulled up at my hotel, the Riki, a wooden, Asian-style guesthouse on the bank of the Tuek Chhu River. Across the road, wooden pylons supported an old, sturdy dock where pleasure craft, sampans, and fishing boats bobbed against the swirling current of the monsoon-swollen, brown water.

After settling in the Riki, I introduced myself to the concierge to ask about a guide. After convincing her the tourist guides she recommended weren't what I wanted and explaining what I did, she seemed to understand. He would be there early the following morning.

'Where would I find the local fruit and vegetable market?' I asked her. 'The one where the local village farmers sell their produce; I'm not looking for the ones where the tourists go.'

'There are several, Mrs Katy. The largest isn't far from here, a little way past the museum. Let me show you on the map. I will say it isn't too clean, but the produce is the best. Be careful of pickpockets there.'

'Is it far to walk?'

'Much better to take a tuk-tuk, or we have bicycles here. It's five minutes or less on a bike.'

Checking the sky, I guessed there must be an hour or two before the rain. So, in a surge of childhood nostalgia, I made my choice. I hadn't ridden a bike in at least thirty years and after my first wobble, I pedalled off, revelling in the simplest of pleasures after the stresses of the last week. An old Chinese folk song, Jasmine Flower, popped into my head and I found myself smiling happily and singing the melody, pulled into the Chavy's World of my imagination…

…Uncannily, I know the way. I park my bike and gaze down the bustling alleyways beneath their hotchpotch of roof coverings. I'm eager to explore. Once under the roof, the hubbub and humidity trapped in the sultry air makes me gasp. It is loud, the customers' voices mix with the sellers' calls, people bargain and joke. I breathe in the wet stench of rotting vegetables laying in the drains and underfoot. They blend into the earthy odours of people and every imaginable produce, all competing with the pungent durian for attention. A few spots of water spatter onto my toes and run into my sandals. Elsewhere, hanging slabs of meat and trays of fish add their dead-creature smells, the shopkeepers seem unconcerned by the flies which settle at will. I breathe in deeply once again, immersing myself in the heady, raw life of this rural market.

I jostle past other shoppers in the crowded, oppressive alleys. I wander up and down and buy rambutan and mangosteens to enjoy later, but mostly I look at people. The stallholders are nearly all village women with faces and skin sun-aged from outdoor life. They haggle with customers or gossip loudly. Others are squatting down nursing young, half-naked children, their sandalled feet and long batik skirts or cotton pants muddied from splashes of water trickling through the shallow gutters. Am I unknowingly walking past one of her sisters or a neighbour who knows her? I step deeper into a pocket of time and space I know is her world where Chavy's mother and older sisters sell their duck eggs and vegetables.

A half-hour later, the humidity under the roof becomes overpowering. I need to leave. The warm air outside feels like a cool breeze on my sticky skin as I free-wheel back down the slight gradient to the hotel. I depart Chavy's World, my plastic bag of treats looped over the handlebars.

Once inside the hotel, a man came over and sampeahed to me. The concierge said he was Munny, the guide I asked for earlier. I scowled at her. I needed a cool shower after the market's sultry air, not an argument with an over-zealous guide arriving a day early.

'My guide's for tomorrow, not today,' I told her, my annoyance showing. She lowered her eyes.

'Pardon me, Mrs Katy,' said Munny. 'The girl is afraid I might not be suitable and you would be angry with her and complain about her poor service. She's frightened she might lose her job and begged me to meet you today. She only knows the usual tourist guides and telephoned me in great distress to ask for my help. She's my niece.'

'Please sit down, Munny.'

Driving down, I'd decided on my story and explained our charity had been helping the daughter of a village family near Kampot with schooling. I told Munny my husband died recently and left money for the family, but I didn't have much information about them, except the daughter's name was Chavy and I was keeping a promise to my husband. Now I needed a guide who could help me find the family.

'All I know is the family lived near the Prek Chha River and their daughter went to a primary school about two kilometres from their farm.'

I gave him the name of the school.

'It may have been several years since she attended there, I'm not sure.'

'If I am suitable as a guide, Mrs Katy, I will be happy to help you. I grew up in the Sovann Sakor district before I became a schoolteacher in Kampot. The place you mention is about eight kilometres from here.'

'Munny, you are exactly the guide I need. Thank you for coming to see me today.'

After he left, I went across to the concierge. She looked apprehensive.

'You did well finding Munny for me. Thank you for asking him to come today.'

The Girl in the Orphanage

Her face lit up; her smile even wider when I gave her ten dollars.

After dinner, I sat on the upstairs deck with a glass of wine, observing the fishing boats moored under the jetty lights as they prepared to leave. A couple of cigarettes glowed red as they are smoked. Watching their busyness and hearing their chatter and laughter carried on the evening stillness, I imagined Chavy's father being one of those fishermen. What did they talk about, these men who lived two lives?

They hauled their nets onto cluttered decks and coiled their ropes, doing those myriad important jobs known to sailors leaving firm ground for the unpredictable, ever-changing one over the horizon. Smoke belched as engines started and foam bubbled from propellors churning in the swirling brown water before their lifelines let go from the bollards, splashing into the river and are quickly pulled on board. Everything in an orderly sequence. When they returned, did those men also stop at the markets to buy clothes or toys for their own daughters?

I supposed Simon had performed these same rituals once on his large boat. Or ship, as he insisted his kind of sailor called them, the ones with guns on their way to war. I realised Simon never told me who waited for him when he came home. I surprised myself when I realised I'd never asked.

No deluge this evening. The storm passed by Kampot to drench the distant mountains beyond the river. I sat for a long time, letting my mind wander, watching the lightning illuminate the peaky skyline. In the gloom, the sporadic flashes made the mountains look oppressive and malevolent. Before the rain, they had appeared soft and curvy in the haze, like reclining women.

The brightly lit pleasure boats attracted passengers again, taking advantage of the weather reprieve; the fishing boats had already transformed themselves into fireflies in the distance downstream. I phoned Clara to let her know how much I was enjoying Kampot.

Munny appeared after breakfast. Donning my wide-brimmed hat against the glare, we boarded a tuk-tuk. Today, we would discover everything or nothing. As if reading my thoughts, I heard Munny's voice.

'I have found the school, Mrs Katy, the one called Trapeang Number Two primary school. We are going there now.'

My pulse quickened. A new feeling I didn't recognise disturbed me.

'I rode my scooter to the Tuekchou district yesterday to look around. Today is a school day and the morning class will finish at eleven o'clock so we shall be a little early and will need to wait. After class, we can speak to the teacher.'

I fell silent, not wishing to say anything. I turned instead to look over the tuk-tuk driver's shoulder as we bumped our way out of Kampot into the countryside. Now I recognised the feeling. Dread. I fought an impulse to tell him to turn around and take me back to the hotel. I kept quiet.

The road rolled beneath us, reeling me in towards destiny like a silver carp hooked on a fishing line. The sealed surface ended after a kilometre and we had to slow down to manoeuvre around deep, stony craters, freshly dug by the rain. The occasional scooter or motorbike passed us going the other way, loaded with vegetables, or ferrying one, two and sometimes three passengers, all of us clumsily pirouetting around the flooded potholes.

I saw dilapidated farmhouses on stilts pass by through gaps in the dense tropical undergrowth lining the road, nestling alongside their palm-fringed, jungle backdrops. In the fields, white, bony-shouldered cows stood around with nothing to do. In others, rice grew tall and emerald-green in made to order conditions. Poverty arrayed in a pleasant setting. Fifteen minutes later, we arrived at a gathering of buildings strewn along the pock-marked road, the houses hiding among tropical leaves so large I could have wrapped them around myself in a waxy, olive-green cocoon.

'This is the commune you are looking for, Mrs Katy. We're early. The school is fifty metres down the main road.'

'No matter, I want to walk for a while.'

I stood in the roadway, looking around at a place I had learnt about from a book. Without a doubt, I knew the answers to *Chavy's Story* lay hidden here, in this tiny hamlet.

'Where's the public telephone?'

'Next to the village general store over there, but you're welcome to use my phone.'

I didn't answer. I shook my head and walked down the road. I saw the public phone inside a perspex shelter fastened to the outside wall of the store, the place Chavy made her phone calls to the person who would betray her trust. I picked up the receiver, forming a mental picture of a little girl's smaller hand gripping the handset instead of mine, pushing the buttons on the pad. She would have needed to stand on tiptoe to reach the numbers. I imagined her talking secretly to her new friend, who pretended he understood her troubles.

'What are these pieces of paper stuck on the front of the store, Munny?'

'The store's the main place for local people to buy everyday items. So people put advertisements here, things for sale, things wanted and jobs available.'

'Are there notices for people seeking friends?'

He looked over the ten or so pieces of paper, scanning each one.

'No, not today.'

'We passed by a coffee shop before. Let's have a drink there while we wait for eleven o'clock.'

Plastic strips hung across the doorway. I pulled them aside and glimpsed a movement in the corner of my eye. A trick of the light. A chill ran through my body. We stepped inside and sat down.

'You're seeking more than the family to give them money, aren't you?'

Munny looked at me, waiting to see if I would answer him. I bit my lip, worried about what might burst free. I sipped my coffee.

'More? Yes, I am. I want to find out what happened to the girl called Chavy. She and her younger sister were taken from this village and my husband died trying to find her. I am also here to give money to her family if we can find them.'

'I understand now, Mrs Katy. I will do my best to find her for you today. The school's the best place and the teacher will know her if she went to this school. If I may suggest, offer the teacher money for school supplies. It will help you in your search. Teachers here earn small salaries and often use their own money to buy supplies for the children because the government gives very little to the village schools.'

I gave him fifty dollars, far too much. I didn't care.

'I doubt she'll speak English, I will translate between you. Come, it's time.'

About twenty children cascaded from the school as we approached, each dressed in a white shirt with blue shorts or skirt, boisterous and happy to be free of the classroom like kids the world over. I waited while Munny went into the main school building. After a short conversation with the teacher, he came back.

'The teacher has been here for several years and thanks you for the money. She remembers a lot of the children but she tells me Chavy is a common name so it may prove difficult without her family name. However, she will help you if she can.'

I walked into the school classroom feeling like a young girl going to school on her first day, excited and a little fearful about the encounter. She sampeahed respectfully to me, gesturing for me to sit down. We settled around her desk. I tried to think of how I could supply information to her which would help identify Chavy. Stupidly, I hadn't considered this problem and my mind went blank from nervousness. I wracked my brain, digging for clues.

'Chavy will be about eleven or twelve years old now. She started school at six... There were five daughters in her family... Her father was a fisherman... He lost his job...'

Our back and forth translated conversation began. The teacher looked at me, helpless, non-recollection in her eyes. She asked what else did I know.

'She had a sister, Peou.'

'Peou isn't a girl's name, Mrs Katy,' said Munny. 'Peou is a pet name we give to the youngest daughter in a family.'

'They had ducks.'

'Do you know her sister's real name?'

'Yes, yes, I do. It's Rangsei.'

The teacher's face changed. A look of thoughtful consideration. A slight smile creased her face. She nodded as she slowly recalled a memory.

'Do you know if she was a clever girl, quite small for her age?'

'Yes, yes, yes. Chavy won a prize for the number one student one year!'

I almost cried and laughed at the same time, remembering the story, biting my lip to control my excitement. The teacher got up and went to a cupboard and pulled down a cardboard box. After rummaging through the contents, she handed me a photograph.

'This is the child you're seeking. Her name is Chavy Pham.'

All awareness of my surroundings melted into the air when I met Chavy Pham. Her eyes bored into mine, burning with a fierce sense of accomplishment. She stood, shoulders back, proud in her white shirt and blue skirt, clutching her first prize tightly against her chest. A writing set.

Within ten minutes of her teacher taking this photo, I knew Chavy would be running home, desolate, unable to share her moment in the sun with her family. Soon after, she would go to the phone box outside the store and meet another person to share her success. And her decision changed all our lives. Looking at Chavy Pham, despair rose again. I knew what she didn't know at this life-or-death moment in her life and I remembered Clara's story about the submarines. I fought to hold back the helplessness and rage boiling inside me.

'I never saw Chavy again, although I heard stories about what happened to her. I never knew if they were true,' continued the teacher. 'I left the school soon after taking this picture to have my own child and stayed away for almost a year. When I came back, her sister Rangsei had joined my class. She never spoke about her older sister and left a month later herself. This must have been half a year ago or could have been a year. Sorry, I don't remember events exactly anymore. I went to their house once to ask about the girls. Her drunken father abused me, so I left.'

'What was Chavy like?'

She paused, searching her memory.

'When she started school as a six-year-old, she was small, yes, more like a little boy. I thought she might be sickly, not enough decent food to eat like many of the farming children. A shy girl at first. The boys bullied her until one day she fought back and surprised everyone, especially the boys. I'm remembering her better now. Chavy Pham was bright, oh yes, always wanting to answer questions even when she didn't know the answer. When she won the prize in her last year, she told me she wanted to be a teacher to make enough money so her mother wouldn't have to work so hard.'

'Where did she sit?'

'In the front row, naturally, so she could call out more easily. Her desk is the one just behind you. She had a big voice for a little one. Chavy had a friend, Kanya, a lazy girl, who would trick Chavy into doing her homework by pretending to be stupid. So I would punish them, sometimes with a stick, or I would make them stand in the corner over there next to the blackboard, on one leg. It made no difference. She still did her friend's homework.'

I turned to look at the desk where Chavy once sat and the corner where she stood on one leg. Was she gritting her teeth, defiant after her punishment for helping her best friend, or meekly taking her punishment?

I smiled to myself. I knew the answer.

'Can you draw me a picture of where the Pham house is, please?'

She got a pencil and sketched a map on a piece of paper.

'You can drive there in ten minutes. There's also a shortcut through the jungle, which is how the farming children along the river come and go. Walk down the jungle path to the river and follow the bank to a small bridge. The Phams live two or three hundred metres past the bridge, about a two-kilometre walk altogether. The way's overgrown by the jungle, but you won't get lost. You'll know the farmhouse, it's the one with the duck enclosure. There are dozens of ducks.'

She apologised, telling us she needed to get ready for the afternoon class and hoped she'd been helpful. She looked at me and smiled, pushing Chavy's photograph into my hands, understanding why I had come. Munny thanked her. After making our goodbyes, we walked outside.

'I'll get the tuk-tuk, Mrs Katy. We can be there in ten minutes.'

'Munny, I'm going to walk through the jungle. By myself. Meet me later at the farmhouse.'

The swollen, mud-coloured river surged and lapped the banks but had not yet burst over the top. The fields looked marshy. Another week or two of heavy monsoon rain and all this would be underwater. The rough track had been well-trodden by years of children, the past palpable. I saw the goosebumps on my skin, half-expecting to see Chavy running along the path after winning her Number 1 Student prize, broken-hearted over her parents not coming to cheer her success.

In the denser jungle, I carefully pushed the heavy undergrowth aside to pass, exploring a magical world. No low-hanging fruit decorated the wild fruit trees, already picked off by passing students. I paused, letting my mind watch Chavy throwing a stick to knock one of the higher ones down for her sister. Other times, I hung back when I sensed her other-worldly presence nearby, watching me intently. I spoke with her under the slivers of sunlight, each of us locked in different times, curiously severed from the here and now. But friends.

I arrived at the bridge. It looked unsafe with only an old rope handrail for balance. I hesitated, queasy. I felt a hand tugging my sleeve and stepped onto the well-worn planks and crossed over the fast-running chocolate turbulence surging centimetres below. A few drops splashed onto my feet. I kept walking. Another hundred metres ahead the farm came into view, half-hidden in a thicket of wild traveller palms and frangipani bushes growing through untidy grass. A ramshackle building with a rusty roof like those of its neighbours. I closed my eyes, imagining monsoon rain cascading over the gutters. I waved at Chavy and Rangsei splashing happily under the waterfalls. A hazy, happy phantom in the grey veil waved back and then turned to laugh together with her sister.

I opened my eyes. A woman pulling weeds in the farm's small rice paddy attracted my attention, her dress pulled up, tied in a knot near her waist. She carried a baby strapped to her back. I smiled at her from the grassy levee as I passed. She looked at me, indifference written on her face. She went back to work. I kept walking. She must be one of Chavy's sisters. I wondered which one of the neighbouring farms I could see had a mother who breastfed another mother's malnourished child ten years ago.

My pilgrimage, for I realised my visit was what it had become, took me over an hour. I lingered several times as Chavy's and my experiences merged into one. She and I talked with each other as two storytellers, hers from a place from where no traveller returned. I stopped again before joining Munny and Chavy's mother, gazing about me at a home I already knew. Everything was there: the rusty bicycles, the vegetable patch, the ducks, the hammocks slung between the house's stilts. If I went up those old stairs, I would see batik sheets covering the walls. I'd discover a bedroom partitioned off by a sheet where Chavy hid from the world, taught her sister English and dreamt about being a teacher so she could make her mother's life better.

Mrs Pham invited me to sit down and handed me a coconut. I took a long drink through the hole she had cut into the top. It tasted sweet. She accepted the money.

'Your husband came here asking about Chavy. I told him we found a job for her and her sister in a house in Phnom Song and I gave him the address. I told him they promised to look after Chavy and Peou, and they would make sure the girls went to school.'

I asked her if she could also give me the address of the house. She went inside to look. A sickness deep in my stomach returned while I waited. It didn't matter. I already knew the address. I had arrived too late again to save Chavy and Peou, only this time my demons had gone. What happened to the girls was tragic, but I wasn't responsible. After my conversations with Chavy, I understood now.

'Do you know where my daughters are?'

Mrs Pham looked at me with the haunted expression of a person living each day with an awful truth and her complicity.

'They have been away a long time. I've heard no word from them.'

'No, I'm sorry, Mrs Pham. I don't know where your daughters are.'

I knew Chavy would never be coming home and I lied to Mrs Pham with no regrets. I had walked in the footsteps of a ghost; I knew the truth as well as I knew the simplest things. I wondered what had become of her younger sister Rangsei, or Peou as I knew her in Simon's book. Could there still be a chance for Rangsei? I hoped so. I would try to find her.

My journey into myself and my quest for Chavy's identity were over. My joy feels profound because Chavy Pham has a name. She had been a real person. I still didn't know the ending to *Chavy's Story*, but I was close and I mourned for everything lost in this wretchedly poor family. I would never walk in their shoes, even so, I fought a battle inside about judging them for the awful decisions they'd made. But I also knew where Chavy's story truly began. It wasn't here in Kampot and I knew forgiveness would eventually come.

Mrs Pham mumbled something as we prepared to leave. I turned to my guide.

'What did she say, Munny?'

'She said Chavy was a filial daughter with dreams of a road they should have travelled together. "Once had high hopes for" would be the best English translation.'

I turned my back, but not my heart, on the tragedies still tormenting this blighted family. And to those other memories now exorcised after haunting me for so long.

'We can leave now, Munny.'

19

CLARA'S LOST WORLD

'What about you, Clara Yehonala? Which ingredients of your genetic soup are also bubbling away silently behind your own mask, waiting to give you indigestion?'

I stared at myself in the bathroom mirror after getting off the phone from my mother, asking myself the question out of concern for her. And myself.

The longer I lived, the more I knew having DNA from Genghis Khan, Nurhaci, and Cixi may be fine for newspaper stories or running a dynasty, but not much help living a normal-ish life in the twenty-first century. Yehonala genes were a disagreeable recipe for lost dads and a worthy challenge for Sigmund Freud.

Still, Ma sounded relaxed and at peace with herself after her first day in Kampot. She described a lightning storm over the distant mountains and let me know about the guide she'd found. I assured her nothing happening in Phnom Penh needed her to be chewing her fingernails over and to concentrate on chasing her demons away. She sounded eager about her visit to the countryside the following day.

As for me, I'd spent the day doing absolutely nothing since blearily wishing her a safe trip earlier in the morning. My most strenuous activities so far had been dangling my toes in the hotel's pool and flicking over the pages of a book I'd brought

The Girl in the Orphanage

with me, liberated from my suitcase for the first time after being forgotten in the recent upheavals. Harry Potter stories enchanted me and my eyes devoured the latest tale of Hermione's road to self-determination. I decided she and Harry would be quite at home in Phnom Penh, plus the odd bit of wizardry would come in passably handy. Oh, I mustn't forget to mention exchanging chatty messages with Elena, who had also dropped in an hour ago for a quick coffee between a break in her heady schedule. We were hovering in some kind of no-man's-land, talking as friends and having a cauldron of desire bubbling just below the surface, as powerful as it had been from the first time we'd met.

The more we chatted casually together and messaged, the more we found we had in common, apart from our shared devotion to charitable work. For different reasons, we were lacking big, supportive families and a wide circle of friends. We discovered we were suspicious, rather than envious, of people who claimed such. I forgave her omission of Adriana as I began to understand her.

Peace reigned. Today's remaining lost soul on my to-do list was Anton, due to arrive in the morning. I didn't remind my mother of Anton's arrival. Not because she needed to be worried about such a handsome man being with me, I thought it best not to give her reason to question why I wasn't tripping over my knickers in hot pursuit. She already had a bee in her head about someone, *anyone* as far as I could tell, doing the grandson-making honours before I joined the ranks of the *cheng nu*. To those of you for whom Mandarin remains impenetrable, it means "leftover women", a fate worse than being force-fed tofu.

About the same time as my mother set off to follow Chavy's trail, I called Martin Lewis to see if Jim's *Don Corleone* get-together with Ambassador Nelson had gone as planned.

'Martin, my mother has run off to the coast for a day or two, so I'm looking for company. I've got two tickets to a classical concert on Saturday night, front row. I wondered if you might like to come with me and soak up some culture, free from her evil eye?'

'Never thought you'd ask. Thanks, I'd love to, but I can't. Something's come up here and I'll be working.'

'Oh. And here I am thinking we were getting on so well. How about dinner tomorrow?'

'Can I let you know? I may be busy for a few days.'

'I'll only ask once. A girl can't beg, you know. If you can spare a little time for me between peeping in bedroom windows, I'm going to be at the Chaktomuk Conference Hall tomorrow and the next day, keeping my hand in on the piano. You're welcome to bring coffee along and listen if you like.'

I hung up the phone. So far, so good. Next, I called Elena. She was thrilled to go with me; there were at least two happy women in Phnom Penh today.

'Malyshka moya! How wonderful to see you again.'

Anton stopped the rehearsal and hurried over, wrapping me in his arms and planting a kiss on either cheek. Vintage Cernzy.

'We have all been so concerned about you for the last three weeks. You look well, my darling, as beautiful as ever. Your mother? She is okay?'

'Yes, yes, Anton, settle down. We're both well and dealing with what's happened. Thankfully, the worst is over now. Thank you for inviting me; I've missed the concert halls.'

'Come along with me and meet the orchestra. There are wonderful musicians here. I'm so happy with their rehearsals, much better than I expected.'

We walked arm in arm towards the stage. Instinctively, I clenched and unclenched my fingers in anticipation of playing the gleaming Steinway my eyes were devouring and my mouth salivating over.

'The orchestra knows you're coming here to help with rehearsals this afternoon, and they're all excited to see you. Nearly as much as me.'

Even as he spoke, all the musicians stood up and applauded. I closed my eyes to take in the atmosphere I remembered so well.

'Is the soloist here today?'

'He's rehearsing tomorrow. His name is Alain Kiry, quite the favourite of audiences here in Cambodia. He's young, eighteen, and plays with all the exuberance of his age.'

I took him to mean Anton had his doubts and if he were a conductor with choices for his soloists, he would have refused this one.

'Still, us beggars cannot be choosers, can we?' said he conspiratorially. 'Perhaps you can inspire him to virtuosity.'

'I've heard his recordings, Anton. He's a gifted pianist.'

'We shall see tomorrow. Now, I propose we rehearse the concerto part of Saturday's performance and you can have the chance to enjoy yourself again. It's Chopin's Second. What do you say?'

A thrill of anticipation ran through my whole body.

'Oh, Anton, I say it is one of my favourite pieces. And you know how no girl can refuse your invitations.'

'You have managed with notable success so far, *malyshka*. I endure my devastation as bravely as I can.'

I shook my head and smiled, Anton spent little time in the depths of despair over his failed seductions of me. He also appeared not to have changed as much as I thought.

I sat at the Steinway frantically massaging my fingers back to life while he cued the orchestra. He glanced over. I nodded.

The next half-hour passed in the bliss of re-discovering Chopin's most intimate thoughts breathed into his piano nearly two hundred years ago and talking to my beloved friend again. I loved his second movement, the *larghetto*, Chopin's indescribably beautiful night music expressing his youthful, passionate feelings for his absent love.

At the end, I opened my eyes, slowly returning to the world I had left behind.

'Clara, as always, you are magnificent. You bring a tear to my eye.'

'Thank you for allowing me to play, Anton; you have no idea the joy you have brought me. I have so missed my music.'

'Come with me. There's someone I want you to meet, the young pianist Alain Kiry. I mentioned to him you were coming here this afternoon and he wanted to meet you.'

He smiled mischievously. *I also wanted him to hear how to play Chopin,* whispered he, pleased with his subterfuge.

'Alain, may I introduce you to Clara Yehonala? Clara, this is the young virtuoso, Alain Kiry.'

'Alain, I'm so happy to meet you. I've heard your music but have never seen you in concert; I'm looking forward to Saturday evening. I hope you didn't mind me playing with the orchestra?'

'Not at all. I'm not due to rehearse until tomorrow. It's an honour to meet you. We all hope you are back in the concert halls of the world soon.'

'Clara, Alain, I'll leave you both to become acquainted,' said Anton. 'I want to rehearse one of the sections for the symphony before we finish today.'

'I've heard you play Chopin's Second before, Clara. I love the interpretation, especially the *larghetto*. Where did the inspiration come from?'

'Oh, do you seriously want the story of my life?'

I smiled, and he did the same. I liked him immediately.

'Maybe the pocket version?'

'Let me see. I believe it all started with a piano, naturally, but not just any piano. My great grandparents were musical and acquired a nineteenth-century Pleyel. It finished up in a sorry state after the Cultural Revolution, so my grandmother hired this man from the French Pleyel factory for the restoration; she couldn't bear to part with it.

'The conservator turned out to be an old man called Shimon Rubenstein, a Holocaust survivor. When he brought the piano back a year later, she asked him to play. He played Chopin for her. Seems he'd been a celebrated pianist until the war when the Nazis sent him to a concentration camp. The piano, he said, was almost identical to the one Chopin first played his second nocturne to *Madame* Pleyel.

'My grandmother told him he played exquisitely. To play music, you must know the stories, he told her. Mr Rubenstein shared one story with her about the lovesick young composer's love for Marie Pleyel and how he wrote the Nocturne, Number 2, Opus 9 and first played it to her.

'As a child, Grandmother and I banged on the keyboard together. She shared the stories too, even before I knew how to read music. So when I play, I'm re-telling stories, like all pianists do.'

'Hard to imagine you "banging on a keyboard" even as a child.'

'You have no idea,' and laughed at the memory of muddling through music sheets, trying to play romantically, instead sounding like a grim funeral dirge.

'The main sounds I produced in those days were only those of Chopin turning in his grave; our neighbours were even beginning to wear black. They would often knock on the walls, especially when my little dog joined in the chorus. My mother would try to avoid them when she went out so she wouldn't have to apologise.'

We both laughed.

'Growing up, my parents pushed me relentlessly,' said Alain. 'There were times I hated the piano. I even resent it today, occasionally. You know, people say I play too aggressively.'

'Playing the way you do is not necessarily a bad thing, Alain. It depends on the work. Despite his fearsome reputation, Uncle Sasha - Professor Berkowitz - never forced discipline on me, except for his gruffness when I made mistakes. He taught me how to listen to opera and told me stories of his friends, Slava Richter and Horowitz. I read the biographies of the composers and I quickly lost myself imagining their love affairs and tragedies. I found myself feeling what they might be feeling with the pen in their hand, trying to capture their emotions in the language of music.

'For example, the piece you're playing on Saturday night, Chopin's Second. Every time I play the piece, I sense the pleading of a lovestruck young man in poor health, nostalgic for his homeland, experiencing another doomed teenage passion. I always picture Chopin the same way. I try to imagine what it must feel like to be him. I believe my job is to help composers tell their stories as well, or better than they could.'

'Aren't you changing the composer's work?'

I smiled at the question I asked myself all the time. 'I hope I'm not so arrogant as to believe I could do a better job at composing.'

'Clara, we all try to get into the mind of the composer when we play their music. What do you mean by telling their stories better?'

'Let me explain it this way. Neither you nor I have English as our first language. Sometimes I can't find the word I want to use, either because I haven't learnt it, or there isn't a word to translate from in my native Mandarin.'

'Happens all the time to me too.'

'Yes. Back when these composers worked, they had limits too. Their instruments didn't always have the words to express their emotions, so they invented awesome harmonic and melodic tricks, especially Chopin. Those ancient pianos also produced a depth of shading a modern piano can't produce and needed a completely different way of playing. For example, it didn't matter how firmly or softly they pressed the keys, the sound volume never changed. I still have the old Pleyel piano and I practise on it, it's amazing how different the music sounds. I try to use our modern pianos to express what I hope the composers would have chosen if they had our instruments. I also try to reproduce the rich, velvety sounds our modern pianos can't make in interesting harmonic and melodic ways as well. If you'd like, we can play four-hands for a while, and I'll show you what I mean.'

One thing I couldn't tell Alain was Max's and my great secret. The stories I imagined included a chilling, intensely personal one. A story needing more than a year of trauma counselling before the raging mental terrors which came perilously close to taking my life were unmasked and tamed. The ones about missing my dad. Max helped me through my agonising time when I was fifteen and I begged her never to tell my mother because I knew even with her strength, it would destroy her. I still haven't shared that brutal episode with Ma, or with anyone, except Max.

The counselling eventually became a cathartic journey. We arrived at the end when I understood the powerful connections I felt in my music were founded on a longing for intimacy with my dad, which I lived out in conversations with composers. Once I grasped the idea my musical interpretations were conversations between myself and my missing dad as well as the composers, my performances soared to new heights, unconscious and personal, as if the audience and orchestra weren't even there. The delusions, suicide attempts and hallucinations left me forever, as did my terror of living my life in a lunatic asylum.

Later, we all sat together, getting ready to leave after the rehearsals.

'Anton, I believe you promised to have dinner with me.'

'Alas, Clara, tonight I have promised myself to Miss Yang, the first violin. We need to discuss one or two aspects of the performance on Saturday.'

'I see. I also see she is remarkably pretty.'

His eyes twinkled.

'You are shameless, Clara, doubting my honourable intentions. I have an idea. Perhaps we can convince Alain to join us to make a foursome?'

'Alain, would you care to be my escort for dinner?'

'I'd be delighted. As a local, I can recommend some excellent restaurants.'

Over a wonderfully social dinner, Anton talked about the world of music I'd been absent from. Alain spoke about his life as his country's budding superstar and I caught up on the gossip. The talented Miss Yang joined the line of starstruck women in the slipstream, and quite probably the hotel room, of the charismatic, devastatingly handsome Anton Cernzy.

I'd barely sat down in the concert hall the following afternoon when Martin Lewis plumped himself down beside me.

'Hello Martin, I didn't seriously expect you to join me here. You do know Chopin's been dead for years?'

'I'd almost forgotten what I like about you. You said your mother was away and I thought I'd be safe. Do you need to be acting like she's sitting next to you *all* the time?'

'You're right, sorry. Good afternoon, Martin. How nice to see you. Jim Preston told me how much you Australians were into high culture.'

He laughed.

'A bit better. Here, I brought you coffee. And I can guess what Jim Preston said. Something about us all preoccupied with meat pies and football?'

'Thanks, coffee's just what I need. No, not quite, though I won't quote him. *Hush*, the concerto rehearsal's about to start. This Chopin piece is lovely.'

To my surprise, I felt comfortable feeling his body next to me, our arms grazing as we listened quietly together. Companionable? I needed to be watchful. Martin Lewis might be a troublesome man in more ways than one. I closed my eyes, letting the music take over.

Alain played well. I could tell from several less-practised parts he'd made changes to his usual style. The music sounded more sensual, Anton would be happy. After the rehearsal, Martin turned to me.

'Thus laid before me is the wondrous world of Clara Yehonala.'

'I had no idea you're a poet, too. I'm impressed. Yes, I'm afraid so. Now you see the other reason I don't have a boyfriend; all I ever do on a date is close my eyes and pretend they're not there.'

'Funny, I had the same feeling myself listening to him play.'

'Well, you've truly mastered the art of making a girl feel special, haven't you?'

Anton and Alain came over to join us. 'Alain,' I enthused, 'I loved your performance. You caught those passionate moments extremely well.'

'Thanks, Clara. I'm sure you could tell I made changes. I need to practise more. If you have the time, could you rehearse with me today?'

'I'd be honoured. Excuse me, Martin, I'll be back soon.'

'How well do you know Clara?' Anton asked Martin.

'Not as well as I'd like. She and I have a…shall we say… problematic relationship.'

'You don't look like a fool. I've never seen her so relaxed with anyone before. I'd bet you're the first man to have ever held her attention for more than a nanosecond. She and I are great friends, though even my charms have failed me too many times with her. Believe me, I know these things. Have you ever heard her play?'

'No, I suppose you could say I'm new to classical music.'

'Then you're in for a treat. Look over there. Rehearsals are over today and the musicians are usually quick to leave. The orchestra's still here, hoping to hear her play even a few measures.'

'I don't understand how one well-known pianist is much different from another.'

'You will.'

'Alain Kiry played wonderfully.'

'He's okay. When Clara Yehonala plays, she pulls music from places only she knows exist. Even now, she still sends a shiver down my spine. *Shhh…*listen.'

20
CATHARSIS

Clara was on the balcony when I got back to the hotel from Kampot on Saturday, dressed to go out. I remembered she must be helping with the concert's dress rehearsal. I put down my bag, sat with her and we gazed across at the river together. She waited for me to say something.

'Her name is Chavy Pham.'

Clara continued to look fixedly into the distance alongside me. After a while, she turned her head to look at me.

'She has a name. I'm glad she has a name, just like you and me. I'm glad she's a real, living person.'

'It feels wonderful for me to hear myself say it aloud. I'm going to finish her story. I also have a new name for the book.'

Clara looked at me curiously. I realised she expected a different truth from the one I knew. I started talking, a stream of words prolonging what I needed to say.

'It's going to be called *The World of Chavy Pham*. When I was a student in England, people often stereotyped us Chinese girls as sex-mad nymphomaniacs. Movies like the Suzy Wong one helped the idea along. The Vietnam War was still fresh and memories of the Japanese lingered with the older generation. English people bundled all of us Asians into the *yellow peril* basket. Not everyone, though I had my problems at the time…'

The Girl in the Orphanage

'Where is she, Ma?'

'Clara, I want people to know little Chavy Pham was a real person, not a racial stereotype, or a nameless Asian trafficking victim, or a picture on a charity poster under a label like "save a trafficked child, give generously". We need...'

'Where is she, Ma?'

'Chavy Pham is dead, Clara.'

The silence hung between us.

'I have a photograph.'

I handed it to her. Clara stared at it for a long time.

'Such a tiny thing. Like a boy with her pudding-basin haircut. How proud she looks, like a gold medallist at the Olympic Games. Look at the passion in her eyes. And the sadness.'

'Yes.'

'Will you tell me her story?'

'Yes. Not today. I'm not quite ready yet, but I will.'

Clara nodded and smiled. Hardly a smile really, more a pinching of her lips. Then she was broken, letting the tears consume her for a long time. Later, she went to the bathroom. I heard the water running. After ten minutes, she reappeared with a new face on.

'I have to go to the theatre for rehearsals with Anton and Alain.'

'Are you sure you'll be all right?'

'Goes without saying, Ma. Don't you know the old story about "the show always goes on"? Besides,' said she with an absent-minded smile, 'I'm one of a long line of Yehonala women. Remember?'

How could I forget?

21

A DASH OF CULTURE WITH A TWIST OF DEATH

I met Elena in the bar at the concert hall. I'd gone along to the final dress rehearsal earlier in the day and saw Anton full of energy and heard Alain mastering changes to his technique. I'll admit to my excitement, and nervousness, about the evening with Elena for more reasons than I wanted to think about.

'*Ciao, bella.* Thank you so much for the invitation. My colleagues tell me the tickets are hard to come by. The international classical circuit doesn't come this way too often.'

She hugged me and kissed my cheek longer than usual. She whispered to me, so close her lips touched my ear, 'please keep trying to be patient with me.'

I sucked in a breath through my teeth and did my best to appear normal as my heart raced.

'You're right, it's a bit off the beaten track for the big orchestras and there isn't much in the way of musical education in Cambodia. Even the musicians in the State Orchestra are mostly Chinese. I know the guest conductor tonight, Anton Cernzy, quite well, we can meet him later. Alain Kiry, the soloist, is a local favourite and is quite talented. I watched the rehearsals earlier.'

'Must be nice to be back into your world again. Which reminds me, I had an idea about our visit to the Vitara Orphanage. Why don't we tell them we're organising orphanage visits looking for talented kids as part of a music program you're sponsoring? I could approach the Chinese Embassy to help and it might be the sort of thing Georgie gets involved with at the Australian Embassy.'

'What a great idea! I'm interested in organising a program. Better you than me talking to them first, though. My family aren't bosom friends of the ambassadors.'

'Don't worry, they're into self-interest, not personalities. If you knew the types of people they get into bed with, you'd wonder if they had souls. Give them something artistic to support to get them into the newspapers to take people's minds off the corruption, or the latest karaoke bar scandal and they'll jump at the chance to help.'

'Speaking of people with souls or not, I meant to ask you something earlier. Back at the embassy, we met George Sorensen. I couldn't help noticing your expression. You don't like him much, do you?'

'You know how you get a feeling about a person? He's one of those people. Nothing to put my finger on. His one redeeming quality is he's not a drunken bore at diplomatic functions due to some kind of liver complaint, which means he can't drink alcohol. Small mercies, I suppose. I'm a little surprised he's not here tonight; he'd usually be at the front of the line for these things. Funny you should ask, Martin asked me the same thing yesterday. Anything I should know?'

'I don't think so. Except my mother shares your view. I'm repaying a bit of female intuition.'

'How's your patience holding up?' asked she, a hesitant smile on her face.

'I'm doing my best. Drink up, I just heard the bell. We can forget about romantic dilemmas for a while and listen to Chopin. My problems pale into insignificance next to his rampaging hormones.'

We took our places for the evening's performance. The packed Conference Hall proved Alain Kiry's popularity among the concert-goers of Phnom Penh. The expatriate community was here in force too, ready to savour their meagre ration of classical music.'

By the time the overture finished, the delectable Miss Yang and Anton had got their cues down to perfection and the orchestra was playing with impeccable timing. I assumed the two of them had found time for private harmonising.

Alain walked onto the stage for his concerto. The audience gave him a generous welcome and I settled down to lose myself for the next half-hour. Full of nuance and sensitivity, Alain played Chopin with polished confidence and a delicate touch, stressing the composer's lyrical beauty in the parts I loved, then with energetic climaxes in his unique style. Unconsciously, I reached over and squeezed Elena's hand. She put her other hand over mine and her nails pressed into my wrist.

At the end, like everyone, I applauded the virtuosity of Alain Kiry. Surely one day, we'd be listening to this artist on bigger stages than Chaktomuk. He stood up to acknowledge the applause and blew me a kiss.

'Did I see what I thought I did?'

'You did. He and I were rehearsing together earlier and we've become friends of sorts. I hope *his* hormones are under control and he never took my Chopin stories too much to heart. I've got enough to worry about already trying to control my own.'

'They do say slow-growing trees bear the best fruit.' She gave my hand an affectionate squeeze before the lights came on. 'There's an intermission now. We can get a drink if you like.'

Elena found people she knew and introduced me to a woman who looked quite at home among strangers.

'Hello, Jane. Are you enjoying the performance?'

'Oh yes. The young pianist Kiry is quite marvellous.'

'Jane, can I introduce you to Clara Yehonala? Clara, this is Jane Nelson. Her husband is Robert, the ambassador.'

'Hello, my dear. How nice to meet you. I've been following your story in the newspapers. I am so sorry about your father.'

'Thank you, Jane. I'm sure the worst is behind us now.'

'I heard you play at the Opera House in Sydney last year.

Liszt. Quite exquisite. This is my daughter, Annie. She's here on sufferance, although I think the handsome conductor caught her eye.'

'Stop it, Mum! Clara, she thinks I spend every moment of my life chasing men.'

'I know how you feel, Annie. My mother is beginning to eye each man I meet as livestock for grandson production. Do you live in Cambodia?'

'No, I'm on a semester break from Sydney Uni. I'm a political science major. Dad imagines me as the Australian version of Henry Kissinger one day.'

'I hope you both enjoy the symphony. Anton's energy and Beethoven's Third are a good combination. As it happens Annie, Anton Cernzy and I are good friends. Elena and I will be having a drink backstage afterwards. If you like, I'll introduce you. Jane, you're welcome to join us.'

Annie instantly cheered up. Jane Nelson sighed with relief. 'Thank you, Clara. I imagine the rest of the night will be much more delightful for her.'

'Your husband's not here tonight?' asked Elena.

'No, some last-minute emergency cropped up. Steve Gray, the military attaché, offered to suffer the agony of classical music with me in Bob's place. The good colonel's over there drinking scotch and avoiding the women's chatter with husbands who also got roped into coming.'

The bell sounded. The break had passed quickly in small talk and handshakes with others of Jane's circle of diplomatic friends.

Never a great fan of these social events, I surprised myself when I realised how much I enjoyed Elena's company. I reached for her hand without thinking as we walked back to our seats.

The final part, the symphony, allowed Anton to rise to the occasion. And he did, full of bold flourishes and high energy, the orchestra responding with a near faultless, dramatic performance of Beethoven's *Eroica*. The magical night came to an end with well-deserved, lavish applause. If Anton could ever rein in his passions outside concert halls, he'd be playing on the world stage.

'Come on Elena, we'll have a glass of champagne and meet Antonio Banderas, otherwise known as Anton Cernzy. Now there's a man who could get a girl to renounce her, *um...*'

'Predilections?'

We laughed together, walking arm in arm to the backstage *après* to regret our own and agreeing we should keep a watchful eye on Annie Nelson's. Personally, I knew Elena was in far more danger from the charm onslaught.

Contentedly replaying Chopin in my head and reading a cute message from Elena about Anton's unrequited offer of blissful union, I found my mother sitting on the balcony, her look a mix between shock and delight.

'What's with the weird expression, Ma? No, let me guess. They've posted Martin Lewis to deepest, darkest Africa?'

'Oh, much better. The police found George Sorensen floating in a stormwater drain.'

'Ma ya! A dead George Sorensen wouldn't have even been my second guess, though it explains why he didn't put in an appearance at the concert tonight. This definitely deserves a drink. What happened?'

'According to Jim, Sorensen went out early this afternoon and Rithy followed him until sure he must be heading towards Phnom Song. Jim told Rithy to go home and leave it to the AFP and the Cambodian police. Seems our George never arrived in Phnom Song.'

'How did Jim find out Sorensen never got there?'

'An hour ago, he got a call from Robert Nelson telling him two westerners had found Sorensen bobbing around in the stormwater drain near his villa on their way home after a night in the local bars. Apparently, they were caught short and stopped for a pee and there was George, large as life. Well, not exactly, but you get the picture.'

'Couldn't think of a better send-off.'

'Your obituary-writing talents are wasted playing the piano. The police say he must have been drunk after a night out, tripped, bumped his head and drowned. They smelt alcohol on him, among other fluids, I imagine. The ambassador called, begging Jim to write the drowning story, not the paedophile one.'

'Hope Jim remembers to include the peeing on him part. Hang on, you said he disappeared on the way to Phnom Song. If he's going off to play with little girls on the other side of town and moments away from being arrested, how did he end up taking a dip in a stormwater drain near his villa?'

'Good question. If we disregard divine intervention, my guess is someone put him there to make it look like an accident.'

'I think in Sorensen's case, we can safely forget divine anything. What are we going to do?'

'You mean after we have a drink to celebrate? First of all, we're going to make sure we have nothing linking us to George Sorensen. Let's double-check I deleted all my photos for a start. Then we're going to meet Jim in the morning at the Fresco Café.'

'Well, Ma, with all due respects to the dear departed black soul of Papa Georgie, this deserves a toast. Can't think of a more fitting end to a blissful evening.'

'*Gambei!*'

22

THE RED ROCKET

With the demise of the unlamented George Sorensen, Jim, Katy and Clara each harboured their versions of happiness mixed with frustration. Sorensen had been the one solid link they had to find out the truth about Simon's murder. With him gone, their hope of uncovering the truth looked bleak.

'I'm not even shedding crocodile tears for him, but what do we do now?' asked Clara, exasperation overcoming the vengeful glee from the night before.

'We go back to square one,' replied Jim. 'We know the Vitara Orphanage is behind whatever's going on, so the question is why Simon got so interested in the Vitara Orphanage in the first place? We know those nice people from the Pink House run it. We don't know for sure, but maybe Simon found out, too. My problem is, as far as we know, the Vitara Orphanage is no different from dozens of other dodgy orphanages run by equally unsavoury pricks. Why be so interested in this one? It's a bloody *shame* we're missing the thread tying it all together.'

'What did you say?' said Katy, suddenly enthused.

'I said we're missing the…'

'Yes, yes, I heard what you said, Jim. I've got it! Shame. We've known the link all along.'

They both looked at Katy like she was about to announce the

winner of the Oscars.

'It's Chavy. *She's* the thread tying the pages together. The young girl killed with Simon in Krong Chey was a little hero called Chavy Pham.'

This piece of the puzzle had fallen into place during her visit to the farm. Katy realised she'd hinted the same to Clara a couple of days ago, now aware of what she meant. Jim and Clara both looked at Katy with similar levels of bewilderment.

'Do you remember what Rithy heard the young girl calling out that night in Krong Chey?'

'Yes, Ma. He heard her calling out *my shame, my shame.*'

'Rithy was mistaken. His mistake's been hiding the truth all along. She wasn't calling out about her shame. Don't you both see?' said an excited Katy.

'Yep, it's as clear as bloody mud, Katy.'

'Not like you to be so slow, Jim. In all the noise, panic and confusion, Rithy misheard. She didn't call out *my shame, my shame* at all. She called out…'

'*Yikes!*' exclaimed Clara as the lights came on for her, too. 'She called out *Mr Simon, Mr Simon.* They knew each other.'

'Yes, *baobei*. There's no other explanation as to why she risked her life running back into the alley. Remember, Simon never told Rithy about Chavy. To him, this was just another rescue. He had no reason to think she called out Simon's name. In fact, he would have disbelieved his hearing when she did. I've no doubt the young girl was Chavy Pham. Those killers also knew Chavy and Simon knew each other. *That's* why they were killed, to make sure the orphanage and the traffickers kept their secrets.'

'As soon as we find out how Dad knew Chavy was in the Vitara Orphanage and how she finished up in the Krong Chey cellar, we'll have most of the answers. I know we will,' said Clara, getting excited herself.

'I know half the answer. The part about how Simon found out she got to the Vitara Orphanage.'

Katy told them the large house in Phnom Song was where Mrs Pham sent Chavy and Rangsei and the same one George

Sorensen visited. While at the Pham's farm, Katy had guessed the traffickers who worked for the Pink House couple were still around the village and they were the ones offering the fake housekeeping jobs to Chavy's parents.

'Mrs Pham gave Simon the address, though she couldn't remember it when I showed up at the farm, except it was in Phnom Song,' explained Katy. 'After Simon left, she knew what she'd done. Her face gave her remorse away when I met her. Simon arrived too late because Chavy, quick to realise the danger, ran away with Rangsei on their second night there. The two girls found themselves at the Vitara Orphanage later at night by accident. Simon must have followed someone from the Phnom Song house, or more likely some children, and he discovered the trail led to the orphanage, which is where he found Chavy and Rangsei again.'

'So that's why he went to Elena asking about the Vitara Orphanage,' said Clara, the pieces falling into place.

'You think Sorensen had nothing to do with Simon's death, after all?' asked Jim, the picture also forming in his reporter's head.

'No, he didn't. Not directly, anyway. George Sorensen was a repulsive human being, but he's also a rabbit hole where there are no rabbits. He knew the children he raped came from the Vitara Orphanage or one of the other places this couple owned; I doubt he knew much about the other activities. Whoever's behind all this killed Sorensen because he'd become too much of a risk. I'm guessing now, Chavy may even have recognised him at the Phnom Song house from her time in the Pink-House and I think because she recognised him, it's part of the reason they killed her too.'

'Somehow, the couple must have known Sorensen was being followed and got worried they would be exposed,' said Clara. 'We still don't know who leaked the news to them, so we're no closer to the truth than before, but his death couldn't be an accident. George Sorensen never had a drink in his life, according to Elena. So him being drunk and falling into the drain simply isn't true.'

'They made it look like an accident,' said Jim. 'The embassy's happy with the drowning story since a serious embarrassment's gone away and Robert Nelson doesn't have a scandal on his hands, just a staffing problem. The traffickers are happy because no one's bringing down the roof on them for knocking off an Aussie diplomat. And no one else will be interested in looking too closely. Everyone's happy.'

'Except George,' mused Katy.

'Especially a few dozen children,' said Clara. 'Sorensen's no more than a disgusting paedophile who got what he deserved as far as I'm concerned, or not what he deserved. He got off lightly in my book.'

'Agreed, but he's not a murderer,' said Jim.

'Next question. How do we find out who tipped off the traffickers George Sorensen spelt trouble for them?'

Katy looked across the table, fixing her gaze on Jim Preston. 'Jim, why don't you give us the answer to Clara's question?'

'Ah, Katy m'dear, you're a bloody legend. Should have known never to underestimate a woman. What was it, the "red rocket" blunder?'

Katy nodded.

'You were clever to pick up on my little slip of the tongue. I realised my mistake straight away, but too late after I'd said it. I never gave you enough credit.'

'My mother never misses anything, Jim, I promise you. However, as for me, I'm feeling like the moron at a Mensa meeting. Can one of you please explain what's obvious to everyone in the world except me?'

'Don't feel too bad, *baobei*, I haven't worked it all out either. And I'm quite sure Jim didn't until George Sorensen turned up in the stormwater drain. Am I right?'

Jim nodded. 'I suspected Rithy was the one behind the betrayals. When we decided to follow Sorensen, I went down to the street outside the villa each night to check on Rithy to make sure he did what you told him to do. I saw you there on all three nights, so I didn't bother about staying. When you followed

Sorensen and after what happened with Katy, I knew Rithy to be the guy I'd want next to me in a foxhole.'

'And how you knew Rithy had a red scooter?'

'Spot on, Katy. Though it left me with the dilemma about who did give you away. I knew when Simon went to Krong Chey, someone must have informed the traffickers. The trouble was, it could have been anyone. So I needed to start getting the numbers down a tad.'

'Do you play sudoku?'

'What?'

'Never mind Jim, sorry. Go on with the story.'

'By the time you two went to Krong Chey, I'd already guessed some bastard tipped them off and why I got so pissed off with you both. Now, I'm quite sure they were watching the place, but I doubted the local police chief or the guy with the reptile shoes would be bothered. They're too important to be hanging around a grubby place like the Paradise Storage Company on the off chance you'd drop in. No, somebody warned them and they were waiting for you, too. The list of possibilities now looked a lot smaller. Rithy was still the obvious one at the time, even though he got a beating. Not a high price to pay to dodge a murder rap.'

'Or it could have been someone he told unwittingly.'

'Dead right, Clara. Someone he spoke to became the only possible answer once I knew he was squeaky clean, except for Martin and the Chinese - and I quickly crossed them off my list. Unless they were tracking your phone or bugging your handbags, there's no way they knew where you were going. Anyway, you thought Martin had no idea you'd been to Krong Chey. He wouldn't have gone along with giving you the phoney official murder report if he had known you'd been there.'

'So who did?' urged Clara impatiently, not wanting the scenic route.

'There were three contestants for the first prize: Rebecca and Ross, Rithy's wife, Jorani, or Simon's mate, the police chief - remember Rithy asked him if he could send an officer to go with you. The only remotely credible one turns out to be the police chief.'

'Come on, Jim, he's been working hand-in-glove with Simon for years rescuing kids, not killing people like Simon. It's not plausible it could have been him,' protested Katy.

'Yep, it looked like a dead-end.'

'Oh, for God's sake, Jim, stop keeping us all in suspense. You're not writing a bloody murder mystery,' snapped Clara, at the end of her patience.

'Settle down, petal. Occam's razor. The simplest solution fitting all the facts is usually the right one. It must have been the police chief, even if it made no obvious sense. I knew not making sense didn't mean it wasn't true.'

'Rithy did tell us the police chief wouldn't spare an officer to go with us to babysit,' remembered Katy.

'Good point. Now we know why. He's happy as a pig in shit getting the credit for cleaning up local brothels with Simon, but drew the line getting on the wrong side of his child trafficking mates. When I left your room with Rithy, he and I had a private conversation. I told him to ask Simon's police chief if he could spare an officer to help watch Sorensen because my newspaper had a tipoff he was a paedophile visiting orphanages for sex. If anything happened to Sorensen, my hunch would be right. I admit to a minor bout of conscience about an unfortunate accident befalling poor old George, but I got over it when I remembered Katy's face back in the hotel room. When I promised you he'd never rape another little girl, I meant it.'

'So now we know who betrayed my father.'

'Yep. The bad news is we still only know half the story. We don't know who gives the police chief orders, for example. He's not important enough to be calling those kinds of shots himself, plus we've got no real proof of anything. Learning the second half is going to be the hard part. The good news is, as far as anyone's concerned, you two are vestal virgins who know nothing or have been scared half to death by the pleasant gentleman from Vietnam and accepted the so-called truth about Simon's death.

We need to keep it that way. You two need to think hard about whether you want to go on. It might get a bit dicey from here.'

'A bit dicey! Jim, three people are dead, including my dad. My mother barely escaped having her eyes cut out, I got way too close to being raped by a Neanderthal, Rithy got beaten up, our room was broken into. And now you're telling us "it might get a bit dicey". How much *dicier* could it get?'

'Ladies, I think Simon discovered the tip of a large iceberg and was only beginning to find out how much of it still sat under the water. Don't forget what happened when you first got here. Neither ambassador wanted you two talking to the media about Simon's death. Now, my guess is they weren't sure how much Simon had told you, which explains why someone, Martin Lewis probably, broke into your room looking for Simon's book once they got wind of it. You were right to be suspicious when they asked you to keep quiet. Now it's clear the real reason must be they, or someone powerful, doesn't want reporters poking around into Simon's death. We're talking about major league people here with plenty to lose. Think about it.'

'What's to think about? We came here to find the truth and we're not leaving until we do. Besides, didn't you read your own Saturday newspaper, or at least look at the pictures? We're bulletproof.'

Clara nodded.

'It's a great article, Jim. But Ma, you might pick your adjectives better.'

'And don't forget what happened to the bloody *Titanic*, ladies.'

'You know Ma, meeting Jim Preston is a piece of good fortune. I know he's looking for headlines, but to be honest, we've been a danger to ourselves.'

Katy and Clara were back at the hotel shortly after midday and decided to relax by the side of the pool, dangling their feet in the cool water. A friendly waiter kept their glasses topped up from a jug of iced lime juice.

'Are you worried about carrying on, *baobei*?'

'Oh, not at all. Quite the opposite. I think we're close to the answers, though I've had one of your *red rocket* moments. How did those traffickers know where George Sorensen would be so they could grab him before he got to the Phnom Song house?'

'I don't know, but it's a great question. One way is Sorensen's driver was part of the gang, which seems too much of a coincidence since, according to Rithy, a regular taxi picked him up this time. I suppose it's possible. The other, more likely one, is Jim wanted Rithy to keep following Sorensen so they could tell the police chief where to find him.'

'Do we want to know the right answer?'

'If we don't ask, he won't have to lie.'

'My lips are sealed.'

'You're not going to like it, *baobei*. There *is* a third possibility.'

'You mean someone else is behind it all? Who?'

'Martin Lewis.'

'What! You can't be serious? I know you don't like him, but you surely can't believe he's a friend of the Vietnamese lowlife. Impossible!'

'Don't be so sure. Did you notice Jim's surprise about Sorensen getting abducted? I don't think he's a good enough actor. What if Jim didn't tip off Sorensen's murderers?'

'There's an easy way to find out. We'll ask next time we see him.'

Jim's ears must have been burning. Katy's mobile phone rang. They spoke for a few minutes before she hung up and turned toward Clara.

'You remember Jim saying he would check up on Rémy Aubert? Well, it seems when the good pastor left his street kids' program to take God to the countryside, there were rumours about molesting children. He doesn't know if they're true.'

'Curiouser and curiouser.'

23

A GIFT FROM GOD

'Rithy, if we cross our hearts and hope to die, will you drive us to Svay Rieng province again?'

'We will all hope to die if we go there, Mrs Katy.'

'I promise we won't be going anywhere near Krong Chey. Me and Clara want to meet Rémy Aubert at his church in Prey Kam village. It's a long way from Krong Chey.'

After more to-and-fro, Rithy reluctantly agreed to drive us if we let him take his old military service pistol with him, a hefty, ancient-looking revolver more at home in a John Wayne western. Neither of us had ever seen a gun up close before. We swallowed hard before agreeing, breathing a sigh of relief when he closed it away in the glovebox, out of sight.

After making doubly sure we'd left no clues about where we were going, I called ahead once we were on the highway. Rémy apologised in advance, in case he was delayed from visiting another border village.

Clara and I had talked about whether we should even go at all; we were under no illusions about what would happen if the traffickers discovered us in Svay Rieng again. Our only reason, foolhardy or not, being a nagging suspicion something must be going on between Rémy Aubert and Martin Lewis, based on a minor slip from Martin about whether or not they knew each other.

Like other villages in the low-lying landscape, Prey Kam hamlet spread itself along the banks of a slow-moving river, the paddy fields swampy from the rain. Mangroves grew dense along the bank and between the old, multi-coloured houses perched on their spindly wooden stilts. Hundreds of wooden stakes decorated the river shallows where a dozen villagers waded knee-deep in the mud, planting smaller mangroves and tying them to more sticks. Further out in the river were roughly-built enclosures Rithy said were fish pens.

Most of Prey Kam itself lay on higher ground behind the banks. We drove slowly down the red-dust street between the dilapidated buildings, attracting the attention of dark-skinned locals unused to strangers, and the curious eyes of skinny children who waved with cheery-white smiles. Rémy Aubert's church was easy to find. A large sign, Prey Kam Mission Farm, pointed the way. What we found surprised us. Far from the stoic house of God pitted bravely against the heathen hordes, an expanse of healthy-looking vegetable fields surrounded his little chapel and a community of local farmers were busy at work under the supervision of a westerner. He came over as we parked, introducing himself in French-accented English; the sort of accent to get women fluttering in movies and, I admit, in remote countryside villages.

'*Bonjour mesdames*, I'm Paul Rocher, one of the farm advisers working with Rémy. He telephoned me an hour ago to say you'd be coming and asked me to make you comfortable.'

Paul looked about Clara's age, good-looking in the layback way of people who do volunteer work, with sun-bleached, uncombed hair and wearing a dirty t-shirt bearing the logo of Agronomique de Montpellier, chopped-off cargo pants and muddy boots. He smiled as we shook hands. I liked him straight away and saw Clara giving him a second once-over. We introduced ourselves.

'This isn't quite what Clara and I were expecting.'

He laughed, near-perfect white teeth showing vivid against his tanned face.

'No doubt you were expecting what I did when I volunteered to come here, getting a dose of fiery preaching on the sins of man, devoting your soul to penury and basking in the glory of God, perhaps?'

'Something along those lines.'

'Well, the penury part's right. Rémy can also get overzealous but mostly does it to maintain his image. That way, people leave him in peace and the university doesn't fight him too hard when he demands funds or people like me to help with his work here. I've heard of you both. It's hard not to read about you at the moment. I'm quite excited to meet you, Clara, all the world knows who you are. You're also as pretty as people say.' He grinned again.

Do I see her cheeks flushing?

'Thank you. However, if you can pay a compliment after my long car ride, without makeup, in a humid village in the middle of nowhere, I think your Gallic gallantry may have got the better of you,' said she, smiling back. *'Je vis principalement à Paris, d'où viens-tu?'*

'Tu parles très bien le français, mademoiselle. Je suis de Montpellier. I'm working on my PhD at the agricultural university there.'

'Paul, while we wait for Father Aubert, perhaps you could show Clara around the farm if you can spare the time. I'm happy to sit under this tree and wait with Rithy.'

'Mademoiselle Clara?'

I knew she missed the company of people like herself, leading a solitary life on the concert circuit and an almost monastic one in Cambodia. Seeing her excitement when Antonin Cernzy turned up gave off a clear enough signal.

As I guessed, they set off like two lost souls finding themselves with a common interest in a strange place, which I supposed we all were.

I sat down next to Rithy, taking in my surroundings. The chapel had seen better days, its white paint faded and curling in places, a small cottage with a shady veranda attached to the side. A recent addition, a wooden cabin with three doors, nestled under a clump of shady palm trees nearby. I assumed Paul lived there with anyone else who worked here. There were a few old sheds full of those tools and sacks of things farmers used, nothing motorised; Rémy ran a hands-on farm on a shoestring. The two acres of fields, dense with healthy vegetables, were an impressive testament to his success.

The distant sound of a noisy motorbike interrupted my idle thoughts. Rémy Aubert emerged from the jungle a minute later, bouncing along a rutted track between the fields, the bike's throaty roar resounding across the quiet landscape, scaring ibis into the air and sending stray chickens squawking for cover. He wore a shirt with the sleeves rolled up, sandals, and old shorts which looked like leftovers from a British Raj movie of the thirties. A Panama hat completed the image. His motorbike undoubtedly hailed from the same era.

Rithy's ears pricked up. I noticed him concentrating intently on the sound.

'*Madame* Yehonala, *salut*. I'm so delighted to welcome you to my farm; I see you've met Paul, one of my helpers and your daughter and Paul already have made friends.'

He turned and waved, gesturing to them not to stop what they were doing.

'We should let the younger ones have their time, yes? You must call me Rémy, everyone does,' beamed he, looking even less like his seventy years than he did at the funeral.

'Please call me Katy and this is my friend Rithy. I must say, this place is far from what I expected.'

'We will talk of the farm later. For now, I'll get you both a cool drink. How do you like my bike? She is a Velocette, very French, nearly as old as me. She never lets me down.'

'I hope she's not the only woman to do so, Rémy.'

He chuckled, pouring us drinks into mismatched glasses from a jug of iced lime juice.

'Sadly, the temptations of the flesh are long behind me, *madame*.'

'Clara and I recently found ourselves on motorbikes for the first time. Except for the storms, we had so much fun.'

'*Eh bien*, the countryside is the proper place for a motorcycle. This old lady has carried me safely up and down the border provinces for ten years. Before me, I think, who knows what stories *Madame* Velocette could tell?'

As we spoke, a young woman joined us. Rémy introduced her as Françoise, the second of his two workers. Smeared in mud from head to toe, she looked too delicate for much more than pouring tea in a French drawing-room.

'You may have noticed Françoise working with the villagers in the river when you arrived, re-planting mangroves. The new mangroves will attract fish and crabs again. Françoise is a divinity student and will eventually be a missionary.'

'*Bonjour* Katy, pleased to meet you. Rémy, I came back to get Paul so we can swim before the rain arrives.'

Rémy beckoned Paul and Clara over.

'Clara, we usually go swimming in the river in the late afternoons after Rémy releases us from his slave labour,' said Françoise, greeting her. 'Do you want to come?'

'But I…'

'Come on, *mademoiselle*, it's an experience not to be missed and quite safe, no crocodiles,' promised Paul, winking at her. 'Perhaps one or two docile catfish to play with if we're lucky.'

'Please come, Clara. Between us, Paul and I have enough old t-shirts and shorts for swimming to fit you. Also plenty of towels and whatever else you need.'

She looked at me, her expression wavering between pleasure and panic. I shrugged. This trip wasn't turning out quite the way either of us expected.

'*Oui, pourquoi pas?*'

I watched the three of them walking arm in arm down the dusty street towards the river, towels slung over their shoulders, laughing and chattering.

'I'm imagining the paparazzi capturing this moment for history. It would make a career to get photos of Clara Yehonala frolicking with a handsome young man in a secluded jungle river.'

'Ah Katy, we are simply looking at what is there when you scratch the surface of anyone, are we not? Kings, queens, piano superstars, you, me. All of us.'

'I can think of at least one person in Krong Chey who might disagree with you, Rémy,' I thought, musing over events of the last week.

'By the time they get back, the rain will be here and driving will be hazardous for an hour or two. Françoise and Paul get few visitors, neither do I. It would be nice to have company; may I invite you to stay at the mission tonight? We can make a barbeque, have a drink or two, and you can all drive back to Phnom Penh in the morning. Clara can stay in the dormitory with Paul and Françoise. The chapel has a spare room you are most welcome to use.'

'What about Rithy?'

'The village chief will be honoured to entertain him in great style as my guest, or he can drive back now and return in the morning.'

When I spoke to Rithy, he insisted he would never leave us in Svay Rieng unprotected and Jorani wouldn't mind if he stayed for one night. Rémy arranged his host for the night with much good cheer.

When the swimming party returned, a thrilled Clara, showered and wearing a baggy t-shirt, flip flops and a pair of shorts, insisted on staying with her new friends, unconcerned about her lack of potions and lotions usually essential for life. Fifteen minutes later, the rain fell. As far as the eye could see, millions of dancing soldiers guarded us against the world.

'Clara, there's an old piano in the chapel. I doubt it has ever been tuned and the occasional key may make a peculiar noise, but you are welcome to play. There's also some music sheets of French tunes Paul and Françoise will know...'

The three of them bounced off into the chapel before he'd finished the sentence. Five minutes later, hollow-sounding notes and laughter echoed back, accompanied by renditions of *Frère Jacques* and *Alouette,* hardly worthy of a school concert, let alone the Albert Hall. Clara's other world seemed a lifetime away.

Rémy dispensed cold beer all around. Soon, crabs were boiling in an aromatic sauce and fish sizzling on his barbeque while I chopped bowls of fresh vegetables pulled from the field. We joined Clara, Paul and Françoise, swapping stories, singing in the chapel and listening to the beat of the rain.

We chatted for another hour until the three of them headed to their cabin as the rain eased, Clara still bubbling with fun and I guessed sleep a long way from their plans. More likely, stories about old people neither of us would care to hear.

Rémy and I settled into two comfortable rattan armchairs on his veranda, looking over the now monochrome fields under a serene moonlit sky, listening to the chirping of distant crickets in the trees.

'You can be proud of your daughter, Katy. The celebrated *mademoiselle* Clara Yehonala is not at all what I expected.'

'I am, though Clara is who she is despite my appalling parenting efforts,' I confessed. 'I could say the same about you, Father Rémy Aubert. I'd like to hear your story.'

'Oh, I'm simply an old, proselyting preacher. It serves my purpose to be thought worse than I am; I doubt I could get anything done without my reputation. A fine line between batshit crazy and Billy Graham, as the Americans might say. You can decide for yourself.'

He smiled, got up, returning a minute later with two glasses and a bottle of what looked more ominous than beer. He poured one each for us.

'It's late. We can talk now the others have gone to bed.

'Like your husband, I love this country and spent my childhood here, back when we French colonialists ran all of Indo-China. My family originally came from Montpellier, a city near the Mediterranean coast; they moved to Phnom Penh to run the family business after the Second World War. My father made his money as a merchant, timber and rubber mostly, and my mother was the daughter of Montpellier's bishop. An unlikely but happy match. After Cambodia's independence, we moved back to France. I was about ten at the time. I attended a religious school, eventually getting ordained and went on to study medicine.'

'Why did you come back to Cambodia?'

'Something about one's roots calling, I expect, or because Cambodia's a magical place. I came back as a missionary in the late sixties, working in a mission hospital in Phnom Penh for a few years before moving here to help the old priest, Father Aquinas, who built the original chapel.

'They were terrible times. The Americans secretly carpet-bombed much of Cambodia back to the Stone Age during the sixties and seventies, particularly Svay Rieng province. The Americans believed the North Vietnamese had their army bases here. When the bombers came, I remember old Father Aquinas and me cowering in tunnels with Khmer families armed with a bible and a prayer.'

'Why did you stay through all the horror?'

'It had nothing to do with heroics, I promise you. In those days, one could see and smell death everywhere. For too many, the war gorged on souls before they even had time to sin. I was scared out of my wits, but much work could be found for a doctor. When the Khmer Rouge took over in 1975, I went to the Thai border camps, helping the refugees fleeing Pol Pot. I didn't take sides and did what I could for the next four years. After the Vietnamese defeated the Khmer Rouge, I returned to Phnom Penh and helped set up missions to help the thousands of orphaned street kids. Later, I heard the Khmer Rouge murdered Father Aquinas, so I moved back to the chapel here in Prey Kam.'

'Do you know people spread stories about why you left?'

'People say what they please, it's not my concern, Katy. I'm a doctor and a priest and what better place could there be for a person like me to do God's real work? People needed food more than God after the devastation of the wars, so I studied agriculture back in Montpellier, believing we could grow crops and teach the farmers to survive.

'My parents had bequeathed money to the Agronomique de Montpellier University, so I convinced the *Conseil* to fund a work-experience program where students could do fieldwork as part of their theses. We've now got four farms like the one here around the poorest regions of the countryside. The old Velocette comes in extremely handy.'

'Elena once told me you know more about this country than almost any westerner. I'm starting to understand what she meant.'

'It's like a sword with two edges. People should know what this country has been through, but no one should have had to live through it. *Mais, c'est la vie.* Even now, there are legacies from those days, one of which I know led to your husband's death.'

I almost dropped my glass.

'What do you know about Simon's death, Rémy?'

'Did you ever hear of the Ho Chi Minh Trail?'

'Simon tried to explain it to me once. Something about it being a road the communists used during the Vietnam War, wasn't it?'

'Yes, but not like a normal road. More like a vast network of tracks, waterways and bicycle paths running from North Vietnam, through Laos and Cambodia, to South Vietnam, over the most mountainous and dense jungle terrain you can imagine. Believe me, I've trekked a good part of it in my time here. Along the trail came weapons and soldiers from communist-led North Vietnam to their supporters in the South.

'There were even underground hospitals and comfort stations for soldiers to hide from the bombs and, ah…restore their vitality, shall we say? The trail's an amazing human triumph with the physical and mental hardships the men and women faced on the journey and the main reason the North won the war.'

'Were you _?'

'I was on the victims' side, Katy. It didn't matter to me what uniform they were wearing.'

'Such a silly question, sorry. What's Simon's death got to do with what happened over forty years ago?'

'Naturally, the trail isn't used for those things today. Nowadays, it's the route for drugs from the Golden Triangle of Myanmar, Thailand and Laos, into Vietnam and Cambodia, where they find their way around the world through ports like Ho Chi Minh City and Sihanoukville. Not only drugs, the trail's open for human trafficking: children, slave labour, brides for women-starved Chinese men and so on. You can pick any number between forty and eighty billion dollars a year for its worth and it couldn't exist without high-level government corruption despite the authorities intercepting a lot. Various gangs fight for the trade, regularly betraying each other. What do they say, "no honour among thieves"?'

'Are you saying Simon stumbled across a billion-dollar criminal operation?'

'A nasty little corner of it.'

'You know what happened in Krong Chey, don't you?'

'Yes, I do, Katy, because I was there.'

I gasped as yet more became clear.

'So Rithy heard *your* motorcycle roaring away afterwards?'

Now Rithy's odd look when he heard Rémy's motorbike earlier made sense. He must have recognised the sound of the old machine and why he refused to leave us here by ourselves. I decided Rithy deserved his own medals for staying around to guard his babes-in-the-woods bosses.

'Rémy, I don't think for one second you're involved with those gangsters. But please, I beg you to tell me the truth about what happened. Don't my daughter and I deserve your charity?'

'Ah, you are unfair to demand charity from a priest in this manner, *madame*. Besides, the police have already arrested the man responsible. What more is there to tell?'

'You know perfectly well what more there is to tell. As you say, you were there. You know the official story isn't true the same as I do.'

I thought I saw a faint smile flit across his face. I decided to risk telling him what I knew.

'Clara and I have been to Krong Chey. We went there to find out about Simon's death. Unfortunately, the same person who betrayed

Simon gave away our visit too and we have since discovered who he is. The man who did kill Simon, a Vietnamese man who wears crocodile skin shoes, threatened us and some policemen beat up our friend Rithy. I'm sure the reason we're still alive today is solely due to Clara's profile with the Chinese Government.

'This man warned us we wouldn't be so lucky the next time we came here. So you see Rémy, we've put a great deal of trust in you by coming to Svay Rieng again. I hope you'll trust us the same way. And please don't tell the story of our visit to Krong Chey to another soul.'

'I've heard about the combative nature of you two. I see it's no exaggeration. Yes, you have my word, I won't mention it. The man you met? He's a Triad monster called Moloch Tran. Without a doubt, you were extremely lucky to walk away from your meeting without an acid bath or donating a part of your anatomy.

'Moloch Tran's the warlord who runs the border area around the Bavet crossing into Vietnam. A truly evil human being and yes, he's the one responsible for the death of your husband and the little girl. Other vicious men are running their territories along the Laotian and Cambodian borders, controlling all the illegal and a lot of the legal trade moving down the trail and across borders in the region.'

'I have three questions for you, Rémy. My first, who *is* the man they arrested?'

'I shall have to tell you a short story first, which will likely answer your second question. I'm assuming the second question is along the lines of how I know these things?'

'Could I have another one of these wonderful cognacs? I think I might need it.'

He poured another for each of us. I rolled the sweet, spicy liquid around my mouth, the smooth texture lingering in my throat, waiting for him to continue.

'I planned to offer you platitudes of what I knew about Simon. Like a preacher trying to soothe balm on a troubled soul, as we might say. I see now I've seriously underestimated you both.

'I met Simon several years ago at a gathering of westerners. I could easily have met him back in those days forty years earlier. I never did, though from what he told me, we were both in the same parts of the world at the same times. I might add we became friends, shared stories and believed similar things, except religious ones. Simon did not see God's grace in wars and what happened to children. I occasionally struggle with my faith too when the victims are children.

'I never saw a lot of him, though I greatly admired his work. He'd come down here and we'd get drunk occasionally and he'd stay over. I learnt about the work he did. The day he was killed, he called me about seven girls he discovered were being trafficked from Phnom Penh to Ho Chi Minh City.

'This particular group of girls seemed especially important to him. They were orphanage children, he said, and asked me if I could find out where they were before it became too late to rescue them. I advised him how dangerous it would be if Moloch Tran were the trafficker, which I believed likely. Regardless, he became quite insistent, so I reluctantly agreed to help him. I had a contact of mine talk to people around Bavet and I'm the one who informed him about the cellar in Krong Chey.

'On Saturday night, I learnt word of the rescue had found its way to Tran. I knew I must warn Simon but couldn't reach him, so I raced there on my Velocette, arriving in Krong Chey too late to do anything. I thought it best no one saw me and I left.'

'And the man they arrested?'

'He passed on the information about the cellar to my contact. Regrettably, he lost his nerve, confessing to the murder after Tran found out, deciding gaol might be a better choice than Moloch Tran's vengeance. He may be safer in gaol, I doubt it. God forgive me for saying so, but I wouldn't lose sleep over him, an evil criminal with plenty of blood on his hands. Tran assumed Simon must have been looking for the information, not me, as he was already known to them. Otherwise, I suppose I'd be in the river feeding the crabs now.'

'Now I understand why you came to the funeral.'

'Yes.'

'I see. I also understand what you do while travelling around the countryside with your farm project. Did you tell Simon about your secret work?'

He nodded.

'I won't press you on those things, so you won't have to lie to me. You're a brave man, Father Aubert.'

'Do you know why those girls were important enough to risk his life, Katy?'

'Yes, dear Rémy, I do now. Especially for one of them. Hers is a story for another time.'

'I feel her story is in good hands, *madame*. It's late, time for bed. Yes?'

'Almost. I still have my third question. How trustworthy is Martin Lewis?'

Rémy looked at me for a long time before answering.

'I trust Martin Lewis with my life.'

The smell of real coffee brewing woke me up. I opened my eyes, wondering where I was, following my nose to the porch where I found Rémy sitting by himself, gazing across the fields. The jungle and fields were violently green again, the sun shining and villagers already working in the mission's vegetable fields. The countryside sparkled in a storybook fantasy.

'Good morning, Katy. A beautiful morning, is it not?'

'A glorious one, Rémy. Where's Clara, Paul and Françoise?'

'They left early this morning to plant mangroves. I believe your daughter may be a convert.'

I joined him and we sat amiably together with our coffees, me unshowered and unselfconscious about my crumpled state. Twenty minutes later, Rithy strolled towards us with a half dozen villagers in tow, chattering and laughing together, looking like they'd enjoyed a memorably social evening. The village leader said a few words in Khmer to Rémy.

'He says your friend spent the night on a chair, keeping watch over the street with his beer and a large pistol, evidently expecting unwelcome visitors. It sounds as if you have the right man on your side.'

I smiled and turned to Rithy.

'Thank you for looking after us, Rithy. You can sleep for a few hours before we leave. Don't worry, we're safe here. And I know all about the motorbike.'

He smiled as broadly as ever before disappearing into the chapel, laying down on a wooden bench and promptly falling asleep.

'I'm sure poor Rithy rues the day he ever met my family.'

'There are one or two diplomats who certainly do, *madame*. Come, we can walk into the village and find a plate of local food. After breakfast, we'll walk to the river to find your daughter.'

24
IT'S ALL GOT A BIT OUT OF HAND...

5.43 pm

Dear Rémy
Thank you! Please visit Western Union in Bavet when you can. Show some ID and quote this number 4534776905. We hope it will help you in your noble work.
Cordialement, your friends Clara and Katy.
p.s. we want you to use some to improve your creature comforts.
p.p.s also use some to tune the piano for when we next visit.

10.37 pm

Dear Clara and Katy
God bless you both.
Rémy

'I had the most amazing time, Ma. The best, except getting up before the sun part was like being in a car crash. I've never been so close to real people like Paul and Françoise before. It's quite inspiring what they do and how much they love their life. I wanted to stay there. Well, you know what I mean. I know I couldn't really do it, but I'm going to do what I can to help. I already sent money to Rémy. Paul told me they struggle with no proper air conditioning in the cabins and basic things like appliances. There's not even a washing machine or a decent refrigerator.'

Clara and Katy were sitting on the balcony back at the hotel, freshly showered and pampered after roughing it in the countryside.

'You'll be an even bigger hit with them than you are already. I must say you look like a new person. I'll bet the mud, fresh air and river water did wonders for your skin. Or maybe the handsome young Paul Rocher is responsible?'

'*Shhh*, Ma. You're seeing every man I meet as breeding stock.'

Katy wondered if she could be right about her Chinese DNA rearing its grandson-seeking head. Clara wasn't getting any younger, after all. She told Clara all Rémy had talked about, including his comment about Martin.

'Well, I'm glad we've cleared up the Martin story. What do you think of those rumours about Rémy molesting children?'

'*Pah!* I don't believe them for a second and I shall tell Jim Preston the same. I'm going to ask him to write a story about Rémy Aubert and his mission in the countryside. Not the spying part, obviously.'

'Do you think Jim knows what Rémy does in his spare time?'

'He wouldn't have told us if he did, *baobei*.'

'No, I suppose not. Oh, I agree about the molesting bit. Speaking about Rémy and Sorensen in the same sentence, well… A good story would help his work a lot. We now also know who else Rémy's undercover work involves, don't we?'

'You mean Martin Lewis? You're right, which explains why they didn't get their stories straight about knowing each other. Martin must have always known the truth about who killed Simon. So why did he lie?'

'Unless they're both Mafia hoods, it must mean Martin, Rémy and God knows who else are working on something bigger than Dad's murder. Another good reason no one wants us making a fuss. It's all starting to make a lot more sense.'

'It does. My guess would be about drug-running from the Golden Triangle. If so, Moloch Tran may be on borrowed time, which is good news.'

'You might have to revise your opinion of Martin.'

'Even if he is a James Bond type, I won't forget he's lied to us regularly. And we still don't know if he's the one who's been rummaging through our suitcases. Never let anyone say I can't change my mind if I must, but your boyfriend has got a lot of explaining to do first.'

'For heaven's sake, Ma, I'm starting to lose count of the men you have queuing up for insemination duty.'

'Sorry. When I let on to Rémy about our visit to Krong Chey, he promised he wouldn't tell Martin about it, so Martin won't suspect we know he's been lying to us. I suppose Rémy will tell Martin we met. Let's wait and see what his next fairy tale will be.'

'What are we going to do now?'

'What we set out to do two weeks ago, *baobei*. We're also going to finish Chavy's story, be like Trappist nuns about spies and lies and stay as far as possible from billion-dollar drug lords. We also need to meet Jim and tell him about our meeting with Rémy. We'll have to decide later how *much* we tell him.'

'Do you think Rangsei is still at the orphanage?'

'We're going to find out. She may be the last one who still knows the secrets and if we're right about Chavy, she must be in great danger.'

'Then you'll be happy to know I have a plan. Hang on…'

Clara's mobile phone buzzed.

'Well, perfect timing. The call was from Elena. She wants to meet me at the Suki Soup shop tomorrow after work, around five o'clock.'

'I'll telephone Jim. We can meet him before you meet her and we'll ask him face to face if he told Simon's police chief friend about George Sorensen.'

'Well ladies, back from the countryside as freshly-minted religious zealots intent on saving my soul? I'll warn you first-up, as far as lost causes go, you'll have more luck with the Tassie bloody tiger today.'

'Aren't you a little ray of pitch black this afternoon? What's happened, Jim? Sophea run off with the postman?' said Clara, a grin plastered over her face.

'Not a good day to be a smart ass. I forgot her birthday. What is it with you damn women? You'd think I'd been caught in a brothel.'

'Forgetting a birthday's worse; you'll get no sympathy from us and your women troubles have barely started. But yes, Rémy Aubert did convert Clara and me, though not to God. We stayed there overnight and saw what he does in the villages.'

'Are you telling me he's doing indelicate things with farm animals as well?'

'Not funny, Jim. People should be singing his praises, not feathering him with tar.'

Katy told a grinning Jim about Rémy's work with his farms. Clara took up the attack.

'We think you should put the record straight about Rémy Aubert. He's his own worst enemy, yet he's got a story to tell about how he set up his farms and is helping those villagers survive across the whole province. People should know.'

'Hold on a sec, Clara. Before you decide to hand Sophea the nails to hang me up on a bloody cross, can I remind you Easter was two months ago? I wasn't even here when those rumours started. And, as you might recall, I never said I believed them. There were plenty of stories in those days about priests molesting small children, so my guess is when he magically disappeared to the countryside, people assumed there must be fire in the smoke.'

'Well, better men than you have been crucified for helping the meek, Jim. How about it?'

'I'll tell you what, it's not my beat, but I'll send someone down to talk to him. Happy?'

'Yes.' Clara smiled sweetly at him. 'And thank you.'

'No problem, you two practically run the *Phnom Penh Times* these days.'

'Oh, we're not finished yet.'

He rolled his eyes and ordered more coffee, waiting for the next broadside. Katy obliged.

'How much do you know about the drug trafficking from Myanmar down the old Ho Chi Minh Trail?'

'Quite a lot, it's hardly a secret. As my editor's not wildly excited about getting fire-bombed and I'm not overly keen to see how long I can hold my breath in the Mekong River, we don't publish much investigative work in *The Times*. We leave it to the major media players and reprint their stories, passing on what we can. We're reporters, not martyrs. We don't have the staff for major investigations; our drug stories focus on the victims, couriers and middle-level dealers in the street trade.'

'So it's a serious problem?'

'Worth billions. Why are you asking, Katy? I hope you two aren't planning to make your next quest exposing the drug cartels. The Vitara Orphanage pair are Hansel and Gretel compared to those bastards.'

'No need to warn us off, Rémy already did. We're not martyrs either.'

'Rémy? What's Rémy Aubert got to do with drug cartels?'

'Settle down, Jim. I don't mean scaring us off as Moloch Tran did. Rémy warned us about how dangerous those people…'

'Whoa right there, Calamity bloody Jane! I'm missing a page from this book I'm reading. Moloch Tran? What the hell does a Triad psychopath have to do with this?'

'You remember saying you thought Simon had uncovered the tip of an iceberg? Well, the man with the crocodile shoes we met in Krong Chey was Moloch Tran.'

'Christ Almighty! Katy, Tran's an evolutionary throw-back to the bloody reptiles. You better rewind and tell me the whole story.'

Clara and Katy explained about Rémy knowing Simon and how he'd discovered the information about the cellar in Krong Chey, deciding not to tell him about Rémy's other work around the border regions. However, for a man of Jim's investigative background, he quickly put two and two together. It took him less than five seconds longer to work out Martin Lewis' involvement and the reason for the fake story about the arrest of Simon's killer.

'This is the greatest story never to be told. Yet. Christ, you two, most amateur detectives are content discovering who pinched the silverware from the vicarage, not unwrapping the world's biggest criminal enterprise.'

'It has all got a bit out of hand.'

He roared with laughter.

'Clara m'dear, you have a delicately Chinese way of putting things.'

'Jim, we need to remember the two heroes of this story, Simon and Chavy, are already victims,' said Katy. 'We must make sure no one else gets hurt, especially Rémy Aubert. I hate to think what would happen to him if his undercover work ever became known.'

'All the more reason to write a human-interest story on him. I'll do it myself and speak to Alex Findlay, my editor, and bring him up to date. We'll need his help. Don't worry, Alex knows where more bodies are buried than ASIO does. He'll make sure Rémy's secrets stay hidden.'

'Can we include ourselves in the "no one else gets hurt" plan, please?' suggested Clara. 'And Jim, we want you to write another article.'

'Why not Clara, as I said, you run the bloody paper these days. What can I do for you this time?'

'We want to go back to the Vitara Orphanage and finish what we started – finding out the truth about Chavy's and my dad's death.'

'You mean how they both got from the orphanage to the Krong Chey cellar?'

'Yes. We think if we can find Rangsei, she may know. According to Dad's book, the sisters were close. She could still be at the Vitara Orphanage and may be in danger.'

'Okay, makes sense to me. What can the paper do?'

'When Elena and I were at the concert, she suggested I could sponsor a music program for Cambodian kids and offered to put me in touch with the Education Department. She also thought the Chinese Embassy and George Sorensen might want to help with a cultural exchange project. Before, you know, his…ah…'

'Murder?'

'I'm still getting over my rabid rat disappointment. Maybe we *could* get both the Australian and Chinese Embassies interested. I've thought about it more and it's a great idea. I want to do it because half the orchestra last weekend were Chinese musicians which won't change unless local children learn music. There's almost none taught in the schools.'

'What d'you have in mind?'

'You could say, "Clara Yehonala is offering scholarships for musical talent among underprivileged children and will be visiting several orphanages and so on", for example. A short article about what we're trying to do would make it easier to get in the door and meet the children. According to Dad's book, Rangsei speaks a little English. We might get lucky and find her.'

'*Baobei*, I have an idea. If we found Rangsei, it might be the time to tell Martin Lewis what we've found out. He'd know what to do about rounding up the owners, Simon's police chief and anyone else involved. After all, he's probably after the same people further up the chain.'

'Slow down, ladies, let's not put carts before horses. I think the music program is a great idea and I'll be happy to help promote it in the paper. Let's see what happens after you visit the Vitara Orphanage before you get Martin Lewis involved. We don't need you barnstorming around like a pair of pensioners at an all-you-can-eat buffet again.'

'There's one more thing.'

'I'm going to demand a bloody salary soon.'

'I can't think of a subtle way to say this, Jim. Did you tell the police chief about Sorensen leaving his villa on Saturday night?'

'What? Come on Katy, do you honestly think I'm responsible for getting him killed?'

'Since you ask, we'd be less surprised finding out you were a transvestite trolling around Street 136,' said Clara. 'You made a promise he'd never hurt any other little girls, remember?'

Jim choked on his coffee.

'Sorry to disappoint you two on both things. I can't deny it crossed my mind, but I thought if the AFP got him before anyone else, we might find out more about Simon's death.'

'Then who did?'

'I assumed the police chief had someone watching Sorensen's place after Rithy talked to him earlier.'

'Pretty unlikely isn't it, Jim? Think about it, if the traffickers wanted to get rid of George Sorensen, all they had to do was knock on his door and bye-bye George. As you said, they're not overloaded with scruples about these things. Why make it so complicated?'

'What's your theory, Katy?'

'Well, we know they did abduct him and dump him in the drain. Therefore, they must have needed a plan to get rid of George they could safely sweep under the diplomatic carpet. You know, to avoid awkward investigations which might trip over more than George the paedophile.'

'You think Martin Lewis gave Sorensen up?'

'I thought about the possibility, though after meeting Rémy and getting my ears scorched by Clara, I know that can't be true.'

'Sweet baby Jesus! You know what you're saying?'

'There are no other possibilities, Jim. No one else knew about Sorensen. Your Occam's razor again. It must either be the ambassador himself, or Martin's boss, Colonel Gray, giving the orders.'

Clara's eyes lit up.

'Robert Nelson didn't go to the concert on Saturday night when Sorensen got murdered. Elena introduced me to his wife; something had come up even though he intended to go, she said. Every other important westerner went as far as I could tell. Now, maybe an emergency did pop up on Saturday night in sleepy hollow. Pigs might fly too. No one else except us, the George-snatchers, Martin, the AFP and those two, knew about Sorensen the paedophile being mixed up with the Phnom Song house. And we can cross Martin and the AFP off the list of suspects.'

'You can also scrub Martin's boss off your list of crime lords.'

'Why?'

'Because Rémy Aubert isn't catfish food; Martin's told his boss bugger-all.'

'Besides, he spent the night at the concert drinking Scotch,' added Clara. 'The only thing Colonel Gray was murdering was his liver.'

25

AN AFFAIR OF THE HEART

I left my mother and Jim deciding what to do next after suggesting a bunch of flowers and some grovelling might pour oil on his troubled domestic waters. I admitted to my doubts about Jim buying into the grovelling bit.

My tuk-tuk is puttering along Sisowath Quay under the gathering storm clouds, taking me to meet Elena at the Suki Soup shop. How much I miss her occupies my mind.

She's waiting for me and kisses my cheek, an affectionate kiss. Her cheek lingers on mine before she pulls away. She's different somehow. I can't put my finger on it. Embarrassed? Her subtle perfume hangs in the air. I breathe it in, hearing her voice from a long way away.

'*Ciao bella,*' says she, greeting me. 'Sit down, a cool drink's on the way. I ordered when I saw you coming. How's Katy? Have you been reading the newspaper stories this week?'

I see she *is* nervous; she's talking too quickly. Unlike her.

'You mean about George Sorensen?' I ask.

'Who else?' replies she. 'Georgie's the talk of the town. You wouldn't believe the wild stories going around. You don't know anything about it, do you?'

'Me? How would I know anything? I read he got drunk, fell in a stormwater drain and drowned.'

'Except he didn't drink. Remember, I told you before.'

'Oh, yes, so you did,' I say, although I remember her telling me perfectly well. 'I suppose there could have been drugs involved and the embassy's trying to hush it up. I imagine the last thing they want are those kinds of headlines involving their diplomats. They aren't shy about stretching the facts a little when it suits.'

'What do you mean?'

'*I'd better be careful, Elena's instincts had found me out before*. Oh, you know, all the stuff about the new laws and keeping us away from the media,' I say as offhandedly as I can. 'We've met Jim Preston from the *Phnom Penh Times* once or twice. He says they couldn't care less what our opinions are about the new laws.'

'I always read the stories about you; you're quite the celebrity in town these days. I must say your version sounds more believable than Georgie being a crime kingpin or a Mafia whistleblower hiding in a witness protection program, to name just two of the current rumours.'

'I imagine hiding George Sorensen from anything would be a challenge, wouldn't it?' I say, both of us not quite suppressing our politically incorrect titters while checking the menu.

'I see there's a Chinese hotpot. If you trust me, I'll order for us,' I suggest. 'It's fun and will give us a chance to talk.'

'Sounds like exactly what we need.'

Within minutes, we have a spicy soup simmering and a luscious array of raw meats, leafy vegetables, mushrooms and seafood heaped on the table.

'I should have skipped breakfast and lunch,' says she, amused. 'Or at least remembered the last time we ate together.'

'And this time there's only two of us to eat it.'

'Yes, *bella*, the two of us.'

She sits quite still. I see she's thinking hard before saying anything else.

'I talked to Adriana last night.'

'Oh, please God, no.'

'We spoke for a long time.'

My stomach unsuccessfully struggles to digest the rejection threatening to make me retch… I gulp back a mouthful of saliva.

'I…'

'*Shhh*, please let me speak first,' insists she. 'Adriana's decided to stay in Somalia. I thought she might. It's the work she loves. I almost said, the work she loves *before me*, but I'd be unfair to her.'

'I'm sorry,' I reply dishonestly but fearing the rest of her story, 'I suppose…' I gag on another mouthful of saliva in my throat, '…I suppose you're leaving Cambodia to join her? *Is this my voice I can hear? I sound like a frog.*'

I try to prepare myself, attempting to straighten my sagging shoulders and shifting my bottom on the seat. We both pause. An awkward silence hovers between us.

'No,' says she, 'I'm staying in Phnom Penh. As I said before, her decision's not unexpected and we haven't seen each other for a year. We were very adult about it and agreed life must go on. Well, life does, doesn't it?'

She smiles, shrugs her shoulders.

'First, let me tell you about your music school plan and get the business side out of the way.'

'Okay,' I say, thankful for a reprieve and anxious to occupy my mind with something, anything, else. 'While you're talking, let's toss these ingredients into the hotpot and mix up our bowls of chillies and spices.'

I recall my jealousy listening to her speak of Adriana and my mind conjuring up pictures of them as lovers, imagining what they did together. It hurt, even made me sick, though I knew I had no right to feel hurt or jealous. From how she spoke about Adriana at Romdeng, I know this is a sincere relationship ending. Even so, I feel an ugly pleasure hearing the news, like a prison door has been thrown open and my chains cast off. Okay, don't say what you're thinking. I admit I'm not having my greatest empathetic moment.

'*What is she telling me?*'

'…in the morning, she's looking forward to meeting you.'

'Sorry, Elena. Who is? What did you say?'

'The Minister of the Education Department, Dr Chantou Heng,' says she. 'She wants to meet you and likes the idea of your music program. We've got an appointment with her tomorrow morning. In the afternoon, we're meeting the director of the Vitara Orphanage.'

'You're amazing,' I say.

'What you're doing with the schools is a wonderful thing,' replies she. 'And I want to help you. What you're doing with the Vitara Orphanage I'm not so sure about.'

'Sorry, I don't understand,' I say, pretending feeblemindedness.

'Come on Clara, I'm not a vegetable. Even after what you told me at Romdeng, I know there's far more going on you're *not* telling me. I hope you know I care about you.'

'What do you mean? *Yikes! My voice still sounds wrong. Get yourself together, Clara!*'

'For someone so bright, you can certainly be a bit dim. Don't you know?'

I can't take my eyes off her, nor dare to breathe.

'I know we've been getting closer, Clara. I've tried not to admit my feelings for you, especially to myself.'

'Please tell me.'

I breathe again.

She sits silently. I see her nervously swallow before she speaks.

'Clara, we… I'm not sorry Adriana and I aren't lovers anymore.'

'Neither am I.'

I betray myself, unable to stop my cheap, self-serving words spewing out. She stares at me. I reach over, grasping her hand.

'I'm so sorry. What a spiteful, hideous thing to say. Do you hate me for saying it?'

'No. I suppose I should. But how can I? I've made life hard for you by staying out of reach, even though I know about your feelings. I've been cruel to you and it's me who should be apologising. I should have sent you away or opened my arms a long time ago. I didn't want to send you away and I've agonised over opening my arms. The truth is, you've been incredible putting up with my pathetic lack of a backbone. The other truth is Adriana begged me to go to Somalia. I said no, a heart-stopping rush of braveness for a coward like me. A month ago, I wouldn't have hesitated for a second.'

'Because of me?'

'Yes,' whispers she.

'Did you tell her about me?' I ask.

'She asked if I had someone else after we finished our conversation.'

'What did you say?'

'I said I was in love, but I hadn't told the person and doubted it would work out because I'm too much of a mouse. She said she wanted me to be happy and hoped it would. I said I hoped so too.'

'Are you sure about me?' I ask.

'What I didn't say to Adriana was when I talked to you the first time at the embassy, you frightened me. I saw the point of my life - I can't think of another way to describe the feeling. Maybe more like my soul had been alone and I just found out for the first time that…. I felt a longing for you tearing through me, which needed the courage of a lion to reach out for and I knew I wouldn't survive if I lost it afterwards.

'You scared me because you know I'm not brave where my feelings are concerned. Let me ask you the same question, Clara. Are *you* sure about what you're doing? You may not be able to turn back; I'm not always easy to be around. I think I'm kind and loving…I have my moments.'

She laughs. Not loud, under her breath.

'I think it may be the Italian bit,' I say. 'I have experience.'

We smile across the table.

'Yes, you told me before. Now you can't use the excuse I haven't followed the rules about fair warnings.'

'No, I won't be able to say you never warned me, will I? I'm not sure,' I tell her. 'Not yet. I'm scared about what I'm feeling for you, in case you hurt me.' Then I add truthfully, 'I'm even more scared because I don't care if you do.'

Our eyes meet.

'What if I asked you to come home with me?'

'What would you like me to say?'

'I want you to say you will. I want you to say you want to be with me as much as I want to be with you.'

'How peculiar life is, thrusting its momentous decisions on us without at least a week's notice.'

I feel a vague fear and a lucid certainty. I realise my life is going to change forever with the next words I say.

'I'll willingly come home with you, Elena. To your bed and into your life. If you'll have me.'

The rain begins to tumble down, a steady rain in the still air, not the torrents of other evenings. We're standing outside the Suki Soup shop with the umbrella up. Trickles of water are running off the edges of the canopy. Elena is looking up and down the darkened street for a tuk-tuk.

'No, Elena,' I hear myself say. 'I want to walk each step of our first journey under my own power. I want to hold your arm and walk home in the rain. I don't care how far it is.'

She looks at me, understanding my meaning and smiles. 'It's this way. Give me your arm, it isn't far.'

Fifteen minutes later, we turn down a tree-lined laneway and pause under an orange streetlight.

'We're here. This is where I live.'

The lane is washed as glossy as a magazine cover under the streetlight's glow and alive with uncountable rain splashes. They play soothing music, bouncing off the umbrella and the ground, a natural melody as beautiful as any concert. I hold out my arm to let the cool drops splash on my bare skin. I look at her modest villa, overgrown with tropical greenery and watch the rain dribbling from beneath the guttering and dripping off the leaves in the garden.

'It's gorgeous. Exactly as I pictured your home would be.'

Perhaps it isn't normal to love a rainy evening so much. I do as we hurry up the path, huddling together under her umbrella.

Passion simmers inside me. My inhibitions and my ache for Elena are at war with each step. She unlocks the door and we step inside, removing our wet shoes and sliding our bare feet into comfortable slippers.

'I'm not practised at this sort of thing,' I say stupidly. *Yikes! Is there a right word for this moment? At least a better one than practised?*

'I mean…sorry. I know my words sound silly, even to me. I don't want to sound silly. Except for Max, I've never been with anyone. Please don't worry, I'm where I want to be. I'm where I've always wanted to be.'

'I…Let me make you a cool drink,' says she.

'Wait a moment,' I say, touching her arm.

I step closer to brush her hair from her shoulder so I can smell the rain on her skin.

'Please kiss me first.'

'I promise I won't ever play games with you again,' says she softly. Perhaps the words are meant for herself.

I hear her words anyway. My nerve ends are exquisitely sensitive to her fingertips caressing my face. Our lips touch. I open my mouth slightly and feel her tongue almost imperceptibly caress mine. Her breasts brush against my blouse, sending a prickle of electricity rippling through my body. I shiver.

'Why did you decide to come here tonight, *bella*?'

Her voice is affectionate. Full of love.

'I'm not brave enough to tell you yet. My hangups are waging war inside me, fighting against what I want to say.'

'Any words will do. Tell me. Please.'

'I would have let you have me on the table in the restaurant and not cared,' I say to her, surprising myself with my boldness. 'I came because I want to feel what it's like when you make love to me. I've had these feelings for you since we first met. I've tried to push them away, I suppose because of Adriana, or maybe Max. I want to forget my taboos so I can feel you intensely. I know if it wasn't you, I couldn't do this because I'd feel ashamed and slutty, but I don't feel this way with you. There's a madness in me,' I tell her. 'I feel gloriously naked for the first time in my whole life....'

Flustered, bashful, I stop the rush of words and stare at the floor, breathing hard, sure I've exposed too much.

'What will she think of me? Oh shit, why did I have to say slutty and that I'm mad?'

She lifts my face with her hand, fixing her gaze on me.

'Please don't stop, *bella*. I'm not only hearing your words; I'm listening to you with all my senses,' says she, a compassionate smile creasing her face. I see her eyes are glassy.

'You cannot imagine my joy when you asked me to come home with you, even with all my hangups and desires fighting their battles. I know I love you with a tenderness I've never known before and there's a fire raging inside me. Will you have me for a little time tonight?'

She kisses me again, softer, longer than before.

'Yes, sweet *bella*. Even for an hour, if an hour is all you'll give us.'

'Will you be in love with me, Elena? You can pretend if you're not. I won't care.'

'*Mettere le catene al vento, amore…* not loving you tonight would be trying to put chains on the wind.'

'… the drink. Please? I can't breathe.'

We sit down opposite each other at the breakfast bar. I look around at Elena's world, my world too, for a little while. She smiles across the space between us.

'I'll stay the whole night if you want me to,' I say.

'I can't bear the thought of you leaving,' replies she.

She watches as I send a message to my mother, telling her I'll be staying at Elena's villa tonight and for her not to worry.

'There, it's done.'

'Yes. I have my clothes for you to wear tomorrow.'

'Will they smell of you?' I ask.

'I expect so.'

'I want them to.'

'It's your turn to kiss me.'

'I may not be as gentle as you,' I say.

'I don't care, *bella*. You can kiss me however you like, wherever you like.'

'I'm going to try. Being with anyone is so new to me. I'm not afraid or nervous about being here now. I am worried I'll disappoint you because I'm not very X-rated and I don't know how to be,' I admit to her, 'and because I don't want you to mistake my ineptness for unwillingness. I'll try to please you like your favourite piece of music pleases you, getting into your soul and playing over and over.'

'You came home with me, *amore*. How could I possibly be disappointed?'

'Will you let me undress you? I want to. Slowly. And…' I say, amazing myself, the words come so easily, 'and I want you to undress me, in the light, so you can see me. I want to shower with you. I've never done those things with anyone before.'

She takes my hand and leads me into her bedroom. I look at the bed with the pillows thrown in a jumble of pastel colours on the pale sheets. A place I'll sleep in Elena's arms tonight and I'll feel her skin against mine. I squeeze her hand. My heart is beating like a drum. I'm certain she can hear.

She turns on the shower and stands in front of me. I kiss her neck, breathing in the subtle notes of sandalwood on her skin. I undo the buttons of her shirt, nervously at first, peeling the silk over her shoulders, letting it slide to the floor. Her eyes follow my hands when I unhook her bra and slip off the straps.

'Kiss them.'

'In a moment.'

I let my fingers comb through her hair. My fingertips trail over her face, follow her cheekbones, trace the line of her nose, each curve of her neck, her bare shoulders, her breasts. I am a sculptor marvelling over a finished masterpiece. She takes my hands and kisses my fingers, one by one. As naturally as breathing, I draw her nipple between my lips, feeling it grow hard in my mouth. I bite it delicately. She shivers.

'Yes, *amore*,' breathes she to me.

'An artist crafted your breasts,' I tell her. 'They taste of you. Tonight I'm going to taste all of you.'

I stand back, free of embarrassment. I open my arms, inviting her to undress me. Mesmerised, I watch her fingers undo the top button on my blouse, the second one and the third. I can hear my heart thudding against my chest.

'Hurry,' I beg her.

'No, *amore*,' says she, teasing me. 'I want to enjoy you, like I'm unwrapping my gift.'

I shrug myself free of the fabric as the last button escapes and kick away my slippers. Her arms reach behind me and unhook my bra; we both look down at my uncovered breasts. My cheeks burn pink, but I feel only the excitement from Elena's pleasure in my body. She pulls down my skirt and underwear. I lift each of my legs so she can remove them from around my ankles. For the first time in my life, I'm standing naked with another person in the light.

'You are a flawless, marble figurine, *bella*,' she tells me.

'My body and my heart are yours, Elena,' I tell her. 'Touch me all over, anywhere you want. I won't stop you or have any regrets.'

Now her tongue is flicking my nipples and I cry out in joy as they respond, hard and ready for her. Urgently, I unzip her skirt and pull her underwear down. We face each other. She reaches down and picks up our underwear, giving hers to me. I hold them to my lips, savouring the thrilling scent of her body. I step back. I want her to look at me standing under her gaze. I'm feeling blissfully uninhibited.

'You're almost too lovely to touch,' she tells me. 'You make the space around us magical.'

My arousal is making me tremble. My breath comes in gasps. I step into the shower, my arms outstretched, waiting for her.

'I'm going to wash you and pretend to myself you're Ming porcelain,' I hear her say.

Her soapy hands massage my neck, my shoulders, my breasts

and move lower. Unbidden, my legs part slightly so she can caress the skin inside my thighs. The water streams off our bodies. She kneels and my hands press her face into me. I cry out as her tongue and fingers part the coarse texture of wet hair to discover the swollen lips buried beneath, then I lose myself in erotic sensations I never dreamt possible.

'Enough, my darling,' I say later, gasping for breath. 'Now it's my turn.'

Afterwards, we dry each other and lay naked on the bed, our faces centimetres apart on the pillows.

'Well. That was…*um*… better than I expected.'

Elena lifts her face from the pillow to look at me.

'Not too bad for a beginner,' says she. 'You've perjured yourself wickedly about the X-rating.'

She smiles, and we both burst out laughing. She moves her hips against me. I can feel her damp heat on my thigh when she leans forward to kiss me, as lovingly as a mother would a child. She lets her lips rest against mine.

'I want to wake up and feel you lying next to me,' says she. 'Just like this.'

'When you wake up, I'll be here as close as I can be,' I promise her. 'The first thing your eyes will see.'

I roll onto my back and turn my eyes towards her.

'Tonight Elena, you must enjoy me. Do whatever you want, anything at all. I don't even care if you hurt me.'

'I'll never hurt you, *bella*.'

'I want you to.'

I roll over onto my stomach and draw my knees up, exposing the curve of my cheeks to her.

'Smack me,' I tell her. 'I must show you I love you enough and you must show me. I'll leave if you don't do it.'

'Please don't force me to hurt you, *bella*, I beg you. I can't.'

'You must. Do it, my darling.'

She brings her hand down and I wince as her slap stings my soft flesh.

'Now harder. Five times. I want you to slap me there as hard as you can. If you don't do it hard enough, I'll make you smack me again and again until you do.'

Each one burns like fire and I feel her anger and despair. I bite my lip hard so I can't cry out. When it's over, I turn on my back. She sees the tears in my eyes and my trembling lips and buries her face in my hair.

'*Oh, mio dio!* What have I done?'

'I'm ready to give you all of me now. I've won the war raging inside me. Now I want you to make love to me and teach me how to make you happy.'

I lift her head and push her mouth onto my breasts.

'Bite them gently, then harder until I call out. Don't be worried,' I tell her kindly. 'I'll stop you before you hurt me. I want to experience every imaginable pleasure with you.'

I push her face lower, nerves in my body tingling with the sensation of her wet tongue tracing a meandering journey down my stomach.

'I'm dripping wet between my legs. It is okay for you there?'

'*Shhh.* You taste divine.'

'Please let me taste myself too,' I say to her.

She puts two fingers inside me and into my mouth. I lick off the salty wetness and arch my body into her face, closing my eyes and groaning in ecstasy. Her tongue and fingers probe deep inside me and a few seconds later I convulse in a shuddering orgasm.

'Too fast, don't stop,' I tell her urgently. 'I'm ready, do it again.'

Afterwards, panting and spent, I pull her back and taste my first ever orgasms on her lips.

'I want you to teach me how to do the same to you.'

She lays back, spreading her legs wide, guiding my tongue, first with her fingers, until I learn what she wants. She wraps her legs around my shoulders. Eagerly, I abandon myself to Elena's most intimate place, letting her wetness smear my face and my tongue flick her delicately. She squirms and sighs beneath me until the spasms I experienced earlier shake her body. The warmth of her orgasm floods into my mouth.

'I want to do it again,' I tell her.

'Yes, *amore*, again,' urges she.

Afterwards, we are holding each other, the steamy smell of sex on our faces.

'I'm not going to clean my face tonight,' I say to her. 'I'm going to wake up next to the woman I have loved with all my heart, still covered in you.'

'*Ti amo, Clara mio,*' says she, stroking my cheek. 'Let's sleep as close as we can to each other. This night I'm so fiercely in love with you I want to remember every sensation too.'

I close my eyes and fall asleep in her arms, my first experience with a woman and being in love burned into my soul.

26

THE MORNING AFTER

The sun had barely risen and shone low through the dusty bedroom window, painting her skin and tousled hair in a hazy circle of light. I gazed at the beautiful woman sleeping next to me and remembered the night before, anxious to wake her yet not wanting to break the spell.

Elena's naked body rose and fell faintly with her breathing. I marvelled at her flawless olive skin and the contrast with mine, an almost magnolia white. We were cappuccino with cream. I couldn't resist touching her, letting my fingers trace the rise of her breasts, over her stomach, stroking her skin with my fingertips. I reached lower, letting her hair tangle around my fingers.

'Your hands feel nice. Please don't stop. Are you happy?'

'*Qin ai de, wo shifen gaoxing.* Blissfully, my darling.'

She turned towards me and reached out to stroke my cheek.

'Do you want me to touch you?'

'Yes, please. Not now though, I'm enjoying myself too much. Do we need to get up?'

'We still have two hours.'

'Good. I'm not ready to end our night.'

I put my arms around her, pressing my body against hers. She held my hand against her breast and looked at me. I leaned forward and kissed her, breathing the taste of our earlier lovemaking. The same passion for Elena's affection stirred inside me.

'I could make love this way each day of my life and never tire of you.'

'Is this how you are with Max?'

'Ohmygod, no! With Max, I'm panic-stricken getting undressed with the light on in front of her. I can't do it. Sometimes I've been naked with her, but only in the dark. Even then, I take off my pyjamas before I get into her bed when I can tell she wants me to, or if she asks me. I've never woken up naked beside her. Or with anyone except you. I don't think she's even seen me undressing in the light or walking around, unless accidentally in the bathroom. I'm too embarrassed and wear pyjamas. We lay together, we kiss and Max touches me with her hands. It's nice, but not like you do and never inside me. I touch her and kiss her breasts. Not desperately, like a lover, like I am with you.'

'I'm sorry.'

'Don't be, my darling. Last night with you was more intense than I ever imagined. Had I known I could love anyone like this one day, I would have happily waited with no regrets about missed chances.'

She put her arm around me and I snuggled in closer, laying my head on her shoulder. We looked at the ceiling together.

'Have you ever been with a man, Elena? I don't care, but I do have a reason for asking.'

'I did once when I was nineteen. We had sex a few times. My family wanted to see me married and producing a herd of grandchildren, which was more than likely since we're card-carrying Catholics.'

'What was he like?'

'Adonis,' replied she, highly amused at the memory. 'He played football, still does. He's a big star now, what we Italians call a *prima donna* and makes millions of dollars a year, last I heard. Alessandro was the same chauvinist egomaniac both on and off the football field, always groping, telling me how to live my life, what to do, what to wear to impress his friends. I had to be Elena the bauble and him, Sandro the Christmas tree.'

'What happened?'

'After three months I told him if I needed advice on how to live my life from someone who chased a ball I'd ask Chichi, our family dog. So, *ciao ciao* to my virginity and Mamma's grandchildren.'

We dissolved into hysterics.

'He didn't think it quite as funny as I did,' said she, the tears rolling down both our cheeks.

'What did your parents say?'

'Oh, they still haven't forgiven me. My parents believe marriage is to be endured, not enjoyed. My mother calls me *pazza* now - crazy woman, not Lanie like she used to. She still shows me the sports pages whenever I go home. I joined UNICEF after I finished university and left home to work in child protection in Calabria. Quite fitting in a cryptic sort of way, now I think about it. I discovered I liked women and eventually met Adriana about three years ago when we both worked in Syria.'

'Lanie?'

'Yes, Lanie's their pet name for me. Or used to be. They only called me Elena when they were cross with me.'

'May I call you Lanie? The name has a beautiful sound, like music. Would you mind?'

'I'd love you to. I always felt cherished when my family did. Well, how about you, *bella*?'

'How about me what?'

'Have you ever had sex with a man?'

'No, never. I'm still pure as the driven snow. Well, more or less, no thanks to you, Ms Accardi. I've only ever had two men kiss me and put their hands on me, each with different degrees of enthusiasm. One was a racing car driver I met at a party; he seemed to believe every activity was a Formula 1 race and we made it as far as the sofa in my hotel room. I decided one lap of the circuit was enough, so no chequered flag for him. The other was a musician who apparently couldn't believe his luck and I was almost bored to bed, so I could sleep through it. That was as close as I ever got to sex. I put both experiences down to market research and champagne.

'The reason I asked you about boyfriends was because Martin Lewis invited me on a date, and I went out with him. Nothing, you know, *happened*. I wanted to tell you I'd been out with him and I had a nice time. I know he likes me. Do you mind?'

She smiled, shaking her head. 'Who can blame him? I saw how he looked at you at the embassy. I've never seen him tongue-tied before. He must have saved up all his courage to ask you out.'

'I didn't make it easy for him. Still, he should have known better than waking a girl up too early to ask her anything requiring a decision. This is nice. Is this how you and Adriana were together?'

'Chatting as friends? Sometimes we'd wake up this way. Not always. Other times we did different things.'

'What different things?'

'Last night not enough for you?'

'I don't intend for you to get away with seducing me once, especially as we have two hours left. I did say you could do anything you wanted and I can think of a place or two you haven't been yet. You're not going to cheat me, are you?'

I looked at her and lifted an eyebrow.

'Don't give me your doe-eyed, docile look, Clara Yehonala, I'm not the only guilty one in the seducing department.'

'So Lanie, what else did you do with Adriana?'

'Are you sure you want to know?'

'Yes, no need to be coy, even if it's pornographic. I'm not jealous of Adriana. We're lying naked together and I'm with the woman I loved last night in ways I never believed possible. And just so you know, I'm going to taste you again before we get up.'

'Go into the bathroom and bring back what's inside the drawer.'

I got up and looked around; she must mean this drawer. I opened it and stared at the contents. Gingerly, I reached inside.

'Did you find it?' called Elena from the bedroom.

'I found something…interesting.'

'Bring it here.'

'You played with this together? God, it's huge. What does it feel like? You know, inside?'

'Wonderful. Even better when two people play together and watch each other. Use it on me first. We can try it later with you if you like. The best part is we won't have to flatter its ego or listen to it snoring afterwards.'

'This is seriously sexy. Show me what to do.'

The most sensual feeling ran through my hands as we rubbed a slippery lubricant along the shaft, imagining it must be what a man's penis feels like sliding between my palms. She guided my hand as I eased it inside her, my heart beating as wildly as the vibrations on my hands as I slid it deeper and deeper inside her body, moving it around as she told me. I watched her face. She closed her eyes and gripped my arm. Her sighs became louder. She kissed me urgently, pressing me tightly against her body. With a shuddering sigh, she fell back, panting heavily.

'Ohmygod! Ohmygod! Ohmygod! I got so excited knowing you were holding it and watching. Did you love watching me?'

'I loved seeing you so out of control. I'll die if you don't put it inside me and watch me, too.'

'Lay back.'

'I've never had anything inside me before.'

She reached for a tissue.

'No. No, don't wipe it. When you slide it into me, I want to know it's you inside me too.'

I watched, my finger hovering over the panic button and insanely aroused as she guided the vibrating toy between my legs. Instinctively, I tensed my body at the first push.

'Breathe, my love. I'll be slow and gentle…'

I exhaled. She slid it inside, filling me. I gasped with exquisite pain and lost myself as the pulses rippled through me, bringing my nerve-endings to a sensitivity I knew would soon overwhelm me. She moved it slightly a second before I lost all control.

'Patience, *bella*. Better if I make you wait.'

She teased me twice before I pleaded with her.

'All the way, Lanie. Please, now, I beg you, deeper. Tell me you love me.'

'*Ti amo, Clara mio*. You are so beautiful. I'm watching, you can let yourself go now.'

I raked her back with my nails, crying out as my pent-up rapture burst out in a primal scream.

'Oh, my darling, did you see me squirm? Did you enjoy me out of control? Did you hear me scream? I was afraid I was being torn apart.'

'More?'

'Oh, yes, please. Not now, though, or I don't think I'll ever walk again. Next time, show me what you did to make it last so long so I can do the same for you. I won't care if you scratch me.'

We were across the breakfast bar from each other, sipping cappuccinos after showering together and dressing for the busy day ahead.

'You look a million dollars in my clothes, Clara. Better than I ever do.'

'Thanks, they smell of you. You have great taste in clothes. I wish I'd been born Italian. And I feel fabulous, not just because of the clothes. I don't suppose we have time for a quick visit to the bedroom before we leave?'

'*Oddio!* Don't you ever have enough?'

'Not as long as you and I are the ones doing all these wonderful things to each other.'

'Our one-night stand?'

'A girl's allowed to change her mind, isn't she? Besides, technically, it's still our one night. I'm sorry about your back. You're lucky I have pianist nails or you'd be needing surgery.'

'My own fault for teasing you for so long. We don't have much time. Come around my side of the kitchen and sit on the stool. I'm sure two smart women can think of something quick and fun.'

I unbuttoned her blouse and unhooked her bra, letting my tongue run wet circles around each of her nipples. I loved hearing her sigh with pleasure.

'In case you're interested, Lanie, I'm not wearing underwear this morning.'

'You're going to make us so late, *bella*.'

'Depends how quickly you get started. I'll even lay on the kitchen benchtop for you to make it faster. I guarantee you won't need more than a minute or two.'

'I've never had sex in my kitchen; I suppose we should fix the gap in my resumé.'

'Yes, you never know when it might be important. Be gentle though, because I'm a little sore. And don't forget, there's still one place your tongue hasn't been. I hope you're not going to disappoint me. A pretty please? I want to experience *everything*. I promise to pay you back later.'

'What are we to do, *amore*?'

'Well for one, I want you to take care of me, my darling, like I want to with you. Teach me how to love you.'

27
IT'S BEEN QUITE A DAY

I called my mother to let her know we'd be visiting the Vitara Orphanage and were on our way to meet the Education Minister about the school pianos program. I assured her I'd be home after we'd been to the orphanage. I'd worry about my story later.

We barely made it in time to meet Dr Heng after hasty makeup and clothing readjustments. Elena outlined our plan and afterwards, the Minister introduced us to one of her senior staff who would be our contact. Rotha would meet with the larger schools in the major cities and come up with a list of six we could work with as a first step in what we were calling my Pianos in Schools program. After taking photographs, we left. Overjoyed with our success and oblivious to bystanders, I threw my arms around her neck.

'Thank you, thank you, thank you, Lanie. You were superb at talking about the program. I could never have explained it the way you did. There will be so much to do. I'm so excited I can hardly talk.'

I hugged her arm, grinning like the village idiot as we walked down the street.

'You know, whenever Dr Heng looked at me, I imagined she knew precisely what we'd been up to this morning. All I could think was it's a good job I looked normal. *Yikes*, I hope I looked normal. Did I?'

'Don't ever play poker, *bella*. Let's walk down to Sisowath Quay for an early lunch, you and I have a few things to talk about.'

Beneath my smile, nervousness took hold, like an unwanted guest moving in.

'Our one-night promise to each other is over, Lanie. Do you still love me?'

'Yes, *bella*, with all my heart. I've loved you for much longer than one night already. I want it to be enough. It isn't.'

After last night, why is she hinting about saying goodbye? A wave of panic washed over me, wiping the remainder of my smile off my face.

We found a café and sat down at a long bar at the window overlooking Riverside Walk. Too afraid to say anything, I gazed out across to the Mekong River, its bustling trade, and studied the passers-by.

'This place has a nice Italian menu. Let's share a *fritto misto* and *bruschetta*. Would you like me to order?'

I nodded, concentrating on my chilled lime juice.

'You've gone quiet, Clara. You were so happy about the meeting five minutes ago. What's wrong?'

'Are you going to say goodbye to me? Are you going to break my heart today?' I could feel my lip trembling and bit hard so I wouldn't cry.

'*Oh cuore mio, neanche per sogno!* No, no, no. Where did you get such an idea?'

'Because when we were walking down the street, you said loving me isn't enough for you. I know it's your perfect right to disown me, but I think I'm going to cry, or else stamp my feet like a stupid little child. You promised you'd never hurt me.'

'Dear Clara, if you think I'll give you up now without a fight, you're sadly misinformed about the Accardis. We have Mafia connections. I hope I won't need to call on them.'

I dabbed my eyes on my sleeve and forced a smile.

'I'm sorry to be so childish and fragile, I don't know where all this fear comes from. Or maybe I do. My passions for you frighten me, for more of you, not less. I don't know what I'd do if you left me now.'

'Let's share this wonderful-looking bruschetta and take a deep breath, shall we? You and I are not going to be saying goodbye if I have anything to do with it, so you can forget that silly idea. You'd be better off preparing yourself for more kitchen benchtops and heaven knows what else.'

'I'm up for anything you have in mind. I even have ideas of my own.'

'I'll need to renew my gym membership. First, I need to be serious about what I meant when I said it isn't enough.'

'Okay, I'm as ready as I'll ever be.'

'Clara, I can't imagine hiding anything from the person I love. If we share our lives, you must tell me what is truly going on with yours. I can't and I won't, live with you if you keep secrets you're not willing to share with me. I don't mean personal secrets like stealing a chocolate bar when you were ten years old or waking up in a strange bed once or twice. I couldn't care less about those things. I mean secrets to hurt you or us if we were together. I would never forgive you if you got hurt and you never told me you were even in danger.'

'We Yehonalas aren't great at sharing secrets, only keeping them; I can see how cruel and unfair it would be. Also, I want to tell you when I made you hit me last night. I needed to show you how sincere I was. I'm truly sorry, Lanie, to hit me or leave me must have been an awful choice for a person like you. I'm a bit of a mess, aren't I? Please forgive me.'

'There's nothing to forgive, *amore*. We both found out how far we would go to prove our feelings. Let's agree we've proved a point to each other.'

'Yes, I like your idea. I know my bum will appreciate it, too.'

I smiled at her.

'Let's cross off one sex game we don't need to play again.'

I touched her hand, sure I never wanted to leave this woman's side. Love simple and pure, intense and kind.

'Now I'm ready to tell you everything. Well, except for one little thing to protect a brave person from harm, though I daresay you'll work it out anyway when I tell you the story. From now on, I promise I'll never hide anything from you.'

The story took more than an hour. The Pink House, the Phnom Song house, Chavy, our visit to Krong Chey, Moloch Tran and the truth about my father's murder, the real George Sorensen, why the Vitara Orphanage was so important, Jim Preston, Martin Lewis, as much as I dared about Rémy, my mother's visit to Kampot, today's visit to find Rangsei. I left out no details and answered every question. Even our suspicions about Robert Nelson. She stared aghast at me.

'You must stop making up horror stories, Clara. You'll give yourself nightmares.'

'Have I scared you away? I won't blame you if you run for your life and be done with me, which may be good advice, by the way. You can't say you haven't been warned either from now on.'

She turned towards me and kissed my cheek. I turned, so her lips met mine. I ignored the people walking past on the street outside who peered at two women kissing briefly and lovingly in the window.

'After your story, I wish I did have Mafia connections. Why do the women I fall in love with have death wishes?'

'I'm a piano player, Lanie, caught up in a quest to find out who killed my dad. I'm not heroic like Adriana, I promise you. I'm scared to death of what might happen to my mother and me if things go wrong, but we won't stop until it's over. I need you to understand I won't stop, no matter what you want. Even if you beg me to.'

'I understand about family, *amore*. I'll never be so selfish as to come between you and Katy and I'll help you any way I can. Are you sure about loving me? I should also warn you I have a temper like an Italian fishwife.'

'As long as you want to make up again afterwards in time-honoured ways, I won't mind too much.'

'Why me, *bella*? Why does a person as famous and beautiful

as you want to be with someone as ordinary as me? You could have anyone in the world you wanted.'

'Excuse me, Ms Elena Accardi, I do have the only woman in the world I want, or hope I do. And you are the most not-ordinary person I'll ever know, even before I count the mind-blowing… other stuff.'

'*Bella*, you know my UNICEF work is important to me. Would it bother you if I said I'd be very uncomfortable sharing the glamorous side of your life? I'm not someone who enjoys the spotlight.'

'Lanie, I don't live my life like a rock star and I expect you'll be disappointed when you see how simply I choose to live. Hopefully, you'll find out soon enough. I live for my music and since I learnt of Dad's work, I spend a lot of time raising money for kids with concerts and you know about my charity work in China and how we support Rebecca's mission work here.'

She looked at me, slowly nodding her head.

'You and I aren't different at all in what we value, Lanie. It's part of why I want to be with you. I can't explain the rest well enough at the moment. The rest is about being naked. I don't mean just my skin, although the naked part is more important than you might think. I mean wanting to expose my emotions, hangups and neurotic twitches to you, for only you to see. I have lots buried under five thousand years of demureness training. As you've already discovered, I'm a pretty messed up girl and I expect you'll regret loving me, but I'll never regret loving you. One day I'll be able to explain better and I'll share it with you. I know right now, I can't get enough of you. I'd probably have sex with you in the middle of Sisowath Quay this afternoon if you asked me.'

'Be careful what you wish for, *bella*; I'm one second away from asking you. I adore you.'

'You're going to make me cry again with a big word like that. I know I adore you too. I'm willing to risk everything to be with you as your partner, your lover, your friend. I know we won't always be so erotic and out of control, and when we end up not making love on the kitchen counter one day and settle for less, I'll still be content. At least I won't get friction burns on my bum.'

'Settling for less might be easier on both of us. How about Max? I won't share you with anyone. I'll be very selfish about being the only lover in your life.'

'It won't be easy telling Max. Later, I'll tell you the story about how she saved my life when I was fifteen years old, so you'll know why she's important to me. Even my mother doesn't know the story. She never will. I'll also tell you why I'll never tell her.

'I hope Max will understand she's giving me my life back a second time. If she doesn't, I'll walk away and I'll need time to mourn her loss. I hope you'll be patient with me if that happens. I promise I'll never blame you. I want Max to remain my friend and my manager. If she does, you'll need to accept sharing me with her, not as a lover, but as my friend who I owe a great deal and who will know me better than you do, at least until you and I grow closer. I don't think it will take a long time.

'I also love her family in Montalcino. They treat me like their daughter and I hope I won't lose them. Do you think you can live with the feeling you might be in second place sometimes? I promise you never will be and it's my one difficult request of you. Oh, and to tolerate my bitchiness when I have my periods.'

She laughed.

'I'll double my usual order of potato chips and ice cream. At least you're not asking me to join the Illuminati, which I was half-expecting after hearing your story. I suppose without Max, I wouldn't have you at all. I can't promise not to get jealous, but I'll try to admit it to you if I am. Perhaps Max and I might become friends one day, so she knows I care for you as much as she does.'

'You mean you're still interested in me? You're tougher than I thought. Or softer in the head.'

'I told you never to underestimate the Accardis. Even our stupidity is boundless. Clara, there's one way I'm not so strong. Well, to tell the truth, there's a huge, long list of them. I know you'll be going back to your other life sooner or later, more likely sooner. I don't want a short, intense love affair, no matter how wonderful it is, I'm not made that way. I couldn't bear to love you like I want to and see you go away.'

'You know as well as anyone nothing's sure in life, my darling. I don't want to lose you one day either, but I'd rather take what's here now instead of worrying about what might, or might not, happen because I'm scared of tomorrow. I'm going to stay with you until you don't want me anymore, then I'll fight you like a tiger so we can stay together. If I'm not here, I'll only ever be a phone call and an aeroplane ride away. And with the music program and charity, we'll be living here together whenever I can.'

She paused for a long time before replying.

'I have one more thing to ask you.'

I took a breath, knowing she'd saved the best till last. Facing all my fears and insecurities had already taken more courage than I owned. I knew what must be coming next.

'I'm ready.'

'Will you tell Katy about us?'

I looked into the hazel eyes of the beautiful woman I loved.

'If you give me permission, I'll tell her about us today.'

'Do you want me to be there with you?'

'God, yes. My perfect coward's way out. Except I know this is my mountain to climb. Trust me, I'm ready to be brave. I didn't feel brave enough with Max, I do about you. I'll also take you to meet my dad and Chavy Pham soon because you need to meet all the people who make me who I am.'

'I'm taking a week's holiday next month; I've already planned on going home to Trieste. If no one's murdered us, or we haven't strangled each other, will you spend time there with me if you're not busy?'

'You'll take me to meet your family?'

'Yes. I could never tell them about Adriana, they'd have carted me off to the confessional promising the flames of eternal hellfire for my mortal sin. I will tell them about you. I no longer care about *Nonna* Accardi's hellfire and damnation. Well, to be truthful, I'm telling a big, fat lie. But after what you've been through, facing the Accardis will be like a bicycle ride along the Amalfi coast.'

'I'll be proud to be there with you, no matter what they say.'

'Will you come home to me tonight after you talk with Katy? I want to hear the story only Max knows.'

'Yes, my darling, I'll come and I'll tell you.'

'We'd best be on our way to Phnom Song. I'll phone my driver and we'll get out to the Vitara Orphanage. Don't we have a little girl called Rangsei to find?'

After the stories, what they'd learnt and what she expected, the Vitara Orphanage didn't look dark and full of foreboding as if copied from a Dickensian novel. Clara felt no nervous anticipation, more the anticlimactic feeling when you've returned from a holiday and pulled into your driveway at home.

Were the ghosts locked away from view? Or was it having Elena by her side? After watching her in action at the Education Ministry, Clara knew she could manage any situation in an orphanage now they were on her home territory. Clara looked at Elena, marvelling at the woman she had spent last night with. Not a lover now, more like an Amazon on a mission.

The Vitara Orphanage had once been quite grand, an impressive three-storey home in another life, back when the French were in charge. Now it showed the ravages of Cambodia's history, the gardens replaced with what could have been dormitories, classrooms and storerooms and a high wall ran around the perimeter. Along one side, children made souvenirs they were busy selling to a dozen or more Chinese tourists from a minibus in the car park.

In the playground, the children looked happy, running around dressed in bits and pieces of whatever had been donated, some clothing almost too threadbare to hold together. A dance class practised in another corner of the compound, the children in traditional Khmer dress. No doubt both were to entice visitors to donate money or to impress the UNICEF lady.

'Well, they seem on their best behaviour, don't they?'

'I'm thinking the same thing.'

'It always happens when UNICEF visits. It's all a pantomime. The nice dolls see the light of day when there's an important visitor or an inspection of some kind. These places get worried we'll give them a bad report and their donors will think twice next time the requests for money come around.'

'I feel being a pianist is living in an alternative universe.'

'Don't give up your music, *amore*. It's what I'm counting on to keep me sane – well, plus a few other things. Come on, let's see what Mr Victor Le has to say for himself. He speaks English but leave most of the talking to me; I deal with these people all the time,' said she smiling, undoing the second button of her shirt. 'Keep your eyes open for anything unusual, but try not to look like you're suspicious.'

They walked into the old mansion. Here, the feeling fitted the pattern of Clara's orphanage. The space stood more ominously, like it had chosen solitude for itself, as if the present inhabitants were a luxury it didn't need or want. Behind their open doors, two large ground floor rooms, she supposed for boys and girls, contained iron bunks stacked two high, each littered with a technicolour mix of pillows, sheets and towels - the unmistakable flotsam and jetsam of children - set against drab, pale green painted walls. Ceiling fans whirred silently.

The floors had once been highly polished parquetry before decades of shoes, the movement of furniture and neglect had scratched the varnish away. An unmistakable sense of disquiet permeated the building as if it waited for exuberant life to enter and meet the ghosts. Clara imagined with a spring clean and fresh flowers, the house might be rid of the odour of dusty, humid air and enjoy the luxury of its children, the playful spinning of their skipping ropes and their shrieks of laughter. Instead, she paused to listen for whispers of the lost souls from the first occupants who lived here, buried long ago in the brick memory.

Here the dolls lying around had no hair, or a few wiry, straggly strands, or hair painted on. Others were missing an arm or a leg where other children had played with them in the past and pulled a limb out of its socket, never to be found again. Not like the nice ones the children held in the playground.

Elena and Clara ascended an impressive mahogany staircase and found the director's office. Victor Le quickly got to his feet, a broad smile on his face, offering a warm handshake and a not well-disguised glance at Elena's cleavage.

'Welcome, Ms Accardi. I'm delighted to meet you and intrigued by your call earlier. Have a seat. What can I do for UNICEF?'

Victor Le looked Vietnamese and a man Clara wouldn't pick as someone committed to a life of caring for the unfortunates of the world from a line-up of such men. He didn't look much pleased to see them either, though did his best at pretending otherwise.

'Mr Le, let me introduce Miss Clara Yehonala.'

'My pleasure, Miss Yehonala. I know you from the stories in the paper. I'm sorry to hear of your father's death. A terrible thing to happen.'

'Thank you. Fortunately, the police did their job and those responsible were arrested, a great consolation to my family. We're now getting our lives back to normal.'

'Good, good. Now, what's all this about a music program, Ms Accardi?'

'Mr Le, no doubt you read in the newspapers about Miss Yehonala setting up a music program in schools here; the Minister of Education recently approved the program for six schools around Cambodia. When Miss Yehonala first envisaged the program, she also had in mind to award ten music scholarships to underprivileged, talented children. She approached UNICEF to ask if we could recommend some orphanage children to be included.'

'I see. Why the Vitara Orphanage?'

'Miss Yehonala is insistent the orphanages have a good reputation. We gave her a list of those with unblemished records, which included the Vitara Orphanage. She asked to visit each one, so I'm introducing Miss Yehonala to you all, over the next week.'

'Well, we're honoured to have your seal of approval. However, we don't have the staff to manage a music program.'

'I understand,' Elena went on, leaning towards him. 'There wouldn't be much to do except help identify talented children. I know you have a theatre and teach traditional dancing here. Perhaps we might look for musical potential there?'

'I suppose it might be possible.'

'If the Vitara Orphanage did have a child selected, you would be included in the media releases for the program and appear in the promotional material and newspapers. I'm sure your donors would be impressed.'

Clara noticed the last part got his interest more than anything else Elena had said.

'Mr Le,' added Clara, 'I would be mentioning all the orphanages whose children received scholarships to the media around the world and I'd visit from time to time for photos with the children.'

They chatted together for the next fifteen minutes, mostly about how the orphanage might benefit from being involved.

'Well, perhaps we could help you discover if we have any talented children here. Our priority is always the children, isn't it?'

'Indeed it is, Mr Le. We won't take up more of your time now, except to ask if you have time to show Miss Yehonala and me around to give her an idea of how the orphanage works. We're so pleased you're prepared to consider the program for your children.'

'I'd be delighted to do both.'

He followed them down the staircase; Clara noticed his eyes never left Elena's hips. They walked around the buildings, Victor Le smiling and making happy gestures to the children while explaining the educational, cultural and skills opportunities the Vitara Orphanage meted out to its fifty-three orphans. Also, not failing to mention the struggle to keep the place going with no funding from the government. Had Clara not known of the darker aspects of this place, she would have been digging into her pockets.

'All the children look well-nourished and happy, Mr Le. I think

Ms Accardi brought me to the right place. I'll look forward to coming back to talk to you again.'

'You'd be most welcome. Perhaps a photograph next time?'

'Yes. Tell me, do any of the children speak English or Chinese? I'd like to meet one or two of them.'

'No, they're all children from broken homes, nearly all from the countryside. Sad to say, we don't have the funds for any language education.'

'Mr Le, a young child is sitting over there by herself,' said Elena. 'She's not playing with the others. Is she not well?'

'Occasionally, the children find the adjustment to orphanage life difficult. She isn't very talkative. We're trying hard to help her settle in.'

'I'm sure you are. Why don't you show Miss Yehonala the entertainment area? I'll talk to the poor little thing for a moment. I speak a little Khmer and I'm a qualified nurse. Perhaps I can help.'

'Ms Accardi, we have a nurse who attends the children regularly. There's no need for you to trouble yourself.'

'It's no trouble. There have been outbreaks of meningitis and tuberculosis in orphanages recently, so I'll need to have a look at her, in any case. It wouldn't do to have a problem here with something contagious and have to quarantine the orphanage. Best to be safe.'

'Yes, yes. As you wish.'

Clara and Victor Le continued the tour while Elena spoke to the child, feeling her forehead, checking her throat and looking as much a nurse as Florence Nightingale at Scutari. Clara saw Victor Le observing them both as he showed her around. After about five minutes, Elena came back.

'Do you know if she's eating well, Mr Le?'

'I'd need to ask the supervisors; I don't manage the children's diet.'

'She seems to be malnourished, as well as lethargic. I noticed some discolouration in her throat as well. It may be nothing, but I'm going to have one of our UNICEF doctors check her tomorrow. Best to be sure.'

The Girl in the Orphanage

'I don't think a doctor's visit will be necessary, Ms Accardi.'

'Mr Le, I hope I won't need to insist? Don't worry, UNICEF will meet the cost if you're concerned.'

'No, the cost doesn't bother me. The welfare of the children is our first concern, always.'

'Good, that's settled. Miss Yehonala, this is how to run a good orphanage. Children first.'

'I'll look forward to coming back and talking to Mr Le more next week and meeting some of the children.'

'Mr Le, thank you so much for your time and for showing Miss Yehonala and me around today.'

They said their goodbyes and headed back into the city.

'Who's this "Miss Yehonala"?'

'Pretending I barely knew you was the hardest part.'

'Well, it seems I scarcely know you either, you never told me you were a nurse. Got any more surprises for me?'

'How about this one? I don't know the first thing about nursing. I didn't need to be clever clogs to work out he didn't either.'

'From what I could tell, he seemed more interested in your breasts and your bum than your nursing skills. Can't criticise him for his good taste.'

'Well, lowlifes like Victor Le are easy to manipulate with an ego massage.'

'Plus, an extra button left undone didn't hurt. So, are you going to tell me why were you so interested in *that* little girl?'

'Can't wait. I've been bursting to tell you for the last fifteen minutes. I may not be a nurse, *bella*, but I know what a traumatised child looks like. It's one of the skills this job gives you. I met Rangsei Pham today. I couldn't risk telling you at the orphanage.'

'What? Ohmygod Lanie, you're the brains in the team. What are we going to do now?'

'First, I'm dropping you off at the Park View and then I'm off to UNICEF to talk to Daveed Khan. Daveed's a doctor and a friend and I'm going to ask him to take Rangsei to a hospital so we can talk to her. Daveed will tell Victor Le a scary enough story to release her to him.'

'How did you know she was Rangsei?'

'A moment of inspiration. I remembered Victor Le saying to you none of the children spoke English, so when I started examining her, I spoke to her in English. She almost answered before stopping herself. I told her I'm a friend and asked her why she looked sad.'

'What did she say?'

'She confessed how scared she was because they're sending her away soon, as they did her sister. I simply asked her if her name was Rangsei Pham and she nodded. I told her I'd come back tomorrow and bring a doctor to see her and asked if she could be brave for one more day.'

The thrill of finding Rangsei almost overwhelmed Clara, although she conceded her joy became somewhat muted after Elena dropped her at the Park View. She took a deep breath, feeling disembodied, standing in the street outside the hotel. The concierge gave her one of those polite smiles people save for the doomed.

Luckily, she'd composed a perfect plan to tell Katy about Elena. Basically, she'd decided to give Katy the great news about Rangsei and see what dregs of courage remained; she admitted to herself her well-thought-through perfect plan might benefit from a little more work. The lift went much faster than she remembered on other occasions. Her phone buzzed.

'*Thinking of you. I bought chocolate xxx.*'

She smiled, gathered herself and stood outside the door waiting for the courage which never comes to anyone waiting outside a door. Taking a deep breath, she went in feeling a mix of excitement, dread, anxiety and bravado. Well, to be fairer to the truth, not much of the latter. Katy looked relaxed sitting on the balcony, feet up, nursing a glass of wine. She poured one for Clara.

'Hello, stranger. Are congratulations in order for your music program?'

'Yes, Ma. The Minister's going to help us launch the program in six schools. Except the music program isn't the huge news.'

'What's happened?'

'Ma, it's so incredible and I couldn't wait to get home to tell you. We found Rangsei!'

Clara went into minute detail about their Vitara Orphanage expedition and how they had managed to find Rangsei, prolonging the inevitable second conversation as long as possible. She finished by telling Katy how Elena had arranged for a UNICEF doctor to get her out of the orphanage.

'You've found her. Oh, such unbelievably wonderful news, *baobei*. I've been trying so hard not to give up hope. Did you say *the doctor*? What's wrong with her? Is Rangsei ill? We must get her into the best hospital straight away. What can I do?'

'No, no, don't worry, Ma. She'll be going to an excellent hospital and she's not sick. Elena thinks she's just hungry. We had to pretend she was sick so the doctor could see her. Once she's safe, we can talk to her and decide what to do next.'

'What's Rangsei like? Is she like Chavy?'

'I'm not sure. Quite small, I'd say. Maybe nine or ten years old. We both had to be careful not to be too interested in the kids in case Victor Le, the director, got suspicious. I only saw Rangsei sitting down with Elena while she pretended to check her for some disease or other. She distracted Victor Le by getting him to show me around the orphanage.'

'Does Jim know?'

'Not yet. We'll tell him when we meet tomorrow.'

'*Gambei!*'

Katy and Clara toasted their success and sat down together, looking over the balcony at the Mekong River, one of their favourite views of Phnom Penh, discussing how they might look after Rangsei.'

'Let's have one more glass of wine.'

'Great idea, Ma... *I'm going to need it*... Exactly what I'm thinking.'

Clara got up, sucked in a big breath and started pacing guiltily around the balcony.

'What is it, *baobei*? Has something else happened?'

'Ma, I need to speak with you. If I stop now, I'll never be brave enough again.'

'Can I get you anything?'

How about a bucket to vomit in? No. No, it's nothing like you're thinking. Last night, I slept at Elena's house.'

'I know, you tol…'

'No, Ma. Last night I slept at Elena's house. With Elena. In her bed. I love her. I'm sure I have since we first met. She loves me too. Are you disappointed in me?'

There, she'd said it. Not in the calm, confident, mentally rehearsed statement of purpose she planned, more like opening a can of Coke after shaking it up. Silence followed. Katy looked at her for a lifetime. An eternal five seconds. Clara's mind imagined a dozen scenarios, from disappointment to anger, even amusement. Instead, Katy smiled.

'I suppose you're imagining eviction, disappointment, anger, shock, plus a few other parenty things?'

'To be honest, I hadn't considered eviction. Pretty much the rest. You won't, will you?'

'Will you please stop flitting around like a wandering ghost. Sit down here, my baby, next to me.'

Clara slid timidly into the chair by Katy's side, inspecting her feet.

'You know, if I rewound the clock twenty-five years or so, I'd be sitting where you are, facing Mama. I expect the thoughts in my head at the time were the same as in yours now. I had to tell her I was pregnant and unmarried which, as you might guess, is on page one of the Yehonala capital crimes manual. The worst part, back then, meant if the local family planning Nazis found out, they would have carted me off for a forced abortion; we would never have lived down the shame.'

'What happened?'

'Well, you're still here,' said an amused Katy. 'She'd already guessed about my pregnancy. She told me "mothers always know these things about their daughters". She must have been right because now I'm a mother too, and we do.'

They smiled at each other.

'We have your *laolao* to thank for the fake marriage plot so I could keep my precious baby. Far from a burden, she said, her grandchild would be a gift. And you are, Clara, the best gift of all. You took our breath away the moment you were born and you still do, every single day. Mama called you a spring day in December snow; she lived an extra few years because of you.'

'I had a lot to live up to, Ma. But unless I missed one of my biology classes in school, you know I can't give you your grandson. You keep hinting about grandchildren. I'm sorry, I have never, ever, wanted to disappoint you.'

Katy shrugged.

'You could never disappoint me, Clara. And grandchildren? They're a matter for fate to decide, not for people like you or me. Are you sure you'll be happy with Elena?'

'I know we haven't known each other long, but I know without a doubt we are right for each other. I believe I knew the moment we met the first time at the embassy. She was the same. I'm going to work hard at being happy with her. Except for you and Dad, she's the only person I've ever loved. I want to be with her for as much time as will be given to us. I hope it will be more, not less. It would be easier with your blessing, Ma.'

'When love comes, what are we to do? You'll follow your heart as I did with Simon and as your *laolao* did. It wouldn't matter if I gave you my blessing or not; we Yehonala women prefer to make up our own minds. I approve with all my heart. Be happy, my baby. I'll welcome Elena into our family with open arms.'

'Would Dad have approved?'

'Oh, yes. Right now, he'll be smiling like a toothpaste advertisement. You have no idea how often he told me he worried whether any man would ever be good enough for his incredible daughter.'

'I suppose this is a novel solution. We had lunch together today at Sisowath Quay and we talked about things I never imagined sharing with a living soul. I told her about what we were doing because I don't want secrets between us. The conversation about me ended up being enormously hard. She's good for me Ma, and she's good to me. You'll never need to worry. You have no idea how quick-witted she was at the Vitara Orphanage this afternoon. We would never have found Rangsei without her.'

'I'm still so excited about Rangsei. We'll all talk more about the Vitara Orphanage with Jim tomorrow. Now, go to Elena. I imagine she's worried sick about what you're going through here with your ogre-mother.'

'She wanted to be here. To support me. I told her this talk with you is my own mountain to climb.'

'She sounds like she loves you the right way. I'll confess, I also never thought anyone deserved you, but I'm pleased to admit I'm mistaken.'

'I'll go after you hug me and tell me you love me. This is so new to me; I'm going to need you more than ever.'

Katy put her arms around her daughter and Clara knew she would be okay. She pulled a tissue from her pocket and dabbed her mother's eyes.

'I love you, Ma.'

'Well, I must say I don't often have two miracles presented to me in one day. Hurry now, don't forget your suitcase.'

Seconds after knocking on the door, it opened. Elena stood there, looking uncertain; Clara had forgotten to call in her hurry. She looked down and saw the suitcase.

'There's enough in there for more than one night. I'll need to rearrange our closet.'

'Yes, for now. We'll need a bigger villa, not straight away, but soon. Our home. So I can play Chopin's love songs to you on an old piano. Will you mind?'

'No, *amore*, I won't mind. Tell me, what happened with Katy?'

'She's on her way over here as we speak, with an axe, and is going to feed small portions of you to the catfish in the Mekong River. She said to tell you if you think you can steal her daughter just because you love me as much as I said you did, you're getting off lightly.'

'I'm glad it went so well.'

'You were right. I should have known. I'm glad you're the one I broke the news to her about and not Max. I hope you'll enjoy getting to know her.'

'You'd better come inside out of the rain.'

'It's raining?'

'You're drenched.'

'Will it involve getting undressed and showering with you?'

'I expect so. But not yet. After I dry your hair, make some pasta and pour a glass of wine for you. I mean, for us.'

'Don't forget the chocolate.'

Clara picked up her suitcase and stepped through the door. It had been quite a day.

Fifteen minutes after Elena and Clara left the Vitara Orphanage earlier in the day, Victor Le had another visitor. This one wasn't offering goodwill; his personality didn't stretch to such niceties.

Moloch Tran's vehicle parked where they had and the two men greeted each other as colleagues. Shortly afterwards, a tourist minibus with a trailer pulled into a parking bay along the wall. Another man stared intently from across the street, feeling a knife in his gut slowly being twisted. He pulled out his phone and anxiously called a number.

28

COMING OUT

My first morning.

I sat up and studied Lanie, sleeping touchably next to me. All the world went on pause in my quiet moment. I was experiencing a wordless joy. I beg each moment, *'stay, please stay a little longer'*.

Last night had been more intimate, without the urgency of wanting too much before our allotted time expired. The night had been more talking than gymnastics. Except once, after I finished telling Lanie the story only Max knew. I pleaded with her to ignore my tears because they were happiness ones and we made love, the tenderness unimaginably beautiful.

'Waking up next to you is like changing from one dream to a better one.'

She stirred, turning towards me.

'What did you say, *bella*?'

'Nothing much, my darling. Just mumbling to myself.'

'I've got an early start today, so I'll need to get a move on. Daveed and I are going to the Vitara Orphanage first, then I have a few internal meetings. Best I shower by myself or I won't get out of here before lunchtime.'

'We're meeting Jim Preston at three o'clock in the Fresco Café. Will you be able to come?'

'I'll meet you there. Are we going to tell him about us?'

'Jim has a mind like a mousetrap. With the colour in my cheeks and the cloud of estrogen billowing around us like the next monsoon, he'd pick it in a second. Trust me, always best to be on the front foot with Jim Preston. Besides, my mother will never be able to keep her mouth shut about us.'

'Should be a more fun meeting than my others.'

I slipped one of her baggy t-shirts over my nakedness and by the time she'd dressed, I'd mastered the espresso machine and filled the kitchen with the smell of freshly roasted coffee. Our first breakfast of cappuccinos, mixed fruits and yoghurt, seated across from each other at the kitchen benchtop. Companionable lovers. The same benchtop we…well, you know…

'I could get addicted to you, *bella*.'

'Just as well, because I'm not going anywhere. But you are. I'll see you at three. Good luck today.'

After she left, I wandered around, running my fingers over the furniture, taking in the Lanie-ambience of my new home. I opened the closet in the bedroom and unpacked my suitcase, filling drawers and racks with my clothes, putting personal items alongside hers in the bathroom, breathing in her smells. I cleaned the kitchen and made our bed, arranging the pillows, first one on top of the other, then neatly overlapping each other, finally throwing them haphazardly in seditious disorder.

'*Much better.*'

My phone buzzed. Rangsei was safe, the message accompanied by an affectionate one. I sent a risqué reply. Who would have imagined? I showered, dressed and hurried off to the busy Russian Market and on to the Ratana Plaza, two places Lanie told me she usually shopped for the Italian food, fresh fruits and tomato varieties she loved. After stocking up our refrigerator and cupboards with my Italian and Chinese grocery treasures, I flagged down a tuk-tuk for the short ride to the Fresco Café.

Clara arrived at the same time as Elena and they strolled inside arm in arm to join Jim for coffee.

'You two look disgustingly chirpy this afternoon.'

'Like fleas on a dog,' agreed Clara with a cheesy grin.

'Oh, for Christ's sake, don't tell me the two most beautiful women in Phnom Penh now both play for the other team.'

'See what I mean, Lanie? Mind like a mousetrap.'

'Another day of mourning for the men in Phnom Penh. Where's the bloody justice in the world?'

'I've met Sophea, Jim. If justice existed in the world…'

'Okay, okay, I got lucky. And congratulations, couldn't be happier for you. Every day's like bloody Christmas with Clara and Katy around. I take it this is one headline you *don't* want splashed over the front pages of the world's tabloids tomorrow morning?'

'Personally, I'd be thrilled if you did Jim, although I hope you'll care about our privacy. And whether you're eager to replace George Sorensen on my rabid rat list?'

Jim roared with laughter. An uncertain Elena looked up as Katy joined them, thoughts racing around her head and feeling like she'd had more caffeine than oxygen. Katy produced a large bottle of wine, a better than passable bearhug and an ear-to-ear smile.

'Katy, I hope you've prepared Elena for life in the Yehonala Women's Revolutionary Army?'

'Are you mad, Jim? Do you think she'd be here if I had?'

'Smart move. Always best to apologise later.'

'They haven't met *Nonna* Accardi yet,' said Elena, surprised to hear the relief in her voice. 'Then we'll see what these Yehonalas are made of.'

'Jim, I've told Elena everything except about Rémy. Though as she's smarter than all of us, no doubt she's worked it out already.'

'Hardly a qualification for Mensa. Also nice to see domestic bliss hasn't blunted your fangs. Which reminds me, we've been speaking to Rémy Aubert and I should have my story out next weekend. People will think he's the reincarnation of Francis of bloody Assisi instead of a lecher.'

'I'm glad. Thanks.'

'No problem. Okay, what happened with you two birds of paradise at the Vitara Orphanage yesterday?'

Elena recounted their visit. She explained she and Daveed had been to the Vitara Orphanage again today and Daveed had convinced them Rangsei may be contagious and needed to be in hospital for tests. Daveed had promised to call Victor Le tomorrow, letting him know the results.

'What do we do with Rangsei now?' asked Clara. 'Can we find a residential care facility for her, maybe even with Rebecca?'

'It's a bit more complicated.'

'Why? Don't worry, money won't be a problem.'

'No, it's not money. UNICEF can't simply barge into an orphanage and remove a child without a good reason. The children are the responsibility of the orphanage. We'd need their permission.'

'Even one as dodgy as a five-dollar Rolex from the Russian Market?'

'Unless we can prove Rangsei's in danger, even one of those. Don't forget, we've just told them they're part of Clara's music scholarship program because they're supposedly squeaky clean; we can hardly claim they're unfit to look after children.'

'Can I adopt her or apply for foster care?' asked Katy.

'You can and I'll be happy to help with the paperwork,' said Elena. 'It's not quick, though. Besides, we know she has parents in Kampot, so I'll need to argue her parents have abandoned her before anyone will agree to foster care or adoption. We can keep her in the hospital for two days according to Daveed. In the meantime, I'll try to think of the options.'

'Katy, if you do try to adopt her,' said Jim, 'and we assume they know Rangsei is Chavy's sister, you'll be back on Moloch Tran's birthday card list, along with the rest of us, including Rangsei. Which, in passing, is more likely than you think.'

'What do you mean?' Katy and Clara played in stereo.

'Well, I haven't mentioned it yet. Now might be about the right time.'

'For God's sake Jim, this *isn't* the right time for another one of your scenic tours around the English language,' said Clara. 'Do you think we might take the freeway today?'

'Fifteen minutes after you two left the Vitara Orphanage, Victor Le had another visitor. Moloch Tran.'

'*Santa madre di dio!*'

'Couldn't have said it better myself, Elena. Now, before we think about getting the hell outta Dodge, there are things in our favour.'

'*Ma ya!*' gasped Katy, a look of near panic on her face. 'In our favour! Do you mean like a passport and a credit card in our favour? You haven't met this man up close and personal. Clara and I still have nightmares.'

'Let me finish, Katy. It may not be as bad as you think.'

'Nothing could be as bad as I think right now, Jim. You know what he threatened to do with us?'

'Listen, ladies. Moloch Tran's territory is around the border crossing at Bavet, not Phnom Penh. It's also a three-hour drive; he was already on his way long before you turned up at the orphanage. Rithy also told me two other men arrived soon afterwards in a minibus with a trailer, so it's unlikely he knew you'd been there. If he did, you can bet he would have been there earlier to say hello. Instead, they drove off together in Tran's SUV, leaving the minibus in a parking area.'

'Victor Le might still tell him me and Elena had been there.'

'He might. But your school music program's been in the newspapers and there's no reason for him to suspect you know anything about the orphanage's history.'

'Jim, you said Rithy told you?'

'Yea, I worried about you and Clara going there, so I asked Rithy to keep an eye on you.'

'Oh, Jim. We'll all be thinking there's a heart buried in there instead of a fire exit if you're not careful.'

'Hate to see a Hallmark Moment killed off so soon, Clara. I guess I'm the last of the great romantics.'

'Your secret's safe with us.'

'Ladies, I think the time has come to call in the cavalry. We're now seriously and I do mean seriously, out of our depth. Whatever Moloch Tran left at the Vitara Orphanage in the minibus and its trailer, it wasn't Jaffas for the kids. I'll call the AFP liaison officer, Melinda Gauci, and get in her ear tonight, away from the embassy.'

'How about talking to Martin Lewis?'

'I'm not convinced he's who he says he is, Clara. Did you get Victor Le's business card?'

'Elena did.'

She handed it over to Jim.

'Did you say Melinda Gauci? asked Katy. 'She came to my home in Melbourne to tell me about Simon. I'll come with you.'

'Lanie, let's see if we can get Rangsei to talk to us.'

'I'll phone Daveed. He speaks Khmer better than me.'

29

MEETING MELINDA

Daveed gave his summation of Rangsei's condition to Elena and Clara.

'I've got Rangsei on a glucose drip; we should have her feeling better by tomorrow. Physically, she's suffering from malnutrition. She says there's enough food at the orphanage, but she's got no appetite. There are a few other things as well.'

'Like what?' asked Elena.

'First, the good news: there's no sign of any infection. Now for the not so good part. I've given her a thorough medical examination and it's obvious to me Rangsei's taken antidepressants, Valium or Xanax, which with the other things, it's as well you got me involved. Her pupils were quite dilated when I first saw her. They're back to normal now and she'll be back on her feet in no time. However, getting her back on her feet might not be such a good thing.'

'Why not?' asked Clara.

'The poor kid's been raped, I'd say regularly. Not recently. She's healed now. At least physically. Psychologically, thank God that's not my field, more yours, Elena.'

Clara drew in her breath, gripping Elena's hand.

'She's no more than a...Can we talk to her?'

'Yeah, she's awake. Given what's happened to her, she's

remarkably cheerful. Ten-year-olds can break your heart with what they can deal with, or what they can hide away. I don't know which one is true with Rangsei.'

'Will you help with translating Daveed? We must find out what's going on at the Vitara Orphanage.'

'Sure. No stress, though. I'll call a halt if it looks like it's too much for her.'

'Rangsei, this is Miss Elena, who you know. The other lady is Miss Clara. Do you feel strong enough to talk to us?'

'Yes, Doctor Daveed, I'm fine now.'

'Rangsei, you remember you told me about your sister Chavy yesterday? Can you tell us more about her?'

'She's gone away now, Miss Elena. She went on the bus, the same one that comes each month for children. They said she went to another orphanage. But I know she's not in another orphanage because Chavy would never leave me alone. She's never coming back again.'

'Rangsei, can you tell Miss Clara and me what happens when the bus comes?'

'Other children come to the orphanage and they all leave on the bus the next day. They come from different orphanages, one girl from each. Mr Victor takes one girl from our orphanage to go with them, too. They have a glass of milk, which makes them sleepy.'

'Rangsei, I'm Miss Clara. Can you tell me if your sister ever met a western man called Mr Simon?'

Rangsei turned and looked hard into Clara's eyes.

'We both know Mr Simon. He brought Chavy home to Kampot a long time ago after he rescued her from the pink-coloured house. He also visited us at the orphanage each day for a little while. He doesn't come there anymore.'

'When did you last see Mr Simon, Rangsei?'

'He came the next morning after Chavy left. I told him she went on the bus. Chavy told him about the bus because she once overheard the men talking. Mr Simon knew it came to take the girls away each month to Krong Chey.'

'Do you remember about the big house your family sent you and Chavy to when you left Kampot?' continued Clara.

'I will never forget the house. When we got there, Chavy made us run away. We found ourselves at the orphanage after we got lost and we slept outside till they found us in the morning. Before Chavy left on the bus, they sent us back there to see the fat man, Papa Georgie. Mr Victor laughed about two sisters going together. Chavy fought with the fat man to try and protect me and later he told Mr Victor about Chavy making trouble. Mr Victor beat her. Then they sent Chavy on the bus.'

'Can you tell Miss Elena and me what happened to you after Chavy left?'

'They said I would go on the next bus ride to be with my sister. The bus is there now to take me away.'

'We're going to do our best to help you, Rangsei,' said Clara.

'Why do you want to help me?'

'My dear little Rangsei, Mr Simon is my daddy. Miss Elena and I want to catch the men who hurt him and your sister.'

'Will I have to go back to the orphanage?'

'Let's get you well first,' said Daveed. 'We'll talk about the orphanage tomorrow, okay?

'Elena, Clara, I think Rangsei's had enough for the moment.'

They said their goodbyes to Rangsei and left the hospital with heavy hearts.

'So now we know the whole story. Will you please take me home, Lanie? I want to lay in your arms tonight and feel how lucky I am to be me. I know I'm selfish. I'm sorry.'

'I've been doing this work for a long time, *bella*. I feel the same way every time we find children like Rangsei.'

After Clara and Elena left to see Rangsei, Jim called Melinda Gauci. They arranged to meet in the garden bar at the Park View. Jim and Katy were now sitting together outside, nursing a drink under the tropical plants, waiting for her. The storms had decided to give Phnom Penh a reprieve and were expending their energy over the Cardamom Mountains to the west, the lightning flickering on the peaky skyline.

'We may need to be brutal with her,' said Jim. 'She's not about to give up information unless she has to. To be honest, I'm not even sure if she knows anything, we'll have to make it up as we go along. I don't know her well, but I can tell you she doesn't get to be in her job by being a princess, so don't stress if we get a bit pissed off with each other. Here she is now.'

'Mr Preston, good evening. Katy, how nice to see you. I'm surprised you're still in Phnom Penh now the case has been closed on Simon.'

'Oh yes, Melinda, still here. A few more odds and ends to take care of before we leave.'

'Mr Preston, what's with all the cloak and dagger crap? You could easily have met me at the embassy.'

'It's so much nicer to get away once in a while, isn't it Agent Gauci? You know, relax away from the office, far from the rat race. By the way, you can call me Jim. I'd prefer it, never been one to stand on ceremony. Are you on duty?'

'I'm always on duty, Jim, but off-duty enough for a drink. A decent red would be nice. I imagine your expense account will cover it. And Melinda's fine.'

The wine turned up and they cautiously toasted each other. Katy watched fascinated as two warriors eyed each other carefully, circling, wondering who would strike first.

'The *Phnom Penh Times* is publishing a story soon, Melinda. It's a beauty. I'm wondering whether you might like to hear about it?'

'I'm not much into media gossip, Jim. What's happened? One of the embassy staff been caught in a karaoke bar again with an underage girl?'

'Hardly rates a mention these days. I hear the Aussie Ambassador's been misbehaving.'

'Tsk. Been putting the hard word on a female staff member after a few drinks at an embassy party, has he?'

'Off murdering a cultural attaché as it happens. Nothing too regrettable as far as we're concerned, since Sorensen also distinguished himself as a paedophile. Bit of an extreme response, don't you think?'

Melinda's face remained expressionless.

'Sounds like a nasty business or a great idea for a movie. A "beauty" as you say. Are you sure you're on your first glass of wine?'

'My first. It's only the first part of the story, too.'

Jim reached into his pocket and laid the photographs of George Sorensen on the table. Melinda gazed at the pictures, then at Jim, sipping her drink. She fidgeted slightly. Jim and Katy noticed.

'Who's this supposed to be, Monsoon Man? I have a home to go to and a couple of kids to put to bed, Jim. I don't have time to admire your happy snaps.'

'Not interested yet? Patience Melinda, the story gets fascinating soon. You'll love the part about why Katy and Clara are still here and why the paper's so interested. The minor matter about what did happen to Simon Bailey in Krong Chey. A good old sex, drugs, and rock 'n roll saga.'

'You should be working at one of the trashy tabloids, not the *Phnom Penh Times*, Jim. I didn't realise writing sleazy exposés was your style. I read your stuff. It's quite good on the odd occasion.'

'My editor thinks so. He loves this story too.'

'I know Alex Findlay quite well. You should be careful pulling a stunt like that on me.'

Jim reached into his pocket again and placed his phone on the table, eyes fixed on Melinda. She met his gaze.

'Alex is on speed dial.'

She picked up the phone, paused and put it back on the table again.

'You know I can't comment one way or the other on this so-called story of yours, Jim. Can't confirm or deny, you know the routine.'

'*The Times* could have published the story earlier, back when you fished George out of the stormwater drain. Or after Moloch

Tran threatened Katy and Clara in Krong Chey, the man who did kill Simon Bailey - which you've known all along – and you lied to her about in Melbourne, the same as Martin Lewis did here. There's plenty more, I promise you. You can ask me why we didn't publish already if you like.'

'Okay, I'll play twenty questions with you. Why didn't you publish this story? Knowing Alex, I'd imagine it had to do with facts and evidence. You know, the lost art of journalism.'

'Melinda, Jim didn't publish the story because Clara and I made a deal with him,' said Katy. 'He won't until we get to the bottom of who murdered Simon and the little girl in Krong Chey and why. She has a name too, Chavy Pham, for your paperwork.'

'I needed to find out tonight how much you knew,' said Jim. 'Now, I'm convinced none of this is news to you. You're working on something much bigger; drug smuggling would be my guess. Moloch Tran's involved, so you went along with the arrest of some poor sod for Simon's murder to keep your secrets.'

'Strictly off the record, Jim. We didn't want to name Moloch Tran as the man responsible for Simon's death for fear it could endanger our agent and a current operation. As it happens, we had another source who gave Simon the information about the cellar in Krong Chey, the one who got himself arrested after Tran found out who betrayed him. He thought gaol might be a safer place to be. Turns out he was wrong. An inmate murdered him last night. No prizes for guessing who paid for the housekeeping.'

Melinda continued.

'At the time, we thought rescuing a few children wouldn't endanger our operation and since Simon became so adamant, we knew he'd try something. Unfortunately, Tran already had him on a list of people he didn't like and he found out about the rescue. We tried to warn Simon, but couldn't reach him in time.'

'Who came up with the story about using the new laws to muzzle Katy and Clara and divert media attention?' asked Jim. 'Ambassador Nelson, I presume?'

'So you know about him too? At the time, we were happy to go along with the ambassador's plan. It met our needs as well.

We didn't question his motives until Clara told Martin about the break-in and the book.

'We hadn't yet connected Robert Nelson to the drug deal and only had suspicions about his other financial activities. Now it's clear he got worried when he learnt Katy and Clara were coming to Cambodia and the problem it would cause if they stirred up too much publicity.'

'What's the deal with the Chinese Ambassador?'

'Lucky leverage for Nelson as far as we know. Clara's a Chinese citizen, the darling of Premier Liu Xiang and Mr Zhao's a powerful man who wants a peaceful life for his political ambitions. He's publicity-shy except where it helps his career, so making sure Premier Liu's favourite girl didn't get herself knocked off on his watch must've been a prudent bit of self-interest. I imagine having photos with Clara, as well as having a couple of his staff following her around, seemed like another bright idea. What are you going to do Jim, cause trouble?'

'I'm a journalist Melinda, not a whistleblower. How I write the story is up to what you and I decide in the next half-hour. These drugs, I assume it's drugs from the Golden Triangle? How much are we talking about?'

'On the street, upwards of a hundred and fifty million dollars. They're heading for Australia. It's the biggest shipment of pure heroin ever smuggled into the country and we've been tracking its production from Shan State in Myanmar for almost a year.'

'Nice to know there's a high enough price tag for ignoring the bloody murder of one of your citizens and a Cambodian kid.'

'Don't get high and mighty Jim. It doesn't suit you. If these drugs ever make it to Australia, the cost to hundreds of lives will be incalculable.'

'Where are they now?'

'Our problem is we don't know. After Simon found out about the Paradise Storage Company in Krong Chey, one of Tran's drop-off points became public knowledge after the publicity and he's hidden the shipment somewhere else. They'll be doubly careful where they store the stuff, especially as the other gangs would love getting their hands on so much heroin without the usual hard work. We're trying to locate the shipment by tracking phones and through our agent working in Tran's organisation.'

'Have you tried tracking Robert Nelson's phone?'

'He's much too smart. How did you work out Nelson's involved?'

'He didn't go to a concert last Saturday. It's a long story. Who is he, anyway? Aren't diplomats meant to be the soul of discretion?'

'You don't do much work in diplomatic circles, do you?' said Melinda with a grin. 'Nelson's one of those jobs-for-the-boys diplomats, like most of them these days. He's always been a big contributor to the Libs; the posting to Phnom Penh is for services rendered. He's got a background in merchant banking, plus some questionable offshore trading operations. Nothing's ever been proven and he's been untouchable with powerful friends, including the Prime Minister. We came to the same conclusion you did after Sorensen died.'

'You knew Sorensen's death wasn't an accident, didn't you?'

'Martin Lewis followed him Saturday afternoon, against Nelson's orders. A police car stopped Sorensen's taxi and they abducted him. I think Nelson panicked when you threatened to expose Sorensen's sex life, his first slip-up. Except for you two, only three people know - me, Martin and my AFP Director. The political damage to the government's going to be pretty ugly when the story comes out.'

'Did Robert Nelson know about Simon's work?'

'I don't know, Jim. I doubt we'll ever know for sure. It would certainly explain a lot, like how Tran even knew about Simon's rescue plan. Maybe Simon mentioned his suspicions to the ambassador at some point, not knowing he had signed his death warrant. Or maybe Nelson knew Simon had his suspicions, which is why he became so interested in the book. Still, we're not into speculation.'

'And Colonel Gray?'

'Steve Gray's harmless. He's seeing out his time till he retires next year. Likes his Scotch with the boys, does Steve. He should have made general, but isn't the sharpest soldier in the parade. Makes a good military attaché, gets on well with most people and is great with the paperwork. He doesn't know anything about Nelson's activities. We couldn't trust him with his Johnnie Walker habit.'

'And Martin Lewis? Is he AFP too?'

'Martin who?'

'Okay.' smiled Jim. 'Listen, Melinda. We'll make a deal with you. You help me finish my story and we won't publish anything until Moloch Tran's arrested. Just to remind you, we could have published the real Sorensen story and the Simon Bailey story, even Rémy Aubert's story, any time before now. If we had, I'd be dusting off my tux for a bloody Pulitzer. Just saying. We're on the same side.'

'Why do you need my help? You seem to have done well enough without me so far.'

'It's in your best interests. We know more than you because we also know where Moloch Tran's hiding your drugs. Our problem is we may be in Mr Tran's crosshairs,' Jim confessed. 'We're all feeling a tad uncomfortable about the possibility.'

'Goodness me, don't you all play in the big boy's sandpit? Sounds like working together is in your best interests, too. I'll need to brief my boss in Canberra before I can give you more information.'

'Let's all meet tomorrow morning at our favourite coffee shop, the Fresco Café,' suggested Jim. 'There's another part of the story I don't think you know yet. We should know more ourselves by then,'

'No, we'll need somewhere private.'

'My hotel room here at the Park View?'

'No good, Katy. This place isn't safe either. I'll book another hotel room and text you the details. The three of us can meet there.'

'You mean the five of us. Katy's daughter and Elena Accardi know too.'

'The UNICEF Accardi? How did she get mixed up in this?'

'Elena and my daughter are… *um*… recent good friends.'

Melinda burst out laughing.

"Oh my God, at least we'll have some light entertainment. I assume no one's informed Martin yet? He's been raving about Clara since they first met. The way he talks about her, your daughter and Martin are practically an item.'

'Hope he doesn't take it as a personal slight on his manhood,' chuckled Jim, thinking about the dark humour of the situation tomorrow.

'Melinda, you'll also need to get on the phone right now to put a monitor on the Vitara Orphanage's phone. A lowlife called Victor Le is the director; here's his business card. He met with Moloch Tran today. Your drugs are at the orphanage.'

'Show me your hands, Katy.'

Katy held them out to Melinda.

'I'm checking you have all your fingers. Most people who meet Moloch Tran have one or two missing afterwards.'

'I told him not to mess with my daughter or he'd have to deal with me. Actually, Clara and I were petrified. He left a calling card with Rithy, our driver. A few cracked ribs.'

'Now I'm impressed. Okay, you two, I'll need to know all you've been up to so I can convince my boss we need to work together. First, I'd better phone my husband and tell him to read the bedtime stories tonight. Jim, order another bottle of red. Alex Findlay won't mind. And you can call me Mel.'

30

RANGSEI'S CHOICE

'Good morning, everybody, I'm Melinda Gauci. I work for the Australian Federal Police. We're not going to have a lot of time for social niceties, so if I'm brusque with anyone, my apologies in advance. And we've changed the name of this exercise to Operation Sandpit, which also means you're all going to find yourselves in an official report later and most likely in the newspapers. So please, let's try not to bugger it up.'

Melinda had arranged them in a small conference room at the Sofitel Hotel at ten o'clock the next morning. She'd also asked Dr Khan to attend. With her, there were two casually-dressed Cambodian men Katy thought had the coldness of Moloch Tran, she hoped without the psychosis, but admitted to herself it was hard to tell. She introduced them as Captain Seng and Lieutenant Khim of the Gendarmerie. No one looked surprised to see Martin Lewis. Jim Preston looked amused.

'Elena, please tell us the story about the young girl, Rangsei. Jim's given me the background. Stick to what happened when you saw her yesterday.'

Everyone finally learnt the story of Simon's involvement with Chavy and Rangsei Pham and how he knew about the trafficking of orphanage girls to Moloch Tran through Krong Chey. Elena also explained Rangsei knew Victor Le would be sending her on the next minibus and what would probably happen to her.

'Thanks, Elena. Now, Jim tells me he believes the minibus has the drug shipment. Given the minibus has a trailer as well, we can assume he's right. Tran's unlikely to be in Phnom Penh unless it's connected to the shipment; his deadline to move the heroin is too tight.

'Captain Seng, can you get your people to visit the orphanage today as tourists to check out the cameras? If it's safe, break in tonight and put a GPS monitor on the minibus. We don't want to lose it in the traffic or if the monsoon's heavy on the highway. We'll also know when it arrives at the drop-off point at the border.'

'No problem.'

'Mel, how will we know when the minibus leaves?' asked Jim.

'Two days ago, we learnt from our contact in Tran's organisation about a ship arriving in the port of Vung Tau, the *MV Sea Rambler*, the day after tomorrow. She's flying a flag of convenience from Vanuatu and will be in port less than eight hours. Shell corporations carefully hide the owners, but they're almost certainly North Korean. We know the drugs will be loaded aboard while she's docked, which means they'll be moved from the Vitara Orphanage to Vung Tau tomorrow or early the following day at the latest. My bet's tomorrow night to allow for delays and under the protection of the rain, otherwise, they'll miss the *Sea Rambler's* time in port.'

'What about the kids? They're going to be on the bus as well,' said Katy.

'Yeah, we can safely conclude the bus will leave tomorrow night with children on their "tour" as additional cover for the drug shipment. We know Tran will hand the minibus over to the Vietnamese who control the port of Vung Tau, before crossing the border into Vietnam. If we can discover the location for the handover, we can get Tran and his Vietnamese counterpart, severely hindering the trafficking of drugs for a long time.'

'Aren't you listening, Melinda? What about the kids? You can't go charging in and risk their lives,' insisted Katy.

'No, we can't,' agreed Melinda. 'And we won't, I'm coming to the children next. We'll need a plan to intercept the bus before it reaches the handover point and remove the kids.

'Martin, get down the highway with Lieutenant Khim and pick the best place for an intercept. We don't want the minibus driver alerting Tran to what's going on, so work with Telecom Cambodia to find someplace along the highway where phone reception is bad, or ideally where there's a dead spot. No, better still, get them to shut down the cell towers in the area you choose when we tell them. We'll need fifteen minutes so we can guarantee Tran won't get a warning about what we're doing. Make sure it's as remote as possible and will leave Captain Seng enough time to get his officers in place at the border. Let's set a minimum of one hour's drive from the interception point to the Bavet border crossing.'

'Right, Mel.'

'Okay with you, Captain Seng?'

'Plenty of time. I'll be moving my teams into the Bavet area tonight and early tomorrow morning.'

'Good. Now, Doctor Khan. How well is Rangsei?'

'We've got her blood sugar levels up and she'll be fine. Elena's still trying to find a way we can keep her from going back.'

'Now listen to me, all of you,' said Melinda. 'Rangsei *must* go back to the Vitara Orphanage. Today.'

The stunned silence and dismay hearing Melinda, turned to anger, then violent objections.

'No! How can you even think of such a thing?' said Clara, appalled at the idea.

'What? Did you leave your bloody soul at home this morning?' accused Jim.

'Melinda, you can't even be thinking something so inhuman,' said Elena. 'She already knows the bus is waiting for her and she's likely to finish up dead like her sister. How can you imagine doing something so cruel to her?'

'There's no choice. Moloch Tran knows Rangsei is Chavy's sister and if Victor Le told him about your visit and you taking Rangsei away, he'll presume he's being watched and change his plans about moving the drugs. Much worse, he'll come looking for all of you. Tran has criminal, political and military contacts throughout South-East Asia. Have no doubts at all, nobody will get out of the country alive, or even make next weekend if he suspects you've betrayed him.'

'Daveed, tell Agent Gauci you won't allow her to send Rangsei back to the orphanage,' pleaded Elena.

'Elena, I can't believe I'm saying this, but Agent Gauci's right. Raising suspicions by not asking her to go back is the last thing we want to happen to her, as well as us.'

'I hate to agree and it's a shitty choice,' said Jim. 'If we can't come up with a better plan, Mel's right. If we don't send her back, she'll be spending her life like the rest of us, looking over our shoulders and our lives may not be long ones. Remember, the couple who owns the orphanage also knows where her family lives in Kampot. She'll never be safe.'

'Listen, Elena, and all of you, I do understand,' said Melinda. 'I'll do all in my power to protect the kids. Elena, I want you, Clara and Doctor Khan to talk to Rangsei and see if she's prepared to go back. Do your best. Please. Unless she goes willingly to not raise suspicions, we'll have to settle on a plan to raid the orphanage before the minibus leaves and try to protect everyone afterwards. We're in a tough place and there isn't an easy answer. On the basis she goes back Elena, I want you to be there when we intercept the minibus on the highway and supervise the transfer of the children to a safe place back in Phnom Penh. So first up, I want you to organise transport for the kids. Have a doctor with you in case the girls are stressed, okay?'

'How about Doctor Khan? Will you help, Daveed?'

'Try and stop me.'

'Doctor Khan's a good choice. Rangsei knows both of you and she can reassure the other kids they're safe and nothing bad is happening to them. Work out a plan down to the last detail with Lieutenant Khim. We can't afford mistakes. Keep what you're doing secret. Tell no-one. I'll make sure you get anything you need.'

Melinda continued.

'Jim, as for the media, Captain Seng will not permit you to go to Bavet or Krong Chey, nor can I allow the media to be there. It will be seen as a publicity stunt, not to mention dangerous. We wouldn't want you missing out on your Pulitzer, would we? Plenty of people would love to throw rocks at the AFP and I'm not about to give them ammunition. Non-negotiable. You can be with Elena at the intercept with your camera guy if you do what we tell you, but no further. The intercept ought to be exciting enough for you. We'll have videos of the border operation and I'll make parts of it available to you. I've spoken to Alex Findlay and he's agreed to play by my rules. You can call him. He's on speed dial on my phone, too.'

She smiled.

'I still hate this idea,' said Katy. 'How you can even think to send Rangsei back to the orphanage is beyond me, Melinda. Does your job take your soul?'

'Sorry Katy, I don't have time for theological conversations. I need to meet with Captain Seng. We've got a lot to organise. We'll all meet here again at nine o'clock tonight when I want to hear a complete rundown of the plans for tomorrow to make sure we've left nothing to chance. Any questions?'

After she left, Katy looked at Martin, incredulous about Melinda being so detached about the lives of seven children.

'Don't be too hard on Mel, Katy. She's also known as Mrs Gauci and has two daughters of her own, one about Rangsei's age. Don't imagine for a second she's making easy decisions; I'm quite sure even she doesn't want her job right now.'

'Well, hello Martin,' said Clara, coming over, wanting to break the tension. 'And here I am feeling terrible about thinking you're a spy and it turns out I'm right all along. Now I know, does it mean you're going to have me shot at dawn?'

'We don't do firing squads these days, Clara. Instead, we generally settle for dinner and a glass of wine. It's much less messy, not to mention the paperwork's easier.'

'I think you may need to know a few things before you decide to ask me out again. We'll save that conversation for later. You have more important things to do.'

'I'll look forward to it.'

'I wouldn't be too sure. At least now I know it wasn't you rummaging through my suitcase, which is a relief. I imagine one of Robert Nelson's acquaintances was trying to discover how much my dad really knew?'

'Yep. And if it's any consolation, if I had, I wouldn't have been careless enough to leave a zipper in the wrong place. You'd never have known I'd even been there.'

'Well, it wouldn't be any consolation to discover someone who took me to dinner had secretly inspected my underwear before ordering the soup. It's too creepy, to be honest. Best you be off to the countryside before my imagination paints more borderline images of you. See you later, Martin.'

After he left, the eavesdropping Jim Preston strolled over.

'Well, Clara, are you saving Martin's good news for a birthday present?'

'Oh, Jim, what am I to do? All my life, I've never had to deal with relationship issues. Now I have gender conflicts.'

'If I can be blunt with you, one of my lesser-known talents, you don't have gender conflicts. Any halfwit can see what's between you and Elena. When you tell him, make sure I'm in earshot. It will be one of my life's treasured moments I'll dine out on for years.'

'You're a scoundrel, Jim Preston. But at least you're my kind of scoundrel.'

'How are you feeling, Rangsei?'

'I am okay, Doctor Daveed. What's going to happen to me? Are you taking me back to the orphanage?'

'If you agree and just for a day or two. We want you to help us stop Mr Victor from sending more girls away.'

'What do you want me to do?'

'Nothing. We want you to go to the orphanage and be like you were before,' continued Daveed.

'Will they send me on the bus?'

'Yes, sweetheart, they will,' said Elena. 'I promise we'll be watching the bus closely when it leaves and we'll stop it on the road later with the police. When we stop the bus, I'll be there with Doctor Daveed, I promise you. We'll be waiting with the police to keep you and all the other girls safe.'

'Will you bring Chavy back?'

'No, Rangsei, nothing we can do is going to bring Chavy back. We are so sorry,' said Clara. 'But you can help us catch the people who hurt her and my daddy. We can both stop other girls from being taken away.'

'I will do it, Miss Clara.'

'Good girl,' said Elena. 'We need you to keep very quiet like you were when I found you. When the police stop the bus, you can help us by telling the other children they are all safe and not to worry, even though it might be noisy and scary.'

'Don't worry, Miss Elena. I won't drink the milk so I can stay awake. And I don't have to pretend about being sad and quiet. I don't care what happens to me.'

They returned to the Sofitel conference room at 9.00 pm. Melinda continued her no-nonsense style.

'Doctor Khan, what's the story with Rangsei?'

'I took her back to the Vitara Orphanage this afternoon. She's okay with what we asked. She's a brave little girl. My fear is once this is over, our little girl is going to need serious help. I'm fairly sure Victor Le isn't suspicious; I told him she needed medication for a slight infection and she'll be healthy again within a day or two. At least no one will want to abuse her for the next couple of days.'

'Good. There will be plenty of attention for Rangsei and all the girls when this is over. Here's an update on what's going on with the shipment. We've been running a tap on the orphanage's and Victor Le's phone and he confirmed the minibus is leaving tomorrow night for Krong Chey. Unfortunately, there's no information on the precise destination yet, so we'll need the information from the driver when we pull it over. Captain Seng's got observers around the orphanage; nothing will get in or out without us knowing. Captain Seng, can you update us on the cameras?'

'We were there today. Cameras are covering the minibus and other areas of the grounds and there's at least one of Tran's men in the compound. Also, the trailer and the minibus are easily big enough to be holding the drug shipment, but it's impossible to get anyone in there without being seen.'

'Okay, we'll need to double up on cars and motorbikes following the minibus tomorrow night. We can't afford to lose it for a second.'

'Already done, Melinda. We'll know every turn it makes,' said Captain Seng.

'I have one question,' asked Katy. 'How will we get the minibus to stop without putting the children in danger?'

'Lieutenant Khim, can you tell us your plan to intercept the minibus?'

'Yes. We're going to fake a car accident at the interception point. I'll have officers dressed as regular police, slowing traffic. Accidents aren't unusual on the highway, so an overturned car should not arouse suspicion, especially in the monsoon season. All the radio stations will announce the accident when the minibus gets clear of the city, advising drivers to travel with care in the area. Most drivers have their radios on during the monsoons when they're on the highway, so there's a good chance the minibus driver will hear the warning and not suspect anything when he sees the police lights. We'll be following the minibus at a safe distance. Two minutes before the minibus arrives at the accident scene, we will switch off the cell towers.'

'What about the girls?' asked Katy.

'We'll replace the orphanage girls with officers from the Gendarmerie. Captain Seng is supplying five female officers who could pass as the orphanage girls if the lights aren't too bright. We'll dress the officers in pretty clothes to make them as realistic as we can.'

'I'll be there with Doctor Khan, Katy. We've organised transport to bring the children back to Phnom Penh,' said Elena.

'Miss Elena's transport for the girls will be the ambulance at the accident scene, which will be hiding the five female officers and the doctor,' continued Khim. 'Mr Jim and his cameraman will be filming the accident to make the scene look more authentic and some of my officers will pretend to be the victims and medical staff. If an escort car follows the minibus, we'll have a standby car with officers inside, in case we damage it in the assault.'

'What if they don't stop?' persisted Katy.

'If the minibus refuses to stop, I'll have other cars two hundred metres further along the highway and they'll stop the minibus in more traditional ways.

'We will confirm the warehouse address with the minibus occupants and contact Captain Seng and Agent Melinda in Krong Chey. Mr Martin and I will continue to Krong Chey. The ambulance will return to Phnom Penh with the children, Miss Elena, the doctor, Mr Jim and his cameraman. My officers will take care of the traffickers. As soon as the operation is complete, we'll tell Cambodia Telecom to reactivate the phone towers. I expect the operation to take less than five minutes before the minibus continues on its way. If Tran is checking the minibus's progress on GPS, he may know about the reported accident and not be suspicious of a minor delay.'

'What if they won't tell you the address?' asked Jim.

'They always do,' replied Khim matter of factly.

'Lieutenant Khim has an interesting strategy,' said Melinda. 'He will say one of them will live and the other will die, depending on whoever answers his question in the next ten seconds. Then he starts to count. It's amazing how well it works. I've thought of using it on my kids.'

'The one flaw in China's one-child policy,' said Katy.

Clara made a rude gesture with her tongue. The thought crossed all their minds whether any of the traffickers would make it back to Phnom Penh in the care of Lieutenant Khim's officers.

'The problem we have,' said Melinda, 'is we know the destination is Krong Chey, but not the exact location, so we'll be relying on the driver to tell us. With luck, the minibus has a GPS map system the driver is following, even if Lieutenant Khim cannot discover the location by asking. These traffickers are very sophisticated. Once we know, Captain Seng's officers will have over an hour to study the streetscape from a satellite map and get into position. The plan's a bit rough but will have to do. If we can't discover the exact location, we'll abort the operation and settle for the drug capture.'

'We'll be ready,' assured Captain Seng.

'Right. It sounds like we have got as close as we can to a workable plan. Now, final points, so there's no misunderstanding.

'First up, Elena and Doctor Khan. When Lieutenant Khim stops the minibus, it will be noisy and you'll naturally want to reassure the children. Wait until Lieutenant Khim tells you it's safe. The driver and guards will certainly be armed, so stay well clear until he's taken care of them. Same goes for you, Jim. You won't help anyone if you get in the way and you may even put the girls in danger. Once they see the Gendarmerie, I don't expect they'll decide to make a fight of it, but we can't take chances. Clear?'

'We understand.'

'Elena, after the rescue, take the kids back to Phnom Penh. On the way, try to discover which orphanages sent the girls. The driver will take you to the Gendarmerie barracks, give the information to the officer there. When I tell you the operation is over in Krong Chey, not before, I want you to take the children back to the Vitara Orphanage.'

'What about Victor Le and the other staff?'

'Captain Seng's officers will have arrested all the orphanage staff before you arrive and all the children will be terrified with the place full of soldiers with guns. Stay at the Vitara Orphanage. Do the best you can until you can organise more staff to help and contact no one until I've told you the operation is over in Krong Chey, which means it won't be until morning before you find help. While on the subject, I want absolutely no personal phone calls made by anyone until we've completed the operation in Krong Chey.'

'How about my UNICEF staff? Can I call them after we're back in Phnom Penh?'

'No. I know the security won't make it an easy night for you Elena, but we can't afford anyone even breathing a word until the operation is over. The soldiers should have two nurses with them, but it will be chaos at the orphanage. I need a person who can take charge, who knows what they're doing and who I can trust. That's you, Elena. Captain Seng has instructed both nurses to take their orders from you. I'm sorry, we couldn't risk involving more than two. I'm sure Doctor Khan will help you. Jim, you and your cameraman stay with Elena too. Take pictures if you want, but try not to make matters worse for Elena. She'll need all the help she can get.'

'Okay, Mel.'

'We'll manage, Melinda.'

'Martin, Lieutenant Khim is in command at the interception. Afterwards, you'll be with him in the minibus and will travel to the location as the security man in the passenger seat. Lieutenant Khim will replace the driver.'

'Right, Mel.'

'Once the minibus pulls up at the location and you're sure the traffickers are there, Lieutenant Khim will message Captain Seng and me and his Gendarmerie will start the assault. They'll close off all the nearby streets, secure the warehouse and minibus. The operation should take two or three minutes. Martin, you and the female officers will be backup and must stay in the minibus. Hopefully, Moloch Tran's men will think the girls are from the orphanage until it's too late. Do you understand?'

'Yea, got it, Mel.'

'Under no circumstances whatsoever do I want bloody heroics from you, Martin. Lieutenant Khim will leave the minibus to take charge of the assault. You will only leave the minibus if it's absolutely essential and the Cambodian officer will make the call, not you. You are solely there as my liaison, nothing else.

Don't be misled by the youth of the female officers. They are well-trained anti-terrorist troops who know what they're doing. Listen to their commander and she'll keep you safe. All Captain Seng's officers are Cambodia's version of the SAS and they're outstanding. You'll be okay if you stay in the minibus and keep your head down. Everyone will be wearing protective vests, including all of you at the minibus intercept.'

'Okay, Mel.'

'Any questions?'

'I've got one,' said Jim. 'What about the couple who own the orphanages and Simon's bent police chief?'

'They'll be picked up at the same time Captain Seng's officers take over the Vitara Orphanage. The fun part is my director and two AFP colleagues are in transit from Australia as we speak. They'll be visiting Ambassador Nelson tomorrow night after the Krong Chey operation. Now, get some rest. Tomorrow will be a long day.'

'We're coming too.'

'Pardon me? Are you crazy, Clara? I forbid it.'

'Melinda, I'm a Chinese citizen. Unless you want a diplomatic incident and want to explain to the Chinese Premier why you've arrested his favourite Jade Princess, you'd best think again. I'm happy to use my celebrity quite brazenly, if I must. I'm sure you know I'm on first-name terms with Premier Liu.'

'And I won't be leaving my daughter's side, Melinda. You better get used to the idea.'

'It's far too dangerous. I'd like even less telling the Chinese Premier why I got China's national treasure and her mother killed. Not to mention explaining it to the Australian Prime Minister.'

'I expect the Prime Minister will have enough to worry about when you arrest Robert Nelson,' smiled Katy. 'We'll stay well away, as far as you think is safe. And we'll have Rithy to protect us. He's an ex-soldier and has a big gun.'

'We want to be there at the end of all this, Melinda,' said Clara. 'We're not going to be storming the building with trumpets and cannons with you. We want to be there to see the book finally closed on Moloch Tran and what he did to Chavy Pham and our family.'

Melinda looked at Martin, who gave a non-committal shrug.

'Plus, we'll be going whether you like it or not,' added Clara.

'From my experience, she's not kidding, Mel. If they keep far enough away, it should be okay. We can't argue they don't know the risks with Moloch Tran. If they agreed to say, staying two hundred metres away from the location of the operation, I can't see any danger. There's sure to be locals closer.'

Melinda reluctantly consented.

'I suppose it's better if I knew where you were instead of not knowing. You stay with me and do *everything* I tell you. Understand?'

'We give you our word. We're not heroes, Melinda.'

'If either of you two disobeys me, even with as much as a blink without permission, Captain Seng's officers will arrest you, with handcuffs and damn the consequences. I promise you they are not gentle. Understand?'

Katy and Clara both nodded dutifully.

31

THE ROAD BACK TO KRONG CHEY

At midday, Victor Le confirmed the minibus would leave at 8 pm.

A white SUV left Phnom Penh for Krong Chey at 6.30 pm. The afternoon rainstorm threatened overhead. By 7.30 pm, the heavy storm had slowed their vehicle's progress along the highway. Inside were Melinda Gauci, Rithy, Clara and Katy. Melinda had decided one vehicle would keep their presence as anonymous as possible. Katy guessed rightly, her motive also included keeping a closer eye on her and Clara.

Katy and Clara hardly said a word on the drive while Melinda talked constantly on the phone to Captain Seng and Martin Lewis and others, who they concluded were her Australian bosses with all the "sirs" being thrown into their conversations. She never mentioned she had Katy and Clara with her to her boss, a sure sign they would question her judgement if something went wrong.

An hour later, Rithy pulled to the side of the road next to several parked vehicles, including one laying on its side. Lieutenant Khim and Martin Lewis came over in their dripping ponchos.

'Agent Melinda, my officers inform me the minibus left the Vitara Orphanage on time. Other vehicles arrived earlier with children inside. If the young girl Rangsei joins them, there will be seven. I have five female officers; I don't think it will matter in this weather. Miss Elena and Doctor Daveed are here with the ambulance and Mr Jim with his cameraman. We have a direct satellite link with Cambodia Telecom. We're ready.'

Clara opened the window as Elena came around to the other side of the SUV. Rain pounded on Elena's umbrella and splashed through the open window.

'How are you feeling, Lanie?'

'From what I've seen of Lieutenant Khim and his officers so far, I'm much happier being on his side. I'm frightened about you and Katy.'

'I'm proud of you, my darling. I'll bet you weren't expecting this when you asked me to come home with you.'

'To be honest *bella*, being in the Yehonala family is a bit more challenging than I anticipated,' grinned she.

'Try not to worry about us and thank you for not getting angry about me wanting to go to Krong Chey. I promise you, my mother and me will stay well away from danger. Before you know it, we'll be back at the Vitara Orphanage to help you. We'll see you soon.'

'We need to go…'

At 9.15 pm, the SUV neared Krong Chey. The rain stopped. Melinda's phone buzzed and she spoke briefly to Martin.

'The cell towers are off. We won't know what's happening for a few minutes.'

The next ten minutes were an agonising wait as Clara and Katy imagined the worst calamities happening on the roadside. Melinda prayed they hadn't overlooked anything which might risk the children's lives. Her phone buzzed again. The relief on her face evident to them all.

'Thank God. Good news, the girls are unharmed. We have the address and the minibus is back on the highway heading for Krong Chey. Rithy, head into Krong Chey and pull into the Shell petrol station on the left side of the road. We'll wait there to pick up Captain Seng at ten-thirty.'

'Melinda, can I call Elena?'

'No. Sorry, Clara. I said we can't risk unnecessary phone calls. Martin told me to tell you Elena's safe and so are the kids. He said she, Doctor Khan and Rangsei did a great job keeping the kids settled and away from harm. Don't stress, if they're not already driving back to Phnom Penh, they'll all be on their way shortly. Even Jim's happy with his pictures.'

They waited for a nervous forty minutes at the Shell station before Captain Seng opened the door and climbed inside.

'We're ready, Melinda. The warehouse is in an alley, easy enough to secure. The doors are open and there are ten men and three vehicles already inside. Lieutenant Khim tells me they should be arriving in the minibus between eleven-fifteen and eleven-twenty. My officers are in place.'

'Good work, Captain Seng. Let's get ourselves in position. Can you show Rithy where it will be safe to park?'

With the lights off, the SUV slid through the pot-holed back streets of Krong Chey, occasionally splashing muddy spray as the wheels bounced into a deeper hole. They came to a stop under a dull, yellowish streetlight in a deserted *cul de sac* and appeared to be the only living souls in the neighbourhood. Rithy turned off the engine.

'The warehouse is about two hundred metres further along, down an alleyway on the left,' said Captain Seng, smiling. 'Now we wait. It isn't like in the American movies, these operations are ninety-five per cent sitting around doing nothing and five per cent frantic action.'

They could all see the five per cent interested Captain Seng. Fifteen more minutes of anxious waiting passed. The five occupants now sweated in the humid air of the enclosed cabin, even with the windows open. Melinda's and Captain Seng's telephones buzzed softly.

'The minibus will be turning into the alley in ten minutes,' announced Melinda. 'You three wait here. Do not leave the vehicle. Don't be concerned if you hear gunfire or see vehicles driving around; Captain Seng's officers will have the situation under control. Come along, Captain Seng. I love watching your officers at work.'

Melinda and Seng left the SUV, slipped into their protective jackets and walked the two hundred metres to the alley. They were both armed with pistols. As they neared the alleyway entrance, six black-clad warriors materialised alongside them. Further along, more shadowy figures moved into position at the next alleyway.

Out of sight of the SUV, men similarly dressed waited in the shadows at the other end of the alley. Nearer the warehouse, another team waited on rooftops or had concealed themselves in doorways, having moved into position under cover of the torrential rains an hour earlier.

Dimmed headlights appeared in the rear vision mirror of the SUV. They grew brighter as the vehicle approached, carefully avoiding the potholes, occasionally splashing into one and bouncing on its springy suspension. Inside, indistinct figures were visible. They might have been young girls with their driver and tour guide behind the windows, the condensation making it impossible to tell. The minibus moved past the SUV. Two hundred metres further along, it slowly turned left and disappeared. They sat in the total absence of any sound.

One minute later, shouting and gunfire shattered the silence. Black-clad men burst from their cover, the orders of their leaders echoing in the night air, their aggressive war cries reverberating between the buildings and intimidating their surprised targets.

The staccato sound of automatic weapons crackled in the air. A crescendo of noise for less than a minute, replaced by intermittent bursts of one or two shots. Within three minutes, silence again. Harsh words replaced bullets as men were bundled together, handcuffed, then forced brutally onto their stomachs in the rubbish and mud of the alley.

Two buses and two ambulances arrived, their flashing red and blue lights casting eerie strobes on the blackened faces of

Captain Seng's men, now assembled in the warehouse. Shortly afterwards, with their human cargoes and captors on board, the buses and ambulances left.

Laughter rang out as the remaining black-clad warriors teased their five colleagues in their frilly dresses and ribbons, part good-natured humour, part cathartic release. A truck pulled into the alley. Transferring the minibus's lethal cargo began.

It was over.

32

RETRIBUTION

'Looks like it's quiet, Ma. Nothing's happened for the last ten minutes since those two buses and ambulances drove away. I'll go with Rithy and look for Martin.'

'I'll stay here, *baobei*. I've seen enough of dark alleys to last me a lifetime.'

'I'll send Rithy back in a few minutes. He won't be long.'

'Tell him to take his cannon out of the glovebox when he comes back and throw it in the river. The bloody thing gives me the creeps.'

Clara smiled, a level of Jimspeak they had both agreed to live with.

'What the hell are you doing here, Clara? I thought Melinda ordered you to stay well away. Don't you damn-well do anything people tell you?' said Martin, not altogether surprised to see her.

'We saw the police and the ambulances leave ten minutes ago. It's been quiet since, so we assumed the battle's over. Anyway, I wanted to make sure you're still in one piece after spending the night with five women and thought you might have some stories to make me blush. I expect all your dream fantasies came true tonight, didn't they?'

'Yeah, right. And don't give me your butter-won't-melt look, Clara. Save it for Melinda. She'll have your guts on toast for

Katy's senses became hyper-alert. She could smell the sweat and the blood, she could hear each laboured breath and her own pounding heartbeats, she could see the stiletto blade and the silver handle and the blood on his fingers.

'*I remember his clean fingernails…*'

She began to shiver, losing control of her body. She knew a grotesque death waited seconds away.

'*What will it feel like? Is it going to hurt? What a lonely place to die, I don't want to die here alone, how can he make me leave Clara the same way I was left alone, it isn't fair to do it again to our family, I'm not going to cry whatever he does, there's so much to do and all will be left behind.*'

A thousand images erupted from deep inside, flashes of thoughts, conversations, dreams for her life. A jumble, looking to make sense of the past, reliving a lifetime of memories and relationships. All treasures hidden in her history and promises guiding her destiny.

No, this night, Katy Yehonala would fight for her life.

She reached behind her back through the open window of the SUV, her panicky fingers frantically grappling around the dashboard until she found the glovebox. After fumbling with the latch, the door dropped down. Inside, her hand touched the metallic, clammy shape of Rithy's gun.

Clutching the handle with both hands, she pointed it towards Moloch Tran, the gun much heavier than she thought it would be. He saw her hands were shaking.

He laughed at her, the effort making him cough. A trickle of bloody spittle ran from his lips.

'Keep away from me. I'll use it…'

He smirked, shrugging his shoulders. Even now, as he struggled to stand, Katy saw he still held her beneath his contempt. She lifted her two arms, trying to steady the old revolver in her trembling hands. The gun was a lead weight. She turned her head away from him, squeezed her eyes tightly closed and jerked the trigger.

The explosion reverberated through her body, deafening her and the gun almost leapt out of her hands. She cried out in agony as the recoil sent a searing pain through her wrist. She turned to face him, pleading to Lady Guanyin for her ordeal to be over.

He still stood there, the same mocking taunt on his face. Katy's shot had grazed his leg. He winced with the effort to keep his balance. His knee buckled.

'You'll need… to do better… bitch.'

She tried to lift the gun again, forcing herself to stare into his eyes, praying she had the strength to pull the heavy trigger a second time. Her wrist screamed in pain, and her arms quivered with the effort of trying to hold them straight.

'Please, my lady, give me your power and courage, please, for one more minute…'

His face blurred and the strength drained from her arms. Katy knew her fight was over.

He lurched the final steps towards her. She watched him stumbling closer, three metres, two metres, waiting for the burn of the knife.

A bright light flashed in her eyes and an excruciatingly painful explosion jerked her body upright.

'So this is what it's like to die…'

Warm drops, like rain, spattered on her face and arms. She saw the swirling red mist and the halo of blue smoke. A jagged hole appeared between Moloch Tran's eyes and a crimson stream of blood leaked down his face. She smelt the acrid stink of gunpowder. He looked surprised, frozen in time, their faces now touching distance away. Defeated, he crumpled at her feet, his arm flailing against her leg, spidery fingers clawing at her ankle.

In horror, she shuffled back, kicking his arm away in disgust and slumping over the vehicle's bonnet, Moloch Tran's gravelly, hate-filled breaths the only sound before the silence. She laughed hysterically, shaking with the shock of being alive.

Unbidden, Katy's eyes transfixed on the man lying in the gutter under the yellow streetlight, hypnotised by Moloch Tran's unblinking stare and the grotesque shadows cast over his mutilated face. She studied the black blood pooling under his head, mixing with the sodden gutter debris.

The gun slipped from her fingers and clattered to the ground. Retching convulsions racked her body. She vomited violently again and again and again until her stomach muscles screamed.

There were arms around her.

It was Clara.

Martin and Melinda stood breathless behind her, holding their guns in a parody of a movie scene.

'Well, Ma, looks like I can't leave you alone for a second before you go getting yourself in trouble.'

Katy and Clara embraced in a mix of laughter and tears, hugging each other like it was the end of the world.

'I'm here, Ma. You can let it all out. I've got you.'

Clara pulled a box of tissues from the SUV and gently wiped the mucus from Katy's lips and chin and did her best with the blood and bone spatterings on her face.

'Did… I do this?' sobbed Katy into Clara's shoulder.

'Yep.'

It was Martin.

'Moloch Tran should have known better than to mess with either of you two. We were all too late to help you. Not as though you needed any…'

Clara glared at Martin, instantly silencing him.

'Here, let me have a look at your hand.'

It was Melinda.

Katy had forgotten about the pain.

'Your wrist's swelling up like a balloon. Let's get you to the hospital and le…'

Katy remembered nothing else. She woke up to the fuzzy outlines of people hovering around her who gradually came into focus.

'Where am I?'

'You're in Bavet hospital, Ma. Rithy drove us here and Martin carried you in from the car.'

'I suppose if he's had his arms around me, I'd best make friends next time I see him. Am I all right?'

'Your wrist's broken. The doctor reset the bones and plastered your arm. She says the injury will take six to eight weeks to heal, but not to worry, you're going to be as good as new. We brought you here Tuesday night, today's Thursday. We've all been anxious about you.'

'I don't remember much.'

'Just as well. It all turned into a bit of a horror show. The doctor gave you stuff to help you sleep. You were in quite a state for a while and you'll be seeing purple elephants until the effects of the medication wear off. You're probably not cut out to be the next *Dirty Harry*.'

'Is Elena here?'

'I'm here, *cara*. Where else would I be?'

'Lanie got here last night, Ma. She hasn't slept for days or left your bedside since she arrived. Before you ask, Rangsei and the other girls are safe. They're in good hands with Doctor Khan and Lanie's UNICEF people. When Jim gets his story out, the world will know little Chavy and Rangsei Pham are heroes.'

'I'm glad. Their sad family deserves some good fortune. I'm sorry Elena, we should have left it to the police and not scared you. You're family now and we need to be taking better care of each other.'

'Will you call me Lanie too? I told Clara earlier being invited into Clan Yehonala is more daunting than she'd let on, so I've been reading the history books and listening to her tales about you and Simon. I'll try to shape up.'

'Loving my daughter will be enough.'

'No complaints so far, Ma. After her heroics on Tuesday night and Wednesday at the orphanage though, I'll have to make an appointment to see her. I also sent Rithy home. He got worried Jorani would be panicking after hearing the news reports. He'll meet us at Rémy's farm later.'

'Rémy's farm?'

'Yes, Lanie and I decided it would be best if you rested for a day or two away from the publicity. Rémy insisted we go there and said he's bought another bottle of cognac for the occasion, tuned the piano and fixed the air-conditioning. I told him it was an offer we couldn't refuse. You'll be safe there. In exchange for the story, the media promised to keep quiet about your part in Moloch Tran's last moments on earth. At least for a while.'

'Seems like you have it all under control. My job as a mother is done.'

'Ha! That'll be the day.'

'Elena… Lanie, will you come too? We could get to know one another and it's lovely on the farm, though I expect they'll make you swim with the catfish. And unless you two have a cunning plan, you and I may need to share a room. I don't think a Catholic priest, even Rémy, will much approve of you two sleeping together. Especially in his church.'

'Catholics! Tell me about it.'

Watery-eyed laughter spilt into the room.

'I'm so happy you're all right, *cara*. I suppose I could live without Clara for one more night. Are you sure *you'll* be safe?'

'You don't get away from me so easily, my darling. As it happens, I do have a cunning plan. Ma, there's someone else who wants to say hello. He's been here since last night, too.'

A familiar face appeared.

'I had a call from a vicar telling me the church silverware has been pinched. Wanted to know if I could recommend a good gumshoe.'

'Jim, the Yehonala Women's Revolutionary Army is officially out of business and my mother's got peonies to prune before July. As for Lanie and me, well, we won't have the time.'

'Ladies, you've already given me way too much information. A pity though, the world's a bit light on Annie Oakleys putting the world right again with a .44 magnum!'

'Looks like you eventually got the story you wanted, Jim. I won't embarrass you with the thanks we owe you and all the other bullshit.'

Clara glanced at Elena, rolling her eyes.

'Could easily have been writing bloody obituaries for you stupid bastards instead of getting a fat pay rise and a fancy award nomination. Won't you two ever have respect for my blood pressure?'

'Nice to see you too, Jim. Come closer.'

He leaned forward so Katy could whisper in his ear.

'Are you up for a fucking cognac?'

33

A PROMISE KEPT

Five days later, Clara and I went to Wat Bagan to say our goodbyes. Morning sunbeams slanted between the lush, tropical trees as we strolled arm in arm past the spired temple into the garden. Stopping for a moment on the path, I inhaled slowly, watching vividly painted swordtail and jezebel butterflies hovering above the flowers in a wonderland of mottled light and colours. Peace.

'Gardens are so vivid after the rain. It's as if the gift of the sky isn't water but magic washing everything clean, showing us nature's artistry has been here all along.'

The words were said barely above a whisper, more expressing my thoughts than speaking to Clara. She looked at me and smiled, both of us immersed in the sacredness transcending the commonplace in holy places.

Tailorbirds and shamas invited themselves into our peace as we meandered the tranquil paths, accompanying us with bursts of birdsong, their hearts rejoicing in the steamy treetops overhead. In this beautiful garden, we both felt the breath of God, letting our senses drink the beauty of his creation.

'Dad and Chavy will be content here, Ma.'

She squeezed my arm and I left her to her private thoughts and prayers. I settled down to my own time with my husband and Chavy Pham.

'Hello, Simon, my dear husband.

'Here I am on my own again, without you, but not afraid. You can see I'm a bit the worse for wear at the moment, what with the sling and plaster. Don't worry, it's nothing. I shall call it my battle scar and carry it with pride. Unlike you, I'll embellish my war exploits outrageously in the years ahead to anyone who wants to listen, even those who don't, until they all politely ignore the silly old woman with her fanciful memories. Or at least I would if Mama's gaze didn't haunt my footsteps.

'I kept my promise to you. The evil people Clara and I set out to find are no more. At least the ones who brought us to this day. It will take longer to uncover them all and sweep them away, though I'm sure with Jim Preston, Melinda Gauci, Martin Lewis and your friend Rémy Aubert on the case, the final accounting will come.

'I've decided to go home. I'm leaving tomorrow, back to Melbourne and the Red Peony Garden; I expect Mr Wang will be pleased with the help and I want to be there for the peonies this year. Now you're resting at peace, it's time. Home won't be the same, but it's our place and where I belong. I doubt the life of the Valkyrie swooping down on the world's wickedness is for me. According to Jim Preston, I'm lucky to get away with a broken wrist.

'"Best leave these things to the professionals in future," he told me, though in rather more flowery language. Did you ever meet Jim? You would have liked each other.

'Hard to believe so much has happened. It seems like yesterday I stepped off the plane at Pochentong Airport and met Martin Lewis. Yes, I know the name's changed; I prefer the airport's old name. Better memories.

'And hello to you, my darling little Chavy Pham, my best friend who I meet in my dreams each night. I expect you both know we found Rangsei. Such a brave soul; I think her big sister taught her how to be a hero. She's safe now and I must tell you both a short story.

'I spoke with the people at the embassy asking if we could arrange to take Rangsei to Australia to live as my daughter, or at least foster care her there. Elena said she would do all she could to help with the paperwork; Clara and I got excited and couldn't wait to tell Rangsei the news. You know, after all she's been through, she looked at Clara and me and thanked us, then said no, going to Australia with me wouldn't be possible. At first, I was astonished.

'She told us she would be going home to Kampot instead, to be with her mother. Do you know what she said? "They're family, Mrs Katy. I need to be with them". Who am I to argue?

'With her mother's permission, we enrolled her in an excellent international school in Phnom Penh. She'll be safe there until she's old enough to look after herself and we're making sure she's getting the help she needs.

'Do you remember the starfish story? You know, the one where the man asks the young boy why he's throwing starfish back into the ocean after the storm and how can he hope to save the thousands washed up on the beach. Well, as the young boy said, we've made a difference for one of them. I have a feeling Rangsei Pham will repay the world many times over one day.

'She'll be going home on school holidays. Elena and Rebecca are going to keep a close eye on her, too. One day, she hopes to earn enough money so her mother can have a good life. You'll be pleased Chavy, I believe your wish will come true. Your sister has your spirit and we let her know where she could find you.

'Simon, I expect Clara's already told you she's flying back to Paris tonight. She won't be gone long; she and Elena are house-hunting in Phnom Penh. She told me Max said their friendship is still strong. They've also agreed to cut back on her concert schedule so Clara can devote time to other things.

'I know you're proud of your daughter, and you should be. I'm sorry you had so few years to enjoy your time together; I'll carry this regret all my life. Little wonder we Yehonalas lost the dynasty if my decision-making genes were the ones they passed down the line. Still, there were a couple of good decisions thrown in among the others. Weren't there?

'Clara told me she'll talk to you in her music. I don't know what she means, but the idea made her smile. I said you'd be pleased with her relationship with Elena, or Lanie as she wants me to call her. I am. She promised me Lanie is good for her and good to her. And she is. I've seen them together enough to be sure. Even though she runs the child protection agency at UNICEF with all the awful stresses of her job, they seem like two children themselves. I remember similar times with you back in England.

'I expect she's telling you all about her plans right at this moment. She'll be in Cambodia as often as she can as patron of her School Pianos Program; once they settle down, you'll be seeing more of them. I hope this will bring some consolation to you and her, to atone a little from before.

'They got the Chinese Premier's wife promising to twist the arms of a couple of Beijing State Enterprises to sponsor her program. Small at first, but you know what they say, each step leaves a footprint. Ambassador Zhao helped; he wasn't so bad after all. There's a good chance the Yehonala name is in safer hands than mine, though I fear I never raised the bar to Olympic heights.

'Max is organising a concert to celebrate Clara's homecoming to the world of music. I know Clara misses performing and she's excited to return to what she loves. She insists it will be a benefit concert to raise money for charity, which appeals to Max's branding instincts. They're arguing whether it will be a classical or a rock concert, with Italian passion pushing against Yehonala steel. Who knows what will happen? Perhaps they'll do one of each. We'll see, but it will be a brave person to bet against a Yehonala girl when she's made up her mind. Especially our daughter.

'Jim Preston put the story of our escapades on front pages around the world. Well-wishers and artists already want to donate their time to her concert. Max says it's beginning to look like a *Who's Who* of music glitterati. I doubt it's going to be as grand as Live Aid, though I'm pleased some good will come from this unhappy time. Lanie and I will be going, to add plenty of cheers from all of us.

'You'll be pleased to hear I finally decided to forgive Martin Lewis. Not for his sins or for carrying me into the hospital like an overgrown baby, but for keeping his courage and silence when it would have been easier to say something. Well, the carrying me part helped; it's hard not to be friends with a man who had their arms around you while you're defenceless. He's got a soft spot for Clara, despite enduring her sharp tongue more than once to preserve his secrets. Don't you think he's moderately heroic, Simon? I do.

'Once, I thought he and Clara had a future together. So did he, but it's no good trying to wrong-foot fate. The only cloud, a little one, is we're unlikely to be blessed by a grandchild, but I'll trade a grandson for Clara's happiness in a heartbeat. I've not given up all hope since fate plays a fickle hand, as we've seen already. Maybe they'll adopt one day. Children are the centre of Clara and Lanie's lives, so I haven't entirely abandoned grandchildren. How else can we live forever?

'We've entrusted the work of the Sunlight Foundation to Rithy, a more loyal friend would have been impossible to find. You did well finding him. He's to become a teacher at Ross and Rebecca's mission and will eventually, we hope, help run the school.

'Did I mention Rebecca got permission to name the community centre at Svay Thom after you? I expect you'll be embarrassed. Too bad my dear, you were outvoted. We all pray when the new laws pass and more light shines into these dark corners of our humanity, children will have better protection and dangerous activities like rescuing them will be unnecessary. Not yet, but one day.

'So you see my love, your work will go on here and I plan to become more involved in future. Now there's one thing I never expected to hear myself say. Truth is, if there are such things as silver linings, one would have to be how much I've grown up over the last few weeks. Not from being a child, more from facing up to a demon who took up residence back in those days. I think Clara has too.

'Oh, I nearly forgot. Jim Preston promised to help me finish writing *Chavy's Story*. Naturally, he writes so much better than me and will do her the justice her story deserves. If you don't mind, I'll call the little book, *The World of Chavy Pham*.

'The new title is part of a longer story I'll tell you next time, one I should have told you ages ago. Except I didn't know it myself.

'Goodbye, my dears. God bless. I'll see you both again soon.'

'Ready, Ma?'

I nodded.

THE END

CHAVY

Her childhood lost
my debt best paid
for innocence cost.
I mourn the end
of little Chavy, my friend.
A precious life stole
from Chavy, sweet soul.
Once a mother's joy made
now a child lovingly laid
into earth's warm embrace.
Leaving no trace.

Katy Yehonala.

Shawline Publishing Group Pty Ltd

www.shawlinepublishing.com.au